Bernardine Kennedy was born in London but spent most of her childhood in Singapore and Nigeria before settling in Essex, where she still lives with her partner Ian and teenage daughter Kate. She also has an adult son, Stephen. Her varied working life has included careers as an air hostess, a swimming instructor and a social worker. She has been a freelance writer for the past thirteen years, specialising in popular travel features for magazines. *Everything is not Enough*, Bernardine Kennedy's first novel, is also available from Headline.

Bernardine Kennedy's website address is
www.bernardinekennedy.com

Also by Bernardine Kennedy

Everything is not Enough

headline

My Sisters' Keeper

Bernardine Kennedy

headline

First published in Great Britain in 2001 by
HEADLINE BOOK PUBLISHING

First published in paperback in 2002 by
HEADLINE BOOK PUBLISHING

10 9 8 7 6 5 4 3 2

ISBN 0 7472 6647 6

Typeset by
Letterpart Limited, Reigate, Surrey

Printed and bound in Great Britain by
Mackays of Chatham plc, Chatham, Kent

HEADLINE BOOK PUBLISHING
A division of Hodder Headline
338 Euston Road
LONDON NW1 3BH

www.headline.co.uk
www.hodderheadline.com

For all my good friends from over the years,
both old and new, here, there and everywhere,
each and every one a piece of my puzzle.

Prologue

As the warm morning sun broke through at daybreak, Cathy Carter, still as a terracotta soldier standing guard, was looking down at her daughter sleeping. It looked a peaceful sleep – no tossing and turning, no screaming out – but how could Cathy be sure? How was she to know if the little girl was screaming inside as mind-demons battled?

Smiling, she lightly touched the shiny hair, fresh and clean from her shower the night before. There was no doubt about it, the child was exceptionally beautiful; the features of both parents jumped out of her face as Cathy stared down.

If Cathy hadn't known better, she would have thought that the pose was faked, it was so perfect. Sammy-Jo was lying on her back with her thick dark hair fanning out across the pillow and fluffy eyelashes stretched across her cheeks like plump spider-legs. Sammy-Jo, her beloved child, with the face of an angel, but occasionally the temperament of a practising she-devil.

As Cathy wondered which of her parents the child would ultimately take after, she prayed silently that Sammy-Jo would be a combination of the best of both of them and none of the worst: her father's single-mindedness but not his arrogance; her mother's resilience but not her lack of self-worth. But Cathy knew there were no guarantees. Maybe just happiness would be enough.

Silently a figure appeared beside her and threaded his arm round her waist.

'Isn't it time you came out? You've been here all night. Come on, I'll make you a nice strong cup of coffee. She'll call as soon as she wakes.' Pulling her close he buried his head in her hair. 'You have to let go; you mustn't pass your own demons on to Sammy-Jo.'

Cathy looked up at him. 'I know that but I can't help it. This is all my fault. I shouldn't have taken her away.' The dark almond eyes filled with tears that she impatiently brushed away. 'I know what it's like to have nightmares about the past, to remember the horrors of childhood. I never wanted that for a child of mine.'

As she spoke Sammy-Jo's eyes flickered open. She looked disorientated.

Scanning the room quickly she cried out, 'Where's Tracy?'

'It's OK, sweetheart, Tracy will come and see you soon. She had a few things to sort out.'

'Can I go out and play today?'

Cathy's heart sank. The last thing she wanted was for her child to be out of her sight. Just as she was about to reply she felt the arm round her waist tighten. He was telling her to be strong.

She gritted her teeth, then smiled down at her daughter. 'After breakfast, OK? I want to have a little chat with you first . . .'

Chapter One

The violent shaking of her shoulders and the urgent voice in her ear brought Cathy out of a deep sleep but it took a second for her to register her sister leaning over the bed.

'Cathy, get up! Move yourself quickly, there's a fire . . .'

The girl blinked, unsure if it was a dream.

'Get up now! The house is on fire! We've got to get out . . .'

The voice was now a scream and Cathy was being pulled roughly from her bed. Suddenly wide awake she could hear the wail of approaching fire engines. Scrambling in the darkness, she felt herself being dragged by the arm from the safety of her room out into the smoke-filled hall.

Thick choking smoke filled the girls' noses and throats as, holding hands, they made their way through the dark towards the front door. Just as they reached the door it burst open and the porch was filled with the shadowy outline of bulky firefighters, who quickly bustled them to the safety of the garden.

'Is there anyone else inside?'

'Yes, my parents are upstairs. I couldn't reach them . . . I don't know where Jane is.'

'Who's Jane?' the fireman asked sharply as he tried to assess the situation.

'My twin sister.'

At that moment one of the firefighters came out with an arm round a young woman who was shaking from head to toe.

'That's Jane, that's her . . .' Alison ran across the front lawn and the twin sisters fell crying into each other's arms. A paramedic wrapped a blanket around Cathy's shoulders and gently led her to a waiting ambulance.

Sitting upright on a trolley in the back of the open-doored ambulance, unhurt but shocked and coughing, Cathy tried to think through what had happened. Just a few hours ago the family had gone to bed as normal, her parents up to their second-floor bedroom, the twins to their room on the first floor and Cathy to hers on the ground floor. Now she couldn't figure out how their beautiful home could be billowing smoke and flames.

Jane and Alison were herded into the ambulance.

'What about Mum and Dad? Where are they?' Cathy asked.

The twins looked at each other before speaking. 'They're trying to get them out now but they must be trapped at the top.'

'What happened?' Cathy started to sob as the full horror of the situation hit her. 'How can the house have just caught fire?'

6

The twins both leaned forward and hugged the young girl.

'We don't know . . . we just don't know. We woke up and there were flames.'

'That's right – flames and smoke. Jane went to wake Mum and Dad and dial 999, and I ran to get you. That's all we know.'

'That's right, that's all we know . . . flames and smoke. I went to wake Mum and Dad but I couldn't get up there so I ran down again. I couldn't see through the smoke . . . I was choking . . .'

The paramedic looked curiously at the trio in his ambulance. The older identical twins, both thick-set and plain with long curly mousy hair, clones of each other in looks, mannerisms and speech, and the tiny teenager with bright red hair and oriental features, looked an unlikely combination to be sisters, even without the obvious age difference.

After covering them in blankets and checking their blood pressure he concentrated on Cathy, who was shivering with shock as she watched, almost in a trance, the drama that was unfolding before her.

High pressure hoses were playing water up to the roof of the house in an effort to hold back the flames as a platform was raised from a fire tender towards the top bedroom window under the eaves. The popping of shattering windowpanes echoed in the night sky like sporadic gunfire.

'Look, they're going up to the bedroom. They must have found Mum and Dad. Do you think they're OK?'

Looking anxiously from one to the other, Cathy realised her sisters were back in their own world – the private world to which they always retreated together when things got tough. Silently holding hands, they were looking at but not seeing the activity that was raging in front of their eyes.

'Ali? Janey? Say something, will you? For God's sake, *speak to me.*' Cathy used the only tone she knew would penetrate, unaware of the sharp look that the paramedic cast at her.

In unison the twins blinked and looked at Cathy, suddenly back with her.

'What did you say?' Alison was the first to speak.

'Sorry, Kitten, what did you say?' Jane followed.

'Look! They're up at the bedroom window . . . They will be all right, won't they?'

The twins didn't answer, just watched as first Bryan, then Elena Carter were passed through the window and lowered to the ground.

Cathy made a move to get off the stretcher but was held back.

'Don't.' The paramedic held her arm gently. 'You have to let them do their job.'

They all watched as the inert forms were roughly laid on the grass and quickly examined.

'Get them to hospital, *now.*'

The transfer of their parents to the second ambulance took only a matter of seconds, then it quickly sped off down the darkened drive, lights flashing and sirens blaring.

'What's happening? Are they OK?' Cathy could feel the hysteria rising; no one was saying anything.

Another paramedic appeared at the doors and closed them sharply before going round to the driver's seat.

'Right, ladies, we're just taking you for a check-up. Soon be there.'

'What about Mum and Dad? Are they OK?'

'I'm sorry, I really don't know. We're going to the same hospital; they'll give you more information there.'

Cathy stared at her sisters, too frightened to close her eyes. She knew the nightmares of the past, nightmares that had taken nearly ten years to erase, were bubbling away in her head, ready to erupt again.

The smell and taste of the smoke, the sound of crackling flames and the rat-a-tat of explosions had brought it all back . . . She could still remember her other life – the bombed and blazing houses, the blood-curdling screams, followed eventually by an eerie silence, accompanied by the smell of death . . . Suddenly she was there again, amid the devastation of the killing fields that had wiped out her entire family in one night.

Eyes wide open she concentrated on the journey. She didn't want to remember.

The three of them were carefully checked, given the all-clear and taken by a sympathetic but obviously uncomfortable young nurse into a small but homely lounge designated for the waiting families of the desperately ill.

'I promise, as soon as there is any news someone will

be with you.' She patted Cathy on the hand and smiled encouragingly. 'They're doing all they can for your parents. Try not to worry too much.'

'That sounds OK, doesn't it?' Cathy looked from Alison to Jane expectantly. 'Doesn't it?'

The twins shrugged silently as the girl walked over to the glass door and peered through the blinds at the accident and emergency department outside. Like any fifteen-year-old, Cathy had paid the odd visit to Casualty over her childhood years, but never before in the early hours of the morning and certainly never for anything more serious than a bang on the head or a sprained ankle.

The nurse returned with a tray of coffee and a warm dressing gown and a pair of thick socks for Cathy. The twins were well wrapped up in their matching purple candlewick wraps and slippers that they had managed to put on before raising the alarm.

'I'm sorry they're not very fashionable, Cathy, but at least you'll be warm for the time being. I'm sure some clothes will get sorted out tomorrow for you all.'

'Have you heard anything yet about Mum and Dad?'

'Sorry, love, I still don't know anything.' The nurse smiled compassionately at the stricken girl. 'As soon as there's any news you'll be the first to know.'

Barely were the words out when the door opened again and the doctor came in, the expression on his face giving them the news before he even opened his mouth.

Cathy screamed, 'They're dead, aren't they?'

Their faces expressionless, Alison and Jane moved

quickly across the room and stood either side of her, each taking a hand.

'I'm really sorry. We did everything we could but the smoke inhalation was too severe. I know it's small comfort but they wouldn't have known anything. They were both still in bed when the fire brigade got in there . . . I'm so very sorry, we really did try . . .'

He gave a few discreet instructions to the nurse as he left the small room, the saddest room in the hospital where news of serious injury and death were regularly delivered to distressed relatives.

The three sisters were admitted to a ward for the night and discharged the next day to a local hotel just in time to see and read all about the fire in the papers and on the news. Cathy hadn't even noticed the photographers and news crews at the time but the devastating scene was graphically portrayed for the nation. A couple of opportunist journalists were even trying to get into the hotel for a quote from the grieving family, but the staff were determined to protect the three sisters.

Watching television on the small screen that flickered in the corner of the unwelcoming hotel bedroom, Cathy found it hard to relate to the fact that the familiar news reporter looking out at her, speaking to her, was actually talking about *her* family. Emotionally detached from the reporting, she watched it all, hypnotised by the drama being played out.

The news report was relayed from outside the still-burning house that bore little resemblance to her home. The report was sensitive and sympathetic, but only

11

portrayed a fleeting glimpse of the tragedy.

'Local business couple Bryan and Elena Carter died last night in a tragic fire at their country home in the heart of the New Forest. The wealthy couple had only recently sold their business, Carter's Haulage, to concentrate on their retirement together.' The reporter hesitated as the camera panned across the front of the property, taking in the scene of destruction. 'Their three daughters, twins Alison and Jane, aged twenty-five, and adopted teenage daughter Cathy, were also in the house at the time. All three escaped unscathed, but obviously deeply shocked. The close-knit local community is finding it hard to accept the death of this popular couple who contributed so much to the area.'

'*Carter's Haulage.*' Cathy spoke the words out loud. It was almost as if she was hearing them for the first time. She had never given much thought to the business that kept the family in luxury. Her father had often spoken proudly about starting the business from scratch with one secondhand lorry, and then slowly building up to a fleet that regularly travelled across the whole of Europe.

Thinking back to when she was small, she remembered having the occasional treat of sitting up high in the cab, waving importantly at any passing vehicle as they trundled down the motorways. But before long her father had given up the driving and she had lost interest. Sitting in an office while her father made countless phone calls just wasn't the same.

Now the retirement that her parents had planned and looked forward to for so long was not to be, and Cathy was well aware that her own future was decidedly uncertain. Suddenly, again, she was homeless, her parents were dead, and she was left to wonder what her future would hold.

Standing together in silence, the three sisters, accompanied by a fire chief and two police officers, surveyed in daylight the house that was now a sodden, blackened shell. The first and second floors were destroyed by fire and smoke, with the ground floor blackened and waterlogged. The gardens surrounding the house, once pristine lawns and perfectly manicured flowerbeds, had been churned up into a muddy swamp by rescue vehicles and big boots.

Tears pouring down her face, Cathy stared, shellshocked, up at the top floor.

'What are we going to do?' she cried to the twins, not really expecting much response. Cathy had spent the last ten years – two thirds of her life – as part of the Carter family, and she accepted her adoptive sisters' strange behaviour, rarely questioning it, but now she wanted to lash out at them, get a reaction. Anything would be preferable to the detached air of acceptance they were displaying.

Although they loved her in their own way – as much as they could love anyone other than each other – and she loved them, at that moment she hated the two unemotional women who were viewing the scene almost dispassionately.

'Say something, will you? We can't live here, we haven't

got anything . . . Where are we going to go?'

The twins suddenly came alive.

'We're going to have the house rebuilt and we're going to look after you.'

'That's right, we're going to look after you, Kitten. It'll be the three of us together in this house . . . I can see it now. It won't take long and it's insured . . .'

Alison started walking around the outside while Jane stayed with Cathy.

'Did you hear that? It won't take long and then it'll be as if it never happened.'

'What do you mean, never happened? Mum and Dad are dead. They died here. How can we pretend it never happened? *I hate you both*.'

Silently the twins just exchanged identical surprised looks.

The fire chief and the police investigator also exchanged glances. They both felt uncomfortable with the twins' behaviour and found it awkward dealing with a fifteen-year-old who appeared to be the voice for all three of them. They had tried directing their questions at the twins but it was nearly always Cathy who answered for them and herself.

Preliminary investigations showed that the fire had probably started in the twins' sitting room on the first floor, which was separated from their bedroom by their own bathroom and tiny kitchen. They had apparently gone to bed, carelessly leaving several candles and oil burners alight and the window slightly open. It had only taken a slight breeze to fan the swathes of gossamer-thin voile drapes into the flames. By the time the twins smelled the smoke and went to investigate it was too late to do anything other than get out. Luckily there had been time to get to Cathy.

When the three girls were out of earshot the fire officer could not resist voicing his opinion.

'Those two are weird, aren't they? It's not normal for even twins to be that alike, especially at their age. Bloody hell, they're adults and still dressing alike and sharing the same bedroom. It's spooky, if you ask me. Even their bloody socks match, and they won't look at us . . . There's more to this than meets the eye. Psychopaths the pair of them – wouldn't surprise me if they torched the place themselves. What do you reckon?'

The other man looked at him distastefully but before he could reply the accompanying policewoman retorted, 'No one's asking you and it's not for us to *reckon*, as you so delicately put it. You're both here to check out the fire and the facts and I'm here to support them all. No one really gives a toss what you think unless it's about the actual cause of the fire. Don't forget they've lost their parents.'

'Yeah, and that's another thing. A fifteen-year-old Vietnamese orphan and twin loons – the parents must have been a bit . . .' He paused. 'It's all a bit odd, if you know what I mean, very odd in fact.'

'No, I don't know what you mean. Now let's get on with the job we're here for.'

Turning sharply away from the men she went over to the three sisters and touched Cathy gently on the shoulder.

'Do you know what you're going to do yet? There's lots of people, organisations, that can help you—'

Before she could finish Alison interrupted her sharply. 'We're fine, thank you, we don't need outsiders. Jane and I will take care of Cathy. We're going to move into the flat over the shop until the house is rebuilt and then move back. We'll manage, thank you.'

She turned her attention to the fire chief who was still a distance away. 'Can we go into the house yet and see what's salvageable?'

His discomfort was almost tangible as he responded to the loud abrupt tone of the woman who spoke confidently but didn't make eye contact. It bothered him immensely that there was no way of knowing which twin was which.

'I'm sorry, Miss Carter, but no, we're still carrying out checks – the investigators are in there now – then we've got to make the property safe. Maybe in a couple of days . . . Now I do have a few questions I have to ask . . .'

Once again the twins looked blankly away as Cathy answered as best she could.

Looking out of the hotel bedroom window as daylight broke, and watching the rain continuing to lash down, Cathy was relieved. It was the day of the funeral and the thought of a nice sunny spring day was too much to bear. At least now the weather was as bad as it should be for a funeral, depressing and sad.

The last time Cathy had visited the hotel in the heart of the New Forest had been on Mother's Day when they'd all gone there for lunch – Mum, Dad, the twins and herself. That had been a lovely sunny day, and afterwards they had gone for a drive to see the ponies and their new foals that roamed free through the woodland. Cathy had loved the quaint old building then, and now, a few short weeks later, it seemed a singularly inappropriate place to be, waiting for the funeral of her beloved adoptive parents.

Hearing a knock on the door, she wiped her eyes and opened it, knowing Alison and Jane would be there.

'We're going down for breakfast. We've still got two hours before we have to leave for the church.'

'I couldn't eat anything, not today. I don't know how you can. The thought of it turns my stomach.'

The twins exchanged glances.

'You must eat or you'll feel ill during the service. Come on, even if you just have some toast.' Jane took Cathy's hand and led her purposefully out on to the landing as Alison closed the door firmly behind her. Cathy knew there was no point in arguing with her sisters.

Heads turned and diners did double takes at the three of them entering the sunny conservatory, where the breakfast buffet was laid out.

Both about six feet tall and fourteen stone, Alison and Jane were swathed identically from head to toe in long flowing black velvet dresses, with the darkest of purple shawls wrapped around their shoulders and black Alice bands holding their uncontrollable curly hair back. Every finger displayed identical huge silver rings and their necks and wrists jangled with matching silver chains and bracelets.

17

In between them was the diminutive Cathy, with her neat oriental features and shocking red spiky hair. Her six-stone frame looked almost skeletal in the skin-tight black trousers and polo-neck jumper she had chosen the day before when the three of them had gone shopping. The knee-high boots that her parents would never have allowed her to have served only to make her look even thinner.

The sisters had had to start from scratch as everything they owned had been destroyed in the fire. It had perturbed Cathy at the time that the twins seemed to be enjoying the shopping trip as they scoured the shops and market stalls, but she knew they could be strange at the best of times so she didn't say anything. She just trailed sadly along behind them, aware that she was all but invisible to them.

Cathy was used to the looks and remarks that the twins attracted, but Alison and Jane never seemed to notice, so now Cathy chose to ignore the attention. It really wasn't the right time to get into a defensive argument with the starers and sniggerers of whom there were certainly a few in the restaurant.

The girls found their table and the twins headed straight for the buffet bar, leaving Cathy to order the tea and coffee for all of them.

Over breakfast, Alison was very matter-of-fact and as unemotional as ever.

'Now, the cars are coming at eleven – I hope everyone is here by then. The service is at eleven-thirty, then back here afterwards. I think we'll have to leave the shop

18

closed today but Tuesday is always a quiet day so it shouldn't affect it too much . . .'

'How can you even think about the shop when we're sitting here waiting for Mum and Dad's funeral?' Cathy burst out. 'You two can be so callous sometimes!'

Jane looked at her in surprise. 'We have to deal with what's ahead. We can't change the past so we have to plan the future. Now it's just the three of us the shop is important; so is the rebuilding of the house.'

'That's right,' Alison joined in. 'Until all the finances are sorted out we have to manage carefully and make plans. Now eat your breakfast, Kitten. We've got a long day ahead of us.'

Cathy picked at a slice of dry toast and tried to clear her mind but the images kept coming back.

Her memories of ten years before were clear as a bell despite the fact that she'd been only five years old at the time.

As one of the older orphans on the airlift from Vietnam to England she'd spent most of the flight helping with the babies and toddlers, who had either screamed with fear or sat silently, shell-shocked by the horrors that had led to their being bustled on to the huge aircraft by kindly strangers and flown to the unknown on the other side of the world.

She could still remember her own fear, sick and petrifying, that had enveloped her as the engines had roared into life and the plane lifted into the sky, pushing her back in her seat. She had wanted desperately to get off and run back to the comforting group of ramshackle huts that had become a makeshift orphanage. It may have been a dangerous and horrific place to be but at least it was familiar territory and everyone spoke the same language.

The twins were fifteen when Cathy was adopted into their family. It was several years before she realised they were different.

Different not just from her, but from everyone else as well. They were incredibly close, even for identical twins. Their lives revolved around each other totally and they spent every minute together, communicating secretly and excluding the outside world as much as possible.

But strange as they were, Cathy loved them and she knew they cared about her in their own way, even if they didn't, couldn't show it.

Cathy racked her brains to try and get a clear picture of her life, but there was just a jumble of images that she couldn't place in order. She couldn't remember much about the time after her arrival apart from being hugged and kissed by yet more strangers and then being whisked away for her first journey in a car. She could, however, remember her first meeting with the Carter family.

'Come along now, Kim-Li. This is Mr and Mrs Carter. They've come to meet you. They would like to be your new parents.' The woman's hand had fluttered about in the direction of the visitors. 'This is Alison and this is Jane – they'll be your sisters.'

The matron of the small children's home had smiled encouragingly as she introduced them all. 'Now I'm going to prepare the dinner, so I'll leave you to get to know each other.'

The still-traumatised five-year-old girl didn't really take in the man and woman – they were just another two well-meaning adults like all the others – but she had been mesmerised by the two identical girls who stood slightly behind them, looking bored and gazing into the middle distance.

They didn't stare at her, they didn't fake cheery smiles and they certainly didn't seem the least bit interested in her as a new sister.

One of the girls had spoken suddenly. 'You said her name was Cathy.'

It sounded like an accusation.

'That's right, darling,' said the woman gently, 'but her birth name is Kim-Li. As soon as she comes to us we'll call her Cathy.'

'Why?'

'Why what?' the woman had wanted to know.

'Why change her name if she's already got one?'

'Because this will be the start of a new life for her. A new life and a new name. We're all going to help her forget the things that have happened to her. This little girl is going to be part of our family.'

Smiling at her, the woman had taken hold of Kim-Li's hand. 'Shall we all go for a walk?'

The child hadn't been able to tear her gaze away from the twins. Already tall and broad, but still with the gawky stature of adolescence, they were exactly the same both in features and dress. She had been fascinated. She couldn't even remember having seen twins before, let alone any like Alison and Jane.

As they had all walked awkwardly around the grounds the diminutive child had worked her way through until she was standing between the two sisters. Tentatively she had looked up at them and smiled first at one, then the other. 'Hello . . . hello . . .'

The twins had registered their first change of expression.

'Hello,' they replied in unison, surprise written all over their faces.

It had been the start of a strange relationship between the three of them.

The funeral cars drew up outside the hotel and, despite her pain, Cathy felt some satisfaction as she saw one of the sniggering couples from the restaurant looking suitably embarrassed as she and the twins climbed into the lead car for the short drive to the village church.

The young girl maintained her composure throughout the service and the journey to the crematorium, but as soon as the matching coffins disappeared one after the other behind the black and purple curtains, the reality of the occasion hit her. She tried to break away from the twins and head for the curtains but they restrained her forcibly.

'Don't let them burn,' she shouted suddenly. 'DON'T BURN THEM!' She screamed and screamed as the twins held her at either side. Helping hands reached from all angles but the twins brushed everyone aside and purposefully led Cathy outside into the porch.

The beating rain had lessened to a drizzle and a weak sun was starting to come out.

'See, Kitten, they're OK. The sun is shining now. Let's go and look at the flowers – there are so many. Come on, Jane, let's take her to see the flowers.'

The rest of the day passed in a haze for Cathy. She felt she was being surrounded and suffocated by well-meaning relations and friends when all she wanted was to be alone with her grief. She wished that the circumstances had been different, that she could have grieved in her own bedroom surrounded by all her familiar things, but all she had was an impersonal hotel room where every sound echoed eerily down the corridors, and little more than the clothes she stood up in.

She desperately wanted to see Sally, the golden Labrador who had survived the fire but was now in boarding kennels on the other side of the Forest, taken there by the police that same night.

Nearly everything she owned was gone . . . again.

Just days later, as far as Alison and Jane were concerned, things were back to normal apart from the inconvenience of having to live in a cramped one-bedroom flat.

'Why have I got to go back to school? Why can't I just help you in the shop? I won't get in the way. I could help with the rearranging.'

'No, Kitten, you have to go back – at least until the end of next year. Then you can decide. Jane and I have more than enough to do sorting this whole business out without having you under our feet.'

Cathy knew there was little point in arguing; when the twins set their minds on something it was always the two of them firmly united.

Wandering round the tiny shop, she picked things up and put them down again aimlessly. It was five years since her parents had accepted the fact that the twins would never be able to find jobs that catered for their eccentricity and had set them up in the shop. Cathy had always loved the dark and mystical atmosphere that her sisters had created. Now she could see that at the time it was probably assumed, and possibly hoped, that the twins would live over the shop but they never did move from the family home and the flat had become a storeroom.

The shop, The Crystal Cave, was a big tourist attraction in the village during the holiday season, a quaint odd-shaped building that looked like an afterthought added to the row of shops that snaked down the steep hill. All but the shortest had to duck as they walked through the doorway and fought their way through tinkling wind chimes into the dark-beamed room. If several customers were in there at once the place was crowded. Shelves and display units bowed under the weight of ornaments, jewellery and books all relating to witchcraft and the occult, and the scented oil burners and candles that were constantly alight added to the atmosphere and the mystique that had grown up around the twins.

The centrepiece of the shop was a smoked-glass cabinet that housed a selection of crystal balls carefully displayed on layers of rich black velvet and gently lit from underneath. Everyone who visited the shop was drawn to it, mesmerised by the flickering lights, and the strange twins swathed in dark flowing clothes and looking for all the world like identical storybook witches.

Visitors were never sure if they were for real but a lot of the locals were certain there really was something dark and spooky about them. Many gave them a wide berth but that suited Alison and Jane: they had always only ever wanted each other.

It had embarrassed Cathy when she first found out they were known as 'the twin witches' but all they would ever say was, 'Why should we care if people are stupid enough to believe that? It's good for business!'

'Kitten, will you leave things alone? If you keep picking things up then so will everyone else. Now go back upstairs and sort out your new uniform – sew on the labels and do whatever else you have to do to get ready for school tomorrow.'

'I'm not going tomorrow.' Cathy stamped her foot and pouted. 'It's too soon. I'll go on Monday if I have to, but not before . . . *and stop calling me Kitten.*'

Alison looked bemused by the outburst and silently ran her fingers through her wild hair, twisting it into a knot over one shoulder. After a few seconds she carried on vaguely shifting and shuffling cartons and carrier bags in an attempt to fit even more into the already cluttered shop.

'OK then, Monday, but only if you keep out of here.

Now we've had to move all the stock out of the flat – we're too pushed for space as it is.'

'Can I go and get Sally back?'

'*No*. How many more times? There's no room!'

Local well-wishers had quickly produced a selection of furniture and essentials so the flat was now as habitable and furnished as it could be in the short time since the fire. Cathy hated it; she thought it was more like a dolls' house. It was all so different from what she was used to. She hadn't realised until then how lucky she had been to live in a big house with a large and pretty room full of things she'd chosen for herself.

As she walked up the small winding iron staircase that went straight into the lounge she thought about the wide welcoming entrance hall of the old house with its spacious lobby and sweeping stairs.

Wandering sadly over to the window she looked out over the street, seeing the holidaymakers roaming up and down, laughing and enjoying themselves. She could hear the twins carrying on downstairs just as usual, and her sadness was suddenly overwhelming as she tried to make sense of what had happened, how her life could have altered so much in such a short space of time.

She picked up the phone and dialled.

'Hi, Tim, it's Cathy. I really need someone to talk to.'

Tim O'Connor was in the same class as Cathy and his adoration of her was the cause of much hilarity at their school. He followed her around like a puppy, and would have walked to John O'Groats over broken glass if she'd asked. It was obvious to everyone except Cathy that he was besotted with her; she simply saw a friend in the painfully shy young lad whose life was blighted by poor eyesight, rampant acne and lank hair.

'Are you OK? I did phone you but your sister said you didn't want to speak to me.'

'I wasn't avoiding you personally, Tim. I didn't really want to speak to anyone until now. Will you meet me down by the river?'

'I'll be there as soon as I can!'

Cathy was tucked out of sight under the small bridge, knees drawn up under her chin, but she knew Tim would find her. She didn't look up as he skidded his precious bike to a halt at the top of the bank, dumping it on its side unceremoniously in his haste before hurtling down the slope, a blur of skinny arms and legs. Silently he took his place beside her. The strands of straw in his hair and the strong smell of horses on his muddy boots and raggedy body warmer were comforting to her, a familiar normality from the past.

'Were you mucking out?' Cathy asked, still not looking up.

He smiled sheepishly. 'Do I smell that bad? Sorry, I just came straight here.'

'You'll get in trouble. I'm sorry—'

'No, it's OK,' he reassured her. 'I explained to Mum and she's fine about it. I'll finish off when I get back unless Julie feels sorry for me and does it.' He looked sideways at her. 'They both send their love. Everyone's really upset by what happened.'

Side by side, they looked into the water at their feet, embarrassed by their shifting roles. Throughout their friendship Cathy had always been the strong one, the one who reassured Tim and stood up for him against his playground tormentors. The delicate-looking young girl never had any inhibitions about wading into the thick of arguments and fights, and was never slow in voicing her opinions. Her reputation as a wildcat and the accompanying respect was well earned.

'Mum said you've always looked out for me and now it's my turn to help you but I don't know what to do.'

Tim looked so miserable Cathy felt more upset for him than for herself and that proved to be the trigger. Suddenly the emotions that she had managed to keep a close rein on escaped and her whole body started shaking as she tried to keep the tears in by tightly screwing up her whole face.

'What have I done?' she wailed. 'Am I a bad person? There must be a reason why God's punishing me – first my parents in Vietnam, now Mum and Dad here. It must be punishment . . . why else would it happen again?'

The teenage boy was at a complete loss. His heart ached for her but all he could think of to do was reach out and touch her tentatively on the hand until she was all cried out.

As the sobs subsided and Cathy pulled a tissue out of her pocket, Tim looked at her curiously.

'You've never mentioned Vietnam before . . .'

'I know. Mum and Dad never really wanted to talk about it, I think they thought that if they didn't mention it I would forget. But you don't forget things like that, you just stop thinking about it all the time.'

'Tell me about it then – if you want to . . .'

Cathy looked off into the distance. 'It's difficult. Because I've never talked about it it's hard to remember what really happened . . . I don't remember much about my other family before the bombing, but I still have the images of what happened afterwards. I wasn't there – I must have wandered off or gone to get something – but there was a terrible noise as the planes swooped over and I ran for cover. Just like I'd been told to do. The noise stopped and eventually I went back, but there was nothing there. Everyone was dead and the village was flattened.'

Tim remained silent as Cathy hesitated and screwed up her face as she tried to think. 'I don't know how long I hid for, but I do know I was starving and so thirsty. Then someone found me and I was taken miles away to some huts where there were loads of other children. Then I was brought to England.'

'Don't you remember what your mum and dad looked like? What about brothers and sisters?'

'I don't know. I just know that everyone was killed, so no one knew anything about me. I was just another orphan.'

Tim's eyes were wide open. 'Someone must have known something—'

'Don't be such a prat, Tim,' Cathy snapped, her black eyes flashing as she glared at him. 'There were thousands of orphans, all the children were rounded up and sent to anywhere that there might be food and shelter. I might not talk about it or even really remember it, but I've read about it. I know what happened.'

'So how did you end up in the Forest?'

'The orphans were dispersed all over the world. I was sent to England and adopted by Mum and Dad here.'

Tim's tone was almost envious as he tried, unsuccessfully, to understand the enormity of it all. 'Well, you did all right then, from a village in the jungle to a rich family here. You've always had everything as far as I can remember.'

Cathy glared at him, her anger written all over her face. 'Yes, Tim. Everything, absolutely fucking everything. Now just think about it before you say anything else really stupid.' Standing up quickly, Cathy aimed a kick at his leg, but missed.

'I'm sorry, Cathy, please sit down. I was only trying to help.'

'Yes, well if that's helping then you're no bloody good at it!' Reluctantly she sank back to the ground beside Tim. 'Just imagine it, I was five years old alone in a new country with a new language, new everything. Not to mention being the only foreigner at school where everyone was under orders to be nice to the poor little Vietnamese orphan!'

Tim's face was bright red with embarrassment. 'I just didn't think . . .'

'It doesn't matter now.' Cathy put her head in her hands. 'Nothing matters now. I'm back to where I started . . . with nothing. Absolutely bugger all!'

Chapter Two

'I am not going and you can't make me,' Cathy stated firmly, tears not far away.

'Oh yes, you are bloody well going. We have to see how the renovations are getting on and that's that.'

Jane and Alison stood side by side in front of the truculent teenager, who was refusing to get up from the pulled-out sofa bed in the lounge. She tugged the quilt up round her chin and glared defiantly.

'I am not going. I'm never going to live in that house again, whatever you say. Mum and Dad died in there – it's just horrible of you even to think it.'

Jane whipped the cover back and threw it on the floor. 'Stop being so childish. It's our home – always was, always will be.'

'It's what Mum and Dad would have wanted, Kitten.' Alison was trying a different tack. 'It was left to us all so it must be what they wanted.'

Cathy pouted. 'No, it was left to you, not to me. The

house is yours. I'm not living there. I can stay here, I can look after myself.'

'No, you can't. We're your guardians and you do whatever we tell you. Now get up out of that bed. You're starting to really get on my nerves!'

Grudgingly Cathy slunk into the bathroom, dreading the thought of having to enter her old home. The twins had no such compunction; as far as they were concerned it was just a building that would continue to suit their needs. Neither was sentimental about anything except each other.

It was this lack of emotion that had led the various investigators to believe that there was something suspicious about the fire but in the end it all came to nothing and the cause was officially accidental, good enough for the insurance company to pay out for the rebuilding. In the will that had been drawn up many years before and not updated, everything from considerable investments and savings to life insurance was left equally to the twins, apart from two hundred and fifty thousand pounds in trust for Cathy that couldn't be touched until she was twenty-one.

Much as she loved the twins, she hated them now having authority over her; deep down she knew that she was more responsible than either of her sisters.

Her final protest was to gel her hair so fiercely it stood to attention in sharp red spikes, and smudge huge amounts of kohl around her eyes and lips. To complete her image of scruffiness she pulled on her favourite jeans with the knees and backside ripped dramatically and a sweatshirt with an obscene gesture emblazoned on the front of it. It made her feel better but as usual the twins didn't even notice.

'Are you ready? Right, let's go. I'll ring for a taxi.'

Cathy pulled a face. 'Why can't we have a car like everyone else? This is stupid . . . Why can't at least one of you learn to drive?'

They both ignored her.

From the outside the old house looked almost the same except for the pristine new paintwork and roof tiles, and the gleaming windows that glistened brightly in the morning sunshine.

The grounds were still a wasteland apart from the few hardy trees and hedges that bordered the once-splendid garden, shading the house from the surrounding lanes and far enough away to have avoided damage on the dreadful night of the fire.

Cathy was surprised to see the new front door was wide open, and as they stepped through, a familiar face appeared in the hallway and smiled happily at them.

'Hello, girls. I just thought I'd pop in and see how things were going for you. Doing a grand job, aren't they? Oh, Cathy dear, you look so thin, and whatever is wrong with your face? Looks like someone's blacked your eyes for you.'

The rounded shape of Sheila Miller, the family's cleaner since long before Cathy was first brought to the house, lunged forward and grasped the girl closely to her. As Sheila wrapped her short chubby arms round the skinny frame and squeezed her tight Cathy felt strangely comforted by the familiar smell of Tweed perfume and furniture polish.

'You poor baby, this must be awful for you. Come into the kitchen with me and I'll make you a nice hot drink while the girls look round. I was just going to brew up for the workmen and I've got some chocolate digestives, your favourites.'

Cathy grimaced at the twins but secretly she was pleased. Sheila's open and loving nature was completely at odds to the twins' lack of emotion and Cathy found it comforting to be cuddled and fussed over again.

'Now, you tell Aunty Sheila all about it . . . How is it with those two sisters of yours? I bet you have to do everything, don't you? Not an ounce of common sense between them, those two. I told 'em, I did, let the poor girl come and live with me, I've got the room – but they insisted you all wanted to stay together. Still, as I was saying to my neighbour Jill the other day – you know Jill, your friend Tim's mum . . .'

Cathy closed her eyes and let the woman's voice wash over her. The familiar Hampshire burr and deep throaty laugh that told of many years smoking strong cigarettes echoed around the room soothingly, and she imagined the kitchen as it used to be. The mental picture of her mother and Sheila Miller hunched over the huge pine table, putting the world to rights over a big pot of tea, was as clear as if it was happening then and there. She could still see herself standing on a stool, mixing and messing about with home-made multicoloured blobs of play-dough and listening to all the local gossip.

It seemed a lifetime away but at the same time it also seemed like only the day before. The woman had never once lost patience with the inquisitive little girl who had followed her from room to room, asking questions about anything and everything. Sheila used to joke that the child was a sponge soaking up information as she meticulously dusted and vacuumed the big house as lovingly as if it was her own.

Widowed after a late but short marriage, she had never had children herself and the young Cathy had filled a void in her life. Sheila had helped the girl get to grips with a new language, a new name and a life that was nothing like the one she had left.

'I've missed you, you know. Why don't you come and stay for a few days? Let me spoil you again, feed you up and get some padding back on those bones of yours.'

'I don't know if Ali and Janey will let me.'

'You just leave them to me. If you want to come back with me then you will! Now, shall we go and look round together?'

Cathy opened her eyes wide to stop them filling up. She thought how nice it would be to be mollycoddled for a while. Just like she used to be . . . almost.

'OK, I'll have a look round but I can't go up to the top floor.' Suddenly Cathy panicked. 'I just can't.'

'No, of course you can't – I understand that. One step at a time, dear; just downstairs for now. You can just have a look at your bedroom. It's almost finished. I've put a few knick-knacks from home in there – only until you get some more of your own, of course . . .'

Cathy stood in the middle of her bedroom and looked around. It bore little resemblance to the cosy girlish room that she had last seen the night of the fire. In place of the pink flowery paper and flouncy drapes the walls were pristine white with a navy-blue patterned border that matched the curtains and bedding, which lay still in the Cellophane packets on the new pine double bed. It all looked very adult, very different, just as she had planned it to be. Apart, of course, from the assorted display of china ornaments lovingly set out on the windowledge by Sheila.

'Now I'm just going to see how your sisters are doing. I'll see you back in the kitchen in a minute.'

As she walked sadly from room to room, avoiding the ladders and platforms that still littered the wide hall, Cathy could hear raised voices from upstairs but she couldn't catch what they were saying.

Suddenly Sheila was beside her. 'I've had a chat with the twins and they've agreed to you coming back with me if you want to. You'll be nearer to that young Tim as well – he'll be company for you during the holidays and it'll give them a break as well. Now I'll just run you all back and you can get your things.'

Looking past the woman's smiling face Cathy could see the twins' matching sullen expressions and guessed that Sheila had put them firmly in their places as only she could. At barely five foot high and nearly as wide, she was one of the few who wasn't intimidated by their over-powering manner.

★ ★ ★

Sheila bustled silently around the kitchen, baking cakes and treats for Cathy who was still asleep upstairs in the tiny two-up, two-down terraced cottage. She was determined to spoil her for a few days, give her a little normality away from Jane and Alison.

When Sheila had first gone to work for the Carter family twenty years before, it was for a little bit of extra money to put away for when she and Ronnie started a family, but it wasn't to be. She could relate to the desolation young Cathy was feeling because her own world had fallen apart when her beloved Ronnie had died under the wheels of a tractor after only two years of marriage. At the time she couldn't imagine ever getting over it, but she had eventually and the young Cathy had helped.

Bryan and Elena Carter had been a tower of strength to her at that time and she had thought she would never be able to repay their kindness – until now. Now she knew she could pay them back by keeping a watchful eye on Cathy and acting as a buffer between the girl and her two very weird sisters, the way their parents had when they were alive.

The footsteps on the stairs alerted her to Cathy on her way down so she hurriedly put the kettle on and fired up the grill that was already laid out with sausages and bacon waiting to be cooked.

'Coo-eee!' she shouted. 'I'm in the kitchen and I've just put the kettle on for you.'

The door opened slowly and Cathy put her head round.

'Sorry,' she smiled apologetically, 'I didn't realise it was so late. It must have been the big comfy bed. That sofa at the flat is so uncomfortable.'

'Now don't you worry about the time. You need sleep, lots of sleep, get your strength back up. Just look at you, all skin and bone, nothing but a skinny little rabbit. Your Aunty Sheila's going to do you a lovely big cook-up for your breakfast – sausages, bacon, the lot – and then you can go and seek out young Tim, who's no doubt down the stables again. I don't know why that boy doesn't just pack up and move in with that old nag of his.'

Cathy walked over and kissed her on the cheek. 'It's good to be here. I'm sorry for not coming over sooner—'

'Don't you fret about that. When my Ronnie died I didn't want to see anyone, do anything, but it gets better, really it does. That's why I left you be. You needed to grieve . . . you still do.'

She went to ruffle Cathy's hair but jumped back, laughing, shaking her hand dramatically and pretending she had been burned.

'Heavens alive, girl, what is that in your hair? Feels like dried-out wallpaper paste. I don't know, when did you go and turn into a teenager?'

Cathy laughed for the first time in weeks. It felt good to be mothered, even if it wasn't by her own mother.

'You are still going to be looking after the house when we all move back, aren't you?'

'Just let anyone try and stop me!' Sheila's jowls wobbled as she planted her hands on her rounded hips and shook her head vigorously in mock indignation.

The agreed few days continued into weeks, and Cathy stayed with Sheila for much of the summer holidays, spending most of her days with Tim and his beloved horse, Champagne, in the stables and fields of his parents' smallholding.

The suffocating misery of the first few weeks abated slowly and was replaced by a gnawing sadness. Cathy dreaded going back to the big lonely house and living alone with Jane and Alison but knew it was inevitable. They were her sisters, after all, though they didn't appear to have missed her. She had called at the shop a couple of times and phoned them but they hadn't been particularly pleased to see her. She felt on a par with Sally the Labrador, who was still in kennels: the twins knew where both of them were and when the time was right they might just go and get them back.

'I don't want to go back to school. I can't wait to leave; I hate it.' Tim's voice had not long broken and Cathy found it hard to get used to the new, deeper tones.

Sitting side by side on a bale of hay in the small yard, they held their hands up high to avoid Fergus the Wolfhound. The size of a pony, he snuffled round them, hoping for a share of the chocolate and crisps that the teenagers were working their way through.

'Get lost, Fergus. Go on, out of it . . .'

As Tim shouted, Cathy held out her hand and gave the dog a crisp.

'Don't do that. You'll only make him worse . . .'

Cathy laughed. 'Come on, Tim, don't take it out on

Fergus just because you don't want to go back to school. It's not his fault. You're lucky you've got him. Sally is still in the kennels . . . Anyway, it's not for long, is it? One more year, that's all, and then we can do what we like.' She looked at him curiously. 'What are you planning to do, by the way?'

'I'm going to work up at Pantiles, at their stables. Dad's sorted it all out for me with Mr Peck, the manager at the farm. I can't wait to get out of that bloody school. It's just like a prison and I hate it.' Tim pushed his straggly hair back from his face as he squinted up at the clear blue sky. 'What about you?'

'I'm out of there too as soon as poss. Then I'm going to do any old job until I meet and marry a rich man who'll keep me in luxury and pay for me to have my stupid face changed. I hate being different. I want to have lovely round eyes with eyelids, and nice fat lips, and masses of bleached blonde curls. I want to be pretty . . .'

She could see Tim was surprised. She'd never said anything like that to him before – in fact she'd only thought of it the previous night when she was sitting with Sheila, watching a glossy American documentary about the impossibly rich and famous and their cosmetic surgeons who seemed to work miracles.

'That's an awful thing to say. What's different about you? You look just like Cathy Carter to me. Anyway . . .' Tim paused and looked down at the ground again, 'I think you're OK, not like some of the dorky girls at school. I suppose you're sort of different but in a good way. What's wrong with that?'

'Piss off, Tim. You know exactly what I mean. If you could find a quick way of getting rid of your spots and sprouting a few muscles so the kids at school would leave you alone I'm sure you would.'

As soon as she saw his face she knew she'd offended him deeply.

He stood up. 'Thanks a lot. Now I know what you really think of me. I'm going to stable Champagne. See ya.'

He walked across the yard with his head down and Cathy felt guilty about hurting his feelings but at the same time she was angry that he couldn't see what she was getting at. He was always being tormented for being so unattractive, so she thought he ought to understand how she felt about being different.

'What's up, chicken? Worried about moving back into the house? Don't be. Me and your sisters have had a bit of a chat and I'm going to come in twice a week to do the housework and then every weekday at tea-time, make sure there's a dinner for you all and keep you company until they come in. How's that?'

'Sheila, I think I've upset Tim. I said something horrible to him.'

Sheila looked at Cathy perched on the edge of the Formica table, looking forlorn and gnawing carefully at her already well-chewed fingernails.

'Don't do that, dear, you'll spoil your dinner,' she smiled as she gently pushed the girl's hand away from her mouth. 'Now tell me what you said and I'll tell you what I think.'

41

Sheila listened in amazement to what Cathy had to say.

'I'm not surprised young Tim was upset but I am surprised at you, dear. Surgery on your face? I've never heard the like. Heavens above, girl, you're beautiful just as you are and young Tim will be really tall and handsome when he grows up.'

Cathy's dark eyes glistened with frustration. 'That's what I mean. Tim can change naturally, I can't. I'm a freak. Mum and Dad thought I was a freak and that was why they wouldn't even talk about my background, about my being Vietnamese. That's why they called me Cathy and let me dye my hair. They didn't want me to be different and neither do I.'

'Cathy Carter, if you were mine I'd slap your legs for you, old as you are. Your mum and dad loved you, the twins love you in their own way, and as for me, you are and always will be the most gorgeous little girl in the world. Now don't you look at me like that – it's true, you silly, silly girl. And what about poor Tim? Anyone can see the poor boy is completely besotted with you. Freak my eye!'

Sheila had always loved Cathy as if she was her own. In fact, she had often wished she had been the one who could have adopted her. When the Carters had brought Cathy home with them she had flirted briefly with the idea of adopting a child herself, but common sense told her that a middle-aged widow who lived in a tiny cottage and cleaned other people's houses for a living had no chance.

Always the plain, overweight one in her family, it had

been taken for granted she would never marry, that she would be the one to stay home and care for her parents. And she had. By the time they had both died within weeks of each other she'd been prepared to spend the rest of her life alone, but then she'd met and married Ronnie, and for the first time ever she had expectations of having her own family.

At first when Ronnie died, she had found it hard to accept that she could have been dealt that kind of blow, but then along had come Cathy, the silent, insular little girl with deep dark eyes that told more of what she'd seen in her short life than words ever could. And without knowing it the little girl helped Sheila get over her loss.

'Rubbish! Tim and I are just friends – we both know that. God, I couldn't imagine anything else, not with Tim . . .'

Sheila laughed out loud. 'Well, my precious, if that's what you really think then you're not as clever as I thought you were. Still, I suppose that's a good thing at your age. You've got all your life ahead of you for boyfriends. Now, enough of this – are you going to come to the house with me while I clear up behind the decorators? Get you used to being there again? It's not long till moving day, is it?'

'I'd sooner live here with you.' The sadness in her voice hurt Sheila deeply.

'Go on now, you'll be fine. I'll see you every day and I'm sure you can come and stay sometimes. I know I can never replace your mum and dad but I'm here for you. Now let's go and see what mess those men have left.'

The sight of the house as they pulled into the drive

made Cathy feel quite sick. She really didn't want to get out of the car but Sheila pulled the passenger door open for her and jollied her along.

Now that it was nearly finished Sheila was amazed to see that the twins had done their best to eradicate all traces of Bryan and Elena Carter. They had taken over the top floor for themselves as well as their own first floor.

The room where their parents had died was now a strange mish-mash of dark purples and reds, with swathes of velvet drapes at the windows and exotic-looking rugs spread over the highly polished floorboards.

Sheila decided the one good thing about the reorganisation was that for the first time in their lives the twins had elected for separate bedrooms on the first floor, but they were furnished and decorated identically and in the same theme as their sitting room. Secretly she thought it looked a bit like a brothel but she knew it wasn't her place to say anything. Her main concern was that she could see Cathy was going to be lonely and excluded on the ground floor, which was at least comparatively normal, thanks to Sheila's input. The twins had virtually isolated themselves upstairs.

Cathy still had to venture past the first floor.

'I don't know how they can use that room, the one at the top.' She paused and looked at Sheila questioningly. 'Do you think they're really odd? You know, like the rest of the village does? Witches and all that?'

The woman hesitated and thought carefully before answering. 'I certainly don't believe all that witches nonsense but they are a bit eccentric, a little unworldly perhaps. Too close to each other really, but then again they do seem to like people thinking they're strange, don't they? Keeps the customers coming into the shop, doesn't it?'

'That's what they say, but they've always been like it, haven't they? I never noticed it so much before, but they don't seem to care about Mum and Dad being dead, and I don't think they even care very much about me.' She glanced around, angrily waving her arms about. 'Look at this place. It just isn't home any more, is it? You must notice that. They've changed everything and I didn't even get a say in it apart from my room, and they even argued about that.'

Silently Sheila agreed. She thought back to the day she had called in when the twins were there issuing instructions and orders to the builders and decorators. She had been so upset on Cathy's behalf she couldn't let it go; she'd had to have her say about it.

'What about Cathy? At least let her choose everything for her own room. She should have some input too, you know. It's her home as well.'

Alison and Jane had looked at Sheila and then at each other in genuine bewilderment.

'But she's only fifteen. We've got to look after her now, we're her guardians . . .'

'Yes, that's right, Sheila. We have to look after her . . .'

Sheila had exhaled loudly. 'Do stop giving me that "guardian" nonsense. She isn't "only" fifteen, she's a teenager coming up to sixteen and entitled to a say in her home. If you want Cathy to stay with you two and, more importantly I might add, be happy, then you have to include her. There are three of you, not just you two!'

'So you think we should let her decide for herself about her room?'

'Yes I do, and what's more, you must let her have some say in the rest of the house. Come on, girls, get your act together and show your poor sister some consideration.'

Jane and Alison had capitulated on Cathy's own room, and even the downstairs décor was comparatively neutral after they had thought about what Sheila had said.

While Sheila got to work cleaning and polishing, Cathy wandered out into the garden. Near to the house it was still as bad as after the fire, although the mud had dried and there were now sturdy weeds forcing their way up among the mounds of debris. She made her way slowly down towards the small stream at the end of the garden where her old swing still hung from the huge oak tree that also shaded the timber summerhouse.

Pushing open the door, she was surprised to find it exactly as it had been left before the fire. Carefully moving the stacked-up garden furniture to get right inside, she inhaled so deeply, she could almost smell her parents. She looked around, touching and moving things as if for the first time.

The small fridge in the corner still housed a couple of bottles of beer, a few cans of lemonade and a half-empty bottle of milk that had solidified into a green mass. Her father's chipped mug was pushed in there out of sight, still with dregs of coffee congealed in the bottom, along with his old enamel plate encrusted with what could have been a half-eaten doughnut.

She could hear her mother as clearly as if she was beside her. 'Bryan, please take your dirty crockery back up to the house. You are so mucky . . . we'll get ants.' The whirly ashtray that Cathy used to love to push down while watching the butts mysteriously disappear still had a couple of cigarette ends inside and Cathy carefully straightened one out and sniffed it, the familiar smell of stale tobacco hitting her like a body blow. 'Why can't you empty the ashtray? It smells like an old ale-house in here . . .' She could hear her father laughing good-naturedly. 'But it's nice to be a slob for a little while every day, Lena – takes me back to that old bedsit we had when we were first married . . .'

Her parents had both loved the summerhouse, and often took the newspapers and a breakfast of big fat croissants down there on warm weekend mornings. Cathy thought sadly about how she used to swing back and forth, watching the squirrels darting around after any morsels they could scrounge before the birds swooped down and flew off with the leftovers. The twins would never go down there so it was always a special time for Cathy when it was just her and her parents, peacefully whiling away the early mornings.

Leaving the door open and everything as it was, Cathy went and sat on her swing. She swung backwards and forwards gently for a while, then suddenly kicked her feet hard into the ground and picked up speed, faster and higher until the ropes flexed, nearly throwing her off.

'Cathy, Cathy, what are you doing? You're going to have an accident . . .'

Cathy was suddenly aware of Sheila making her way cautiously down the path, wary of tripping on the uneven stones.

Cathy kicked again as her feet touched the ground and was off, backwards and forwards as the branch creaked in protest.

'*Now*, Cathy! Stop it *now*! I want you down here off that swing. You're frightening me, you'll kill yourself!'

'I know,' Cathy shouted back, almost happily. 'That's what I want.'

Sheila glanced in the open summerhouse and realised what was going on. She could remember going into Ronnie's potting shed after his accident. She perched carefully on the arm of a sun-bed and watched through the open door, hoping against hope that she was right – that Cathy would take all her anger and frustrations out on the swing, that when she had done that she would come down.

The woman heaved a sigh of relief as eventually the swing slowed to a standstill. Cathy stayed in the seat, her little chest juddering as she breathed in and out rapidly.

Sheila pulled herself up, walked slowly over to the girl and put her arms tightly round her, pulling her close.

'It'll be all right, trust me. It'll take time but it will be all right, it really will.'

Chapter Three

'Should we wait for them, do you think? Did they say what time they'd be back?'

Sheila asked the question innocuously enough but Cathy could see she was getting fidgety. The dinner was already starting to shrivel up in the oven and Cathy was all too aware that it was bingo night in the nearby town and Sheila hated to miss a session and the chance to win a few extra pounds. It was also her big social event of the week, the opportunity for her to get dressed up and have a good gossip in the social club afterwards.

'Do you want me to phone them? I'm sure they're still at the shop. They're changing the flat round so they can use it for reading palms and cards and things. They probably forgot the time again – you know how they get distracted. It's just the way they are . . .'

Sheila reached out her hand and touched Cathy lightly on her cheek. 'Shhhh, you have to stop making excuses for them, you know. Alison and Jane are two big grown-up women who are old enough to have some manners. It's not your job to apologise for them. Anyway, I'm not so sure that all this eccentric behaviour isn't deliberate.'

Cathy hesitated. She knew she was always making excuses for the twins and suddenly she hated having to do it.

'Tell me about them, Sheila. When Janey and Ali were young, what were they really like?'

Sheila patted her freshly permed hair nervously. 'That's a hard one to answer . . .'

'Go on, I'd really like to know what you think. All I ever hear are the stupid remarks.' She could see that Sheila was thinking about it, thinking carefully how to word her answer. Deep down she knew the woman wasn't too fond of her sisters.

'Well, when they were little they were cute, and it was lovely to see two little girls so fond of each other, but if they had been mine I would have tried to discourage it a bit as they got older. Don't think I'm criticising your mum and dad at all – we all do what we think is best – but they were never seen as individuals. It was always "the twins" or, even worse, when people couldn't tell them apart they called each of them "twinnie".'

'But they are alike. In the old photos I couldn't tell them apart; I even have trouble with them now sometimes.'

'I know, absolutely identical, but if they'd been dressed differently, encouraged to have different friends . . .' Sheila paused.

'Go on – how do you think that would have changed them?'

'I'm not sure . . . Anyway, take no notice of me. I've never had children so who can say how I'd have been if they had been mine. Maybe that's the way they would be whatever. Now, what about this dinner . . .?'

Jane and Alison were sitting side by side in the lounge above the shop in comfortable silence. Both were engrossed in books about fortune-telling, which they would soon swop and then compare notes on.

The tourist season was at an end so the shop was now open only four days a week but the sisters still went there most days to potter around both the shop and the flat.

'It's much better here, isn't it? Much cosier than the house.' Jane looked up from her book and glanced around the junk-filled room.

'You're right, and it's quieter without Cathy and Sheila twittering on all the time, playing happy families.'

'Do you think we ought to get rid of Sheila? She's taking over and mothering us all and that's not how we wanted it, is it? Not outsiders . . .'

Alison looked at her sister and shook her head. 'No, it's not, but if Sheila wasn't around we would have to do everything ourselves and we don't really want that either. Perhaps we did the wrong thing by renovating the house. We could have lived here without any outside help and Cathy could have stayed with Sheila. God, it's nearly as bad as having the parents around.'

'We have to think about it, decide what's best for all of us.'

'Mmmm . . . we'll think about it.'

They sank back into the companionable silence and picked up their books simultaneously.

Instead of changing the flat back to a storeroom they were now planning to open it up for fortune-telling; they were both studying reading the tarot cards and palms, and crystal-ball gazing. It was a customer who had given them the idea and suddenly it became an obsession, as things always did with them. Once they became focused on something, everything else faded into the background.

The ringing of the phone made them both sigh at the same time.

'That'll be Cathy.'

'I know. She'll be looking for us. You answer it.'

Jane snatched up the phone and almost barked into it, 'Crystal Cave.'

'Hi, it's me. Sheila wants to know if you're coming in for dinner or should she put yours in the fridge?'

'Cathy, can't we have five minutes' peace? We're busy at the flat and you can tell Sheila that we pay her so we call the tune. We come home when we're ready; we don't have to answer to the bloody cleaner.'

It took all Cathy's willpower to keep her voice calm and her face straight.

'Fine. I'll tell her you won't be back just yet.'

Cathy firmly replaced the receiver and turned to Sheila, smiling. 'They're not sure when they'll be back. They're a bit tied up at the shop but they said they're sorry and thanks for cooking their dinner.'

Sheila threw her head back and roared with mirth.

Cathy couldn't help but smile. When Sheila really laughed, her eyes nearly disappeared as her round cheeks rose up towards her eyebrows. At the same time, her huge belly and boobs wobbled in slow motion.

'You're not a very good fibber, chicken. I can only imagine what they said but whatever it was, it certainly wasn't that!' She wagged a finger at Cathy, who looked sheepishly at the floor. 'You don't have to spare my feelings as far as the twins are concerned. I've known them too long. Too wrapped up in themselves by far, those two. Still, you can have your dinner and I'll sit with you. You can tell me all about this fortune-telling nonsense.'

Cathy felt angry. Once again her sisters had put her in a difficult situation.

'I'm all right. They'll be in soon and you've got your bingo and I've got homework so I'll be in my room anyway. Go on, I promise I'm OK.'

'Ooooh, little Miss Bossy Boots! OK, if you're sure, I'll just dish up then.'

She handed Cathy her dinner plate before quickly snatching off her apron and grabbing her coat from the back of the kitchen chair.

As soon as Sheila had left, Cathy gathered up her dinner on to a tray and headed for the lounge, where she clicked the remote control to the TV. She had no intention of doing her homework; she could never be bothered to do it any more.

Eating her meal idly with one hand and changing channels with the other, Cathy thought about how boring her life was virtually alone in the big house that used to be a happy family home. Despite the TV blaring out in the corner of the lounge, the silence in the rest of the building was overwhelming. Everything was neat and tidy – Sheila made sure of that – and the twins, with unlimited funds at their disposal, had ensured nothing was overlooked in the restoration.

Thick off-white carpets lay throughout the house and the gloomy greys and browns painted on the walls and draped around the windows were offset only by a selection of ornaments that reflected the twins' taste: elaborate pewter and crystal statues of magicians and witches, wrought-iron candlesticks and glittering glass figurines. There were no personal mementoes, no photographs, nothing familiar at all, and Cathy hated it. She hated the bare look of it, the cold feel of it, but most of all she hated the loneliness. By being totally unsociable to everyone most of the time the twins had ensured that few people bothered to try to help them, and there were rarely any visitors.

When Jane and Alison were at home they were closeted away on the top floor most of the time, plotting and planning their latest venture, totally oblivious to their young sister's presence. Cathy was left to spend her time either with Tim or at home on her own.

After picking half-heartedly at her meal and leaving most of it, she went into the kitchen and tipped it into the bin, carefully covering the remains with a page of newspaper to save Sheila's feelings. The advertisement at the bottom of the page caught her eye: 'Local Amateur

Dramatic Society needs young, enthusiastic members for youth-orientated production. Auditions Thursday night.'

It sounded as though it might be fun. After thinking about it for a few minutes, Cathy picked up the phone.

'Hi, Tim, it's Cathy. Guess what, I've seen an ad for an amateur dramatics group and I don't want to go on my own – can you come with me? Please? It's tonight at the community centre in town.'

Once they were actually standing outside the old brick building it suddenly didn't seem like such a good idea.

A young couple walked past them giggling, and went inside hand in hand.

'Romeo and Juliet,' Tim sniggered, looking at Cathy, waiting for her to make the first move towards the doors. She glared at him and he laughed quickly. 'Sorry, just a joke! Come on, shall we go in or have you changed your mind? We can always go to the youth club instead.'

'With all those dorks from school? Nope, we'll go in. Deep breath and let's go, but if they're all boring then we're not stopping.'

Tentatively pushing the heavily sprung door, they entered the small lobby and peered through the grubby square of glass into the main hall.

'There's not many there,' Tim whispered.

'No, but maybe some more will come later. Come on, before I bottle out.'

They tried to get in quietly but as the door creaked open everyone turned and looked.

'Jolly good, another couple of young people,' a theatrical voice echoed across the bare floorboards. 'Come and join us, we're just about to start the auditions. We've got a perfectly wonderful play to put on.'

Cathy and Tim exchanged glances, trying hard not to laugh.

'Come on now, chop chop, take a seat and we can all start getting to know each other.'

Waiting outside for Tim's mother to pick them up at the end of the evening, they both fell about laughing hysterically.

'My God, he was just so over the top. You'd think it was a big London show he was putting on, not a poxy little amateur play. Who does he think he is?' Cathy could hardly get the words out.

'I don't know but I'd bet that's not his real name, and when he kissed you loudly on both cheeks I thought you were going to pass out.' Tim put on a silly voice and pranced around the pavement air-kissing. 'Darling, you simply must come again, you're just perfect, perfect. You'll be the best Julianna ever . . . a gift from heaven to the company . . .'

'Leave him alone. He was only doing what he thinks directors should do. Still, that other fella, Nico, was OK. He made us feel quite welcome and the rest of the group seemed friendly enough. I enjoyed it. Shall we go next week?'

'I'm not sure. I don't think it's really for me. I prefer horses.'

'Well, I'm going, with or without you. It's better than staying home.'

When Cathy got back Jane was in the kitchen making coffee and piling sandwiches and cakes on to a tray.

'Where did you get to?'

'I went out with Tim. We went to a drama thing. Didn't you read my note?'

'No. Now listen, Kitten, we have such a lot to tell you, all about our new business. We're going to be real fortune-tellers. We think we've got the gift – you know, psychic, seeing into the future and all that . . . It's really exciting and it'll be up and running right away in the flat over the shop. It'll look fantastic once the decorators have been in . . . Oh, and guess what. We're changing our names. From now on we're Zara and Zeta, the twin psychics.'

Dressed in an ankle-length black kaftan, and with her hair pulled back into an elastic band, Jane moved quickly around the kitchen, opening cupboards and drawers as she searched nervously for crisps to go with the sandwiches. She waved her hands around wildly as she spoke and her normally expressionless face was animated and glowing.

'It'll be wonderful, just you wait. You could be our receptionist . . . Mind you, we'd have to do something about that awful hair of yours and those clothes, make you look the part . . . Oh, and of course we'll have to change your name as well.'

When the twins were in the grip of excitement it

worried Cathy; she was all too aware that extreme happiness and hyperactivity in the twins were usually followed at some point by an encompassing silent depression that affected everyone around them. And if Jane was flying high then so was Alison.

'We'll see,' Cathy replied cautiously, knowing the time was certainly not right to get into a debate that could last for hours. 'Do you want to hear about my evening?'

'Not now, I'm going up. Don't stay up too late, school tomorrow. Night night.'

Jane blew her a happy kiss, picked up the heaped tray of snacks and was gone, leaving behind her the cloying scent of her heavy perfume and a relieved Cathy.

Instead of getting into bed Cathy grabbed her quilt and a pillow, and curled up in the big armchair in the corner of her room.

She decided she had really enjoyed the evening with the drama group. There were no sympathetic smiles and embarrassed silences, and no smart-arses calling her Susie Wong and thinking it was the most original remark in the world. Even Justin was OK in his own way. He was probably quite good at directing. Everyone took notice of him when he spoke dramatically in his perfectly enunciated voice that carried all around the hall.

And then, of course, there was Nico, Justin's friend and sidekick. The dark and handsome Nico, with his casually perfect clothes and a shiny sports car carelessly parked across the pavement outside.

They hadn't been seated long before he had come over to introduce himself.

'Hi there, I'm Nico. I've been dragged along to help Justin.' He paused and pointed in the direction of the small stage. 'He's a good friend of mine and I felt obliged to help him out when someone let him down.' He smiled conspiratorially at Cathy and Tim. 'And you are . . .?'

'I'm Cathy Carter and this is my friend Tim O'Connor. We saw the ad and just came on the spur of the moment.'

The man smiled again, but this time only at Cathy, his unusual, not-quite-hazel, not-quite-green magnetic eyes looking deep into hers until she felt uncomfortable. No one had ever looked at her like that before.

'I'm pleased you did. You might just be what I'm looking for. How old are you, Cathy Carter?'

She felt the blush rise from deep on her chest and slowly make its way up to her hairline.

'I'm fifteen, but I'll soon be sixteen; so will Tim. We're in the same class at school but we're both leaving next summer . . .' Her voice trailed as Nico kept staring at her, his eyes slowly travelling over her body, a slight smile on his lips.

'Nico, darling, stop chatting up the girls and come and help. That is what you're here for, isn't it? To help?' Justin's distinctive voice echoed across the hall.

Nico looked over at his friend. 'Just coming. I'm making the newcomers feel welcome to our little drama group . . .' Cathy saw a flicker of annoyance pass across his face but then he looked at her and winked before jumping to his feet and making a very dramatic walk across the hall.

Everyone laughed. He was obviously the life and soul of the party, and very popular with all the youngsters.

'Smarmy bastard! Why didn't you ask him how old he was? You could have made him squirm, dirty old man.'

Cathy could see Tim was angry so she laughed. 'Don't be so touchy. I thought he was quite nice, actually. At least he came over and talked to us.'

During the rest of the evening Nico caught Cathy's eye several times and when she read for the lead female part of Julianna in the comedy play *Party-time*, he smiled encouragingly from the edge of the stage, making eye contact at every opportunity.

'See you next week I hope, Julianna.'

Cathy laughed. 'I haven't got the part yet. There are others who have been coming a lot longer than I have.'

'It's talent that counts and that is what will make you Julianna, take my word for it.'

As he spoke his hand brushed against hers. It was so subtle she wasn't sure if she had imagined it, but it made her jump, intentional or not.

Now Cathy snuggled down in the chair, hugging her quilt close, and smiled. She was looking forward to the next meeting but she had to try really hard to push out of her mind the hope that Tim would decide not to go. She wondered what it would be like to have a boyfriend, a real boyfriend. She thought about Nico – surely a good-looking sophisticated man like him wouldn't be interested in a fifteen-year-old?

Cathy arrived home the next day to find a very grim Sheila waiting at the open front door.

'Exactly what have you been up to, my girl?'

'What do you mean? I haven't been up to anything . . .' Cathy tried to think on her feet; surely Sheila hadn't found out that she had bunked school.

Sheila took her hand and led her into the kitchen.

'What's that then?' She pointed accusingly at the sink where a huge bouquet of flowers was standing in a bucket of water.

'That's nothing to do with me.'

'Oh yes it is. Look . . . it says "Cathy Carter" on the envelope.'

Cathy unstapled the small envelope from the Cellophane and opened it.

'For Cathy, the best Julianna. Nico.'

'Oh my God . . .' Cathy's hand flew up to her mouth as she gasped.

'Too right. That's exactly what I thought. Now then, who are they from?'

Tempted though she was to tell Sheila to mind her own business Cathy could see she was really worried. She giggled nervously.

'It's from the drama group I went to last night. They thought I was good, that's all. Nico – he's the sort of stage manager and general helper to the director – must have sent them on behalf of everyone.'

The relief was written all over Sheila's face. 'Oh, dear

Lord, you had me worried there. I thought for a minute you'd found yourself a wealthy admirer. These must have cost a fortune.'

Her mind at rest, Sheila plucked at the girl's cheek affectionately. 'I'm so pleased you've found something to do that you enjoy. You deserve it. Now we'd better find a vase for these although I don't know if there's one here that's big enough.'

'What about the one in the lounge? The one with the dried flowers in? I'll just go and get it.'

Cathy rushed out of the kitchen, pleased to get away from Sheila's gaze. She could feel herself going red again and she knew she was going to have problems keeping the silly wide grin off her face.

'You don't have to come if you don't want to, Tim. I really don't mind going on my own.'

Cathy and Tim were in the burger bar after school and she was unsuccessfully trying tactfully to stop him going to the drama group that evening.

'No, it's OK. I'll come with you. Mum said I should give it another go. Anyway, how would you get home after? The buses don't run after eight o'clock.'

'It's OK. I'll get Jane or Ali to give me the money for a taxi. It's not a problem, really . . .'

Tim looked at her, trying to puzzle out what was going on. 'Don't you want me to go? You did last week when you didn't know anybody.' His tone was accusing.

'Don't be daft, of course I want you to come if you want to, but you don't, do you? Not really.'

'Of course I do. We'll pick you up at seven from the top of the lane.'

Cathy tried to sound enthusiastic. 'Thanks, that's great.'

Cathy dressed carefully. The previous week she had gone as she was, with scruffy clothes and no make-up, but this time she intended to make an effort. It was frustrating that for once the twins were at home early but she hoped they wouldn't take any notice. Sheila was a whole different ball game. Cathy was all too aware of her eagle eyes and good intuition. If anyone was going to spot that Cathy had more on her mind than just amateur dramatics then it was definitely Sheila.

She heard Sheila shout goodbye through her door but she didn't open it.

'I'm just getting changed. Bye, Sheila, see you tomorrow,' she shouted back happily.

Cathy didn't have much choice about what to wear. All her clothes had been lost in the fire and she had replaced very few; there had not been any need and she had no enthusiasm for shopping. The twins had spent like mad women to replace everything but Cathy had resolutely refused to have more than the essentials. For the first time she regretted it.

After pulling her few clothes out of the wardrobe she decided on the black trousers and top she had bought for the funeral and not worn since.

Tucking the trousers into the high black boots and breaking up the black with a big wide scarlet belt buckled around her hips, she looked in the mirror and was pleased with the effect. She thought she looked older, despite her lack of height and boyish figure, but as usual she focused on her eyes and they depressed her again. Everything else looked good except for the black oriental eyes that could not be disguised.

She attacked with the kohl pencil again, and spiked her hair with gel, pulling the fringe down as far as she could past her eyebrows and pushing the rest back behind her ears. A touch of pale lipstick swiped over her lips finished off her preparations and although she wasn't over the moon at her appearance she knew she had done the best she could.

'You look nice, Kitten, where are you off to?' Cathy nearly fell off her boots in amazement as Alison looked her up and down and smiled.

'It's the drama group again, remember I told you? I went last week. It was really fun and I might even get a good part. That's who sent me the flowers . . .'

The twins looked at her, almost as if they were seeing her for the first time.

'You look older!'

'That's right. That's what's different – you look more grown up.'

'That sounds like an accusation. I'm nearly sixteen, you know – soon be leaving school and going to work.'

Cathy grinned back at them. It was nice when they noticed her and were interested. It made her remember how much she loved them, even if they did drive her crazy most of the time.

'And then you're coming to work for us.'

'Hang on, I never agreed to anything. I might want to do something else. Maybe I want to be an actress. I've been told I'm good.'

'Don't be silly, we have to keep it in the family. We don't want outsiders working with us, we want you.'

Cathy wasn't keen to discuss it, especially as she was about to go out, but she didn't like to upset them either, so she kissed and hugged both of them and headed for the door.

'I have to go; Tim's mum is giving us a lift. Bye, both. See you later.'

'Bye, Kitten. Behave yourself.'

She knew that by the time she shut the door they would have forgotten her but she was pleased they were at least a little aware of her even if it was only for a short while.

Cathy was pleased that Tim looked the same as usual. At least Nico couldn't think that he was her boyfriend. She was aware for the first time that although they were the same age they were light years apart in experience.

Tim had been born in the New Forest and brought up in a secure and happy family. She knew he was unhappy about being teased and bullied at school, but she also knew that would pass for him. Her background was chequered and tragedy-ridden; none of that would ever pass for her. He was still a child really and she felt like an adult. She wondered if that was why she was attracted to the much older Nico.

'You're not listening to me, are you? We're there.'

Tim's voice brought her sharply back.

They climbed out of the car outside the hall and Cathy was surprised to see Nico waiting outside, leaning on the railings. His faded blue jeans and white T-shirt were immaculately laundered, and the black tassel loafers casually elegant and very Mediterranean. Cathy thought he was the best-looking man she had ever seen.

He walked round to where the car had pulled up and opened the door for Cathy to get out.

'You're early, you two – the first here, in fact, apart from Justin and, of course, moi. I came out for a breath of fresh air to get away from Justin. He's convinced, as always, that no one is going to turn up.'

As he stood back politely to let Cathy and Tim go in through the doors first he lightly placed his hand in the small of Cathy's back as she passed, an innocent guiding movement but enough to make her look round sharply. Standing close to him she was surprised that he was quite short, about five foot six or seven but lean and confident and smiling directly at her.

'I'm sorry, did I make you jump? I didn't mean to. Looking forward to rehearsals?'

'Yes, we both are. It was fun last week; we really enjoyed it.' She smiled nervously.

'I'm pleased. I think we're looking at utilising your young man behind the scenes . . .'

'He's not my young man, he's my friend.'

'Good, I'm pleased to hear that.' Nico smiled and then wandered off over to the stage and Justin, leaving Cathy

66

to try to decide what he meant. Was he pleased that Tim wasn't her young man? Or was he just pleased that Tim was her friend?

More important, was she making a fool of herself? He was probably just being friendly and kind to the newcomers. Perhaps he was like that to everyone in the beginning, and she was kidding herself.

After all, she thought, why would a handsome, charming and obviously successful older man fancy a fifteen-year-old who looked about twelve and had never had a boyfriend in her life?

If Cathy had heard Justin and Nico talking in the changing room she would have known why.

'For fuck's sake, Nico, can't you ever leave the young girls alone? Jesus, they're getting younger and younger. How old is that one? Thirteen? Twelve? One day you're going to get in deep shit . . . It was a close call last time; you nearly got caught out.'

'Actually, she's fifteen, nearly sixteen, she just looks a lot younger. Come on, admit it, isn't she gorgeous? I don't know how you can resist, she's just so childlike and innocent, so . . .' He frowned and hesitated as if he was having trouble articulating. 'Untouched by human hands, if I'm not mistaken,' he smiled slyly, 'and soon-to-be-legal. What more could a guy want?'

Justin tried hard to keep control of his temper.

'That's certainly not what I want, I can assure you. Fucking jailbait? You're kidding. Please, please, behave, Nico darling. You promised to keep your hands off the kids. I really want this play to work. It's for charity, and in any case, I don't need irate parents battering down the doors and dragging their little darlings out of here.'

'I'm sorry, Justin, but I really am going to have that girl. She's just what I'm looking for, and anyway,' he smiled, his capped white teeth glinting against the perfect tanned features, 'she hasn't got any parents, just two batty sisters!'

'You know, my friend, you're starting to get a reputation for drooling over schoolgirls. The local Chinese whispers are coming up with the word "paedophile" time and time again . . .'

Nico's face darkened and his handsome features suddenly looked quite evil. Justin took a step back as the man in front of him clenched his fists.

'Don't *ever* use that word about me. Paedophiles abuse children. I don't. I have never touched anyone underage – do you understand? Read my lips . . . I AM NOT A PAEDOPHILE, and I've never forced anyone to do anything they didn't want to.'

The door slammed and Nico headed back to the main hall.

It was lucky he didn't hear Justin mutter under his breath, 'Methinks he doth protest too much!'

Chapter Four

Young Cathy Carter was in love, completely and madly in love with Nico. Thoughts of him occupied her every waking moment and dreams of him filled her nights. She was besotted in a way she could never have imagined, even at the height of her teenage crushes on pop stars and soap actors. The worst part was not being able to confide in anyone but she knew that if she did they would either laugh their socks off or be totally horrified so she had to hug it all to herself. There wasn't a single person she could trust with her secret, not even Tim.

Every hour was a countdown to the next rehearsal, the moment when she would see him again. Her doubts that she might be imagining his interest in her always evaporated as soon as they came face to face and he smiled into her eyes and touched her fingers – intimate, meaningful gestures that said more than words ever could.

Nico had been nothing if not completely respectful to her, the perfect gentleman in fact. He had never even so much as tried to hold her hand, let alone kiss her, and they had never been alone together but they had talked and talked in the corner of the hall and she knew, she just knew, that he felt the same.

She had plans to move the relationship on. Her sixteenth birthday was coming up and she was intending to throw a party, an ideal opportunity to be close and together without anyone taking too much notice. She imagined the situation all the time: a fast dance, then hopefully a slow dance, followed by a walk in the garden, maybe holding hands, and then she hoped, a kiss, her first kiss with Nico. She plotted and planned constantly in her mind how she was going to make sure that something happened at the party.

Everything was organised down to the smallest detail – the guest list, the food, the drink, what she was going to wear and how she was going to do her hair – but there was still the most important thing to do. Cathy had yet to broach the subject with her sisters whose permission she needed, and Sheila whose help she wanted, but whose presence she didn't. When the opportunity presented itself it was totally unexpected and she nearly wrong-footed herself.

'What are you going to do for your birthday, Cathy? Are you going to have a party? Sixteen is a big birthday, you know . . .'

Sheila was in the conservatory carefully mopping the perfectly clean floor while Cathy perched on the windowledge with her feet out of the way.

'You could invite your school friends – Tim, of course – such a nice boy. You're a really lucky girl to have such a good friend, and who knows what will happen in the future, eh?'

Cathy avoided Sheila's questioning glance and tried not to get annoyed. Sheila was constantly matchmaking the two youngsters and no matter how hard Cathy reiterated that they were just friends Sheila would just smile knowingly.

'He's OK, for a friend. Do you think Ali and Jane will let me? Have a party, I mean? I'd love to have a proper party, and it'd be a great opportunity to really get to know the others at the drama group . . . and have round some of the kids from school, of course.'

'If you want a party I'll talk to the twins. I take it you don't want them there?'

'What do you think?' Cathy smiled nervously. 'I love them both, I really do, but they can be so embarrassing. Can't you just picture it? They'd have that bloody crystal ball out.'

'Cathy Carter! You mind your language!'

Cathy giggled and continued, 'How can I get out of it without hurting their feelings? I really want to have a proper party, not a kid's birthday party.'

'Oh, I'm sure I'll find a way. I'll do a special dinner for you girls on the actual day and then you can have your party at the weekend. I'll offer to supervise, that should do it. I'm sure they won't want to be surrounded by a crowd of teenagers, anyway. They'll prefer to either lock themselves away upstairs or stay at the flat. Just you leave it to Aunty Sheila.'

Cathy tried to smile gratefully. She knew she had more

chance of putting one over on the twins than on the eagle-eyed Sheila, but at least the party was now a real possibility.

The next rehearsal went well for everyone except Cathy, and Justin was starting to lose patience with her. She found it hard to concentrate with Nico's gaze on her constantly, watching every movement.

'Cathy, darling,' Justin bared his teeth in a sarcastic smile as he spoke slowly and carefully, 'you really must concentrate just a teeny bit. Julianna is lively and fun, the life and soul of the party, not a distracted lovesick teenager. This is acting, dearest, acting. On stage you are Julianna, not Cathy.'

For an awful moment Cathy felt her bottom lip wobble, the thought of crying in front of the whole cast was just too humiliating, but Nico leaped to her rescue just in time.

He was standing behind Justin and suddenly he put his thumbs in his ears and waggled his fingers while at the same time sticking his tongue out at the posturing Justin's back.

Cathy smiled.

'That's better,' Justin smiled back, completely unaware of what was going on. 'Now let's try again, shall we? We don't have many rehearsals left to get it right.'

Nico went over to her afterwards and gently patted her on the back. 'Take no notice of Justin. He can be a prat sometimes and he takes all this, and himself, far too seriously, but he doesn't mean it.'

Cathy felt the heat rising slowly from her chest up towards her face.

'Where's young Tim tonight? You two are usually joined at the hip.'

'He's away for a few days at some horse show.' She still found it hard to meet Nico's direct gaze so she studied her hands as she spoke. 'And we are not joined at the hip, we're just friends, I've told you before.'

'And I believe you! How are you getting home?'

'I've got the taxi fare.' She glanced at her watch. 'Actually I'd better call one now; it's nearly time to leave—'

'Oh no you won't,' Nico interrupted almost angrily. 'I don't know what you're thinking of. I'm not having you go home in a taxi on your own. I'll give you a lift. Just wait while I help Justin clear up – in fact you can help, we'll get it done a lot quicker that way.'

Cathy couldn't keep the grin from her face. She felt flattered that he was concerned about her safety and she was sure that showed that he felt something for her.

She watched him surreptitiously as he moved about the hall, stacking chairs and picking up the odd bit of litter. Impeccably casual as usual, he looked, with his tanned face and arms, as if he belonged on the deck of a yacht in the sun. His jeans and shirt were immaculately laundered and ironed and held in place by an understated but very exclusive-looking leather belt. She suddenly wondered who looked after his clothes, who looked after him. Was there a wife? A girlfriend? A mother? She realised she knew nothing about him other than that he was handsome and kind and liked her, and that she was in love with him.

Just as they were ready to go Cathy darted into the cloakroom quickly, touching up her lipstick and spiking up her hair. She pulled a face at herself in the mirror and ran back out to find Nico waiting impatiently.

'What kept you? I thought you were going to be all night in there . . .'

The tone took Cathy by surprise. 'I'm sorry, Nico, I was just—'

'Just tarting yourself up?' he almost snarled. 'You don't need to do that.' Just as quickly his tone changed and a slight smile started at the corners of his mouth. He reached his hand up and very lightly touched her cheek. 'You're lovely without any of that muck caked on your face. You're young and gorgeous – don't go and spoil it by growing up too soon.'

The warm glow that seeped through her body at the words continued on the drive home. The sleek red Lotus snaked easily through the quiet tree-bordered lanes as she guided him to where she lived. The car slowed as he looked for the entrance, hidden from the main road.

'I think you'd better drop me here. My sisters might not be too happy that I got a lift from a strange man instead of a taxi.'

Cathy was starting to panic. She wanted to get out of the car before anyone saw her. Her instincts told her no one would approve of Nico but she also knew that as long as he was a secret then she was safe.

He pulled the handbrake on and turned off the engine

before leaning slightly towards her.

'So, you think I'm a strange man, do you? Exactly what do you find strange about me?'

Cathy laughed nervously, not quite sure what to say, not quite sure if he was joking or not.

'I didn't mean . . . It wasn't meant . . .'

Nico raised his finger to his mouth. 'Sshhh, I was only joking, I'm sorry. Go on, off you go, I can see you're getting jumpy.' He patted her thigh. 'The last thing I want to do is get you into any bother.'

Cathy hesitated. 'Nico, it's my birthday soon and I'm having a party. Would you like to come? And Justin and the group, of course. There'll be all sorts of friends there . . .'

'Sounds good to me, sweet little sixteen! I look forward to it. Now go! I'll see you on Thursday. Be good in the meantime.'

She stood freeze-framed at the side of the road as she watched the car roar off rapidly, waiting until the tail-lights disappeared round the sharp bend before she headed towards the house.

'Nico? Is that you?' The voice echoed down the hall before he had even shut the front door.

'No, it's the phantom of the opera . . . who the fuck do you think it is?'

Justin appeared in the doorway, his gentle features unusually angry, the pale blue eyes wide open. A large dog was standing behind him, growling half-heartedly.

'Thanks a lot for just leaving me in that poxy hall. I had

to get a cab all the way back. I suppose you were sniffing round that kid again. I'm sorry, Nico, but if you want to continue to take advantage of my hospitality here, in *my* flat, then I expect a smidgen of good manners in return.'

Nico burst out laughing. 'Just listen to yourself, you pompous dick – *a smidgen of good manners*. Who do you think you are?'

'I know exactly who I am. I'm the stupid pompous dick who gave you somewhere to crash when the lovely Simonie showed you the door for the one hundredth time.'

'Soon to be sorted, my friend, soon to be sorted. You know how it is – give her another week and she'll be begging for me to go back. Just a minor misunderstanding . . . You know she can't resist me.'

Nico walked over to the drinks cabinet and opened the flap.

'Scotch? I could do with a nightcap, calm me down after a ride through the Forest with the delectable Cathy. We've been invited to her sixteenth birthday party, how about that? A celebration of legality.'

Justin looked at him distastefully. They had been friends for nigh on twenty years but Justin couldn't get to grips with Nico's ever-increasing appetite for teenage girls.

He found it even harder to understand, considering Nico had Simonie at his beck and call. Justin wasn't surprised that she had thrown him out yet again, this time after discovering his secret stash of hard-core child-porn magazines direct from Amsterdam, but he also knew that

Nico was right, she would have him back shortly. She always did. It was a volatile relationship that erupted at regular intervals, but Simonie was always the one to apologise and always the one to plead with him to go back.

Justin could never understand it. The woman was young, beautiful and intelligent, and addicted to Nico Marcos. But at twenty-five she was not young enough for him. Nico just seemed to use and abuse her and push her to the limits, but still she would have him back.

'Will you be inviting the little sixteen-year-old Cathy to your fortieth in a couple of months? A celebration of middle age?' Justin threw the remark at him casually.

Nico just laughed. 'Jealousy will get you nowhere, my friend. If you could stop camping it up as a pseudo stage director for five minutes and take lessons from the master then maybe you too could have a Simonie or a Cathy instead of living alone with just a mangy mongrel for company. Here, take your drink and chill out before your face curdles the milk!'

'Arrogant bastard!'

'Not so much of the bastard, thank you.'

Justin felt his anger slowly abate as his friend, still chuckling, passed him a glass. Nico could have charmed Godzilla if he'd set his mind to it.

Justin was unlucky when it came to looks. He had blond hair and blue eyes and was tall and rangy. It should have been a good combination but somehow it all missed and he looked nondescript. Rarely did anyone notice him and if they did they certainly never remembered him.

The suave and darkly sexy Nico always made him feel inadequate, and Justin envied him his confidence.

Nico himself was well aware of the dynamics of the friendship and he enjoyed the power and control he exerted over Justin, the same power and control that he had every intention of exerting over Cathy very soon.

However, the sexual excitement that he found in just thinking about the young girl had almost been over-powered by the sight of the house she lived in. In the dark it had been hard to get the full impact but he did see, swathed in the outside lights, a huge house set back from the road in its own grounds. A house that, although not ostentatious, reeked of money.

Then and there a plan had formed. His insurance and finance business was not getting his full attention and he thought he could boost his falling bank balance in one hit while at the same time giving himself unlimited access to a gorgeous young thing who barely looked twelve when she wasn't done up to the nines trying to be sophisticated.

The day of Cathy's sixteenth birthday party finally dawned. Cathy had been counting the hours ever since Nico had accepted her invitation and the time had gone painfully slowly.

Just before the invitation time of eight o'clock Cathy started to march around nervously. Supposing Nico didn't come? Would he really want to spend Saturday night with a group of teenagers? She decided it had been a stupid idea and at that moment would have given anything to be able to call the whole thing off, unable even to imagine the pain of having to get through the party without Nico. Nico, who it was all for!

Even though she hadn't quite achieved the supervision-free setting that she had wanted she had the next best thing. The twins were staying completely out of the way upstairs, by choice, and Sheila was leaving once everyone had arrived and got settled. A tiny stabbing of guilt niggled away because Cathy knew the woman would love to be there and be motherly, but she kept smothering it. An eagle-eyed Sheila watching her every movement certainly wasn't in the plan.

Sheila had prepared all the food for a buffet and laid it out on the extended table in the dining room while a bar for soft drinks and beer was set up in the conservatory. Cathy was pleased; it all looked very adult. She prayed desperately that Nico would turn up and be impressed, that he would realise that she could be cool and sophisticated, not just a silly teenager.

As soon as Sheila left, and if Nico showed, she intended to dim the lights and light the scented candles that she had begged from the twins, and produce the bottles of vodka and brandy that she had stashed away in the unused summerhouse. But by the time it got to 9.30 all the guests had arrived bar Nico and Justin. Sheila had grudgingly left but Cathy was so disappointed she just wanted to go to bed and leave everyone to it. She had stopping running to the door every time the bell rang and was quietly collecting dirty plates and glasses for the dishwasher.

'What's up, Cathy? You're not enjoying your party, are you? Is it because of your mum and dad?'

Tim had silently appeared behind her and she had nearly dropped the crockery.

'Shit, you shouldn't creep up on people like that . . .' As soon as she had shouted at him she regretted it. He was looking at her just like a sad puppy, a bedraggled little spaniel, all dark floppy hair and big sad eyes. His glaringly new shirt and trousers hung loosely on his gangly frame and she could see he felt uncomfortable out of his old jeans and comfortable T-shirt. She couldn't fail to notice his adoring gaze and for the first time she felt self-conscious in front of him, aware that she was dressed up and made up for Nico, not for him.

'Sorry, Tim, I didn't mean to shout. You just made me jump. I'm fine, really, just having a bit of a breather.'

'Fancy a dance? I know I'm not much good . . .'

Cathy smiled at him. 'Later perhaps. Nothing personal, I just want a break for a minute. You go back through, I'll be in shortly . . . promise.'

She watched him walk dejectedly out of the kitchen but her guilt was soon forgotten as the outline of Nico appeared in the doorway with Justin close behind him. Resisting the urge to fling her arms around his neck and grin from ear to ear she just smiled nervously, her heart palpitating so much she was sure he would notice.

'It's nice to see you both. Drinks are in the conservatory, food is in the dining room and dancing in the lounge. Oh, and the garden is lit up so if you get hot you can go out there . . .'

She knew she was babbling but couldn't help herself. Nico was standing in front of her, looking straight into her eyes, the corners of his mouth twitching slightly in amusement. 'Happy birthday, beautiful Julianna.' He leaned forward and reached out his hands, taking hold of her bare shoulders before kissing her gently on both cheeks. 'Sweet sixteen and yet to be kissed properly . . . I hope!'

Before she could react Justin pushed him out of the way, laughing.

'Put her down, Nico, it's my turn. Happy birthday, Cathy. Here's a little something to help the party along.' He handed over two bottles of champagne before he hugged her.

Over his shoulder Cathy could see Tim standing stock-still in the doorway, his young face frozen as Nico looked hard at him. His lips were drawn back over his teeth in semblance of a smile but his eyes were piercing through the boy, almost threateningly.

Cathy couldn't understand what Tim could have done to upset Nico and made a mental note to find out.

Suddenly Nico was aware of her looking; his expression changed in an instant and he reached up and ruffled Tim's hair playfully. 'How's it going then, Tim? Where are all your little friends? Bopping away to Abba in the other room?'

The point wasn't lost on Tim and he flushed angrily before turning quickly and leaving the kitchen.

Nico turned to Justin. 'Didn't you say you were starving? There's food around somewhere if you go and look for it . . .' The two men's eyes met. Justin held his gaze for a few seconds before bowing to the inevitable and leaving Cathy and Nico alone together.

The girl was flustered. 'Shall I introduce you to everyone? There's loads of people here . . .'

'I didn't come tonight to meet anyone else. I came to see you, the birthday girl. Come with me . . .'

He took her by the hand and led her out of the house to where his car was thoughtlessly parked with two wheels in one of the carefully restored borders squashing the plants flat. Opening the car boot he reached in and with a flourish handed her a bouquet of red roses.

Cathy squealed. 'Oh my God, they are just so beautiful, thank you, Nico, thank you . . .'

Immediately he reached in again and took out an elaborately wrapped and ribboned square package.

'Don't open this now, beautiful, save it until later, when everyone has gone and you're on your own. This is just between us, from me to you . . . you'll understand when you open it!' He leaned forward and brushed her lips with his. 'Now, let's get back to the party and celebrate.'

Nico could feel himself getting aroused just looking at the young girl hanging on his every word and gazing up at him, oblivious to the loud music and raucous laughter of the party. Oblivious also to Tim, he thought triumphantly, the spectre at the feast, who was almost shadowing them, a picture of misery in the background.

He also got very excited when he sneaked off to have a look around the house. It was everything he had hoped for and he guessed there was a lot of money floating around in the family, but how much was Cathy's? He knew there were three sisters and he wondered if Cathy had an equal third.

His mouth was almost watering in anticipation. He decided that would be his next project – to find out how much she was actually worth and when she could get her hands on it.

'Who are you? What are you doing up here?'

Nico jumped. He tried to remain cool but it was hard when he was confronted by a woman of Amazonian proportions who stood head and shoulders above him, swathed in a black silky kaftan, with mad hair spread out over her broad shoulders.

'I'm a guest at Cathy's party and I'm looking for the bathroom . . .'

'Not up here you're not. Are the three downstairs not sufficient for you? This part of the house is private. Now piss off to wherever you came from.'

The woman stared at him and didn't move her eyes even when she took a long-drawn-out puff from her cigarette.

Slowly she turned to go back up the flight of stairs where he had been creeping about, and he was aghast to see there was a second woman behind her, a clone. Fuck, he thought, it's the twins. He wanted to laugh but his heart was pounding. He had heard about them but never seen them before, never taken any notice of the rumours about witchcraft and bizarre behaviour.

Suddenly his confidence in his ability to ensnare Cathy,

and her money, wavered as he wondered how he could possibly get on side with the two of them.

'I am so sorry. You must be Cathy's sisters, Jane and Alison, isn't it? Cathy comes to my drama group, very talented young lady . . . she'll go far.' He smiled his most charming smile, hanging his head very slightly in deference. 'Anyway, I am sorry, I didn't mean to intrude. I really did get lost. Cathy said to use the bathroom upstairs so I thought . . . Sorry again . . .'

The twins looked at one another and then back at him before turning silently and heading up the stairs.

Nico was stunned. He couldn't remember the last time his charm hadn't worked, that he had been completely cold-shouldered. He was angry but he was also very perturbed. He could see that they really were weird. They were also Cathy's guardians. Right then and there he knew he would have to rethink his plans. If those two were the sisters then Cathy wasn't quite the vulnerable orphan he thought she was. He had definitely underestimated the situation.

Quickly composing himself and straightening his thoughts, Nico made his way back down to the party and to Justin. Cathy was nowhere to be seen.

'Nico, my friend, just what are you playing at? Cathy's been looking for you. I thought you must have done a runner, had second thoughts about deflowering yet another little virgin . . .'

The smile on Justin's face faded as Nico turned towards him, eyes wild with rage.

'Shut your fucking mouth and keep out of my life . . . Go and get a life of your own for once.'

'Maybe I'll do just that. I'll keep out of your life and you get out of my flat, deal?'

Justin turned his back on his friend just in time to see Tim disappearing into the conservatory. He wondered how much he'd heard and hoped, for the boy's sake, that it wasn't much and that he didn't repeat it. It wasn't healthy to have Nico as an enemy.

'Nico! Where have you been? I've been looking all over.' Cathy bounced into the room, her eyes bright and her voice loud from one drink too many.

'Sorry, I got lost en route to the bathroom and bumped into your sisters. They weren't too pleased to see me, I don't think. But I'm afraid I have to leave now.' A feeling of satisfaction swept over him as he saw the naked disappointment on Cathy's face. 'How would you like to have lunch with me tomorrow? It is your actual birthday tomorrow, isn't it?'

She nodded, feeling the red glow warming her face once again.

'Good! I'll pick you up at the top of the drive at twelve-thirty . . . you can let me know if you like your present.'

As soon as the last of the guests had gone Cathy went out into the kitchen and retrieved the present Nico had given her. Turning it over and over she savoured the anticipation of what was inside, almost frightened to open it in case she was confronted with disappointment.

After looking around at the mounds of party debris she carefully extinguished the candles, locked all the doors and turned off the lights. Then she went to her room, promising herself she would get up early in the morning to start clearing up before the twins surfaced and Sheila arrived.

Slowly she pulled one end of the palest pink ribbon and then the other before peeling back the corners of the gift box. Inside was a square velvet box that she quickly snapped open.

Although alone she gasped out loud. Inside was a yellow and white gold brooch of the two theatrical masks, happy and sad. A card was under the brooch: 'For Cathy. You were sad but I'll make you happy again. I love you. Marry me. Nico.'

After what seemed like hours, just staring at the box and reading the card over and over again, Cathy eventually went to bed with the box clasped tightly in her hands and a huge smile on her face.

Nico had no intention of begging Justin to let him in so he headed for the one person he knew he could get round. He rang the bell and waited for a few seconds before calling through the letter box.

'It's only me. I have to see you. I love you and I want to be with you. Please let me in.'

Slowly the door opened and a face appeared, bleary-eyed with sleep.

'Darling, darling, please let me in. I'm so sorry . . . Honestly, Simonie, I swear nothing like that will ever happen again. It was all Justin's fault . . . he talked me into keeping the stuff for him.'

The woman opened the door wide to let Nico in. Triumphantly he flung his arms around her and nestled into her neck. He would have been happier if the first move had come from her but under the circumstances he told himself she was better than nothing and certainly better than a night under a frosty tree!

He was still awake as dawn broke. The gentle rays of light spread fan-like across the room and he looked down at the young woman curled up into him, one arm slung across his chest in an unconscious gesture of ownership.

Her long natural-blonde hair partially obscured her face but her naked body was there for him to look at and admire. But the long legs and boyish hips that had once turned him on now held less appeal.

All he could see was Cathy, tiny unrounded Cathy with virtually no breasts and the face of a twelve-year-old when it wasn't covered with inexpertly applied make-up. He jumped out of bed, aware that if Simonie woke up and saw his erection she would think it was for her and he really didn't fancy making love to her now, not when little Cathy was waiting in the wings.

Prior to Cathy he had even considered marrying Simonie.

After Joanna had divorced him he had sworn never to give another woman that kind of control over him. He missed his two children like crazy but that had been part of the agreement. He didn't see them and she didn't go to the police.

She sold the house and moved away, wiping him out of their lives for ever, and he had to start over again. After heading back to Hampshire and his old friend Justin, he eventually met Simonie and quickly moved in with her while still pursuing the secret vice that he couldn't live without, despite the close calls of the past.

He silently pulled some clean clothes out of the wardrobe and dressed quickly before looking down at her and trying to rouse some feeling. But it was impossible. She was too sophisticated now, too experienced – too old, in fact. He knew he had to have Cathy, to own her and mould her – the young innocent oriental girl who could fulfil his fantasies and, he hoped, pay off his debts into the bargain.

He was sure he could train her to do everything he wanted.

'Come back to bed, darling. We've got so much time to make up and I've missed you.'

Nico already had his hand on the door when Simonie's sexy voice floated across the room. He looked over his shoulder. She was leaning up on one arm and pouting beautifully as she playfully twirled her hair.

'I can't, darling, I've got a lunch meeting. There's a big deal going down and I want to be part of it. It might mean megabucks.' He walked over and leaned down to kiss her on the cheek but she grabbed his arm and playfully pulled him back on to the bed.

'Ten minutes, just give me ten minutes, and I'll relax you ready for your silly meeting . . .' Reaching down she slowly and sensually unzipped his trousers.

Nico closed his eyes and thought of Cathy – Cathy, whom he would be meeting at 12.30; Cathy, just the thought of whom turned him on like no one had ever done before.

Chapter Five

'You're mad, Cathy.' The twins looked sharply at each other, their shocked expressions mirrored.

'Do you really think we'd agree to you getting married? You're just a child . . .'

'That's right. No way, Cathy, no way, and especially not to that . . . that . . . old man.' Alison almost spat the words out as she stammered in disbelief. 'Christ, he's old even for us, let alone you!'

Cathy had anticipated their reaction and had her counter-argument prepared. She was going to marry Nico, as soon as possible, before he changed his mind, whether they liked it or not.

'Well, if that's how you see it then good luck to you,' she smiled nonchalantly. 'Gretna Green, here we come . . . Nico has asked me, I've said yes and that's all there is to it. I was only trying to be polite by mentioning it to you. I'm marrying Nico, like it or bloody lump it. We love each other.'

Cathy kept her voice calm and level. The twins were

incensed but it was exactly what she had expected.

'Don't you dare talk to us like that! Mum and Dad would turn in their graves if they could hear you. Married indeed! Be sure you're not even going to see him again. Married! No way, José. Christ Almighty, you're only just sixteen and we're your guardians. So no, no, no!'

Jane's face was so red with anger and frustration it almost glowed in the dim room where the curtains were permanently closed tight.

'Yes, yes, yes.' Cathy spoke quietly, determined not to lose her cool. 'I am sixteen and old enough to spend most of my time here on my own while you two are playing shop and fucking about with crystal balls. I'm old enough for you two not to care about where I am and who I'm with but not old enough to make my own decisions? I think not!'

With that she laughed and slammed out of their sitting room, stomping noisily downstairs. She knew the twins and she knew how to handle them and she had thought out her strategy before confronting them.

Aware that they were both far too self-absorbed and preoccupied in their own world to put up a fight for long, she hoped to wear them down until they gave in about both the wedding and the money.

As Nico had pointed out to her, it was only five years until she got her inheritance and then she would be completely financially independent. Meanwhile, he had suggested she could try to get access to the interest and maybe even a one-off withdrawal with which to start married life. After all, it was hers; her parents had left it to her alone. She had been a little surprised when he had asked her if the twins had made wills in her favour but he had quickly reassured her that it was sensible for them all to know where they stood financially for the future.

Smiling, she went back down to her own room, curled up on the floor and went over everything for the hundredth-odd time. It was all she could think about.

The day after her birthday party, following a disturbed night where her thoughts and dreams had become confused, she had woken with a start to banging on her door. It had taken several minutes for her to separate fact from fiction, to realise she was in her own bed and to remember the card.

'Marry me,' it had said. She tried to get her head round the words. Did he mean it? Or was it just a silly joke? He had said he would take her to lunch . . . would he be there? Should she just ignore the note? Laugh about it?

The knocking on her door got louder.

'Cathy? If you don't get out of that bed soon, my girl, and come and help with the clearing up, then I'm coming in to get you.'

Cathy groaned, wondering how on earth she was going to present a normal face to Sheila and the twins when she had such a huge, delicious secret she knew she couldn't share with them.

'Coming, I'm up already . . .' She really wanted time to herself before going to meet Nico but she knew she wouldn't get it. She could remember the mess she had turned a blind eye to the night before!

'Happy Birthday!'

Sheila and the twins were in the lounge waiting for her. The room was spotless and there was no sign of the party. Cathy knew Sheila must have been there at the crack of dawn to clear the debris on her own. She also knew she could safely have put money on the fact that the twins would only just have surfaced themselves, and that that was probably under duress from Sheila.

Cathy laughed and hugged all three of them in turn. 'I had forgotten, I had really forgotten, what with the party and everything . . . I was going to clear up, honestly. I didn't mean to leave it to you, Sheila!'

Sheila's eyes glistened, tears dangerously close to the surface. 'How could I possibly let you do the housework on your birthday? Come on, there's presents for you, and Tim has already phoned. He's on his way over with a present as well. Why don't you ask him to stay to lunch?'

Cathy looked at the clock. It was eleven o'clock already; she was due to meet Nico in exactly an hour and a half.

'I'm actually going out to lunch today, if that's all right with you all. A couple of friends from the drama group have invited me, only they haven't invited Tim so don't say anything . . .' Her voice faded as she was confronted by silent disapproval from Sheila, but the twins, noticing nothing, carried on happily.

'Come on, Kitten, you'd better get your presents open then if you're going out. Here's ours . . .'

When Tim arrived Cathy made an effort to act pleased,

but all the while her eyes were on the clock on the wall, counting down the minutes. At twenty-nine minutes past twelve she jumped up, said her goodbyes, and was out of the door before Tim could even open his mouth to ask where she was going.

Cathy made it up the drive just as Nico roared to a halt at the entrance. He jumped out as she reached the car and wrapped his arms around her gently.

'Happy Birthday again. You look lovely – is that new?'

She looked at him nervously, her embarrassment making her feel quite sick. She concentrated on looking down at the new jumper as she spoke far too rapidly. 'Yes, Sheila gave it me, you know Sheila, I told you about her, she's our housekeeper and a sort of surrogate mother . . . and Jane and Alison gave me money for clothes and Tim gave me that cassette I wanted . . .'

'Ah, puppy dog Timmy, the little boy with the adoring eyes that sadly follow you everywhere. A portrait of unrequited love if ever I saw one.'

The spiteful sarcasm in his voice was almost, but not quite, overridden by the wide smile on his handsome face.

'That's mean,' Cathy said quickly, feeling suddenly defensive. 'Tim has been a good friend to me since Mum and Dad died – both he and Sheila. I don't know what I'd have done without them. In fact Tim is my best friend.'

'I'm sorry.' Nico managed to look quite contrite. 'I'm sure he's a really nice boy, but you don't need him now, you've got me. In fact you don't need anyone else any more. I'll take care of you and be your best friend.'

He raised his hand and touched her cheek with his index finger, running it slowly down the line of her jaw. Cathy felt herself stiffen. Quickly he withdrew his hand and laughed.

'Right, let's go and really celebrate your birthday.'

He took her arm and helped her into the car solicitously before going round and getting in himself. He didn't look at her as he revved the engine, spinning the tyres on the gravel as he accelerated sharply away from the house and on to the main road.

'Thank you for the brooch. It's fabulous, I love it . . .'

He looked sideways at her. 'And what about me? Do you love me too? I meant it, you know. I want to marry you and I won't take no for an answer, my sweet little sixteen!'

'But I don't really know you, and you don't know me. How could I marry you?' She slowly and carefully shredded a tissue in her hand as she spoke, not daring to look at Nico beside her. 'Anyway, the twins would never let me. They're my guardians and they wouldn't even let me go out with you, let alone marry you. You're crazy.'

'That's right, crazy about you – and I will marry you, just wait and see! I knew the second I set eyes on you that I would marry you.' His confident laugh filled the car as he raced carelessly around the lanes.

At the restaurant Nico took Cathy's hand and held it tightly as they walked across the car park. Just as they reached the entrance he pulled her towards him and carefully kissed her on the lips for the first time. The tension in her was electric but just as she started to relax and respond he pulled away and looked down at her.

'How many times have you been kissed before, Cathy?'

'Never,' she replied emphatically as she gazed up at him. 'Never ever.'

Nico could feel the excitement building up. He had been right about her: pure and innocent. The thought of being the first was nearly too much for him but he was nothing if not disciplined in his seduction techniques, and the car park was certainly not the right place to start her education.

'Good. Now let's get celebrating!'

The heat of her earlier embarrassment changed slowly to a warmth of happiness. She knew then and there that she would marry him whatever they all said.

Sitting cross-legged on the floor of her bedroom she looked at the engagement ring he had presented her with. The shiny diamond sparkled up at her and she knew there was no way she was going to give it back as her sisters had demanded when she had told them earlier, and there was certainly no way that she was going to finish with him.

Somehow she was going to get her own way. She loved Nico and he said he loved her.

'You're what?' Justin spluttered. 'You're a fucking lunatic, Nico. I didn't think there was anything left that you could do to surprise me, but this? Jesus, you've got kids her age . . .'

Nico laughed. 'Not quite. Don't exaggerate, my friend.

Cathy is sixteen, old enough to get married legally, so what's the problem? If I was some crumpled rock star or ageing actor no one would bat an eyelid. Anyway,' he smiled slyly, 'she's agreed. We just have to get over the hurdle of those fucking barmy sisters of hers.'

'But what about Simonie? You're still living with her, for Christ's sake, and no doubt still screwing her – what does Cathy have to say about that? And come to think of it, what has Simonie got to say about it?'

Justin was up and pacing the floor. He could see the situation coming back to haunt him. Whatever devious, dishonest Nico did, straightforward Justin eventually got the blame.

'Compartments, my man, compartments. Simonie is one part of my life and Cathy is another. I'll deal with it when the time is right. I'm just hedging my bets for the moment!'

'You are just the pits, Nico. You've got no fucking morals at all. She's a child – she's not even your average sixteen-year-old – and as for Simonie . . . she doesn't deserve this.' Justin almost spat the words out. He would have given anything to be in Simonie's bed, the beautiful, kind and caring Simonie who thought Nico was the best thing since sliced bread and honestly believed every single untruth that spouted from his mouth.

'Trust me, Justin, Cathy's not a child. She just looks and acts like one because those witches won't let her do otherwise!'

Justin looked at his friend, leaning back in the huge

leather armchair with his feet casually propped up on the matching footstool, a huge grin on his face. Once again he could feel himself being won over against his will and he hated himself for being so weak.

'All I can say is, I hope you're prepared for her sisters, because from what I've heard they're not averse to the odd hex or two. You might just find yourself impotent, or even worse, in a short space of time.'

'Oh, I can deal with them – they're no problem – but the housekeeper, she's a whole different ball game; the substitute mother-hen with no kids of her own, who's turned Cathy into her life's project. But I'll get round her. I'm always quite good at charming fat old widow women and if that fails – well, tough, she'll just have to get used to it!'

Justin knew there was no point in arguing further. Nico would get his own way as usual. And anyway, a tiny selfish seed was growing in his mind. When Simonie found out about Cathy then maybe he could be there to step into the breach and comfort her.

'Fine, if that's what you want, but fuck up my life and you'll regret it!'

Nico knew he had won – again. Justin had always been a pushover.

'I tell you what, I'll do you a deal, my friend. You don't fuck it up for me with Cathy and Simonie, and I won't fuck up your whole life or break your legs. That way everyone's happy. How's that?'

Justin looked unhappily at the smug man sitting opposite him. 'There's not a lot I can say, is there? But please promise me you'll go easy on Simonie and at least try to be fair. She's never done anything to deserve what you are about to do to her.'

Nico jumped up and held out his hand to the uneasy Justin, who shook it reluctantly.

'It's a deal, Justin, my friend, and who knows, I might even put in a good word for you at the same time.' He looked at Justin with a mockingly quizzical expression on his face. 'That is what you're thinking, isn't it?'

With that Nico swaggered out, grinning widely.

Sheila had been completely taken aback when she received the telephone call from the twins, mysteriously summoning her to the shop with the proviso that Cathy was not to be told.

Knowing how the twins could sometimes be irrational, she wondered fleetingly if they were going to sack her, and by the time she got there she was on the defensive, ready to plead her case for the sake of Cathy. By the time she came out she was in a state of shock.

Little Cathy wanting to get married? To a man old enough to be her father?

On the way home Sheila thought about it, and the more she thought about it, the more she thought she could see what had happened.

From the very first day she had joined the Carter family Cathy was 'Daddy's girl'; Bryan had doted on her, giving and receiving all the love that Alison and Jane were never capable of. Now she was alone and was looking for a replacement for her father. Sheila could understand that. But as for the man – what on earth was a forty-odd-year-old, apparently good-looking and affluent man doing chasing after a girl of sixteen?

After she had nearly run into the back of a slow-moving tractor Sheila stopped the car in a lay-by and tried to gather her thoughts. The twins had said they didn't know what to do, which to Sheila meant they didn't want to deal with it, so she had promised to do her best. She also knew she owed it to Bryan and Elena to look out for young Cathy.

The first step, she knew, would be to talk to this Nico Marcos. She wasn't sure where to find him but she knew where to start looking.

It didn't take long. Sheila did listen to Cathy and she knew all about Justin.

'I'm coming, I'm coming . . . Stop banging on the door.' Justin put a restraining hand on the barking dog's collar as he opened the door.

'Are you Justin?'

'Why, darling?' Justin stood hands on hips and affectedly looked the woman on his doorstep up and down. 'Who wants to know?'

'Don't you darling me, sonny. Just tell me, are you or aren't you Justin from the drama group?'

'Well, yes, I am but—' Before he could finish the sentence the door was pushed open and Sheila, flushed and breathing heavily from the two flights of stairs, was in his hall.

'Good! Now you can shut up.' She made eye contact

and pointed at the barking dog who cocked his ears up but stopped instantly. 'And as for you, I want to talk to you about your slimy friend Nico and Cathy Carter.'

Suddenly Justin was the one breathing heavily as he started to panic. The woman pushed past him and was walking ahead. He had no alternative but to follow her into his own living room and watch in amazement as she plonked herself heavily on to his sofa, still puffing and panting.

He had no idea who she was but he was well aware that there was no way the woman was paying a social visit!

'Now, young man, I want you to tell me all about your so-called drama group and all about your friend Nico Marcos.' Sheila smiled grimly at the bewildered Justin. 'Come on, I want to know everything there is to know and I'm staying put until you tell me.'

Cathy was in a quandary. The twins and Sheila were all watching her like hawks and any time she could grab with Nico was taken up with him ranting and raving about her 'mad' family. The vague fear that she felt when Nico was in full verbal flow was quickly stifled when he apologised, which he always did after an outburst.

She had been so proud of Nico when he had visited the twins and tried to reason with them, but they had simply refused to speak to him other than to call him an opportunist pervert and to order him out of the house.

Cathy also desperately wanted to stick up for them when Nico was stamping about calling them the most awful names she had ever heard, but she loved him so much she was scared to say anything.

Now Nico had even fallen out with Justin, insisting Cathy had nothing else to do with the play and, to compound her misery, Tim wouldn't speak to her.

She was helpless in the middle, a fox caught up in the chase of the hunt, unsure which way to go for safety.

Alone, with no one to talk to, she was becoming completely dependent on Nico.

Cathy knew she was pushing her luck, bunking off school yet again, but she didn't care. Nico had come in round the back, skirting the edge of the grounds down towards the stream and they were both safely in the summerhouse with the door firmly shut against detection. Curled up tightly on a garden chair she gazed at Nico who, elegant as always, was crouched in front of her, his hand gently resting on her leg and his eyes intensely focused on her face.

'I've told you before, my angel, Justin has his own agenda. He's always been jealous of me, and having Sheila turn up on his doorstep gave him the greatest opportunity to twist the knife . . . Truth be said, he probably wants you himself. He's always wanted whatever I've had.'

'But he said things about you, about your ex-wife, and what about that Simonie? He said you lived with her, are still living with her . . .'

'Look at me. Now who do you believe? Me? Justin? Because if it isn't me you believe then we might as well finish this here and now. If you don't trust me then there's no point in us having a relationship.'

Cathy nearly fell off the chair as she tried to get up quickly.

'Don't say that, Nico. Of course I believe you, and I trust you—'

'Then don't question me,' he interrupted sharply. 'If you believe me then there's no need to keep going over it all again and again. The last thing I want is a nagging wife before we're even married.'

Smiling the smile that he knew always worked, he continued, 'The future is what matters now – our future, together – and we will have a future because I think I have a plan.' He pulled her to him. 'Now tell me again about the fire and how it all happened.'

Chapter Six

Three days after she had officially left school Cathy stood on the steps of the register office, looking more like a wide-eyed child at her confirmation than a new bride. The expensive off-white trouser suit that she had chosen fitted neatly on her barely pubescent frame, the shoulder pads adding some width and the high-heeled white patent shoes adding some height, but there was still no disguising her age.

'I can't believe this is happening,' Alison hissed at her twin sister, loud enough for the immediate ears to hear. 'It's not right.'

'I told you that from the start.' Sheila's face was a portrait of pain and misery. 'You should never have given in. Bryan and Elena would never have let this happen. I don't know what possessed you.'

The twins glared in unison. 'We had no choice, we told you there was no choice.'

'Of course there was a choice, you silly girls, but it's too late now. It's done and all we can do is be there for her when it all goes wrong . . . which it will. As sure as night turns into day it will all go wrong. Just look at the expression on his face, smug and victorious. Young Cathy is going to rue this day for the rest of her life and so are you!'

The three of them watched unhappily as Cathy and Nico posed for the photographer. Nico was also dressed from top to toe in off-white, apart from an emerald-green silk tie and kerchief that matched the blouse Cathy wore under her suit. They actually made a stunning couple, despite the obvious age difference.

'Come on, you three. I want at least one photo of us all together.'

Cathy smiled brightly and Sheila tried hard to respond in kind and smother her feelings of impending disaster.

'Come on, you heard your sister, let's have our photos taken.' Sheila grabbed the twins and propelled them to the top of the steps. 'Now smile. You've let it happen so don't spoil the day for her now. Let her enjoy it while it lasts.'

The twins had made few concessions when it came to their clothes for their sister's wedding day. They were still swathed in black but they did pin carnations on, and they did dump the shawls for the day and pin their hair up at Cathy's insistence.

The four of them linked arms and it was obvious that the photographer would have a tale to tell in the pub that evening. Four faces looked at the camera; the diminutive Cathy smiling happily in white, the statuesque and sullen twins in black, and Sheila, colourful and rotund with a bright smile that couldn't quite disguise her obvious discomfort.

As the camera clicked Nico stood a few paces away, nonchalantly smoking a large cigar but at the same time keeping a suspicious eye on Cathy and the strange clan that surrounded her.

Sheila still couldn't understand why the twins had agreed to the wedding. She found the whole idea preposterous, especially after she had told them everything she had found out from Justin. But once they had agreed then Sheila was helpless. That Nico was divorced, with two children he didn't have anything to do with, was bad enough, but the fact he was actually living with someone else when he proposed to Cathy was completely beyond her to condone. But despite all that, the twins had eventually caved in and agreed to Cathy and Nico getting married, leaving Sheila feeling distraught and impotent, unable to persuade any of them to think again.

She hadn't even wanted to go to the wedding at all but she knew she had to bite her tongue and try to befriend Nico if she didn't want to lose Cathy altogether. Nico had made it perfectly clear to Sheila that if she didn't co-operate then he would make sure she never saw Cathy again.

Deep down Sheila knew that it would only be a matter of time before Cathy really needed her and she wanted to make sure that she could be there when the time came. She made a silent promise to herself that when it did happen she would personally nail Nico to the wall one way or another. Just the thought of Cathy getting hurt made Sheila dig her nails into her palms so hard she almost drew blood.

After the photograph the twins drifted into the background again, but Sheila put her arm around Cathy and leaned across as if to kiss her, but instead whispered urgently and quickly, before Nico came into earshot, 'Remember, Cathy, I am *always* there for you, whatever. If you need me just let me know.'

She could see Nico approaching so she pulled Cathy to her and kissed her dramatically for his benefit. Then, as he got close she put out her hand to him. 'Congratulations, Nico. Now you look after her, won't you?'

Sheila's mouth was set in a wide smile but her eyes were cold as they pierced into his.

Nico smiled happily back. 'Of course I will, Sheila. After all, she is my *wife* now!'

The dark and threatening emphasis wasn't lost on Sheila but she kept her eyes locked into his until he looked away.

Nico had done his homework well. The tiny seed of suspicion that Cathy had unwittingly planted in his mind had quickly germinated into something much bigger. He had got to know family friends and neighbours and charmed his way into their confidences. He had spoken to other shopkeepers around the vicinity of the twins' shop and he had checked back on all the newspaper cuttings he could get his hands on. He had even gone to the trouble of looking up an old friend who worked in the fire service and who owed him a favour.

Then he had decided to take a gamble and hope that he was right. He had made his move a few weeks before the date Cathy had optimistically chosen for their wedding.

'What the fuck are you doing here?' Jane had turned round when she heard the bell tinkle to be confronted by Nico in the doorway.

'We've already told you, piss off! You're not welcome at our house and you're certainly not welcome here.'

Nico sauntered through the shop and stood in front of the counter with his hands in his pockets. There were no customers inside – he had made sure of that before going in, and he had also made sure there was no way Cathy was going to be there. He put his head on one side and frowned.

'I'm sure you don't mean that. After all, I'm going to be your brother-in-law. Don't you think we ought to try to get on?'

Hearing voices, Alison came through and joined in.

'Brother-in-law my arse. Now get out before we call the police. You're trespassing.'

Nico stayed on the spot and smiled. 'Oh no, big sisters, I know you wouldn't dare call the police. That's the last thing you want, isn't it – the police back in your lives, asking questions again and maybe this time finding out the answers . . . the right answers about one of your least savoury antics. Now I think it's time for a lunch-break. We've got a lot to talk about.'

Three large paces took him back to the door that he

gently shut, pushing up the catch and flipping the sign over to 'Closed'.

'Right, which one of you is going to make me a coffee? Two sugars and just a dash of milk, please, and then we can get down to business.'

Up until then Nico had been playing a hunch based on guesswork, but as soon as he saw the look that passed between the twins he knew he could be on the right track. He hoped so, anyway. From that moment on, however much they tried to bluff it out, he was determined to have the upper hand.

Nico looked curiously around the dimly lit room. Despite the daylight outside, the windows were fully draped over, and the red-tinged lights cast eerie shadows around the walls.

The twins perched stiffly on the edge of a small sofa, both fiddling with their hair, while Nico settled himself at the chenille-draped table that had as its centrepiece a large velvet-covered crystal ball.

'This is all very spooky, girls. Business doing OK? I hear there's a big market out there these days for phoney fortune-tellers and make-believe witches.'

'You're wasting your breath trying to insult us, Mr Marcos. Just get to the point and then get out. You're interfering with our livelihood, you know. We've got appointments!'

Nico threw back his head and laughed long and loud, an affected and humourless laugh that had scared many a person in the past.

'Call this your livelihood? This is just a little game, a

pastime. Your livelihood is courtesy of your dead mummy and daddy's will and insurance payouts. Call yourselves fucking fortune-tellers? Don't make me laugh. You're no more fortune-tellers than I am. If you were, you'd know why I'm here, wouldn't you? Ah! But then thinking about it you probably do know, don't you? Spooky, huh?'

He looked from one to the other. He felt slightly disconcerted by their complete lack of response and vacant expressions but he continued, 'Actually I'm quite good at crystal gazing myself. Shall I tell you your fortunes? Past and present?'

Nico whipped away the piece of soft velvet and threw it across the room in the twins' direction, smiling as it floated gently to the floor at their feet. He looked towards the ceiling and closed his eyes, his neatly manicured hands hovering theatrically over the crystal ball.

'I can see a fire – a big fire, a house fire,' he droned gently, waving his hands over the glistening glass globe. 'I can see two sisters – twin sisters, mad sisters . . . They are torching the family home, making it look like an accident, frying their parents in their beds and getting away with it, pocketing all the money . . . lots and lots of money.' He paused as if in thought, then peered at the crystal ball. 'Now I can see two prison cells – separate cells in separate prisons, two sisters locked away from the world and each other for life, convicted of murder . . .' He stopped and looked at them before continuing in his normal voice, 'I'm right, aren't I? See? I'm just as good as you. Maybe we ought to go into partnership! Now I can almost admire the fact that you got away with it, but it was very, very naughty, wasn't it?'

Still they didn't respond.

'Now then, Jane and Alison, about me and Cathy getting married – oh yes, and let's not forget her dowry . . .' This time he didn't smile. 'Now, you agree to Cathy marrying me and you give me a cash payment of one hundred thousand pounds and we'll say no more about it. How's that? You scratch my back and I'll scratch yours . . . Oh, and I want you to take steps for Cathy to receive the interest from her inheritance. She'll be a married woman soon and that can be really expensive.'

'You're mad,' Alison was the first to respond, 'stark raving fucking mad if you think we'd agree to sell Cathy to you. That is what you're proposing, isn't it? You're asking us to sell you a child?'

Nico was across the room in a flash, his face screwed up in positive hatred as close to hers as it could be without touching.

'You will agree. I'm telling you that for a fact because if you don't I shall go to the police without a second thought, and worse than that, I shall tell Cathy. Sweet innocent little Cathy, who thinks her sisters walk on water.' He moved away. 'Oh yes, you will agree.' He threw a business card on to the table. 'You've got until eight o'clock tonight to agree and then we can all play happy families and start planning the wedding. However, if I don't hear from you . . .' He held both his hands out in a gesture of feigned helplessness before continuing, 'I'll have no choice but to see you in court! Anyway, ciao for now. I'm sure you have plenty to talk about so I'll see myself out.'

'What are we going to do? He's bluffing, of course, talking nonsense . . .'

The twins were both up from their seats, their large masculine faces set in matching expressions of anger.

'I know, but someone might believe him. Look, it's not as if it's not what Cathy wants, so we might as well agree, give him the money as a wedding present and let them get on with it. We don't need this hassle.'

'You're right, it's what she wants. What about Sheila? She'll crucify us . . .'

'Sheila is the cleaner, nothing more. It's none of her business. We're Cathy's guardians.'

'What about the money?'

'A small price to pay for Cathy's happiness. Anyway, she'll reap the benefit of it if she's married to him.'

When the twins called Cathy up to their sitting room that evening she went reluctantly, expecting yet another row about Nico. Going on the attack she was quickly deflated and completely taken aback by their pronouncement.

'We've been thinking about it, Kitten, and we've decided that if you really want to marry Nico, and you think you'll be happy, then we give our permission.'

'That's right, we've changed our minds.'

Cathy was dumbstruck; it was the last thing she had expected. Eventually she managed to speak.

'Why? Why have you changed your mind? This isn't a wind-up, is it?'

The twins looked at each other and then at the floor.

'No, it isn't. You can marry him if you're sure, but please be sure—'

Alison interrupted her sister. 'It's not what we want and we're not happy about it, but we don't want you running off and disappearing so that's what we've decided.'

By the time she had finished speaking Cathy had tears streaming down her face.

'Thank you, thank you. I know you'll really like him when you get to know him. I know he's a lot older than me but we truly love each other. Oh God, I'm so happy. I have to go and phone Nico. He'll be thrilled!' She kissed each of them quickly on the cheek and was gone like a small whirlwind.

The twins, as always, were thinking identical thoughts: One day we'll get our own back on that bastard, you see if we don't! One day in the future, Mr Nico Marcos is going to regret crossing us.

When Simonie Cameron eventually answered the persistent ringing and banging on her front door she'd already guessed it was Justin. The look on his face made her glance at herself in the mirror by the door. The image that looked back surprised her but she just silently walked away back into her bedroom, leaving Justin to follow her.

Jumping straight on to the bed, she pulled the duvet up to her chin and buried her face in her hands.

'Simonie, darling, you can't carry on like this, wasting your emotions on that useless piece of shit. Nico's no good and deep down you know it. Same as I know it . . .'

'Maybe you're right but I can't help how I feel. How could he do that to me? And why didn't you tell me?'

Justin went over and sat on the edge of the bed, gently stroking her forehead and brushing her hair back off her face. The usually sleek and shiny blonde hair was a dirty, matted mess, and once it was away from her face revealed puffy, bloodshot eyes and mottled skin.

'How could I tell you?' He carried on stroking her face and hair gently and softly as if comforting a sick child. 'Nico said he was going to tell you weeks ago. I can't believe he carried on living here as if nothing was wrong.'

'They're getting married today, aren't they? Who is she?'

Justin paused, unsure how much to say. He had already crossed Nico once and paid the price; he didn't want to do it again. He wanted Nico as a friend not an enemy. 'I don't know too much about her except that she's very young. Too young for him and she's besotted with him.'

Simonie sat up sharply. 'How young exactly?'

'I'm not sure.' Justin couldn't look her in the eye. He hated not telling her the truth.

'Liar! You know exactly how old, or rather how young she is. *Tell me.*'

He hesitated for a second. 'She's just sixteen.'

'*Sixteen? Fucking sixteen?* He's lost it, hasn't he? He's in a mid-life crisis, surely. Unless of course . . .'

Justin could see her brain ticking over through the fug of her hangover, the result of half a bottle of Scotch in the middle of the night. She was trying to piece together all the things that had been bothering her.

'Justin, tell me the truth now: whose were the magazines I found? Those godawful paedophile mags from Amsterdam – were they yours? Or were they really Nico's? Were you taking the flak for him?'

The questions were flying like bullets across the room and Justin was having difficulty weighing the situation up quickly enough for his self-preservation.

'Which magazines?'

'You know exactly which filthy magazines. The ones I found in my garage, the ones Nico said were yours. *Were* they yours?'

Simonie's huge blue eyes focused sharply on Justin's face and he could feel himself getting hot and bothered. He could never have imagined a time when he would be in Simonie's bedroom and wish that he wasn't but at that moment he would have given anything to be somewhere else, anywhere other than face to face with Simonie's realisation.

He looked away. 'No, of course they weren't mine, they were Nico's. I'm not into schoolgirls. He had hundreds of them stashed all over the place but he always said he only liked looking. He swore he never actually did anything like that, it just turned him on to look . . . same as the videos.'

Simonie got out of bed and ran into the bathroom. Justin could hear her retching but he stayed where he was until she returned, her face washed and her hair brushed and tied back.

'So the great Nico Marcos thinks I'm so thick and

114

dumb he can get away with all this, does he? Well, he is oh so wrong. I might have given him the benefit of the doubt when he was hanging round that other young girl but now . . .' she looked around wildly, 'now I'm going to ruin him. Does he really think I'll let him off scot-free? That I'll let him carry on with our business together? Forgive him? Again?' She was pacing the floor, alternately running her fingers through her hair and chewing at her once elegantly manicured fingernails.

'I don't know, Simonie. I really have no idea about Nico any more.' Justin stayed where he was, looking at the floor, scared he was going to be sucked into Simonie's revenge but she carried on as if he hadn't even spoken.

'It was my father's money that started the business and I'm going to get rid of Nico in that, and I'm going to take his reputation as well. Mr Financial Consultant will never work again if I've got anything to do with it! Christ, I wish I still had those magazines. Daddy would castrate him single-handed if he saw them.'

Flinging open her wardrobe she started dragging clothes out at random and throwing them around the room. Designer clothes floated to the floor and were trodden underfoot, expensive shoes were thrown fiercely at the walls as she got dressed.

'I'm going to find him now. I'm going to cause such a row at that wedding—'

'Simonie, don't do this to yourself.' He took her by the hand and pulled her down beside him. 'Look, I'm sorry but the wedding's already over. They got married first thing today and they're going to the Caribbean . . . on honeymoon. They will already have left. I'm so sorry . . .'

Justin watched helplessly as the beautiful young woman dissolved into a hysterical heap beside him.

'You know how he told me, don't you? He came here when I was out on Wednesday and cleared out all his things, plus a few of mine, and he left me a note – a fucking note scribbled on the back of an envelope – saying he was getting married on Saturday. I thought he was going to marry me. I really thought we could get it together. Justin, I loved him so much . . .'

At that moment Justin hated Nico so much it scared him, but he also knew he was too cowardly actually to do anything about it.

'I know you did, Simonie, I know you did, but if it's any consolation to you I think you've had a lucky escape. He's been my friend for so long I tried not to see what was going on, but we have to admit it now, the man's a shit. He's got big problems and before long he's going to get into real heavy trouble.'

'Too right he is. I'll make sure of it!'

'Simonie, trust me, just let it be. Revenge is useless if it backfires and it will backfire – on to you. That's how Nico works. Just leave it. He'll get his just deserts one day.'

As the plane rumbled down the runway, gathering speed ready for take-off, Cathy closed her eyes and gripped the armrests, hoping Nico would not notice the all-encompassing terror that engulfed her. All Nico knew was just the bare bones of her life before adoption.

Something stopped her from telling him about the horrors that had taken place before that. In fact she had never spoken to anyone about it, apart from Tim, briefly. It was something that couldn't be put into words.

Her parents had accepted her fear of flying and she had never been on a plane of any description since the day she had arrived in London from Vietnam, but with Nico it had been different. Cathy had tried telling him she didn't like flying but he had brushed her fear aside, turned it into a joke, and had booked the honeymoon in Jamaica regardless.

'You'll be OK as soon as we get going,' he had said dismissively. 'No one is really frightened of flying. It's all in the mind. Trust me, it'll be fine, and we'll have a wonderful time together, alone, just the two of us for the first time. I can't wait . . .'

She had tried to block out the thought of the flight by concentrating on the wedding but as soon as they got to the airport the memories started coming back again.

Nico was happily showing her around, airing his knowledge of international travel, showing off, almost as if she was his child rather than his bride.

But Cathy could hardly think straight. She just felt sick with fear at the thought of getting on the plane.

'Confront your fear,' she kept telling herself, 'you have to confront it.' But the images kept coming as they always did when she was stressed or frightened.

She wasn't sure if she could really picture her parents in Vietnam or if it was her imagination but she hoped it was them, she prayed it was them. By closing her eyes and concentrating she could picture them together, see them sitting on their haunches side by side in a tiny cramped room surrounded by several solemn young children. But as soon as she tried to get any faces into focus or count the children, the image blurred and disappeared and she could still hear gunfire, such realistic gunfire that each time it made her jump.

'Look out of the window, darling. Isn't it great? I love flying. I remember flying Concorde to New York – man, that was something . . . I think I'll start taking lessons when we get back, learn to fly, that'd be good for business and I'm sure we could afford it . . .'

Nico's persistent voice brought her back to the present. As the plane banked and rose Cathy tried to look out of the window, at Nico's insistence, but instead of the green fields of the Home Counties she could only see charred trees and scorched earth dotted with burning huts, and people running. They were running in all directions, panicking and shouting, screaming and falling . . .

Trying hard not to grab Nico's arm, she closed her eyes and took deep breaths, waiting for the pounding heart-beat to subside and the images to disappear.

It seemed to take for ever but at last the flight was over and Cathy was almost back to her bubbly self and looking forward to the actual holiday. She was determined not to think about flying home. It was only the thought of two weeks in the Caribbean, and, of course, not upsetting Nico, that had given her the courage to get on the plane. When the terror had threatened to overwhelm her she had focused on just her and Nico with nothing to do but be with each other, love each other.

Although the Carter family was wealthy, there had never been much show of it and Cathy had never actually realised how rich her parents were until they died. Her life had always been focused around the home in the New Forest, winter holidays in Scotland and summers in the West Country. Now she was actually halfway across the world in the Caribbean and couldn't quite believe it.

'This is so beautiful.' She looked all around the honeymoon suite in childlike wonder, touching and stroking the furniture. 'Look . . . flowers and champagne, even chocolates . . .'

Nico smiled indulgently. 'See, I told you that you'd love it once we got here. Now it's just you and me alone for the first time with nothing and no one to interfere with us. I've ordered a late snack to be sent up to the suite so if you want to go and get unpacked and freshen up—'

Opening the door to the balcony with one hand and holding the other to him she interrupted happily, 'Let's go and have a look round first. I can't wait to see the whole resort and paddle in the sea. I'm so excited I'm really not hungry. I just want to see everything. We can eat later. I want to walk along the beach in the moonlight . . .'

Nico's response was sharp. '*No*, we cannot eat later!' He took Cathy by the arm and pulled her away from the balcony. 'I told you exactly what we're going to do so don't argue with me. Now go and get unpacked like I said, there's a good girl.'

'What do you mean, "there's a good girl"? I'm your wife, not your daughter.'

As Cathy looked at him, bewildered by his tone, the grip on her arm tightened and Nico's face darkened. For a second their gazes locked, but then suddenly he regained control and smiled.

'Darling, you *are* my wife, *my wife*,' he emphasised the words with a jabbing finger at her chest, 'and I know best. You have to accept that, so we're going to have something to eat and then we're going to bed. It's our wedding night, don't forget.' He smiled his most charming smile, the smile he knew from experience worked well, but at the same time smacked her on the bottom so hard that it stung. 'Then tomorrow we shall have a look around. We've got two long weeks here, don't forget.'

That night, their first night together, was totally bewildering to Cathy. Innocently she anticipated romance, hearts and flowers and whispered words: what actually happened was something she had never even heard about in her short, sheltered life, let alone experienced.

After the meal Nico disappeared into the bedroom to 'get ready' while Cathy lounged on the balcony in the moonlight, taking in the sights and smells of the Caribbean. Blissfully happy, she was convinced the romantic mind snapshot of couples walking hand in hand along the beach to the faint sounds of a steel band in the distance would stay with her for ever, a reminder of the happiest day of her life.

Suddenly Nico was behind her, kissing her neck.

'Come on, my baby, let's go to bed now.'

Cathy nearly jumped out of her skin when she turned round to find him stark naked with a confident but smug smile on his face and a huge erection.

'*Nico*, people will see you—' Cathy screamed, and was up from the lounger in a flash, the horror she felt reflected on her face.

'I don't care about other people, I want you to see me. We're husband and wife – what's wrong with that? I want you to look and admire. This is all for you . . .'

Cathy ran into the room, her embarrassment overwhelming, but he followed and pulled her to him, kissing her hard. 'Now off you go and get ready. I'll see you in the bedroom . . .'

Her heart was thumping and her knees wobbly as she stood in the bathroom with her back to the door, suddenly unsure of the man to whom she was now married. Nico had only ever kissed her gently before, and he had never so much as touched her, and suddenly it hit her that he was expecting more, much more, than she had ever considered in her childlike fantasies.

If the sight of Nico naked had shocked her it was nothing compared to what she felt when she eventually crept into the bedroom to collect the new negligée that she had bought for her wedding night.

Carefully laid out on the bed in place of the delicate cream and lace silk creation she had carefully chosen was a tiny unfamiliar school uniform complete with navy-blue serge knickers and short white socks. On top of the pile was a new pink teddy bear. Even worse, though, in pride of place at the foot of the luxurious four-poster was the shiny expensive video camera that Nico had bought to film the honeymoon. It was set up on a tall tripod and was pointing threateningly at the bed.

Holding both his arms out in front of him Nico walked over to her and pulled her towards him.

'My beautiful little Cathy, I've been waiting so long for this . . .'

Despite being only sixteen and not very worldly wise, Cathy was intelligent and intuitive and what she saw definitely didn't feel right. Suddenly she felt frightened of the adult man she was with, the man who was now tugging quite forcibly at her arms, dragging her in front of the viewfinder – the man who, for better or worse, was now her husband.

Chapter Seven

'Cathy, Cathy, oh I'm so pleased to see you. I thought you'd forgotten all about your old Aunty Sheila.' The woman's face lit up with delight at seeing Cathy on her doorstep. She hugged her close for a few seconds before holding her away and looking her up and down. 'My, oh my, you look all pale and pasty. You should be blooming. Are you feeling OK? No problems, are there?'

Cathy smiled up at her. 'I'm fine, Sheila, really I am – just a bit tired. I came over on the bus and I had to change in town. I'm knackered. Do I get a cup of tea then?'

Sheila laughed loudly and turned back into her tiny lobby, pulling Cathy behind her by the hand as Sally, Cathy's dog, barked excitedly. The ageing dog had settled happily into her new home after the twins had refused point-blank to let her live with them, but still went berserk when Cathy visited.

'Come on, I'll put the kettle on and you can give me all your news. It's been weeks and weeks. Look, even Sally can't understand why it's been so long. She misses you!'

When Nico had casually informed her that he was going abroad on business for a few days without her, Cathy had felt quite guilty at the wave of relief that had swept over her. Despite being concerned at what he might actually be going away for, she had also savoured the thought of time to herself, time to go out without facing the third degree about who she'd seen and what had been said to whom. Despite trying hard to convince herself it was because he loved her, cared about her, deep down she knew he was jealous of anything she did that didn't involve him.

Ever since the wedding the previous year Cathy had not had any freedom. Although not literally under lock and key she had found herself having to account for every minute of every day and every conversation she had. A visit to her sisters or to Sheila warranted such in-depth interrogation that she had almost given up talking to them. It was much less tiring, especially now.

'Your bump's not very big!' Sheila made it sound like an accusation. 'Are you sure you're looking after yourself and that baby of yours? You've not got long to go. What is it? Another six weeks?'

'Spot on.' Cathy tried to smile and look happy but ended up looking even more dejected. 'Six weeks and then I'll be a mother. That seems so strange. Nico's gone away for a few days to Denmark, on business.'

'Aah, so you're off the leash for once, are you?' The words were said gently but Cathy was suddenly alert. She was not prepared to give anything away; as always, she defended her husband, regardless of her secret doubts and fears.

'That's not fair! We like spending all our time together – that's what being married is all about, isn't it? Nico loves me, that's why he worries when I'm not with him. Anyway I've got more than enough to do in the new apartment.'

'Mmm, if you say so. Here's your tea. How about a nice big slice of ginger cake? I've not long made it . . . or how about the chocolate one? I made that yesterday for the twins.'

As Sheila fussed around, talking about nothing in particular but constantly glancing in her direction, Cathy knew she was marking time, waiting for the right moment to ask questions. Eagerly wanting to know but not liking to ask outright.

Cathy, at the same time, was desperate for someone to talk to but had no idea how to put her unhappiness into words to the much older woman. She also knew that Nico would be furious if he found out. Suddenly she missed her close friendship with Tim, the only person she used to be able to confide in, her best friend for so long and now a total stranger who ignored her if they met.

'How's Tim doing, Sheila? Is he OK? I saw him the other day but he didn't see me.' She framed the question casually but she still sensed Sheila's ears prick up like antennae, trying to tune in to hidden messages.

'He's fine.' There was a pause as she bustled about, putting every little treat she could find in her cupboard in front of Cathy before sitting down herself. 'He loves his job at the stables and he's got two horses now. You know he still goes to the drama group, gets on really well with that Justin fellow, apparently, and is having a bit of a social life away from his animals for a change. He's even been out with a girl a few times – Petra from the hotel, you know, that new receptionist at the Hall – she's been going to drama with him. It's such a shame you gave it all up.'

Determined not to show her disappointment, Cathy raised her eyes and patted her swollen stomach gently. 'Not many parts for me now, are there? Anyway, Nico wouldn't let me go any more. He prefers me to be at home for him. I'm married now and I'm going to have a baby.'

'I know that only too well.' Sheila spoke sharply and instantly regretted it. She smiled gently to take the edge off her words before carrying on, 'But that's still no excuse for a girl your age to be cooped up at home all hours of the day and night. It's not right. You should still be able to enjoy yourself, for heaven's sake. It's supposed to be a marriage, not a jail sentence, you know!'

Cathy couldn't have turned up at a better time. Sheila had been off her head with worry but try as she might to raise the twins' concern, it had been nigh on impossible. Their joint response was always the same: 'She's OK. It's what she wanted.'

The lively young Cathy who had smiled happily and bounced around on her wedding day had disappeared from their lives that day. She had returned from honeymoon almost a child again with not a trace of make-up, and her hair pulled back off her expressionless scrubbed face. Minus the clumpy shoes she was barely five foot and looked about ten again. Cathy was back to being the quiet, frightened little girl who had been adopted all those years ago and Sheila was worrying herself sick over it.

Sheila looked on her as her own and she loved her with a passion – she had done since the very first time she had seen her. Now, seeing Cathy looking so young and frail that the bump of pregnancy appeared almost obscene, she hated Nico Marcos with the same passion. She noticed too the huge dark rings under her eyes that were all the more noticeable now Cathy had grown her coal-black hair to her shoulders and scraped it back in two bunches. Although she had always slightly disapproved of the girl's appearance when she was growing up, Sheila would have given anything to see the old Cathy with bright red spiky hair and eyes ringed with thick make-up instead of tiredness.

'Are you sure you're OK? Have you been to the clinic lately? You've lost weight since I last saw you. Mind you, that was months ago. I've missed you so much, you naughty girl.' She saw the defensive look that flashed across Cathy's face, and changed tack.

'Come on then, tell me, do you want a boy or a girl? If it was me I'm sure I'd want a little girl, a dainty little doll just like you—'

The interruption was so quick and vehement it nearly made Sheila jump. 'I don't want a girl, I want a boy. It has to be a boy. It just *has* to be a boy!' She was on her feet, her eyes wide and wild. 'I don't want a girl!'

Standing as quickly as her vast bulk would let her, Sheila, bewildered by the outburst, moved round the kitchen table to comfort her.

'It's OK, it's OK . . . Let's wait and see before we get upset about it, mmm? You've got to stay calm for your baby, whatever it is, and once it's here, well, I'm sure everything will all be OK. Boy . . . or girl . . . just so long as it's healthy. Is it because Nico wants a boy that you're so upset?'

It was as if a warning light had gone on. Sitting back down quickly Cathy smiled her brightest smile. 'Take no notice of me, Sheila. Nico says I'm probably hormonal! Anyway, I don't want to talk about me any more. Tell me all about you, what you've been up to, and what about the twins? I'm going to the shop next. I haven't seen them for so long and, as you know, they're useless on the phone! Come on, Sheila, give me all the gen on everyone. I've missed all the gossip – and you, of course!'

Sheila played along with the change of subject. The last thing she wanted was to lose Cathy completely.

'Nico, wake up!' Cathy pulled frantically at his arm, 'Nico, quick, I think the baby's coming! I need to go to hospital.'

Cathy had taken note of all the information the midwife had given her and knew that the patch of blood and the griping pains across her tightened belly meant something was happening even if there were still a couple of weeks to go.

Eventually he roused himself although Cathy could sense the indifference. Nico's obsession with her had waned noticeably since the pregnancy had started to show and she sensed that he just wanted it over and done with, with the minimum of disruption.

'I'll call an ambulance for you.'

'I don't want an ambulance.' She was almost screaming. 'I want you to take me in the car. I want you with me. I'm frightened!'

'For fuck's sake, Cathy, keep the noise down. You're only having a baby, for God's sake.' A cold chill enveloped her as she saw the undisguised loathing in his eyes.

'Now like it or not I'm calling an ambulance. I'll come as well but I'll follow right behind in the car, then I can get home again. Just get dressed and get your things together quietly.'

Cathy went in the ambulance, unaware that Nico wasn't close behind.

As soon as she had gone he went straight back indoors and poured himself a drink, but his frustration and anger at the situation he had got himself into got the better of him and he threw the glass full force at the wall. As it shattered and the golden liquid slid down the expensive embossed wallpaper he watched in fascination until it reached the wood-block floor and settled in a pool.

It went against the grain for Nico Marcos to admit that he had screwed up but this time he had no choice. He had married Cathy, young, innocent and eventually to be wealthy, seeing her as his child bride, to be moulded into his fantasy plaything but he had got it wrong, very wrong. She had conceived and that spoiled it all.

It was the very youth and naivety that had obsessed him that ensured she hadn't even realised she was pregnant until it was too late to do anything about it and now she was sullied for him. Her swollen stomach and engorged breasts spoiled everything, and the thought of her childlike body giving birth made him feel physically sick. He knew he couldn't be there to watch. It was Cathy the child he desired, not Cathy the adult. It was only the thought of her inheritance that prevented him from kicking her straight out – an inheritance that he couldn't get his hands on for years. He had the money the twins had given him and he had the interest off the capital that the executors had agreed to pay into a joint account, but the lump sum was still so far off.

He picked up the phone and dialled the number that had been buzzing around his head for weeks.

'Hello, sweetheart. It's me, Nico. I've made a terrible mistake – can I come and see you?' The fact that Simonie slammed the phone straight down didn't deter him in the slightest. In fact it made her even more of a challenge.

With Cathy safely pushed out of his mind he went down to his car and drove straight round to Simonie's flat. He was sure that he could talk her round, that she would soften. She always had before! The thought of the challenge of getting round her excited him. He loved the thrill of the chase. Before getting out of the car he checked himself in the mirror and was satisfied he looked tired and dishevelled enough for sympathy.

He was momentarily taken by surprise when Justin answered. Opening the door a fraction, just enough to look through the gap, he made sure Nico was aware that he was unwelcome.

'Hello, Nico! We were expecting you. Now goodbye, Nico. Simonie really doesn't want to see you.'

Ignoring the open hostility on Justin's stony face, Nico smiled and put his foot in the door.

'But I want to see her. Let her come and tell me herself.'

Justin's face was white with anger. 'Read my lips. Simonie wants you to fuck off back to where you came from. Just piss off back to your childwife and leave Simonie in peace.'

'Come on, just let me in. I've missed her like crazy – and you too, of course! I've missed both of you. I don't know what came over me. Please, I just want to be able to put my side. I want to explain to Simonie, I made a mistake . . . a big mistake . . .'

As Justin pushed the door hard against the blocking foot, Simonie appeared in the background and looked over his shoulder. Nico smiled at her, looking directly into her hostile eyes.

'Let him in, Justin; see what he's got to say.'

When Nico wanted to be penitent and humble he was in a class of his own and he knew that it wasn't the time to gloat at Justin if he wanted Simonie back on side.

'Come on, Justin, we go back a long way – surely I'm entitled to a fair hearing? I must have been mad, barking mad. Let me in and we'll all talk . . . clear the air . . .'

Justin stepped back and, against his better judgement, allowed the apologetic Nico inside.

Cathy was exhausted and sobbing her heart out. A doctor and two midwives were with her, trying to calm her down and reason with her.

'Where's my husband? I want my husband . . . where is he?'

'I'm sorry, Mrs Marcos, but he must have been held up. We've tried phoning but the answerphone is on. We can't wait any longer, you have to go to theatre for an emergency Caesarean section if we're to save the baby. It's in distress; we have to deliver it straight away.'

Cathy sensed that they were losing patience with her but she didn't care. Despite being tired and in pain all she could think of was Nico and why he wasn't there.

'Not without Nico, I can't. I can't agree to anything without Nico . . .' Cathy could barely get the words out she was so distressed and confused.

'Mrs Marcos – Cathy – your baby is going to die if we don't act now. Please sign the form and we'll carry on trying to reach your husband. I'm sure he'll get here but we have to act now. Please? For your baby's sake? And yours?'

Cathy reached out for the pen and paper.

'Will you phone my sisters as well? Please?'

'Of course we will. Now sign the consent form, we're running out of time . . .'

Tears streaming down her face, a mixture of anger at Nico and fear for herself, Cathy signed the piece of paper and handed it over reluctantly.

Suddenly the small side ward was a hive of activity and in no time Cathy was being wheeled along the corridor by a jovial porter who took it on himself to make the child smile. He didn't succeed and as Cathy faded off under the anaesthetic she was still crying.

Jane and Alison arrived with Sheila just as Cathy was being taken back to the ward, still bleary from the anaesthetic. She opened her eyes and looked around.

'Is Nico here?'

'No, we don't know where he is. Sheila brought us in the car.'

'We haven't seen him, Kitten. Does he know you're here?'

Cathy looked around, trying to focus her eyes. 'Did they save the baby?'

Sheila sat beside the bed and took her hand. 'The baby's fine. You've got a little girl, but they're keeping an eye on her. She's quite tiny, barely five pounds . . .'

'But I didn't want a girl.'

Suddenly without warning Cathy opened her mouth and howled. There was no comforting her and before long she had to be sedated.

'Don't worry about your sister,' the nurse spoke kindly and gently, 'it's all been a bit much for her and she is so young. What happened to her husband, by the way? She was waiting and waiting for him. We nearly didn't get to the baby in time.'

The twins looked at each other vacantly, leaving a

furious Sheila to respond. 'We haven't a clue what happened to her so-called husband, but we sure as hell are going to find out!'

Despite his obvious anger Justin kept very quiet. Nico was in full flow, wide-eyed and innocently explaining to Simonie how young Cathy was not as sweet and naïve as everyone thought, how she had trapped him and black-mailed him into marriage and then proceeded to get pregnant.

Justin was equally wide-eyed listening to it all. Nico kept glancing in his direction, waiting for a reaction, prepared to counteract any arguments but none came. Justin uttered not one word and neither did Simonie until Nico suddenly found the silence too much.

'Aren't either of you going to say anything? Come on, be fair, say something.' Leaning forward in the chair he held both his hands out towards them, palms up, and shrugged his shoulders affectedly.

Simonie stood up, wrapping her full-length white satin wrap around her body and pulling the belt tight. Walking over to Justin she tousled his hair affectionately.

'Shall I tell him or will you?'

Justin looked up at her and smiled broadly. 'Tell him what? To fuck off and never show his face here again?'

'Well, maybe, but once he hears what I have to say I'm sure he'll go willingly enough.' Walking over to the chair where Nico was lounging, she stood in front of him, hands on hips and her head to one side.

Looking from one to the other, Nico was suddenly

aware of something different in the atmosphere between them. Simonie obviously had nothing on under her wrap, and although Justin was wearing jeans and sweatshirt he was barefoot. Nico laughed harshly.

'Oh, I get it now. You two were screwing, weren't you? I've interrupted you! Christ, it didn't take you long, Justin – dead men's shoes and all that.' Grimacing slightly he focused his attention back to Simonie. 'Still, I suppose I can understand it – you are quite irresistible – but it's back to square one. I'm back for good; you won't need him any more!'

This time it was Simonie who laughed. 'No, Nico darling, I don't think you do understand. We're not just screwing, as you so delicately put it, Justin and I are getting married and it's you we have to thank for us finding each other. So, thank you and goodbye, you lying, thieving little pervert. The door's over there. Get out now before I call Daddy. He's got many a bone to pick with you and you know what happens when he's upset . . .'

If looks could kill, Justin would have expired then and there. Nico just couldn't believe it. He had been so sure that after a few minutes he'd have full access to Simonie's bed and bank account again.

'Simonie darling—'

Justin stood up. 'You heard her, now OUT!'

Nico left with as much dignity as he could muster. He even smiled and wished them both well. He didn't even slam the door behind him.

Justin and Simonie getting married?

After being unceremoniously ejected out of the business

venture, funded by Simonie's father, with nothing he had shrugged it off. Then, he had still had his sights happily focused on Cathy's trust find. But the vision he had had of instant access to a vast amount had proved to be a fantasy and all he had pocketed was the one hundred thousand from the twins, which hadn't gone far after buying the apartment and paying for the honeymoon.

His business acumen for wheeling and dealing barely kept his head above water but whereas previously he had always just about stayed inside the law, lately he found himself straying over the line into dangerous territory.

He needed funds urgently and Simonie had more than enough for both of them but now good old Justin was going to get it instead.

And Cathy was no longer the innocent child he so desperately desired. Nico was backed into a corner. No money to support his extravagant lifestyle, no child bride to satisfy his ever-increasing perverted needs and now no Simonie, whom he had hoped could provide both, to fall back on.

The rage built up inside him as he got in the car and raced off. The more he thought of Justin and Simonie together the faster he went. The powerful engine revved loudly as he crunched gears and accelerated fiercely round the winding lanes. He thought about Cathy, the little girl that he had wanted to own, giving birth. He thought about all that money just lying dormant in a trust fund. It was just too much to take. He thought his head was going to explode. His hands gripped the steering wheel so hard they were nearly numb, and the speedometer registered higher and higher until it touched ninety.

Suddenly, as his rage peaked, he veered across on to the wrong side of the road just as a pair of full-beamed headlights came straight towards him. Pulling hard on the wheel he managed to miss the car but headed straight off the road through a hedge. The last thing he remembered was the sleek, shiny bonnet going up in the air and then tipping down and down into a water-filled ditch.

The twins and Sheila were still with Cathy on the maternity ward when word came through that Nico was in casualty following a car accident. He wasn't seriously injured, just concussed from a bump on the head, and he had cuts and bruises. The impact of the crash had been lessened by the fall into water and the other driver had stopped and called for help.

Cathy's tears of relief when they woke her up to tell her the news were quickly replaced by anger.

'See, I told you something must have happened. Nico would never have left me here alone without a good reason. You thought he'd deserted me, didn't you? You all thought he'd run off!'

Cathy looked accusingly at the three women around her bed. Much as she hated what Nico did to her, and made her do to him, she still loved him and desperately wanted him still to love her, the way he used to before they were married. The way she was sure he could again now the pregnancy was out of the way.

Anyway, she wasn't going to let them know that she

had been thinking the same thing.

'Of course we didn't think that, Kitten, but now you know what's happened you have to rest. You've just had an operation. Baby's being taken care of so you get some rest. Jane and I are going now. We'll probably see you tomorrow.'

Alison and Jane both blew her a kiss as they walked out of the small side ward accompanied by a red-faced Sheila. As soon as they were off the ward she confronted them.

'There's no way he was coming here to the hospital. The accident was on the other side of town, nowhere near here. I wonder what he was really up to.'

The twins exchanged startled looks. They were constantly aware of the secret that they shared with Nico, the secret that no one, least of all Cathy, must ever find out.

'That's none of our business. Tomorrow he'll be able to see Cathy and the baby, and then everything will be OK. I don't know why you have such a down on him—'

'Absolute twaddle,' Sheila interrupted angrily. 'Why do you always stick up for him? You know as well as I do that he's no good. How can you just let everything go like this? He's making the poor girl's life a misery.' Sheila stopped in her tracks and glared at the twins. 'She's your sister and she's still only a child – can't you do something?'

'There's nothing to do. Nico probably just took a different route from the ambulance, had an accident and didn't get to the hospital. That really couldn't be helped,' Jane said.

Alison glared at the frustrated older woman. 'Anyway, Cathy and the baby are both OK and so is Nico, so no harm's been done. Now, are you going to stop sticking your nose into our family business? It's nothing to do with you.'

'Alison is right. So are you going to give us a lift home or not?'

Lying in a cubicle in the casualty department Nico tried to take stock of what had happened. Daylight was dawning and the nurse had told him he was lucky to be alive and facing a new day. She also broke the news to him that mother and daughter were OK at the opposite end of the hospital, unaware that he didn't really give a toss, that his first thought had been one of regret. He quite cold-bloodedly could see that it would have got him out of a really tight spot if they had both died.

Instinctively he had known that the pretty young nurse fancied him and automatically turning on the charm, despite aching from head to toe, he had thanked her with a tear in his eye. At the same time he was making a mental note to check out where he stood in relation to his wife's trust fund if she did die, especially now there was a child in the equation. He decided he needed to have another little chat with the sisters from hell.

'Do you want me to arrange for a porter to take you up to the maternity ward, Mr Marcos? I know you must be itching to see your wife and new daughter.'

Groaning slightly, Nico reached his hand up and gingerly touched his face. 'Not just yet. I'm a bit of a mess and I don't want Cathy to see me like this. It'll upset her. No, I'll get a taxi home and have a wash and brush-up first, get into some clean clothes.' He groaned again. 'How bruised is my face? I feel I've just gone twenty rounds with a prize fighter.'

'It's not too bad,' the nurse smiled caringly as Nico surreptitiously looked her up and down with admiration. 'The bruising will soon go down and you'll be as good as new. The stitches on your forehead will need to come out next week but the scar won't even be noticeable in your hairline.'

Even Nico realised that it wouldn't be a good time to turn on the charm too much – not as she knew about Cathy – but he made a mental note to add a young nurse to his list. He hadn't had one of them before and the uniform was always an added bonus when he sold the films on afterwards.

'Well,' she hesitated slightly and looked at him before continuing, 'if you're sure you want to go home first, Mr Marcos, Doctor has discharged you so you're free to go . . .' She handed him a leaflet. 'This is about concussion. Now if you have any problems come straight back.'

He swung his legs off the trolley bed. 'I will, thank you, but I'm sure I'll be fine.'

Leaning forward, he kissed her lightly on the cheek and was satisfied to see her blush.

He paid the taxi off at the top of the drive and limped to the front door, the gravel scrunching loudly underfoot. Ignoring the doorbell he hammered hard on the huge brass knocker several times before calling through the letter box.

'Come on, girls, I know you're in there. It's your friendly brother-in-law come for breakfast and a chat.' He hammered harder. 'Come on now, out you come. I haven't got all day.'

The door opened and he was confronted by Alison and Jane defensively standing side by side, arms crossed, presenting a united front against his intrusion.

'We have things to talk about.' Unsmiling, Nico pushed straight past without even looking at either of them. Exchanging helpless glances, they followed him into the kitchen.

He leaned casually against the worktop, smiling menacingly. 'I want more money and I want it now. Any suggestions from either of my favourite sisters-in-law? We are family, after all!'

'No way. We had an agreement, now the matter's closed and you're leaving—'

Nico interrupted Jane sharply. 'Oh, please, don't try that again. It's just so boring. Let's just cut out all the threats and promises and get down to business. I need money, you have money, it's time for a little redistribution. All we have to do is iron out the technicalities . . . like when you're going to hand it over. Call it an investment for the future, your future *outside* of prison!'

Waiting at the top of the drive for the taxi he had victoriously summoned in front of the two frightened and silent sisters, Nico smiled smugly.

Nothing excited him so much as when he was exerting his power. He loved the feeling of being in control, being able to intimidate, and now he was on a high, the pain from the accident forgotten in the adrenaline rush that engulfed him.

The twins had submitted once again. It didn't really matter that it was the twins, it could have been anyone. It was the thrill of someone being frightened of him that gave him the buzz, and the twins had been terrified.

Almost wistfully, he thought about his father, the supreme bully, the undefended champion of whipping women and small children. Much as Nico never wanted to see him again, other than in an open coffin with a knife through his heart, he knew his father would have been proud of him. With threats, intimidation and even violence when necessary, Nico Marcos Junior could make anyone do anything.

Nico Marcos Senior. The man who had beaten and humiliated him for fifteen years under the guise of making him strong enough to stand up for himself. The man who had constantly mocked his son for being small and skinny, for being his mother's favourite. The man who had even got away with murdering his own wife by terrifying his children into agreeing that she had fallen down the stairs, curiously battering her own head to a pulp on the way down.

A mere few days after the funeral, where he had wept and wailed appropriately, Nico Senior had happily turned his sexual attentions to his terrified twelve-year-old daughter.

The isolated farm cottage up in the hills of the small island was tiny and inadequate for a large family. There were no neighbours to be aware of what went on up there, but within the overcrowded cottage itself there was no privacy, no secrets.

Nico could still remember hearing his sister's stifled moans as her own father grunted and groaned his way to satisfaction whenever the mood took him. All the other children had studiously ignored what was going on for fear of being the next. They all knew, but self-preservation stopped them from speaking out.

Nico could also remember the excitement that he himself had experienced. He hadn't wanted to be aroused by the abuse of his own sister, but he couldn't help it. It happened every time – he had even started to eagerly anticipate it, to wait for it and then to enjoy it. The guilt that had always enveloped him afterwards when he had been confronted by his bruised and cowed sister had been instrumental in his running away. A part of him wanted to protect her, but another, darker, part of him wanted to participate. He had even thought about trying it for himself, but eventually one lash from the heavily studded belt too many and Nico Junior had disappeared to the mainland and eventually ended up in England. He had left his old life behind but the damage was done.

Nico Marcos Junior was unaware that he was scarred for life and oblivious to the fact that he was now being his father's son, perpetuating the traits that he hated most about his father.

143

As the taxi pulled up Nico flung the back door open. 'Where the fuck have you been? I phoned half an hour ago. To the hospital as quick as you can. I've got a new-born daughter to meet.'

Chapter Eight

'Please, Sammy-Jo, please settle down, my love. You have to go to sleep . . . Go night-nights for Mummy now.' Cathy looked at her daughter as she pleaded with her. The two-year-old gazed up at her, huge dark eyes in a tiny angelic face peering out from under the covers.

'Daddy coming soon . . . See Daddy . . .' Giggling, she threw the covers back and tried to get off the bed but Cathy restrained her gently.

'No, Daddy's not coming soon. Now go to sleep, baby. You can see Daddy tomorrow.'

Every night Cathy prayed that Sammy-Jo would be settled and asleep when Nico got in. That way she didn't have to watch the spectacle of Nico playing with her, tickling her and throwing her up in the air.

The little girl adored her father and would clamber all over him, laughing as he blew bubbles on her stomach and playfully smacked her bottom.

But Cathy was always paranoid about leaving them in the room alone together and always tried to keep watchful eyes and listening ears, never lowering her guard. The feeling of panic and sickness that overcame her when Nico took the child into the bath with him would get worse and worse until, when she could stand no more, she would intervene on any pretext. She knew that he did a lot of it to wind her up, that he found it all amusing, but she couldn't ignore her fears, no matter how hard she tried.

In a normal family, the things he did wouldn't raise an eyebrow but with Nico they sent Cathy into a blind panic.

Hearing the key in the lock she physically jumped, alerting the now sleepy Sammy-Jo.

'Daddy, Daddy, Daddy,' she called in a high-pitched excited squeal as she wriggled away from Cathy and headed out into the hall.

'Hello, my precious. You still up for Daddy? That makes a change . . . I must have beaten the clock!'

Picking the child up swiftly, he cuddled her close and looked at Cathy, a victorious smile on his lips and a coldness in his eyes that made her shiver.

'Please don't excite her, Nico. She's not been very well today. I think she's sickening for something; she'd be better back in bed.'

'Cathy, darling,' Nico replied sharply, sarcasm to the fore as always, 'if I believed you every time you told me this child was sickening for something I'd have to sell her to medical science. Now you go and put the kettle on like a good girl and I'll spend some time with my daughter . . . alone.'

She did as she was told, as always, but whenever she

was in a separate room to Sammy-Jo she was on the alert, listening for the slightest sound out of the ordinary.

Nico had sworn that he would never touch his daughter, that he had never touched a child, but Cathy wouldn't, couldn't, trust him. Deep down she knew that soon, very soon, she would have no alternative but to find a way out, a way to leave him and take Sammy-Jo to safety somewhere, even if it meant sacrificing her sisters.

The giggling stopped and there was a silence that sent her back into the room, her eyes wildly scanning for something out of the ordinary but there was nothing. Sammy-Jo was on the floor playing with a doll Nico had given her and he was reading the paper. He looked over the top of it at Cathy.

'By the way I forgot to mention, we're going out to dinner tonight. I need you to be happy and smiling, the perfect executive wife, in fact. Do you think you can manage that?' He smiled a huge fake smile, pulling his lips back over his even white teeth. 'Like this. Happy. Can you manage happy? I'm getting really pissed off at your morose little face following me everywhere. Now go and put your glad rags on, my darling, and smile. The babysitter will be here in half an hour.'

'Why didn't you tell me? I could have got Sheila over or asked the twins. I hate having strangers looking after Sammy-Jo.'

'Nancy isn't a stranger, and, anyway, I prefer not to have my daughter sucked into the fucking crazy coven of Carters.' He stood up and Cathy knew the subject was closed.

'I hope my suits are back from the cleaners.' He put his arm round her waist and hugged her almost affectionately before turning the knife. 'I'll just put Sammy-Jo back to bed while you get ready. Off you go, I can manage on my own!'

Laughing, he scooped up the little girl and took her to her bedroom, shutting the door tight behind him.

Cathy was beside herself trying not to think the unthinkable, trying not to remember.

The date of the pivotal day could easily have been tattooed on Cathy's forehead or carved on her arm. She remembered it and the time, exactly what she was wearing and where Nico was, or maybe wasn't.

It was as if a photograph had been taken of the exact moment that Cathy grew up and was confronted with evil for the first time, and she really hated herself for getting so close to the edge of doing the right thing and then pulling back.

Sammy-Jo was nine months old and Cathy was looking through the video tapes, trying to find the one of her christening. Among the jumble of tapes she pulled out from the cabinet was one with a label written in an unfamiliar hand. It read simply 'Kids'. Curiously Cathy had pushed it into the video recorder and pressed play.

The flickering picture of a cheap home-made recording couldn't disguise the images that would be imprinted on her brain for ever. From that moment on Cathy knew she would be confronted by the images whenever she closed her eyes: images of huge adult men performing the most obscene acts on little girls, some not much older than Sammy-Jo and some wearing the same sort of clothes that Nico made Cathy herself wear. Grown men leering and laughing as the children tried not to cry.

It took a few seconds for Cathy to realise exactly what she was seeing, but it was there confronting her in full graphic colour. Even the expressions of ecstasy on the men's faces as they systematically brutalised the children were not as shocking as the tortured looks on little faces as they looked into the camera lens, silently pleading with their tear-filled eyes for it all to stop.

Her hands shaking, Cathy could barely work the remote control to turn the video off before rushing to the bathroom. She vomited and vomited until her stomach ached and her throat bled.

Straight after the birth Cathy had found it hard to relate to the little creature that was placed in her arms. The pain from the Caesarean and the despair that enveloped her when Nico hadn't shown at the maternity ward after his accident was compounded by a constantly crying baby whom she didn't recognise or even understand.

She had half-heartedly blamed Sammy-Jo for wrecking her relationship with Nico. Although deep down she'd known the fault lay with Nico himself, she hadn't been able to accept that, and the fretful baby had been an easy target.

But the constantly grizzling tiny baby that demanded everything and gave nothing soon turned into a chuckling lovable little girl with huge dark eyes and masses of dark brown hair, who loved everyone, especially Cathy and Nico, and before long Cathy was completely besotted with her daughter.

Suddenly her life had meaning again and even Nico was taking an interest in their daughter. In the beginning Cathy had been wary of this, aware as she was of Nico's penchant for her pretending to be a little girl, but over time she convinced herself that it wasn't a problem. Nico always told her it was only a game and she wanted so much to believe him.

They had a lovely apartment in a converted country house that was tastefully and expensively furnished. Nico had bought the showflat at a knockdown price to make up for all the people who had marched through it, and it included all the show furniture and fittings. Cathy accepted it all gratefully and didn't even try to make any changes. Nico had told her that it was wonderful so she had accepted it, even though it wasn't her taste.

The décor reminded her of the cold and unwelcoming look the twins had created in the big house, but Cathy still believed Nico knew best. She was almost content until the day she played that video tape. In one split second everything became crystal clear and she saw the real Nico for the first time.

When Nico came home that evening Cathy was so calm and collected she surprised herself.

'When did you say you were going abroad again?' With her back to him in a pretence of laying the dining table, she framed the question carefully, starting the conversation she had been practising in her head for several hours.

'I'm not sure. Why do you ask?'

'Oh, I just wondered. Where will it be this time? Denmark? Holland? Germany even? You seem to do a lot of business in the porn hot-spots of Europe . . .' Still calm, still carefully laying out the cutlery, still not looking.

'What the fuck do you mean by that? You know what the insurance business is like—'

Sharply she interrupted. 'Yes I do, but what exactly is it you insure, Nico? Houses? Cars? Life? Children's lives? Do the little abused children receive payouts for the pain and suffering caused to them? Do the children get compensation for being raped? Or are they killed afterwards? You disgusting little ponce, *I've seen the film*! I thought Vietnam was my worst nightmare; I thought I had seen enough torture and cruelty but now I have this . . . this filth in my home.'

Turning to look at him in disgust, she felt almost triumphant as she watched his face blanch, but it was only a few seconds of triumph before deathly pale turned to beetroot red and he was across the room with his hands around her throat.

Cathy tried to scream but couldn't. He was strangling her vocal cords and she could feel herself blacking out before suddenly he let go and she slumped to the floor. 'Don't ever talk to me like that again, you little whore.' He deliberately spat at her, aiming at her face, but missed. 'All men watch those sort of films, *all men*. It doesn't mean anything, it's just something we all do, a male thing. Now just grow up and join the real world, you big baby. Give me the film.'

'I can't. I've put it somewhere safe. I should have put it out with the rubbish just like I should do with you, but it's safe, ready for me to take to the police.'

Walking away from her he sat down on the sofa but she could see through the red mist in front of her eyes that he had an erection and was slowly touching himself.

'Just go in the bedroom and get ready for me. I'll give you five minutes.'

'No way, Nico. The only place I'm going is to the police.'

To her amazement he started laughing. 'Oh, I think not, little Miss Holier Than Thou. If you go to the police then I shall just have to tell them all about your precious sisters, the murdering old witches from The bloody Crystal Cave.'

'What are you talking about?' She frowned, still rubbing her throat. 'What have Ali and Jane got to do with this? They'd be the first to call the police if they saw that tape.'

Nico put his fingers to his temple and screwed up his face in mock contemplation. 'Mmm. I know!' He threw his arms up in the air. 'Ring them and ask them. You phone your sisters, tell them all about it and see if they think it's a good idea to go to the police. Go on,' he passed her the phone, 'go on, phone them. Phone the old crones in their coven and ask them what's the best thing to do.'

'This is nothing to do with them,' Cathy screamed, but it came out in a whisper her throat was so sore. 'I'm phoning the police and handing it over. Nico, it made me sick, physically sick. It is just so perverted and it's yours. Suppose it was Sammy-Jo? How would you feel? No, don't answer that. I'm not putting her at risk. It might be her next . . .'

The more Cathy railed at him the louder he laughed.

'Just answer me, Cathy, why do you think your crazy sisters agreed to us getting married? Where do you think the money came from to buy this place?'

Shocked into silence, Cathy stared at him.

'Not only did they agree to us getting married, they gave me one hundred thousand pounds to do it and do you know why?' He was on his feet, face to face with her, so close she could feel his breath on her skin. 'They did it because *I know*! I know they deliberately set fire to the house and murdered your parents. So don't get all self-righteous with me because one more word and I shall go to the police myself . . . about them. Now GIVE ME THE FUCKING FILM.'

'I can't. I've cut it up – look in the bin. I lied to you.'

As Cathy obediently dressed up as a little girl and silently endured the ritual that she hated so much, her mind, for once, was far away.

Was he telling the truth or bluffing? Could she take the chance, bearing in mind the number of times in the past she had wondered herself at the circumstances surrounding the fire and the twins' total lack of emotion over it?

She vowed to do nothing until she had spoken to her sisters.

★ ★ ★

'The man's mad, completely mad. Surely you don't believe him, do you, Kitten?'

'He's lying. I don't understand why he'd say a thing like that . . .'

Cathy looked from one to the other, surprised by the vehemence of their denial. Normally disinterested and vacant, this time the twins were emotional, pacing the floor and wringing their hands.

'So if I take the film to the police there's nothing in what Nico said?' But as Alison and Jane looked at each other in horror, Cathy wondered if maybe everything Nico had said was true. 'Did you do it? Did you kill them – Mum and Dad? TELL ME!'

'You know what happened. It was our fault, we always said that. We left the candles alight—'

'*I know that*,' Cathy was crying hysterically, 'but I thought you did it by mistake, that it was an accident. Nico says you meant to kill them, that it was murder . . .'

There was a short standoff between the three of them as they were all suddenly aware of the implications of the word. It was Jane who broke the silence.

'That's rich, coming from a blackmailing little fortune-hunter like him. Kitten, it was an accident but Nico threatened to go to the police and say it wasn't. We couldn't face that; we couldn't have coped with outsiders prying. You know how much we hate anything like that and it would have ruined our business, so we paid him.'

'That's right, we paid him. But now he wants more and we don't know what to do.'

Cathy couldn't remember ever seeing either of the twins cry or show emotion, so seeing Alison weeping openly stunned her.

'Why didn't you tell me at the time? Why did you let me marry him?'

'Because you were determined to anyway, that's why. So before you start criticising us just remember it was you who brought him into our lives.'

The twins put their arms around each other and hugged closely. Not for the first time Cathy felt completely excluded and alone. She realised that Nico had all three of them under his control.

The one single thing that saved Cathy's sanity was her secret meetings with Justin and Simonie. It had started when she had bumped into Justin in town and he admired the baby in the pram before taking her for lunch with Simonie. Despite being naïve in many ways, Cathy knew well enough that Justin was probably right when he suggested it wouldn't be a good idea to tell Nico.

The meetings were not as frequent as she would have liked now Sammy-Jo was starting to talk but sometimes, when Nico was away 'on business', she would take the child to Sheila's and leave her there while she sneaked off to meet her friends just to have a coffee and a chat about nothing in particular. Her real relationship with Nico was a no-go area, and she never discussed that with anyone.

Surprisingly she had built quite a rapport with Simonie and was sometimes pleased when Justin wasn't around and they could be girlie together. She envied Simonie her stunning looks and bouncy blonde hair, she envied her amazing self-confidence but most of all she envied her normal marriage, the one thing she had wanted herself.

They were sitting together in the shabby but clean café at the back of the local charity shop, the regular morning meeting place for local pensioners and the one place that Cathy was one hundred per cent certain Nico would never be.

'Justin's gone up to London today but he sends his love.' Simonie smiled across the table. 'So, how's it going now? Everything OK? I haven't seen you for weeks. I wondered if anything was wrong . . .'

Cathy smiled tentatively. She only ever confided in Simonie up to a point. 'Oh, you know, in fact you probably know as well as I do. So long as everything is going Nico's way he's OK. Anyway, at the moment he's away in Berlin.' She paused and reached out to touch Simonie's hand. 'I wish we could be real friends, not have to sneak around like this. I hate it—'

Embarrassed, Simonie interrupted her quickly. 'Never mind, just believe me, it's best like this. I like you, I hope we're already friends, and Justin is very fond of you so let's leave it at that. Now tell me all about Sammy-Jo. I miss seeing her . . .'

Simonie smiled affectionately as Cathy went into overdrive about her daughter. It was so easy to distract her that the older, more sophisticated woman felt quite guilty, but she didn't want Cathy to know all the sordid details unless of course the time came when she had to.

'Now you tell me, Simonie, how's Tim? I know he still

goes to the drama group but he just ignores me if I see him out.'

'Well, of course he does. He's always been in love with you and unrequited love is painful! But seriously, he's fine. Maybe one day you two can make up.'

Cathy laughed. 'Can you really see Nico allowing that?'

'Thinking about it, no I can't, not until hell freezes over!'

The first time she had met Cathy, when she had gone to meet Justin for lunch one day and found her sitting there with him, Simonie had been furious with her husband. Still harbouring a deep desire to make Nico pay, she couldn't believe that Justin could be so insensitive and, despite warming to the young girl with a tiny baby in tow, she'd told him so afterwards.

'I can't believe you did that to me, Justin. How could you just invite Nico's wife along? Shit, you know what happened. I hate that man so much . . .'

'I know exactly what Nico did and what he's like and that's exactly why I did it. She's a child, and you and I both know what he's probably putting her through. She's a good kid and she's got no one. Anyway . . .' he'd looked at Simonie sideways, 'one day she'll want to nail him, just like we do! I just hope she does it before her trust fund pays out. But be honest, darling, didn't you feel just a little bit sorry for her?'

Simonie had smiled and reached out to Justin, pulling him close. 'You're nothing but a big softie, you. To think I had such a near miss with that bastard.'

'I know, but it still makes me laugh when I think of his face when you told him we were getting married . . . Talk about double bluff! If you hadn't said that I would never have plucked up the courage to ask you.'

They had both laughed. 'Obviously it was meant to be,' Simonie had said. 'I can't believe how blind I was for so long. Tell me, Justin, how could I have been taken in?'

'I don't know but he took me in as well. Still, that's in the past. Apart from Cathy. I really think we should keep an eye on her – and her daughter, for that matter. Over time I'd forgotten just how young Cathy was – still is, in fact. I wouldn't put anything past Nico.'

'Oh, come on. I mean, you and I both know that he married her mainly for her money, and as for the baby, that's his daughter!' Simonie had shaken her head in disbelief. 'No, not even Nico would do anything like that . . .'

Justin had looked at Simonie and rolled his eyes upwards. 'You've seen some of the stuff he looks at. Every child in those photos is someone's child. If he doesn't have principles when it comes to looking at it, why should he have them at all? I hope I'm wrong, I really do but . . .'

Simonie had been surprised by how much she loved Justin, the man she had never taken a lot of notice of when he'd lived in Nico's shadow. What she had previously perceived as weakness and lack of character she'd now seen was actually kindness and lack of ego. He didn't want to take over her business or raid her bank account, all he wanted was to love her and for her to love him.

'OK,' she'd kissed him on the nose, 'you win. We'll keep an eye on Cathy and Sammy-Jo.'

Cathy glittered through the business dinner the way she always did, the way that ensured she wouldn't get a torrent of abuse when they got in. She watched Nico in action and wondered anew at his charm and persuasion that had his prospective clients and their wives, especially their wives, eating out of his hand.

When Nico was like that Cathy could still feel the old attraction and hated herself for it. As always Nico was immaculately turned out and Cathy was aware that other women in the hotel restaurant were eyeing him admiringly. The dark hair was now flecked with pewter highlights, especially around the temples, and he was wearing a midnight-blue suit and pristine white shirt that emphasised his permanent tan. There was no getting away from it, he was the best-looking man there; he knew it and so did everyone else.

Cathy had long given up trying to understand him or to figure out why he did what he did. She knew that he watched the videos and read the magazines and although she knew they were illegal she was aware she could do nothing about it if she wanted to protect her sisters.

'Cathy?'

The voice filtered through and she shook herself back. She smiled disarmingly. 'I'm so sorry, I was just wondering whether I ought to ring home, check on my daughter. What were you saying?'

'I was just asking where you bought that wonderful

dress you're wearing. It's a cheongsam, isn't it?' The woman smiled. 'It's so different. It really wouldn't suit everyone – mind you, with your Chinese features—'

'Vietnamese, actually, my features are Vietnamese, but really I'm as British as you are, adopted and raised in England, not the least bit Chinese in fact!' Although she said it nicely she felt Nico's eyes piercing into her face. Pretending not to notice, she continued, 'As for the dress, Nico chose it for me. He has such good taste; he chooses most of my outfits—'

'Darling,' Nico interrupted, 'would you and the ladies like to go through to the lounge for coffee? Then we can talk business without interrupting your conversation about ladies' things.' As he flashed his wide, charming smile at the wives of his two business associates they preened and almost twittered out loud. He stood up and pulled their chairs out for them attentively before standing back with a slight bow to let them all past.

'Be nice to them. A lot depends on this and if it goes wrong I shall be furious, if you understand my meaning.' Anyone watching Nico whispering in Cathy's ear would never have guessed what he was saying; the smile never left his lips as he solicitously held his arm out to point the way.

While the women were busy admiring Nico the men were all watching Cathy as she walked confidently through the restaurant. The skin-tight black dress with a slight silver thread emphasised all the curves she had gained from motherhood and the silver high heels clicked seductively on the parquet flooring. There was no middle road for Nico when it came to clothes and styles for Cathy. They were either ultrasophisticated or childlike. Full make-up and overdressed hair or scrubbed face and plaits.

Tonight was definitely ultrasophisticated and made up to the hilt, and Cathy, aware of the admiring stares, felt good about herself. She was also aware that Nico was watching her as well.

'Now our good ladies have departed shall we get down to business? Brandy, gentlemen?' Nico smiled and pulled his briefcase on to the table.

'Not here, Mr Marcos. Let's go up to the suite – a little more private, don't you think?'

'If you wish. I didn't feel it was my place to suggest it but I agree, some privacy may be appropriate. Is there a VCR up there as well?'

'Of course, we always ask for one. We never know when we'll need it for some quality control. We have to test the merchandise, see that it's up to standard.'

Both men threw their heads back and laughed loudly and coarsely.

Nico tried to hide his disgust. He hated anything less than perfect, and these two were, in his eyes, ignorant obese slobs with bellies bulging precariously over the top of their trousers and fat red necks struggling to stay put inside overtight collars. Even their wives were the caricature overmade-up brassy blondes with big boobs and skinny hips in short tight skirts that rode up the second they sat down. These men represented everything he hated but he had to do business with them so he smiled and pretended that it was the funniest thing he had ever heard. He had watched the men watching Cathy and realised with a start that she was a beautiful and classy woman. He also realised that he didn't like seeing them ogle her, his wife.

When they got home Cathy put the coffee-maker on and they both sat and chatted with Nancy for a while, mostly about Sammy-Jo, but Nico was on top form, describing his two business contacts, the alleged insurance salesmen. Even Cathy was laughing, and when she joined in with her imitation of the two wives Nico smiled appreciatively at her mimicry.

As Nancy left, Cathy started clearing away but Nico came over and pulled her down on to the sofa with him.

'Let's just sit and have a coffee on our own, like we used to . . .'

Cathy froze, dreading what was coming next.

'You were really good with those old whores tonight. Without you I couldn't have dealt with them.' He leaned away from her and looked her up and down. 'We make a good team, you know. It's just a shame all the other stuff gets in the way. But it needn't. I've always had compartments in my life; if you did the same we could be OK.'

'We couldn't, Nico. I can't accept what you do, what tonight was about. Insurance business my arse! I'm not stupid, I'm not silly little Cathy any more. I'm a grown woman, in case you haven't noticed, and a mother. I can't accept it.'

'Do you still love me?' The question was quick as a gunshot.

'I hate you—'

'I know that,' he interrupted, 'but do you still love me? You can do both.' He paused. 'Well? Do you?'

Cathy sat silently. She didn't want to confront her feelings for him, especially when he was sitting beside her, looking at her in the same way he used to when they first met. 'I don't know,' she said eventually. 'I hate what you do and I hate what I know about you but most of all I hate the way you treat me.'

'I take it the answer's yes then! Cathy, we could make this work and we'd both be a lot happier if we were friends, like we used to be. We could be good together, you know, and we do have a daughter in common.'

She looked at him and a flicker of power flashed through her, a feeling of having him on the run for the first time. It felt good.

'We could try, I suppose, but you have to treat me like an adult, and I don't want any filthy books or films in my home again and I want your word about Sammy-Jo.'

'Compartments then?'

Cathy smiled cautiously. 'I'll try but I can't promise. I don't know if I have enough compartments.'

That night they made love for the first time as two adults and Cathy was ecstatic. It was just how she had imagined it would be when they got married and she decided then and there – against her better judgement, and knowing full well she was betraying herself and her principles – to give it a go. He was her husband and he had promised it was only business.

As Cathy slept quietly, a peaceful smile on her face, Nico leaned on one arm and looked down at her. He could see she was a beautiful young woman and he knew that she still loved him, despite everything. That was exactly what he had intended.

He wanted her in his life for the moment but not in his bed, not now she had grown up. The sex had been offensive for him: he found her dirty, her body was no longer innocent but he had enjoyed the game. His control of Cathy had been fading but the change of strategy had brought her back in line. Victoriously he grinned down at the sleeping woman. 'Gotcha,' he whispered gently. 'I win again!'

He knew it was time for another fishing expedition. After all, Cathy had agreed to compartments and this time he would keep his females separate. Everything would have been fine if he had married Simonie and kept Cathy secret.

Whenever the thought of Simonie with Justin came into his head he turned it all over and over in his mind, unable to dismiss them. He determined to get her back eventually and make Justin pay for taking her but he was going to bide his time. Once Cathy had her inheritance then he would make a move; until then, Cathy would do.

Cathy and the pubescent he had yet to find. Nico decided he would look for another youth project like the drama group.

Chapter Nine

Alison and Jane were becoming so bizarre that they were the talk of the village and beyond. Whereas previously they were regarded as fairly harmless eccentrics, now they were acting as if they were positively batty. They had an equally strange woman helper in the shop itself and spent most of their time upstairs telling fortunes and reading about witchcraft, and when they did go out they would speak to no one.

Dressed in black from head to toe, they floated along the street with their heads down, avoiding any attempt at conversation or any eye contact. They were fast becoming local celebrities and even the most cynical would think twice about laughing openly at them. They wouldn't even respond to Sheila unless she referred to them as Zeta or Zara and, although she tried to be tolerant, she was fast losing patience with their behaviour, convinced it was all an act. The only person who could get through to them was Cathy, and she resolutely refused to use the invented names.

After Sheila had telephoned in a panic and told Cathy the twins were now completely bonkers, Cathy had gone to visit them at the big house and been horrified at the scene that confronted her. The house was in darkness bar a few candles, and she had found the twins out in the garden sitting on the ground on opposite sides of a small fire burning on the once-pristine patio, chanting and rubbing their hands in the dirt.

'For Christ's sake, you two, what are you up to? You're going to burn the whole fucking place down again. You're bloody mad, the pair of you. Wasn't once enough?'

Cathy was so angry she went over to the fire and started kicking it out.

'Don't do that, you interfering little bitch. This is our house and we can do whatever we like.'

Alison hadn't looked up as she'd spoken, but Jane did: 'What are you doing here anyway? I thought your pervy husband kept you locked up at night.' She looked at her twin and laughed. 'And she's got the nerve to call us mad when she's actually married to that . . . that thing?'

Cathy refused to rise to the bait. 'Let's just go inside in the warm. You don't need an open fire – that's what the central heating's for, isn't it? Come on, I'll put the kettle on.'

The twins looked at each other and then clambered to their feet, obediently following a dispirited Cathy into the house. Just lately she had begun to feel she was responsible for everyone: Sammy-Jo, the twins, Nico, even Sheila, whom she had to protect from the truth. They all demanded bits of her until there was nothing left for herself.

Although Sheila tried to mother her there was no way Cathy could ever bring herself to let down the barriers to her. There were too many secrets to keep track of and keep to herself.

Putting two steaming cups of hot chocolate in front of the twins on the coffee table covered in congealed candle wax, Cathy sat opposite on the huge white sofa that was now covered with a black sheet marked out with hand-printed symbols.

'So, are you going to tell me about it? Tell me why you're behaving like this? It's all getting a bit surreal now, this witchery nonsense. You're becoming a laughing stock.'

'It's not nonsense. We *are* witches – we're white witches. Just because you don't understand—'

'You're wrong, I do understand, believe it or not. You're looking for something – I don't know what, but I do know this is not it, this mumbo-jumbo. You're being sucked into something dangerous and evil.'

'Just listen to you,' Jane sneered, 'little Miss Innocent. You're the one sucked into something dangerous and you're too blind to see it. That thing you're married to is what's evil, not us.'

'I never said *you* were evil.'

'No, but that's what you meant – what they all mean, especially that sneaky spying Sheila. I bet it was her that sent you round, interfering old goat.'

The smell of incense permeating through the house was so overpowering it was making Cathy feel quite nauseous. Jumping up from her seat she quickly extinguished the

167

candles and joss sticks that were all over the room and turned the lights full on. The twins blinked in unison but stayed silent.

'Don't you think Mum and Dad would be really unhappy if they could see you both behaving like this? This house was their home, a family home. Now it looks like the bloody black hole. No wonder everyone thinks you're a joke . . .' As soon as the words were out, Cathy regretted them. After spending all her life getting upset over the way people treated her sisters she was now doing the self-same thing. 'I'm sorry, I didn't mean that.'

'Yes you did. You're so full of yourself lately it won't be long before it's beneath you to even talk to us,' Alison retorted. 'I don't know what's happened to you, Cathy, but you're as hard as nails. Have you completely forgotten where you came from? How our lives were totally fucked when Mum and Dad took you in?'

For once they weren't in unison. Jane looked horrified. 'Don't talk like that.' She spoke to Alison but looked at her young sister, sitting opposite, biting her nails and looking stunned by the outburst. 'She didn't mean it; you've just upset her. Why don't you just go and leave us alone? We're not hurting anyone—'

Alison was on her feet waving her arms about and shaking her head furiously. 'We're not hurting anyone but she is. She's always hurt us. She took over Mum and Dad and made them lose interest in us, and now she's wrecked everything again by bringing that blackmailer into our lives. He never leaves us alone – money, money, money, always wanting money . . . I hate him! We both hate him! We wish he was dead!'

Cathy stood up abruptly, her face set in a deep frown as she tried to take on board what Alison was saying. 'Look at me! Are you trying to tell me that Nico is *still* demanding money from you?' The silence was deafening. 'Tell me!'

'Just go home, Cathy. We can't take much more of his threats. He threatened to go to the police again the last time. We can't have that, so just go home and forget about it. Every time you upset him he comes after us for some more, tormenting and tormenting us. Please, just go away and leave us in peace!'

'When was the last time he was here? *When?*'

'Last week – he was here last week. He wanted money again. He told us we were murderers and that he had proof. He can't have proof but he said he did. We've given him so much . . . You must have known; you must have had some of it as well!'

Alison and Jane were both looking at her, the accusation clear in their eyes.

'I didn't know, I swear I didn't. I thought it all finished years ago.' She hugged them both but they remained poker-stiff. 'I'll sort this out, I swear it. I'll sort it out for good. Nico won't come round here again!'

In the taxi on the way back to Sheila's to pick up Sammy-Jo, Cathy thought over everything that had been said – maybe said in anger but said just the same.

Sheila was looking out of the window as the car pulled

up and quickly opened the door.

'Sshhh, Sammy-Jo has just dropped off. She's been running mad with Sally and they've worn each other out. How did it go? Were they really dancing round a fire?'

Cathy tutted furiously. 'Of course they weren't. You should know better than to believe silly old Ben. He may be a good gardener but he's a crap gossip. Yes, there was a fire but they were just sitting there. I'm going to have a word with Ben.'

'Cathy, don't be unfair! Old Ben is one of the few who always, always sticks up for the twins in the village. He's fond of them, that's why he was worried.'

'I know, I know,' Cathy sighed. 'To be honest, I'm a bit worried too. This witchcraft nonsense is going too far. They're both too unstable to get involved in things like that. Sheila . . .' she tried hard to find the right words, 'you know when I was adopted, did they resent me? Be honest – it's just something that Alison said . . .'

Sheila was looking thoughtfully out of the window, wrestling with herself about what to say. 'Well, to be fair to everyone I'm not too sure,' she said eventually. 'I wouldn't have thought they took enough notice of what was going on around them to be exactly resentful, but having said that . . .' She stopped mid-sentence lost for words.

'Well, go on,' Cathy replied impatiently. 'Did they or didn't they?'

'As I was saying, I'm not sure, but they were very self-sufficient, those two, so your mum and dad did make more fuss of you. But fuss wasn't what Alison and Jane wanted. You filled a big gap for Bryan and Elena and if that silly pair resent it now, well, too bad. It was their own doing; they only ever wanted each other.'

Cathy leaned back on the kitchen chair and looked up at the ceiling, talking almost to herself.

'It seems so strange. I spent most of my life wishing I was really like them, looked like them, wishing that we could really be three matching siblings instead of the loony Carter twins and Susie Wong, the novelty Vietnamese orphan, the token foreigner in the village. But all the time they just wished I wasn't there at all.' The forced rasping laugh almost disguised the sob that was forming in her throat, but suddenly tears were rolling down her face. Leaning forward she folded her arms on the table and leaned on them crying uncontrollably.

Before Sheila could do anything to comfort her a small figure appeared in the doorway.

'Aunty Sheila, why's Mummy crying? Has she been naughty? Did you smack her like Daddy does?'

Blinking sharply, Cathy sat up and looked away from her wide-eyed daughter.

'Mummy's not crying, Aunty Sheila just said something funny. I was laughing and you know Daddy doesn't smack Mummy so don't say things like that. Come along. Now you're awake it's time to go home.'

Sammy-Jo stumbled over sleepily to her mother and laid her head in her lap. Petite like her mother, with a head of thick black hair, she also had Nico's handsome, even features and dark impenetrable eyes. Unfortunately, despite being only three years old, she also had a lot of

Nico's ways about her – the flashing smile and the slightly downcast face that could be turned on at will.

Cathy often feared for her daughter because she was so undeniably gorgeous and knowledgeable beyond her years. Heads turned wherever they went and complete strangers would come up and pat her on the head. Sammy-Jo lapped it all up and had quickly learned how being wide-eyed and cute could be quite profitable when it came to little treats.

Sheila's face was a picture of restraint as she tried not to pick up on what the child had said.

'Why don't you stay a while longer? I'll run you home later, and you did say Nico was away on business . . . again.'

'We'd be grateful for a lift, Sheila, but I really must get back. I've got a lot to do.'

Sheila sighed and leaned against the old gas cooker, struggling to cross her arms over her huge bosom.

'Cathy, darling, I wasn't born yesterday and I certainly don't need a three-year-old to tell me what is in front of my eyes, but if you don't want to talk about it, that's your choice. All I will say is, don't accuse your daughter of lying if she is telling the truth. You'll confuse her. Now . . .' Sheila turned away and bustled in the small kitchen, 'tea or coffee? And what about my precious little Sammy-Jo? Do you want one of Aunty Sheila's special, special drinks for big girls?'

'Yes, please.' Automatically the child opened her eyes wide and smiled what Cathy called her 'Nico smile'. 'Can I have a chocolate bar as well? Pleeeeeze, Aunty Sheila?'

★ ★ ★

That night, after Sammy-Jo was tucked up in bed and Cathy was in the apartment as usual with only the television for company, she decided to risk the wrath of Nico, should he ever find out, and look through his study.

The door was always locked but Cathy had long ago found a spare key taped to the back of Nico's chest of drawers in the bedroom. She had never looked in the study before – never wanted to for fear of what she might find – but this time it wasn't tapes and magazines she was interested in.

She wanted to try to find out about his business, his finances, anything that might give her leverage when it came to the big confrontation that she knew was bubbling away. Nico had promised the moon and come up with nothing, and although deep down Cathy still loved him and wanted to believe him, every time Sammy-Jo precociously opened her eyes wide and almost flirted with her father, Cathy could see the children in that film.

Her ongoing nightmare was of Sammy-Jo getting caught up in it. She wanted to hurl herself across the room and beat to a pulp the so-called business associates of Nico who would sit in her home and, laughing at the child's antics, pull Sammy-Jo on to their knees and tease and tickle her while her father just watched, smiling proudly.

No matter how often she raised the subject Nico would just laugh and tell her she was paranoid, that because she was so uptight about sex she imagined it everywhere. Cathy could still feel the tenderness down the side of her

173

face where Nico had cracked her one and broken her cheekbone the last time she had complained about it.

Despite the fact that she knew Nico wouldn't be back for days, the hairs on the back of her neck tingled and the thumping of her heart echoed throughout her body as she unlocked and opened the door. She felt a surge of power as she entered the forbidden zone. Even though the room was completely unoverlooked, she closed the curtains quickly before turning on the light and looking around.

Considering Nico's ridiculously high standards in the rest of the apartment, his study was quite disorganised. The huge pseudo-Edwardian desk that was his pride and joy when he bought it was covered in papers and folders, and the drawers of the matching filing cabinet were slightly open with files and folders sticking out at all angles. If Cathy hadn't known better she would have thought that the place had been ransacked.

Not really knowing where to start, and certainly not wanting to leave anything different from how she found it, she decided to begin with the desk, gingerly moving bits and pieces and then making sure they went back in exactly the same place.

There was nothing out of the ordinary apart from a selection of hard-core paedophile magazines in the bottom drawer, but Cathy knew she had to ignore them if she didn't want to be sidetracked by her own abhorrence. She just took one from the bottom of the pile.

Slowly but surely she went through the whole room, even the bookcases, mentally making notes of where anything that might be relevant was located. The shelves of videos looked innocent enough but, being well aware of Nico's habit of putting his disgusting films into innocent cases, she wasn't deceived. But again she had to make a conscious effort to ignore them, just taking one at random and shuffling the others along to fill the space.

Finally Cathy had covered the whole room and pulled out the only files she really wanted to get her teeth into: the ones concerning Nico's business dealings and his finances.

Carefully locking the door behind her and putting the key down her bra, she went through to the bathroom with the files tucked under her dressing gown, still irrationally paranoid that Nico might appear and catch her in the middle of her search.

Two hours later she emerged grim-faced. The incriminating evidence she wanted was there – details of various bank accounts, letters, names and enough proof to confront him with. All she had really wanted was to have enough leverage to stop the blackmailing of her sisters, like with like, but she now had changed her mind.

The single most disturbing item she had found was an envelope containing a set of seemingly innocent photographs of a child standing in the shower stark naked, laughing and posing for the camera. The child was bending forward, leaning back, arms and legs stretched wide as the water rained down on the skinny little body. There was a complete set of twenty-four. They could easily have been the sort of photos that most parents have and laugh about, but in the context of the filth in that room Cathy was shocked into true realisation.

The child was Sammy-Jo.

Cathy had no idea they had been taken and she was stunned by the almost provocative poses the child was adopting. She knew then and there she had to rescue Sammy-Jo and herself, and she hated herself for being so weak and believing everything Nico said.

Simonie answered the first call of the day, cursing as the phone rang that she hadn't left the answering machine on a little longer to give herself time to clear some of her huge backlog.

'Good morning, Forest Property Management. Simonie speaking. Can I help you?'

'Hi, it's Cathy. Can we meet? I need to ask you a favour, a huge favour in fact. Can I come to your office as soon as I've dropped Sammy-Jo at playschool?'

Once Simonie had got Nico Marcos out of her life and then out of her system she had concentrated on getting her business back on track. Without Nico around raiding profits it had been onwards and upwards, and after Justin had joined forces with her they had gone on a roll. Combining her insurance brokerage with his luxury estate agent and property management company had been Simonie's idea. They had put a lot of work into it, the timing had been spot-on and they were really reaping the rewards.

The business was successful and she and Justin were happy. It often surprised her quite how happy she was, considering that it wasn't too far in the past that she had viewed Justin as a bit of a chinless wonder.

Simonie had barely had time to open her post before Cathy was shown into her office. She smiled as Cathy was suitably impressed with the surroundings.

'Wow, this is one really great office. How do you manage to get any work done with that fucking marvellous view?' Cathy gazed all around the low-ceilinged, oak-beamed office that looked out on to a village green littered with grazing ponies.

'With difficulty!' Simonie smiled, and gave Cathy a quick hug and a peck on the cheek. 'It's a shame really but to be honest I don't notice it very much. You know the old saying: familiarity breeds contempt. And, of course, I'm out a lot of the time. Now what can I do for you? It must be something good for you to take a chance on being seen coming in here.'

'I've got some things that I want photocopied but I need you to swear to me that this won't go any further. If Nico finds out he'll kill me, he really will.'

Simonie's face was suddenly grave as she looked Cathy in the eye. 'You should know me by now, but I swear I would never ever betray you to Nico. Don't forget, I know what he's like . . .'

'You're right, of course. I think I know what he's like but what do you know about him that you haven't told me? There must be lots of information you haven't shared. It would be helpful if you did, you know.'

Simonie hesitated, unsure exactly how much the young woman actually knew. How could she possibly tell her that Nico married her for her money, that her innocence was a bonus and that he only dumped Simonie just before the wedding? How could she possibly tell Cathy her husband was a paedophile?

Suddenly the phone rang and her sigh of relief was almost audible as she snatched it up and willingly got caught up in a meaningless conversation with her assistant in the outside office. Then, clicking the phone sharply back into its cradle, she turned back to Cathy and smiled brightly.

'Now, where were we? Oh yes, you want something photocopied but I'm sworn to secrecy. Let's see if the photocopier's free and I'll show you how to use it. That way it'll be between you and the machine.'

'You know that's not what I meant, and anyway I want your advice, or at least a listening ear. I've discovered Nico is involved in some very dodgy imports and exports, porn magazines and films, hard-core stuff, I mean *really* hard-core . . . with children.' She paused, waiting for Simonie to be shocked but her expression didn't change.

'I can't do anything about it officially,' Cathy continued. 'For various reasons I can't go to the police or anything, but I want copies of all his documents, bank accounts, et cetera. I've got them all here but I have to put them back pretty sharpish.'

'No problem. Come on, we'll do it now.' Simonie took her hand and led her to the photocopier, asking her assistant en route to go and put some fresh coffee on, telling her that they would be some time.

'Simonie, you don't look very shocked; did you know about all this?'

By concentrating hard on lifting the lid and placing the papers in one by one Simonie didn't have to look up. She felt like a traitor and knew that Cathy would be able to tell from just one glance at her face that she had kept secrets.

But Cathy was suddenly like an alert little terrier that had just caught its first rat, and she wasn't going to let go.

'Simonie? You're not answering me . . . Tell me what you know. He *is* my husband, and I have Sammy-Jo to think of.'

Fiercely pressing the start button, Simonie turned and faced her. Taking a deep breath she launched into speech.

'I knew Nico was into some bizarre dealings and that he had strange reading habits, but he had always blamed Justin. During what I laughingly used to think was a relationship he ripped me off for thousands of pounds. Then he married you for your money.' Simonie gently reached out and took both Cathy's hands in hers. 'So yes, I did know a lot more than I let on but you were already married to him by the time I got to know you as a person, not just a name, and of course you were in love with him. You wouldn't have believed me. In fact, I think you still are in love with him and I can understand that. He's a charismatic bastard, is Nico Marcos.'

'I see . . .'

Simonie knew Cathy was evaluating the information.

'Everyone seems to know more about him than I do and everyone seems to think I need protecting from bad news. Well, I don't. How did you all expect me to deal with this fucking nightmare, to protect my daughter, if you insisted on treating me like a child? I thought it was only Nico who wanted to treat me like a little girl but it seems even you and Justin think I'm ten years old.'

Stunned into momentary silence Simonie stood stock-still, her mouth agape. For several seconds the only sound was the clunking of the photocopier. Despite everything Cathy wanted to laugh.

'Bloody hell, Simonie, do you really think I'm that silly?'

'You're certainly not that, Cathy, but you are loyal to a fault where that man is concerned.'

'Not any more, Simonie, not any more. Now let's get on with it. I won't feel happy until all this is back where it came from and then . . .' she smiled triumphantly at the other woman, 'then I can plan my new life!'

'Cathy, I know you think you know him, but please be careful. Nico Marcos is a driven man. He is quite ruthless and will do anything at all to get where he wants to be. Don't underestimate him, will you?'

'Don't worry.' Cathy hugged her. 'I know what I'm doing.'

'I hope so, and please, don't forget that Justin and I are always there for you. Anything you need – any help at all – just ask.'

After meticulously putting everything back where it had been, Cathy locked the door and stuck the key back behind the chest of drawers. Only then did she heave a sigh of relief.

Placing in a carrier bag all the photocopies, the video

tape and magazine, one of the photos of Sammy-Jo and the spare key to the study that she had had cut, she called a taxi and took the bag over to Simonie for her to put in the private safe at her and Justin's new home. The expensive thatched cottage in the middle of the Forest that Nico didn't know they owned.

'What are you planning to do, Cathy?'

'I'm not sure yet. I have things to do and people to see first, but I promise as soon as I've decided I'll let you know. By the way, you don't happen to know where his ex-wife Joanna lives now, do you?'

Simonie paled visibly and started fidgeting with her long flaxen hair, twisting and twisting the end of a long strand. 'No, I've no idea, but Cathy, please don't do that. Nico really will kill you. Please. The only time I ever mentioned her he flew into such a rage he broke a couple of my ribs among other things and put me in hospital. Apparently the nasty, nasty lady sold his home from under him, took all his money, abducted his kids and disappeared for absolutely no reason.' Smiling sarcastically she continued, 'And if we believe that then, well, we're really ultra, *ultra* stupido!'

For the first time that day they both laughed but it was hollow laughter bordering on hysteria.

Next stop for Cathy was The Crystal Cave. The Closed sign was on the door but she could hear noises coming from inside so she knocked loudly several times until Jane came over and peered out.

'What do you want?' The aggressiveness of her question did nothing to deter Cathy.

'Stop fucking about and let me in. This is important.'

Shocked, Jane opened the door and Cathy pushed past into the shop, then through to where Alison was standing looking bemused.

'Well? What's so important you had to practically break the door down?'

'I need to talk finances with you. I want all your bank statements that prove how much money you've handed over to Nico and I want to talk to you about my trust fund. I want to make sure Nico doesn't see a single penny of it.' Banging her hand ferociously on the glass-topped counter to emphasise that she meant business, Cathy continued in the most authoritative voice she could muster, 'You're both trustees – we're going to go and see the bank managers, accountants, solicitors, whoever – even the courts, I don't care who – and we're going to sort this out. I'm going to screw that low-life but I'm going to do it so well he won't realise until it's too late.'

'And why now all of a sudden, after everything that's gone on?'

Cathy raised her eyes to the ceiling and sighed loudly. 'Because I'll soon be twenty-one and as soon as that happens Nico will be away with the lot. Now quickly give me the bank statements. I know you keep them here so just give.' Holding out her arm she clicked her fingers impatiently. 'Come on, don't worry about Nico. He's about to learn the true meaning of the word blackmail!'

Hot-footing it back to Simonie's to get the bank statements copied and safely filed away with everything else, Cathy started making plans. Her main concern was the twins. They were definitely the weakest link in the chain. Would they co-operate or would they cave in to their concerns about Nico going to the police? She knew she would have to keep harassing them until they were so fed up with her they would concede. The one thing about her sisters that she knew she could depend on was their hatred of anything interfering with their lives. Now Cathy was determined to *keep* interfering with their lives until they did as she wanted.

Nico was feeling particularly pleased with himself. His trip had gone well and, as always, he had mixed business with pleasure. He enjoyed his European sorties, but he viewed visiting Thailand as the biggest perk his business could offer. The merchandise was dirt cheap and he could selectively sample the goods.

Now he was home and smugly aware that his profitable purchases were trundling their way over to Britain via a long and complex route across Asia and Europe, and he was going to make a huge profit when they eventually arrived at his hideaway in Devon. The dilapidated farmhouse on its own land in the back of beyond had been a good investment. No one knew he owned it and the neighbours took absolutely no notice of lorries delivering bales of hay.

And he was lucky enough to have Paul. Recently out of prison and with nowhere to go, Paul was more than happy to potter about down on the farm in return for a roof over his head and the promise of a substantial bonus each time a consignment arrived for distribution. There was also the promise of a trip to Thailand in the future to take his pick of the available children who filled the streets and bars, eager for cash.

All in all everything was going great guns. Nico was satisfied that he had found a way of having the best of both worlds. As a wife Cathy was a business asset – a soon-to-be wealthy business asset – and his business venture ensured an endless supply of nubile young oriental girls who would willingly do absolutely anything they were told, especially when there was a burly minder stationed outside the door. He even had the twins and their money on a long piece of elastic that he could tweak whenever the mood took him, reeling them in sharply to bail him out.

Cathy had seemed so happy to have him home and so had his gorgeous little Sammy-Jo. After weighing up all the options he had decided he would keep Cathy, even after he had relieved her of her inheritance, and satisfy his other urges away from the home.

Looking out of his study window he smiled to himself. All he had to do now was totally fuck things up for Simonie and Justin. He chuckled. A little revenge would be the icing on the cake!

Chapter Ten

Walking down the local high street Cathy spotted a familiar figure not far ahead of her going in the same direction with his back to her. The shoulders were broader and higher, the hair tidier but she would have recognised him anywhere.

She decided to take the bull by the horns. Every other time she had seen Tim O'Connor in the street he had pointedly ignored her and she had accepted it, aware that she deserved his cold shoulder, but this time she wanted to talk to him. It mattered to her to set the record straight before she went away.

Breaking into a jog she weaved through the pedestrians to catch him up. Gently she tapped him on the shoulder.

'Hello, Tim. Remember me?'

The young man turned round with a smile on his face but it disappeared the second he saw her.

'Please don't walk away and ignore me, Tim. It's been a long time. Time to forgive and forget, don't you think?'

The tall and muscular young man who stood head and

shoulders above her bore little physical resemblance to the gawky adolescent who had been her friend for so many years but the blushing cheeks and downcast eyes were exactly the same.

'I really don't think . . . I mean . . .' He turned his face to her but his eyes were anywhere but on hers. 'Really, Cathy, there's no point in pursuing this. We've both moved on and I certainly don't want your godawful husband after my blood again.'

'What do you mean "again"? When was Nico ever after you?' Her inbuilt antennae, perfectly honed after years with Nico, twitched suspiciously.

'Cathy, it doesn't matter, it's history. I'm pleased to see you're looking well but I have to go. I'm in a bit of a rush . . .' He moved to one side to walk away but she moved also.

'Please, Tim. You were a good friend to me; I want to explain, set the record straight before it's too late. Just half an hour of your time, that's all . . .'

She could see from his expression that he was hesitating. She had always been able to read him like a book.

'Please? My car's in the car park. I've only just passed my test and can't quite manage parking in the street.' Laughing gently she continued, 'We can drive up to the picnic area – you remember the one? Up where we used to ride the horses and annoy the tourists with their picnic baskets and Primus stoves! Nothing like a bit of horse dung to put them off their tea and sandwiches.'

Tim smiled and Cathy knew she had succeeded.

'I'll meet you there. My car's just up the road, but then

I passed my test at seventeen!'

'Show-off! I'll meet you there in half an hour.'

As Cathy drove through the lanes her mind was hyperactive as she tried to decide how much she could tell Tim, how much she could trust him. She needed someone who could reassure Sheila and keep her informed without giving her too much information for Nico to force out of her. The twins would be OK – they would soon forget about her and, anyway, they had Sheila – but Sheila had no one and she didn't want any of them knowing about her friendship with Justin and Simonie.

It was Nico who had taught Cathy about compartments and now she was doing it for herself. For their own protection as well as hers, she had to share only selective information with selective people, or, as Nico always put it, work on the 'need-to-know principle', or 'what you don't know you can't tell'. How she used to hate those convenient little phrases but now she was discovering the usefulness of the lesson. The twins knew some of the facts, Sheila knew some, and Justin and Simonie knew more than most. However, no one knew it all and it had to stay that way to protect everyone from Nico.

The big question was, could she trust Tim? Would he even be willing to help?

Tim was there first, his the only vehicle parked up at the picnic area on the chilly autumn day, so she pulled in beside him and wound down her window.

'Which car shall we sit in? It's a bit nippy for a stroll and I haven't got a coat with me.'

'You always were a chilly mortal! Better come and sit in my dilapidated old heap. I'll feel less at a disadvantage than in that sporty thing of yours!'

Clambering in beside him, ignoring the bits of hay and straw littering the seat and floor, Cathy thought how the vehicle was typically Tim. Hard-working and practical, with no concession to fashion or status, his old Land Rover said a lot about him.

The uncomfortable silence lasted a few seconds as they both looked studiously ahead through the windscreen. Tim was the first to speak, tentatively and slowly.

'How is everything with you? You look well—'

'I'm fine,' she cut in quickly. 'Has Justin said anything to you about me and my . . . well, my situation?'

Tim turned sideways in his seat to face her. 'Justin? No, never a word. I don't really see him so much now the drama group has folded. Anyway, what situation?'

Cathy was relieved to see the obvious surprise on Tim's face. Now she was certain she could trust Justin as well as Simonie.

'Things aren't good between me and Nico. They never have been, not since the day we got married. I was so stupid – in fact, I really was the silly little girl that everyone thought I was. I was well taken for a ride.' She smiled sheepishly. 'Just like you all said at the time, eh? I am just so sorry for the way I treated you. You were my friend and I walked all over you.'

Tim looked away from her, avoiding eye contact as she continued, 'Anyway, I got my comeuppance in the end. I've more than paid for my stupidity.'

'Yes, well, that's all water under the bridge. I can't say I wasn't hurt but I got over it. I was young and stupid. Still, you've lasted longer than I expected and I know you had a baby. Needless to say I got that from Sheila and my mum, keeping me up to date between them! Ever hopeful, that pair.'

'Yes, I have a daughter, Sammy-Jo, and yes it has lasted longer, mainly because of her, although now it's because of her that I have to think again. Tim,' Cathy paused, trying to think of the best way to phrase what she wanted from him, 'I know I was a little shit to you and I'm truly sorry. I should have listened to you, to everyone. Nico is a no-good low-life—'

Tim interrupted her with a snort. 'Huh! I don't need you to tell me that, Cathy. After the way he treated me I hate the man, I really hate him.'

'But what did he do to you? I know he was horribly snide to you, and demoralising. He always was – and still is, for that matter – king of the one-liner put-down.'

'Snide and demoralising? You're kidding, aren't you? That I could cope with. He threatened to have the barns torched and the horses shot if I didn't stay away from you! He banned me from even saying hello and, stupid kid that I was, I took notice of him. I was so frightened each time I even saw you in the street that I rushed home to check them, always listening out for fire engines in the distance and sniffing for smoke!'

Cathy's eyes opened wide in disbelief. 'I wonder if there's anyone that he didn't threaten? He blackmailed Alison and Jane and got money out of them, he

189

threatened Sheila and now I find out about you. Why didn't you tell me at the time?'

'Yeah right, Cathy, and I'm sure you would have listened! That's why I'm not all that comfortable sitting here with you beside me waiting for a double-barrelled shotgun to appear through the window!'

The uncomfortable silence was broken only by the lively wind outside whistling through the badly insulated vehicle.

Eventually Cathy said, 'Tell me about you. What have you been doing, Tim? Anyone special in your life that Sheila hasn't found out about yet?'

'No, not really. I'm still young, free and single and enjoying it, and even if there was someone I'd have to keep her under wraps to avoid the third degree from Mum and Sheila!'

Once again the ice was broken as they laughed together about Sheila and Tim's mother, Jill.

Eventually Cathy plucked up the courage. 'Tim, I want to ask you something – a favour. You can say no if you want to, I'll understand, only it has to be between you and me.'

'Fire away. I can't promise to help but I can promise to stay shtoom, sawn-off shotguns permitting, of course.'

'I'm leaving, going abroad. Well, to be precise I'm running away from Nico and taking Sammy-Jo with me. I don't want the twins or Sheila to know where I am because Nico will never leave them alone and it wouldn't take long for him to get it out of them, but he wouldn't think of you.' Her tone was steady and neutral but her eyes pleaded with him. 'Can I just phone you sometimes so that you can reassure Sheila and the twins that I'm OK? And vice versa? I won't tell you where I am – that way you don't have to lie for me – but if you could pass on messages . . .?' Her voice tailed off as she saw the bewilderment on his face.

'What, for good? Are you leaving for good?'

'I don't know. I know where I'm going but I have to wait and see what happens here before I can think of coming back. I'm going to divorce him but I don't want him having anything to do with Sammy-Jo. I don't trust him.' Suddenly she was gabbling, getting the words out quickly as if to lessen the impact. 'The only time I talked about leaving him he threatened to kill me or have me killed. That's how he threatened, continues to threaten, to wreck the rest of my family, and I've lost count of the times he said he would take Sammy-Jo away from me.'

'But, Cathy, surely that's what the law is for? Go to the police, tell them everything. For Christ's sake, they'll protect you.'

'Maybe, Tim, maybe. But that's not all. There are things I can't tell you but they concern the twins. I have to protect them as well. I simply can't go to the police; I can't chance it. I have to disappear completely – it's the only way. If I don't get out of Nico's life he may well take Sammy-Jo and disappear himself before anyone can do anything.'

Looking at him intently, she wondered again at the change in Tim. The once-weak features had filled out, and the lank greasy hair had disappeared, to be replaced by a shorter cut. As he lounged back in his seat with one boot-clad foot up on the dashboard, she realised that the skinny, painfully shy young boy had turned into a very attractive man. Very fleetingly she thought about where they could have been at now without the appearance of Nico Marcos at the most vulnerable time in her life. As quickly as she thought it she dismissed it. There was no time for sentimentality at this point in her life.

'Tim, I have to go now, but think about it . . . please? You can contact me via Justin and Simonie. They've been good friends to me.'

Jumping out of the Land Rover, she walked round to the driver's side and waited for him to wind down his window. Leaning in, she kissed him on the cheek, touching his arm briefly.

'It's been good to see you!'

Tim smiled properly for the first time since she had pounced on him in the high street, the smile that Cathy remembered so well and suddenly realised how much she missed. A bright pink blush rose over his cheekbones as he spoke. 'You take care, eh? I'll be in touch.'

The heat in the solicitor's office was almost unbearable. On the second floor at the top of a listed building the wooden floor creaked alarmingly, despite the thick utilitarian carpet, and all the windows were shut tight. Six people were crammed in sitting close together on an assortment of chairs grabbed from other offices, all arguing the toss about Cathy's trust fund.

The twins had tried to get out of the appointment with

the solicitor, but Cathy had insisted. She knew they were terrified about how Nico would react when he found out but, as far as she was concerned, they would just have to deal with it as best they could.

After what seemed like hours of debating, decision-making and tut-tutting by the legal eagles and the trustees it was arranged that Cathy's trust fund money be transferred directly to an offshore account well out of reach of Nico.

It took a deal of arranging, especially as Cathy wanted to be able to access it from abroad and couldn't tell them that. But eventually it was done, just as Cathy had convinced herself that if she heard the phrase 'we really can't recommend this' one more time she would throw herself straight out of the window.

Sitting quietly at the buffet bar that divided the open-plan kitchen and dining room Cathy went down her checklist once again.

Finances – sorted.
Passports – up to date.
Money – cash and traveller's cheques.
Details of new accounts – numbers and cards.
Clothes, etc. – new things bought and put away.
Suitcases at Simonie's.
Letters to: Nico (to write); Twins (written); Sheila (written); Solicitor (written).

The sound of a key in the lock sent Cathy scampering

into the bathroom. Folding the piece of paper small she returned it to its hiding place inside the tampon box.

Sammy-Jo's high-pitched squealing penetrated the locked door. 'Daddy, Daddy, have you got any sweets for me?' Cathy could imagine the expression on the child's face as she threw herself at him, opening her eyes wide and smiling expectantly at her adoring father. Adoring? She wondered if that was a good choice of word. *Lecherous? Predatory? Paedophile?*

Flushing the toilet with a fierceness that nearly broke the handle off she straightened her clothes and ran her fingers through her hair before dragging it back with a white velvet Alice band. A quick dab of concealer under her eyes and a touch of gloss on her lips and she was ready to play the part again: the all-forgiving, ever-loving housewife and doting mother.

'Nico! I didn't hear you come in. Have you had a good day?' Smiling cheerily she walked across the lounge and planted a polite kiss on his cheek.

With a look almost of dislike on her face, Sammy-Jo focused on her mother while at the same time moving closer to Nico. 'Don't touch Daddy. He's *my* daddy, not yours.' She flung herself around his legs like a baby monkey and Cathy felt the usual cold chill in her veins as Nico smiled and reached his arms down to pick the child up. Sammy-Jo wrapped her skinny little legs around his waist and buried her head in his neck. '*My daddy.*'

For a moment Cathy wondered if she was doing the right thing taking her daughter away from the father that she obviously adored. But then she saw Nico gazing down at the child and remembered the photographs.

Not for the first time Cathy cursed her crazy, disturbed sisters. Without the threat hanging over them she could have gone to the police and got Nico locked up, but she knew that her parents had always protected the twins and that was what she had to continue to do.

Often, lying awake in the darkness, she thought about the fire. Had it been an accident? Or had it been deliberate? She couldn't believe that they would have started it deliberately, knowing the family was inside – that she was inside – but if it was an accident why had they let Nico continue to blackmail them? As daylight dawned she would always be certain they had let him get away with it because they were simply terrified of being separated from each other. There was no way they could ever have killed their parents. It was just an accident, and their paranoia and a bullying Nico had confused them.

But then again, what if they had done it, committed the perfect murder? Round and round it would go in her head, leading nowhere.

But she also knew she couldn't take the risk of Nico going to the police and the twins getting taken in for questioning. That could drive them over the edge into total madness. No, the only way was to blackmail Nico in return and run for cover, taking the ever-vulnerable Sammy-Jo with her . . .

A voice penetrated her thoughts and she was back with a jolt.

'You're not listening, are you? You were miles away. I was saying we ought to think about celebrating your twenty-first in style. How about a big do up at the Hall? I've made a few enquiries and we can have the Saturday before.'

Thinking on her feet, Cathy smiled. 'That sounds lovely. Then on the actual day, Thursday, we could go out for a quiet dinner, just the two of us.'

The fleeting panic passed and Cathy thought smugly what fun it would be to celebrate happily with all Nico's slimy friends and business acquaintances. No doubt Nico would really push the boat out in anticipation of the two hundred and fifty thousand that he still thought was due on her twenty-first. Then, two days later, the day before her birthday, she would fly out of Heathrow with Sammy-Jo.

Smiling the wide friendly smile that had females of all ages falling at his feet, Nico continued, 'I thought we might take a holiday soon, to the Caribbean, maybe Cuba. I fancy Cuba – how about you?'

Cathy could imagine the cogs turning inside Nico's head as he thought about how to spend his anticipated windfall, her parents' money that they had worked long and hard for.

She smiled back. 'Sounds good to me. Do you want to book it now? We could sort out some dates tonight, if you like, but why not really go for it and book a Caribbean cruise? That would be fun. Let's go and do it tomorrow!'

'Oh, I don't know, it's a great idea but maybe we should leave booking it until after the party; wait until we're sure exactly what we want.'

Yeah, right, you big dickhead. Wait until after my money's come through. But still she smiled.

'Whatever you say. I'm sure Sammy-Jo would like a holiday, wouldn't you, darling? We'll go on a big plane a long, long, way away and then have a lovely time at the seaside. Remember last time we went?'

'Yes, yes, yes.' Jumping up and down, she clapped her tiny hands. 'Can I take my bucket and spade?'

Nico was feeling strangely unsettled as the conversation between mother and daughter batted back and forward in front of him. He felt he was missing something. There was something different about Cathy and he couldn't quite put his finger on it. It was almost as if she was playing a game. He wondered if she'd got wind of Tracy, his latest plaything, and was waiting to confront him. He hoped not because she was really something and he thought he had chosen wisely for a change.

Ever since Nico had got involved in the youth project in Southampton he had been looking for his next victim, and the young Tracy presented herself as a gift: thirteen years old, from a poverty-stricken dysfunctional family who didn't know, or care, where she was from one minute to the next, and streetwise enough to act out all Nico's fantasies happily providing the rewards were good enough. For Nico she came very cheap: the occasional outfit from the local market or some tacky gold jewellery always kept the girl happy, along with the odd twenty-pound note and the occasional poor-quality dope.

He made sure this one knew nothing about him – just knew him as Nicholas, or even Nick – so he was sure he was safe.

His import business was now doing extremely well and he had a large cash fund buried away, waiting to be laundered, and that was without Cathy's money due very soon and his own Carter bank courtesy of the crazy twins.

Cuba? He had heard that young girls and boys desperate for a little cash were up for anything when it came to the lucrative video market. He had already decided to visit and research. Taking Cathy had only occurred to him just now, to keep her happy, make her feel she was getting something out of her trust fund. Also a pretty young wife and daughter would be much less suspicious than a middle-aged man travelling alone.

Everything had turned out right in the end. Marrying Cathy hadn't been such a disaster after all. He didn't sleep with her any more – didn't want or need to – and she never complained. Each kept studiously to his or her own side of the bed on the nights that he was there, and sex was never mentioned. It had taken longer than he had anticipated to break her in but a few well-placed kicks and punches and the regular heavy reining-in had broken her eventually. It was a shame about the maturing but now she was beautiful and good-mannered she added a touch of class to his business entertaining, and Tracy provided everything else in abundance.

Once the money was through they could move to somewhere more impressive.

'By the way, I've got a bit of a business meeting tonight. Max and Wally are due here about nine thirty. Can you sort out some drinks and nibbles and then make yourself scarce? You can go out if you like. Sammy-Jo will be asleep by then. Go and visit Marge and Maisie – oops sorry, it's Zara and Zeta, isn't it now?'

What, and leave you and your perverted friends alone in the apartment with my three-year-old? she thought. *Not a fucking chance. And don't take the piss out of my sisters; at least they're not fucking child abusers.*

Her mouth said, with a forced bright smile, 'Actually I'm a bit whacked today. I'll just have an early night. Anyway, I saw Jane and Alison yesterday. Don't worry, I won't disturb you. I'll be the perfect hostess and then I'll disappear. That way, if Sammy-Jo should wake up I can deal with her. I'm sure the last thing you want is a little girl running around in front of your businessmen friends?'

Again Nico had that sense of something, an undercurrent, but as he looked at Cathy she was smiling and humming softly as she pottered about tidying up, to all intents and purposes without a care in the world.

The snacks were ready; a large tasteful selection of finger foods specially ordered from the local delicatessen was laid out on the long, lace-covered dining table along with crystal glasses and decanters at one end and delicate bone-china plates and condiments at the other. Checking that everything was in order and carefully turning the central flower display just a fraction to the left, Cathy smiled to herself at Nico's delusions of grandeur. The likes of Max and Wally would be better suited to a backstreet clip joint followed by a cheap greasy burger from the hot-dog van, but Nico always had to put up a front and play the game of being a high-flying entrepreneur.

His two guests would have been surprised to find that instead of a businessman straight and simple who was in it for purely financial reasons, Nico was actually into the stuff himself.

The buzzing of the intercom made her jump.

'Get that, Cathy. It'll be the lads . . .'

Yes Nico, no Nico, three bags full Nico.

Cathy picked up the handset and welcomed the men, inviting them upstairs and greeting them at the door while Nico lounged in the armchair, a glass of Scotch in one hand and a cigar in the other. Standing up, he greeted the two men as if he was face to face with captains of industry instead of a couple of sleazeballs.

Looking at Nico with the two men, a huge wave of sadness swept over Cathy that someone so handsome, so personable when he wanted to be, and so intelligent, was chasing the pound at whatever cost.

The sparse details of his background that she had gathered pointed to a poor but brutally strict upbringing where the belt ruled and Nico had done exactly as he was told until he was old enough to get out. He had never returned to the small Greek Island since the day he left at fifteen with nothing but his wits and a pocket of stolen loose change.

Suddenly, feeling quite emotional, she had to shake herself back to the reality of what Nico had turned into.

'I'm going to leave you gentlemen to your business

now.' She smiled charmingly at them all in turn. 'I hope you have everything you need but if not, then I'm sure Nico can accommodate you. Good night!'

Max looked her up and down, a lecherous smile on his face. 'Need any company, sweetheart? It's a pity to see such a pretty little thing go to bed alone.'

With great difficulty Cathy kept her cool, but inside all the hatred returned in full force the instant Nico joined in the laughter.

Fortunately Cathy had never had any expectations of her twenty-first birthday celebration actually being just that so she wasn't disappointed. In fact she quite enjoyed it. Hugging her secret to herself she watched the proceedings more as a detached observer than as the guest of honour. She hadn't put up any argument – it no longer meant anything to her – instead she looked forward to the next day at her old family home with just the twins, Sammy-Jo and Sheila, and then the next day she would be gone.

Hardly anyone she knew was at her party. Nico had been adamant that the twins and Sheila be excluded, even the few friends she had made through Sammy-Jo. It was purely and simply an exercise in networking for Nico Marcos, the guest list including anyone whom he thought might be good for him.

'Well, that went off quite well . . . did you enjoy it?' Nico was slurring his words and staggering slightly. The champagne had flowed all evening and he had gone from table to table without pause. Cathy wondered to herself how much the total bill would come to. She guessed many thousands and felt satisfied at the thought of the bill arriving after she had left. Nico would have to pay it himself!

'Yes, it was lovely – plenty of food and drink, the catering was great, although the company left a lot to be desired.' As soon as the words were out and she saw Nico's face darken, she could have kicked herself.

Nico stumbled towards her. 'What did you say?' In her high heels Cathy was the same height as him and he put his face right up close, eye to eye. 'Well, come on, you fucking smartarse, tell me again what you just said, and what you meant.'

'I didn't really mean anything.' She backed away, her eyes never leaving him. 'Just that I didn't really know anyone there. They were all your friends . . .'

'It's not my fault you haven't got any fucking friends, you stuck-up little Chink.' As she retreated against the wall his hand was up and he backhanded her across her face before she even saw it move. At the same time his knee rose quickly into her groin. Falling to the ground as the pain erupted she curled up into a ball and waited for the kicks, trying not to make a sound, desperately not wanting to give him the satisfaction of even one tear. Each drunkenly aimed kick prefixed with an expletive, he covered the whole range of insults he could think of until he nearly fell to the floor himself.

Wordlessly he grabbed her hair and twisted it in his hand, pulling sharply until she had no option but to get to her feet and allow herself to be led painfully into the bedroom.

The bright red numerals on the clock shone 4 a.m. and the bedside light glowed gently pink, casting an eerie shadow over Nico's face. He lay beside her on his back, still half dressed and snoring loudly with his mouth wide open. The smell of alcohol on his breath made Cathy want to gag but still she looked at him, her emotions running back and forth between hatred and gratitude.

The brutal beating and violent sex had strengthened her resolve to run away, and had easily removed the slight cloud of guilt that had been hanging over her. Rolling her tongue around gingerly, she wondered vaguely about her front tooth that felt a bit loose. The dried blood in and around her mouth felt gritty and sour, and she hoped her lip wasn't cut again.

She debated if there was an alternative, whether she could call his bluff and involve the police but immediately dismissed the idea. Nico was dangerous and to stay would endanger both herself and Sammy-Jo. One more day to go was the thought that kept her from total despair. Just one more day and they would be out of his reach. She had done her best by her sisters and tried to protect them but from now on they would have to fight their own battles.

Justin and Simonie had promised to keep an eye on Jane and Alison from a distance, and Tim had agreed to do the same for Sheila. Cathy knew she could do no more except cross her fingers and whisk Sammy-Jo out of

Nico's life and away to a safe haven.

Creeping into the bathroom, Cathy closed the door quietly and turned on the light. Touching her face and body she checked there were no broken bones, no permanent damage. The tenderness was spreading and her bones ached. The lump in her groin was the size of a pigeon's egg, and the ugly weal across the side of her face shone a purply red. She hoped she could cover that with make-up for her birthday lunch – her farewell lunch with the twins and Sheila, with whom Sammy-Jo had stayed overnight. The last thing she needed at this point was to have to answer any difficult questions. Cathy knew it was unbearably sad that none of them was aware that it was the last time they would see her but that was how it had to be.

Climbing into the shower, she washed herself all over gently, soaping the bruises and bumps, determined that she had been abused for the very last time, ever, by anyone.

'Monday is the first day of the rest of my life,' she murmured to herself as the fierce jets of hot water beat down on her head.

Chapter Eleven

'Cathy, I wish you wouldn't. There must be some other way. It's not too late to change your mind.' Justin looked in the rear-view mirror at her pallid face etched with stress and tiredness.

She made eye contact with him and shook her head, silently warning him not to say too much in front of the apparently sleeping Sammy-Jo who was strapped in beside her. It was going to be a rush to get to the airport in time through the morning traffic because, as always, the best-laid plans had gone slightly awry.

Everything she was taking was either already in Justin's car or her handbag, and Nico had told her he had to leave for Devon early that morning. All she had to do was ring Justin as soon as Nico had gone and that left plenty of time for the journey.

Except that Nico changed his plans at the last minute and was getting the train to London instead, so expected Cathy to give him a lift to the station! By the skin of her teeth she had got there and back, praying that Justin wouldn't turn up before they left, got herself and Sammy-Jo dressed and ready, and had flown out of the door, doing a quick check as she went.

The carefully worded letter was in a large envelope propped up against the extravagant and ostentatious mantel clock that nestled tastelessly amid the crystal glassware on the sideboard and was Nico's pride and joy. It gave her a perverse feeling of satisfaction to place it there.

Nico,

I have left you and taken Sammy-Jo up north with me. You won't find us so there's no point in looking. No one, I repeat, no one knows where we've gone. I cannot risk Sammy-Jo's safety any more, taking into consideration your predilection for little girls, and to be honest I also fear for my own safety and sanity.

Before you go heading off to my family and friends please be aware that:

1) Videos and photographs from your office are lodged in a safety deposit box along with copies of all the paperwork that relates to your blackmailing of the twins and also your dubious import/retail/insurance business. (What on earth possessed you to keep all that at home? And I always thought you were so clever!)

2) My trust fund has been relocated and I hope you have no expectations of benefiting either now or in the future. I will ensure Sammy-Jo benefits appropriately but you will not get a penny.

3) One single threatening visit to the twins or Sheila will result in all the contents of the box being forwarded directly to the police. The same applies if you consider approaching the police about the twins.

Nico, I really loved you but now I despise you. I would like to see you turn your life around but I fear it's too late. I shall take care of Sammy-Jo alone. From now on, as far as she and I are concerned, you no longer exist.

As she was trying to hurry, her daughter was pulling back, wary of the sudden panic rush.

'Come on, Sammy-Jo. We're going on holiday. You said you wanted to go so we are! We've got a lift to the airport waiting. We have to go now or we'll miss the plane.'

'What about Daddy?' The child looked up at her and all Cathy could see in her daughter's face was Nico.

'Daddy can't come. He has to work but he's given me five pounds' spending money to give you – how about that? Five whole pounds! Now *come on*!'

'I don't want to go without Daddy. I'm not going. I'm not going with you. I want Daddy . . .' As Sammy-Jo stamped her feet and shouted loudly, Cathy, for the first time ever, slapped her legs, a sharp stinger across the back of her skinny little thighs. The screams echoed round the walls as Cathy pulled her forcibly through the door and down into the car park where Justin and Simonie were waiting and pushed her into the car, roughly pulling the seat belt across her little chest.

They were halfway up the motorway before Sammy-Jo

stopped screaming and dozed off.

Simonie swung round in her seat and whispered quietly, 'Cathy, you will keep in touch, won't you? I'm going to miss you.'

'I'll miss you too. You've been so good to me – kept me sane, in fact – and eventually I'll let you know where I am but it's safer for now if no one knows.'

They reached Heathrow airport in record time and Cathy bundled the fractious child out of the car as Justin unpacked the suitcases.

'I'll phone in the next couple of days. Don't forget to post the letters to Sheila and the twins, will you? Oh, and give my love to Tim.'

They all hugged and Simonie tried hard not to cry in front of the little girl who was suddenly looking around with interest now they were actually at the airport.

Cathy too looked around and hesitated for an instant, but before the enormity of it all made her change her mind she blew a kiss and waved before turning to walk through the large glass doors into the building.

'Justin, I'm sorry, I know we promised but I have to know where she's going. I'm going to follow her to check-in.'

He smiled at Simonie. 'Exactly what I was thinking. We'll just stay for a while. If we get caught we can say we were looking for the restaurant for a meal before the journey back.'

They separated slightly as they walked into the terminal and followed at a safe distance, keeping an eye on mother and child. It was easy to see them. Cathy, as always, was unaware of how stunning she looked even at her most casual. Her hair, parted in the middle, hung long and black past her shoulders and moved gently as she walked purposefully, her tiny denim-clad body swaying slightly against the weight of the trolley that now had Sammy-Jo perched on top. Even if they had lost sight of her it would have been just as simple to follow the high-pitched shrieks that Sammy-Jo was emitting at regular intervals, and the usual hustle and bustle of Heathrow made it easy for Justin and Simonie to stay hidden in the crowds.

However, Cathy was too preoccupied with a wonky trolley and a hyperactive child to look around. She knew she had to focus her thoughts on practicalities to avoid changing her mind and taking the easy option.

When Tim had contacted her and offered to help she had at first been wary. Supposing Nico found out and went after him? Would he be able to hold out? But eventually the offer had been too good to turn down. Tim was spending a lot of time giving riding lessons and had a lot of wealthy contacts. He was teaching someone to ride whose friend had a villa in the hills just outside Marbella. It was available for an initial let of six months, cash up front, and if anyone asked she was related to the owner.

Tim had persuaded her that she would be better giving herself some breathing space before making a more permanent move and common sense had told her he was right.

Cathy and Sammy-Jo checked in for the Malaga flight and immediately became Kit and Jo Carter.

Simonie and Justin read the flight details from the board over Cathy's head as she handed over her passport and tickets, and then quickly turned and headed back to the car. At least they knew roughly where she was heading.

'I wonder if this has anything to do with Tim,' Simonie said. 'He was talking months ago about someone with a villa in Spain somewhere, do you remember? He asked us if we were interested in a holiday there.'

Justin looked at his wife and smiled. 'I sincerely hope so because if that's the case then she's not completely alone with no back-up. Come on . . .' He took her hand as they walked out. 'Let's go home and hope that Nico doesn't find out that any of us had anything to do with this. Nico as a friend is trouble, as an enemy – well, whatever he may do to us would pale into insignificance if he got wind of Tim being part of the equation . . .' His voice tailed off but Simonie squeezed his hand reassuringly.

'We have to deal with that as and when. At least Cathy and Sammy-Jo will be safe!'

They got back to the car just in time to see a traffic warden slap a ticket on the windscreen. Screeching 'Bastard!' at his departing back, Simonie got into the car and punched the windscreen hard.

'This is all my fault. If I'd dealt with Nico at the time, done something about him instead of believing every lying word that came out of his mouth, none of this would have happened. I should have gone to the police then and there.' She flicked the designer sunglasses that were balanced on the top of her head in place of a headband down over her eyes but Justin could see the tears rolling out from underneath.

'I'll tell you again, my darling, it's not your fault. It's Nico's fault plain and simple and one day he'll get his comeuppance. Trust me.'

The journey back to Hampshire was long, slow and silent, with both of them completely immersed in their own thoughts and each thinking they should have done something, but neither knowing what.

Nico was on a high. His trip to London had been a roaring success and his new contact in Soho had promised he could shift every single item that was stockpiled at the Devon farm ready to make way for the next delivery.

Heading home the same day, he had been unable to resist a pit stop in Southampton to see Tracy. He phoned the mobile that he had given her for that purpose and made the arrangements.

She'd been ready and waiting for him as ordered outside the small discreet hotel tucked away up a side street that he always took her to. As usual she had looked decidedly tarty. The short black Lycra skirt and purple skinny top had been grubby and worn, and the dingy blonde hair pulled up into a ponytail on the side of her head had looked decidedly common, but he knew a quick shower would soon alter all that. Once he had stripped and washed her and scrubbed off all the make-up, he knew she would quickly be transformed back into the thirteen-year-old that she really was, the thirteen-year-old that he couldn't resist.

With the video camera that he took everywhere on the off chance clasped tightly in his hand, he had climbed out of the taxi a little way away from both the hotel and Tracy.

She had been pleased to see him, so pleased that, as always, he had been able to do whatever he wanted to her and she had joined in with gusto.

Now he was on his way home with another riveting piece of film for his private collection and it was Cathy's birthday this week, the day she, and he, officially gained access to her inheritance.

As the taxi pulled up Nico jumped out, whistling happily, especially as he saw Cathy's car parked in its allotted space. He thought about taking her out to dinner . . . or maybe even to a club . . . keep her happy for a little while.

Deep down he knew he shouldn't have behaved the way he had after the party although he justified it by telling himself that she had asked for it, backchatting him like that when he'd had a few drinks. Really she should have known better.

Skipping up the stairs two at a time he rang the bell at the same time as putting his key in the lock. Quickly he realised there was no one there. The silence and darkness struck him first, and then the absence of Sammy-Jo running full speed down the hall to meet him.

Looking all around the flat, he was bewildered that Cathy's car was outside. She never went anywhere without her car now. It was only when he went into the dining room to pour himself his usual large Scotch that he saw the envelope with 'NICO' written in red on the front in Cathy's scrawling handwriting.

This time it wasn't just the glass of Scotch that got smashed, it was the whole set of crystal glasses, along with the decanters and several expensive ornaments for good measure.

The rage that built up inside him, the chest tightening and head throbbing were so fierce that at one point he thought he was actually going to have a heart attack.

By the time he had calmed down enough to give the situation some thought it was too late to start making calls. The phone socket was ripped out of the wall and his mobile lay battered on the kitchen floor.

Grabbing a fresh bottle of Scotch from the cabinet, he proceeded to drink himself into oblivion.

Coming to in the middle of the night, fully dressed on the couch, it took Nico a few seconds to remember. He reread the letter, making sure he didn't miss a single word, and then staggered through to his study as fast as his hangover would allow. Everything looked in place; he started pulling papers out and throwing them around the floor as he tried to figure out exactly what, if anything, Cathy had seen.

Running into the bedroom, he frantically dragged the chest of drawers away from the wall, but his euphoria at seeing the spare key still there was quickly replaced by dread when, after looking closely, he saw the fresh Sellotape that was far too new and shiny.

For once he agreed with Cathy – he was stupid, but she was dishonest and ungrateful, and he promised himself that she would pay for what she had deprived him of: his daughter and, more importantly, a quarter of a million pounds.

By the time Cathy had walked out of Malaga airport into the searing afternoon sunshine she was worn out. Sammy-Jo had played up at the airport, on the flight and now she was pouting and whingeing as the taxi weaved and hooted its way to their destination.

Cathy promised herself that as soon as they were settled and Sammy-Jo had accepted the situation, then the child would have to be taken in hand. The behaviour she had learned to use to get her own way with her father would have to go. As more than one person had noted out loud within earshot of an embarrassed Cathy, the three-year-old was really one spoiled little brat!

The pretty little whitewashed, single-storey villa that the taxi eventually deposited her outside was a lot smaller, and somehow newer than she had imagined. Piling their baggage on the patio, Cathy took Sammy-Jo tightly by the hand and went warily over to the gates of the huge villa next door to pick up the keys as Tim had instructed her.

'Hello, I'm going to be staying next door. I've come to collect the keys . . .' She tailed off as the old woman looked at her quizzically through the wrought-iron keeper door. 'The keys to next door? I was told to collect them from here . . .' Pointing and making an exaggerated turning action with her hand, Cathy suddenly hated herself for not having the foresight to learn at least a few words of Spanish.

'*Ah, sí,* keys.' The woman disappeared but returned quickly and silently handed Cathy the keys through the elaborate black wrought-iron gates.

'Great!' she said to Sammy-Jo as they walked back. 'She's not going to win a friendly neighbour award, is she? Old grumpy-grumps.'

'Mummy, Mummy, look at the swimming pool. Can I go in it?'

'Sorry, sweetheart. That belongs to next door, but I'm sure I was told we had one we could use. Let's just get all our stuff inside and then we can have a look round. Come on, please.'

Once inside the cool marbled villa Cathy turned on the huge ceiling fan and collapsed exhausted on to the long wooden-framed sofa.

'Come and give Mummy a cuddle . . .' The child lunged on to her lap and promptly fell asleep, the heat and the excitement finally getting to her. Loath to disturb her, Cathy sat quietly mulling over the events of the past few months before dozing off herself, leaving the bags and baggage on the patio where she'd dumped them.

'Coo-eee! Anybody home?'

The voice filtered through and Cathy wriggled away from Sammy-Jo and crept over to the doorway.

'Hello, I'm Amanda O'Brien, but call me Mandi – absolutely everyone else does. I live next door. Sorry I wasn't in when you collected the keys.' The woman's smile revealed a set of perfectly capped and straightened white teeth that glistened alarmingly in the sunlight. 'It didn't take you long to get into siesta mode, did it?'

The loud estuary-accented voice and big grin reminded Cathy instantly of the wives she had disliked so much, the ones she used to criticise to Nico as all big hair, big boobs and no brains. Her heart sank as she took in the vision in front of her decked out in white Lycra and gold chains that emphasised the deep brown tan.

'Sorry I'm whispering,' Cathy apologised politely, 'but my daughter is asleep and I don't want to wake her yet.' Cathy went out on to the front patio and held out her hand grudgingly. 'I'm Kit Carter and that's my daughter, Jo, who's crashed out. The journey proved a bit much for us.'

'No problem. Do you want me to come back later? No, I've got a better idea – as soon as she wakes up, come over. The little girl can have a swim and I'll fill you in. We don't usually rent the guest villa out to people we don't know – tax reasons and all that rubbish – but we were persuaded. Mind you, I didn't realise you were bleedin' Chinese. I've already told everyone you're my cousin . . . whoops.' Before Cathy could respond the woman was laughing her way back down the stone steps, her strappy high-heeled sandals staying on her feet more by luck than anything else as they clattered loudly on the cool hard tiles. 'Just come round the back when you're ready . . . through here.' Waving happily over her shoulder she made her way carefully through a gap in the perfectly manicured hedge.

'Shit, shit, shit,' Cathy muttered to herself, inwardly cursing Tim for persuading her to head for Marbella. He hadn't told her the next-door neighbours were also her landlords.

Cathy's spot judgement of Mandi was temporarily reinforced when she and Sammy-Jo later made the trip through the hedge. Mandi was laid out full length on a huge padded sun-bed with an attached sunshade and matching side table. A minuscule leopard-print bikini barely covered her obviously reinforced breasts, and the statutory Raybans were carefully placed on top of her bleached blonde candyfloss hair.

As soon as she heard the approaching footsteps she sat up and waved.

'Over here, darlin'. I'll get Anita to bring some more drinks.' Turning her head in the direction of the main building she shrieked with all the ferocity of a building site foreman. 'Anita! ANITA!'

The woman who had handed Cathy the keys came waddling out of the house, a sullen look on her face that reminded Cathy of a truculent Sammy-Jo.

'More drinks . . . iced water, iced tea, and lemonade for the *niña*, *comprendes*? Oh, and bring biscuits and cakes.'

'*Sí señora*.' Anita turned slowly and made her way back to the house, her expression fixed on bored.

Mandi looked at Cathy and grinned. 'She's all right is Anita really. She just plays up when I'm here on my own. My Benny flirts with her and she twitters all round him, does anything for him, but me? Oh no. Everything is too

much effort for me. And for that I pay her a bleedin'
fortune!'

Laughing loudly she turned her attention to Sammy-Jo.
'Now, little Jo, can you swim? 'Cos if you can, just get
your kit off and get in there!'

Cathy still hadn't managed to get one word in.

'Now. Tell me all about yourself and what you're doing
here. What are you running away from? And don't say no
one. A little girl like you who pays cash up front for six
months through someone else is running away. Bloody
'ell, I've got a son older than you!'

Cathy could feel the rising panic. She wanted to grab
Sammy-Jo and get away as fast as she could. She had never
imagined for a minute that she would be questioned on her
first evening. But before she could think of an answer
Mandi was in full flow again.

'You're all right, girl. You don't really have to tell me.
Lots of us have secrets in this neck of the woods and no
one really gives a toss apart from the odd bit of idle
curiosity . . .' Laughing loudly again she stood up as
Anita made her way over to the terrace with a heavily
laden tray.

Cathy made eye contact for the first time. 'So what's
your secret, then?'

Without a blink Mandi answered straight away as if it
was the most natural question in the world.

'My Benny was a bit of a naughty boy in London and
we had to get out quick but that was years ago. This is
home now. We love it here and we've got lots of mates.
Are you thinking of buying? If you are, my Benny can

help you. He dabbles in a bit of property.'

Cathy smiled and started to relax. 'I don't know what I'm going to do. I just need some breathing space while I decide. You don't mind me renting your villa, do you?'

'Course not, darlin'. Stay as long as you like. This is the best place in the world for chilling out and you'll have a ball at the same time. You're so gorgeous you'll be fighting all the men off before you know it. You can do as much or as little as you want. I love it here – two villas, two sporty Mercs in the garage and a classy little boat down in the harbour. Beats the crappy old council flat in Peckham where I was brought up, that's for sure.'

Mandi dragged Anita back out to keep an eye on Sammy-Jo and then took Cathy indoors to show her around the villa.

It was only then that Cathy realised she was actually going to be staying in the guest villa of the main house that had been separated in the grounds by a hedge and given its own entrance.

The villa was big and beautiful. Set in its own grounds, it was spacious with several en-suite bathrooms and glorious roof terrace that looked out over the surroundir countryside to the sea in the distance.

But the furnishings nearly made Cathy gasp out l In every room the floor and furniture were cover animal print, and the largest and loudest vases fille both fresh and artificial flowers littered the place. corner there were potted plants from floor to cei the vast satin drapes at all the windows were c

out of place in the Spanish heat, despite the air-conditioning.

'Well, darlin', do you like it?'

'I'm impressed. It's a beautiful villa . . .' Cathy tried to be as tactful as possible. She could just imagine the place decorated tastefully. 'I love the view. How far is it to the sea?'

'Ooh, about two kilometres as the crow flies but if you want to avoid the tourists it's easier to go the longer back way. Are you going to get a car? And what about the girl and nursery? They're all the things you have to consider . . . Still, plenty of time for all that. I tell you what, I'm going into town tomorrow for lunch with a couple of me old mates. Why don't you join me? Anita can look after Jo.'

Swept along on Mandi's enthusiasm Cathy agreed, only to regret it straight away. She knew she had to spend time with Sammy-Jo acclimatising her to the change of circumstances, not just dump her with a Spanish house-keeper whom she didn't know.

'Don't talk crap, girl,' was Mandi's response when Cathy retracted. 'It'll do the kid good. Anita loves kids and she'll teach her Spanish and introduce her to her hundreds of grandchildren. Sometimes it's more like a bleedin' crèche in my kitchen. The sooner your Jo gets used to the change of lifestyle the better – and you too. The sooner you get over that fella and get your life ~gether the better.'

Cathy nearly fell off her chair. She hadn't given any-ing away to Mandi. 'What fella?'

'The one you're running away from, of course. There's always a man involved, trust me! Been there, seen it, done it, worn the T-shirt.'

Smiling sheepishly Cathy didn't answer.

Nico was beside himself. It had been nearly three weeks and he had heard nothing. Cathy and Sammy-Jo had disappeared without trace.

He had tried the twins but after half an hour of nonsense conversation he had come to the conclusion that they were really both barking mad and probably knew nothing. They certainly didn't seem that interested one way or the other, especially as he didn't dare mention money to either of them.

Sheila was a whole different ball game. The woman was so offensive it had taken all his willpower not to smash her straight to the floor and kick her head in.

'Nico Marcos, if I ever see you near me again I shall call the police. I don't know where Cathy is. I wish I did but I don't, but I do know it's your fault she and Sammy-Jo have gone. Now GO, before I really lose my temper.'

He finally convinced himself that Cathy would come back eventually with her tail between her legs and bringing her bank account with her as an apology. In the meantime, the best thing to do was to make the most of it. The money would have come in handy but at least he wasn't broke. The merchandise was moving well and he had another trip to Thailand coming up in the future to look forward to. This was the trip he had promised Paul;

keep him content for life down on the farm.

And there was still Tracy. He wished she was old enough to move in for a while . . .

Sheila was at the big house giving the twins what for.

'How could you have let that poor girl down like that? If you'd stuck to your guns she couldn't have married him and wouldn't be in this situation now, all alone God knows where with Sammy-Jo. Why won't you tell me what's going on?'

Alison was the first to her feet. 'We don't know any more than you do, so just shut up, you old crow. Cathy will be all right. She's twenty-one, she's got lots of money . . .'

'Money isn't everything – what about family? Good God, she's never been on her own since the day she arrived here, all those years ago. How do you expect her to cope?'

'Sheila, for the last time, it's none of your business. Now leave us alone and do some housework or just piss off and find another mug to employ you.' Jane was standing beside her twin sister and they both glared at her.

'That is exactly what I'm going to do.' Sheila could feel the tears pricking. 'There's no reason for me to stay here any longer. You can get on with it yourselves. I'm sick of you both, you selfish, selfish pair.' Sheila grabbed her coat and bag and headed for the back door. 'See how you manage without me to wipe your backsides every step of the way!'

As the door slammed Alison and Jane looked at each other in amazement.

'She'll be back.'

'I don't think so.'

'I do. Now, where were we before the hag interrupted us . . .?'

Justin and Simonie were just starting to relax. They had heard briefly from Cathy and she had assured them that she was fine. Much to their relief they had heard nothing from Nico, although they both knew him well enough to stay alert.

Cathy had nearly panicked when she'd phoned Tim, and his sister had answered, but she'd successfully bluffed her way by pretending to be a mum interested in riding lessons for her children.

He'd told her that he had heard nothing from or about Nico, and promised to contact Sheila in due course.

Chapter Twelve

Cathy looked around the restaurant. The charity fashion auction arranged by the Marbella ex-pats to raise cash for the local animal shelter was in full flow and she was loving every minute of it. It was glamorous and fun, and she was part of it on her own merit. She was now Ms Kit Carter, instead of the deferential arm-candy wife of Mr Nico Marcos.

'Kit, KIT.'

The voice echoed across the room and Cathy let her eyes roam until they settled on its owner, Peter, Mandi and Benny's visiting son. Smiling, she waved across the room and mouthed, 'It's too crowded. See you later.'

'Quiet, please, everyone. Tea break over, back to your wallets . . .' The alcohol-fuelled crowd laughed uproariously as Mandi's husband, Benny, standing to attention at a makeshift podium, banged his glass theatrically. Peter caught Cathy's eye and grimaced good-humouredly.

After Cathy had done her bit by paying a large sum to 'adopt' half a dozen ageing cats she leaned back in her chair to watch the rest of the proceedings and the participants. Far more quickly than she could ever have imagined, she had settled into the ex-pat life in Spain and loved it. She felt she was her own person for the first time in her life and she had developed a healthy taste for shopping and socialising, but, more than that, she spent time with Sammy-Jo who loved it here equally.

And Mandi had been right: there was certainly no shortage of men hanging on her every word and offering her the moon. She didn't actually want a man, but the attention was flattering and did her ego no end of good.

She often said a silent thank you to Tim for sending her in this direction.

As the auction finished and everyone gravitated into the adjoining bar, Peter came over and affectionately slid his arm round Cathy's waist.

'So, what exactly are you going to do with half a dozen mangy senile moggies, hmm?'

Grinning confidently, she elbowed him gently in the ribs. 'You know as well as I do they live in their little retirement home. I'm just paying their bills for them. I hate it when people bugger off back home to England or wherever and just abandon their pets . . . Selfish bastards. If that's how they treat their pets can you just imagine how they treat their kids—' .

Eyes wide, Peter interrupted the flow, holding both his hands up in mock surrender. 'Whoa there, I was only joking, you know. No need to get off your trolley. Dear me, you'll be a candidate for high blood pressure at this rate.'

Cathy relaxed instantly and smiled as he continued, 'Fancy a drink? Or shall we go for a stroll and get some fresh air? It's like an opium den in here.'

'A stroll, I think. Let's go and look at the yachts. They're all so . . . I don't know, ostentatious, I suppose, but I love them just the same. I wouldn't mind one myself.'

'You and me both, but a dinghy is more my mark at the moment, I'm afraid.'

They slipped out of the side door into the warm fresh air and walked across the main road in the direction of the harbour. It was still hot, but comfortably so, and although the multinational crowds were thinning there was still a buzz of activity.

At six foot four Peter towered head and rugby-playing shoulders above Cathy, even with the highest shoes she could find on her feet. All the women, young and old alike, took a second glance at him.

'So, Peter tightwad, tell me why you didn't bid for anything.'

'I was only there under duress from Mum and Dad. I'd sooner have gone into town to Shakers, the new nightclub down near the front. Much more my scene than the old Saga louts convention.'

'Don't be so judgemental, you.' She pushed him sideways, making him stumble slightly. 'Your mum and dad have been great to me – and their friends as well. Ageism is as bad as sexism, you know.'

Bantering comfortably, they walked along the harbour until they found a vacant bench to sit on. Peter, ever the well-trained gentleman, brushed it down carefully with his handkerchief first.

'Honestly, I am not ageist, or sexist or any other ist, I just like having fun with my own peer group, and you should too sometimes. You're far too young and pretty to be hanging about with the oldies. Anyway, my hols will soon be over and it'll be back to grey old London for me so I want to enjoy it while it lasts.'

The lights on the harbour and the yachts twinkled as their reflection rocked about on the surface of the water. Looking at Peter, Cathy was sorely tempted to give in to the holiday romance she knew he was looking for. Classically hunky, with sun-bleached blond hair and unusually dark blue eyes, he had the kind of skin that tanned at the merest hint of sun and after six weeks under the Spanish skies he looked more like an Aussie beach bum than a London student.

'How much longer have you got before you get your piece of paper and head out into the big wide business world?'

'This is my final year – I'm a post-grad – and then I'll look for a job in the City. I really want to get into the money markets 'cos, funnily enough, that's where the money is. Dad wants me to go into business with him but no way. That's a recipe for disaster if ever I heard one.'

He looked at her closely and the intensity of the gaze made her blush the way she used to as a teenager.

Smiling easily, he continued, 'What about you, Kit? Are you going to stay in sunny Spain living the life of Riley for ever, or is this just a happy interlude? Will you still be here when I come out at Christmas?'

Cathy hesitated. Her wariness of everyone was still there. It had mellowed slightly over the months, but she still stuck to her original story, which was basically true: she was starting a new life after the end of an abusive marriage. The community she now lived in was not really interested in pasts; there were too many of them around and most of them were far more interesting than hers.

'I think I'm going to stay, for a while at least. I've tried persuading your mum and dad to sell me the bungalow but they don't want to so I think I'll start looking around for something to buy. I love it here, don't you?'

'Not really my cup of tea for permanency, but great for holidays. I love London. My poky little flat in the Barbican suits me fine for the moment, right in the centre of it all.'

His gaze settled on her face and as she looked at him she could read the question in his eyes as easily as if it had been stamped across his forehead. She wanted to say yes but couldn't. She still wasn't sure. She looked away and moved along the bench a fraction.

'We'd better get back before your mum and dad start adding up two and two and making eight.'

They both laughed at the same time.

Peter's arm was already along the back of the bench so he let it drop a fraction and pulled her to him, pecking her on the cheek at the same time.

'They're so transparent, aren't they? My mother has always been a matchmaker. As far back as I can remember she's been eyeing up girls to see if they're suitable – even when I was still at nursery school! Anyway, are you up for a night out at Shakers before I fly back? Let your hair down and have some fun?'

'Yes, why not? One last celebration before you have to get back to the real world!'

Mandi tottered straight over as they tried to creep back in unnoticed.

'And where have you two been? I was looking everywhere for you. Then Benny said he'd seen you both sneak out!' Her tone was accusing and questioning at the same time.

Cathy and Peter both giggled.

'What's so funny?'

'You are, Mother dearest! You are. We didn't *sneak* out. Kit and I went out for a breath of fresh air away from the stench of cigars and cheap Spanish fags. We didn't run off to get married or anything!'

Mandi held her hands together and bowed sheepishly. 'Sorry, babe!' Mandi loved her only child with a passion and her pride in his every achievement was overwhelming. Benny had had his moments of minor villainy more by need than choice, and Mandi didn't want that for Peter. She also didn't want him getting tied up with any of the money-grabbing Marbella beach babes that swarmed around him on the strength of her and Benny's lifestyle.

She thought Kit was a lovely girl with class, and the best one in Marbella at the moment for her precious Petey.

The three stood comfortably together until Cathy

looked at her watch and shrieked.

'Mandi, look at the time! I have to get home. I can't keep putting on Anita for babysitting.'

'Jeez, Kit, she doesn't mind. She loves every minute of it, and little Jo loves her to bits. Strange, isn't it? No offence, but Jo was a bit of a mare when you first got here, but now she's a different child!'

'No offence taken, Mandi. I know she was a nightmare but her life is so much freer and easier now. This place has been good for her. Anyway, I must go.' Looking around she offered generally, 'Anyone want a lift? What about you, Pete?'

'Thanks, but I'm off to club it. Drive carefully now, won't you? You know what that road is like.'

Having kissed her affectionately on the cheek and squeezed her shoulders, he walked away and immediately approached a leggy blonde perched on a bar stool, who flashed a look of triumph in Cathy's direction.

Cathy was surprised to feel a touch of disappointment and envy.

The blonde slid gracefully off the bar stool and wrapped herself around Peter before pecking him on both cheeks, still looking at Cathy.

'I wondered how long it would take you to break away from Miss Wong over there . . .'

Peter smiled at her. 'Put those claws away, Jilly-Jill. She's just a neighbour and a friend.'

'Yeah right, just a neighbour! It all looked more than neighbourly to me just now.' Shaking her thick mane of

Farrah Fawcett-style hair sexily, and running her beautifully manicured pink nails round the nape of her neck she smiled widely at Peter and continued, 'What I'd like to know is . . . where does she get all her money from? How old is she? Twentyish? She's got no bloke to fund her, no job to earn from, and a kid in tow to boot. It doesn't add up.'

Peter looked round and checked that Cathy had left before reaching out and stroking Jilly's hair gently.

'Who really cares? I'm sure I don't. Now let's get out of here. I'm bored and I think it's time for some serious fun.'

Jilly Holden was one of the many Marbella beach babes on the lookout for a rich husband, regardless of pedigree, or rather lack of it, and a life of luxury. It was this that had brought Jilly to the Costa del Sol in the first place on a cheap charter flight, but it was proving harder than she thought as competition was so fierce.

The beach babes all looked alike, were clones even: long blonde hair, deep suntans and model figures that were either being displayed topless on the beach during daylight hours or virtually nude in the many lap-dancing clubs at night.

It was this that annoyed Jilly so much about Kit Carter. She didn't have to do any of that. She didn't have to kowtow to the lecherous old bastards with overhanging bellies, skin like tanned hide, and more gold than Hatton Garden on their wrists and necks, who constantly grabbed and groped at Jilly day and night. Kit Carter didn't have to smile gratefully and fake orgasms for a trip on a yacht or a decent meal out, and she certainly didn't have to share a back-of-beyond two-bedroomed villa with six other beach babes all after the same thing.

Kit Carter had even been given an invitation to the auction evening, unlike Jilly, who had flounced in confidently, trying to look like a guest, and then spent most of the night waiting to be thrown out for gatecrashing.

Jilly Holden had set her sights on Peter O'Brien and there was no way she was going to let him out of them. Young, good-looking and wealthy, if his parents' lifestyle was anything to go by; and it ate her up each time she saw him hanging around the beautiful and elegant Kit Carter, who oozed money and class from every pore.

No, no, no, Kit Carter didn't need Peter O'Brien but Jilly Holden definitely did and Kit Carter was not going to get in her way.

Mandi O'Brien watched the scenario and it panicked her into searching out Benny.

'That bloody tarty bimbo is draped all over our Petey again. Just look at her. And he's so bloody naïve he's falling for it. What are you going to do?'

Benny patted her on the backside affectionately. 'We're not going to do anything. He's a young lad, Mandi; he's gonna put it about a bit at his age. Leave him be. He'll be back in London next week and she'll be history.'

'But she looks serious, and he is quite a catch for someone like that.'

'Trust me, Mandi. If you make an issue out of it then it

might just turn into something. Now credit the lad with a bit of common sense and let him enjoy himself. Christ, we've all done it in our time.'

Mandi slapped her husband on the arm indignantly. 'You speak for yourself, mate, 'cos I certainly haven't. I was only seventeen when we got hitched, if you remember!'

Benny screwed up his leathery face in a frown for a few seconds before his throaty guffaw echoed round the room. 'Well, bugger me. I do remember, now you come to mention it!'

Peter and Jilly both heard the laughter and looked over, just in time to see the couple snogging happily in full view of everyone.

'Mum and Dad are at it again,' Peter commented, amusement in his voice.

'Doesn't it embarrass you, all that nonsense at their age?'

'No, why should it? They're happy; let them get on with it, I say. Christ, they've been married over thirty years. I think it's great.'

'Well, I think it's gross and I think it's sick the way they keep trying to pair you off with that Chinese cow. She's got a child, for God's sake, and all that money must have come from somewhere. Has to be illegal, I'm sure.'

Peter laughed at the beautiful but irate young woman who was still wrapped around him, pouting prettily and smelling expensive. He knew full well it was her night off from writhing around poles and waving her boobs about but he didn't mind. She would do for the night again in the absence of anything better!

'Jilly dearest, I doubt it very much but at the same time that's her business. Let's have a little realism here. If all things illegal offend you then you're in the wrong place and mixing with the wrong people. Now are you coming with me or staying here to grind your teeth with jealousy?'

Benny saw them leave but didn't tell Mandi. He thought it was much healthier for his son to be sowing a few wild oats rather than getting involved with Kit Carter and child. And anyway, he thought Peter and Jilly looked rather good together – both tall and blond and both looking for a good time. Just how it should be at their age.

As she drove back to the villa round the unlit and unmade road that ensured seclusion for the people who lived there, Cathy wondered again whether she was being silly not getting involved with Peter. After the trauma of life with Nico she wanted to have a fling, have a little romance in her life, and also some fun, but at the same time she couldn't help stepping back and looking at the Marbella beach babes and their reputations. She didn't want anyone to think of her like that.

Mandi and Benny were great, and so were the majority of their friends who were now Cathy's friends as well, but they were all older than she was with lives that revolved around coffee mornings, siestas and all-night socialising. Cathy wanted more than that but at the same time she didn't want to be associated with the beach babes. It seemed as if there was a choice of two extremes and all

Cathy really wanted was something in the middle.

Pulling up on to the drive as quietly as she could, she crept up to the door and knocked just loud enough to alert Anita but not to wake Sammy-Jo.

'Is Jo OK?'

'*Sí*, she sleeping now but she want her daddy . . .'

Cathy's heart plummeted. Just lately Sammy-Jo had been asking for Nico more and more, and Cathy was running out of excuses. She knew the time was coming when she would have to be honest with the little girl.

Anita looked at her disapprovingly. 'Why *la niña* no see her daddy, eh?'

Cathy shrugged her shoulders helplessly. 'Anita, I cannot explain to you but he is gone from her life.'

'You tell her then, *sí*?'

'*Sí*, I'll tell her. Thank you for looking after her, I'll pay you tomorrow. *Gracias*.'

The woman lumbered out of the villa, her lips pursed as she tut-tutted to herself for Cathy's benefit, pulling the door quietly behind her, leaving Cathy feeling depressed and guilty.

Sammy-Jo had settled into a small private nursery school nearby that picked her up and delivered her back each day. Brown as a berry and outwardly happy, she had made friends with other children, and her time spent with Anita's grandchildren had given her a fluency in Spanish that completely eluded Cathy. But it was always at night, just before she dropped off or if she woke with a nightmare, that she wanted Nico.

Tomorrow, Cathy decided, tomorrow I'll deal with it.

Absently she padded barefoot around the villa that she had come to think of as home. Although compact, it appeared more spacious because the living area was completely open plan – lounge, dining room and kitchen all in one, divided only by a long tiled breakfast bar. The cool marbled floor had just a couple of colourful rugs to break up the solid light brown and there were no curtains, just shutters at all the windows and doors. It was plain and basic and Cathy loved it.

She decided that she would have one last try at persuading Mandi and Benny to sell.

Nico knew he had had too much to drink and it irritated him. He hated not being in control, not being one hundred per cent alert to his surroundings but once again he had been pushed too far.

Clicking the remote control to the video recorder he leaned back in his armchair and pushed the recliner button that raised the integral footrest. Head back, feet up, drink in one hand, cigarette in the other he watched the film he had recorded with a detached and critical eye. He had seen it and the scores of others like it that he had recorded with Cathy and Tracy many times for pleasure, but this time the images that writhed and moved on the screen went almost unnoticed as he tried to judge the quality. He decided it was definitely substandard. It was good enough for personal viewing and for selling on the cheap but not for real distribution.

The ones of him and Cathy had sold quite well in a back door kind of way, and it had satisfied him immensely to think of the little bitch's image being savoured by hundreds of men masturbating in front of their television screens. But now it was time to move up a notch – to be professional, to stage-manage the performances and to charge accordingly. There was no doubt in his mind that Tracy would agree but she was time-limited now and he needed more young girls – an assortment, in fact, that he could use and then discard as soon as the initial freshness wore off.

He made a mental list of his requirements.

He needed good equipment and someone to operate it professionally.

He needed an isolated studio with no immediate neighbours.

He needed a constant supply of prepubescent innocents.

He needed a front.

Suddenly he knew what he needed . . . *a child model agency*!

As soon as the idea flew into his head it started growing. Quickly he rushed through into his study and set up what he needed for a line of coke. A clear head was essential if the idea was going to work and he didn't want to waste any time. Inhaling the white powder deeply through a crisp twenty-pound note he could feel the rush of it coursing through his body. Suddenly his head felt clear and sober and the ideas were spinning.

A model agency for children could make a fortune. He figured he could use it as a sorting house for silly little young girls, maybe even boys, whose naïve parents indulged their every whim and blindly believed that their little darlings would make loads of money in the model-ling world.

A smart set of photographs that cost a fortune would keep the parents happy and give Nico access to the names, addresses and copies of the photographs of the most likely candidates. Everything he needed in fact.

Nico's grin stretched from ear to ear in anticipation. All he had to do was set it up, but not in Hampshire where too many people knew him. It had to be some-where where the parents weren't streetwise enough to suss him out.

He decided on Devon – a nice anonymous town in Devon for starters, and then he could expand, have networks all over the country and the pick of the crop beating a path to his door instead of him having to go out looking.

Picking up the phone he dialled quickly.

'Paul? I've got a brilliant idea to run past you . . . We may just be rolling in it yet, my friend!'

Justin was bemused. He had heard on the grapevine that Nico and Cathy's apartment was up for sale as a vacant property and much as he hated the idea of Nico being around he hated even more the idea of not knowing where he was. All the information he had was that Nico had moved away from Hampshire.

'You don't think he's found where Cathy is, do you? You don't think he's heading for Spain?' Simonie was pacing the office, pulling at her fringe the way she did when she was upset.

'I doubt it. He would have just taken off there instantly, not hung about and waited to sell first. No . . . but I think he's up to something. Perhaps he's met someone else to string along and rip off, probably a ten-year-old this time!'

Simonie was visibly shocked. 'Don't even joke about things like that. I still think we should have told the police about him. He's dangerous. Imagine how you'd feel if he got his hands on our child.' She rubbed her rapidly expanding stomach dreamily.

Justin looked at her in total adoration. He still found it hard to believe that they were happily married and expecting a baby. It was all too good to be true and it was this feeling of incredulity that made him constantly aware of the spectre of Nico Marcos, who he knew would spoil it all if he possibly could.

'Should we tell Tim? I'm still sure he knows exactly where Cathy is. Maybe we should warn her, just in case.' Simonie thought hard. 'Or do you think we might then be worrying her for nothing? I don't know . . .'

Justin leaned across the desk and entwined his fingers in hers. 'Let's just wait and see. The most important thing to me is you – and, of course, the baby. You don't need this. Let's leave it for a while. Cathy would soon get in touch if he turned up there, I'm sure, and last time she called she seemed perfectly content.'

'Mmm.' Simonie loved Justin dearly but was well aware of his ability always to look on the bright side. 'We'll see, darling, we'll see. But I think we need to at least let Cathy know he's on the move.'

★ ★ ★

Cathy was caught between a rock and a hard place. There was no way she was ever going to let Nico near to her daughter again, but at the same time she felt guilty at depriving Sammy-Jo of her father.

She decided to ring Simonie.

As soon as Simonie told her the news about Nico she also swung between the two emotions: the desire for Nico to be out of her life for good and the concern that swept over her at what he could be up to.

'I'm sorry, Cathy, that's all I know. We can't ask too many questions in case it gets back to Nico and he gets wind of us knowing something. Apparently the apartment is up for sale and he has already moved away – disappeared.'

'Oh well, at least that solves one of my problems. Now I can look Sammy-Jo straight in the eye and tell her I don't know where Nico is. Shit, it makes me feel so mean, depriving her of her father . . .'

'You're not depriving her of her father, you're protecting her. Remember that. Now if Nico has gone are you going to come home? Take a chance?'

'I have to think about it, Simonie. I'm actually quite happy here. In fact, I may stay for good by choice.' As soon as the words were out Cathy realised what she had said and that it was true. She genuinely was happy, apart from the shadow of Nico. 'I'm going to phone Tim in a while, see how he's doing and get all the info on the twins and Sheila. It's nice to think I may soon be able to relax and contact everyone myself – maybe even pop home for a catch-up. Perhaps Nico's given up on me and my money now: perhaps he's glad to see the back of us. That would be great, wouldn't it?'

'Yes . . . it would.' Simonie wouldn't have dreamed of saying it, but she truly doubted that Nico would leave Cathy alone if he actually knew where she was. She was sure he had moved on for the time being but would be back if he got the slightest hint of where Cathy and Sammy-Jo were. Nico just didn't forgive and forget, he was a vendetta freak.

After she had put the phone down, Cathy excitedly started to dial Tim's number but before she could get through there was a knock at the door.

'Anybody home? It's only me on the search for caffeine and good company, so here I am, at your door.'

Putting down the phone quickly she turned to see Peter framed in the doorway on the other side of the security gate. Still smiling widely from Simonie's news, she let him in.

'You look pleased with yourself,' he said.

'Oh, it's nothing important, just some good news from home. A friend is expecting a baby. Take a seat and I'll put the kettle on.'

But Peter roamed around the room.

'You know, it always seems strange to see you living here. I used to stay here sometimes when I came out for the hols; gave me some freedom from the never-ending mothering.' Idly he picked up a brightly coloured pottery vase. 'Isn't this just awful? I bought it for Mum and Dad one Christmas. I bet Mum was thrilled to be able to have it on display in here where she doesn't have to look at it!'

Cathy laughed gently. 'You're so lucky. Mandi and Benny love you to bits.'

'I know, but sometimes I think it would have been nice if there had been more kids so they wouldn't have had just me to concentrate on. Have you got any brothers and sisters?'

Cathy stopped pouring coffee into the cups and looked round. 'Why do you ask?'

'It's OK, I'm only making conversation. Don't be so prickly . . .'

'Sorry.' Cathy pulled a face at him. 'I had blood brothers and sisters in Vietnam but they were all killed along with my parents. Then when I was brought over to England my adoptive parents already had twin daughters, so the answer is yes on all fronts!'

'Husband?'

'Pardon?'

'I said "husband": have you got a husband stashed away somewhere?'

Suddenly Cathy was flustered. 'No, I haven't got a husband, not any more.' Turning her back to him she picked up the mugs. 'Now that's enough about me, here's your coffee. Shall we sit inside in the cool or are you after the final tanning top-up before you head for wet and windy London?'

They took their drinks out on to the patio and settled comfortably into the loungers, Cathy in the shade and Peter in the sun.

From behind the safety of her black-lensed sunglasses

Cathy studied Peter. He had slipped his cotton shirt off and was wearing just his long baggy beige shorts. They looked as if they were well past their use-by date, but they emphasised his long and muscular legs, and the baggy waistband hung loosely off his flat and fit belly. Cathy definitely found him attractive – in fact she thought he was rather gorgeous, the complete opposite of the much older, shorter and darker Nico, and maybe just what she needed to exorcise herself of her husband.

At the same time Peter was studying her from behind his dark glasses. To him she was mysterious and exotic, and he fancied her something rotten. He pushed his glasses down on to the end of his nose.

'Are you up for it tonight then, Kit?'

'I'm not too sure about that.' She looked at him, pretending to be bewildered. 'Up for what exactly?'

'Whatever you like,' he laughed, 'whatever you like! But shall we start off at Shakers?'

'Sounds good to me but I'll have to check out Anita for babysitting duty . . . again!'

Twelve hours later Cathy lay in the darkness listening to the rhythmic breathing of the man in bed beside her. The man who previously had made love to her both gently and fiercely, the man who had made her feel desirable as the sexual adult woman she was, naked and free of the constraints of silly clothes and pigtails and video cameras. Thanks to Peter she now knew what making love was really all about and it had been fun and enjoyable.

Shakers had been just what Cathy needed. It was a

night out mostly with people her own age, lots of alcohol and loud music. Because the nightclub was a little way out of town there had been few tourists there and Peter had seemed to know everyone.

Laughing, they had fallen into and out of a taxi, both a little tipsy, but neither too drunk to not know what they were doing.

Peter had politely said goodbye to her at the door for Anita's benefit, exaggeratedly shaking her hand, and had then hidden round the back until Anita had disappeared out of sight.

'Sssh, I don't want Jo to wake up. Let me shut her door, you go and pour a couple of drinks. Bacardi in the cupboard, Coke in the fridge.'

They had giggled like schoolchildren as they'd sat in the dark on the patio until suddenly Peter had pulled her from her chair and kissed her hard. Without any hesitation she had responded, standing on tiptoe and wrapping her arms around his neck.

'God, Kit, I fancy you . . .'

'I thought you'd never say it,' she'd laughed. 'Come on, let's go to bed, *quietly*!'

Turning on her side she could just make out his profile in the dark. With even features and a strong jawline he really was good-looking. The now dishevelled blond hair fell over his forehead and emphasised the long thick eyelashes that rested on his cheekbones. Cathy decided he was really a lovely man and she fancied him like crazy. It wasn't the same feeling that she had had for Nico in the beginning, the all-encompassing besottedness that causes sleepless nights and dreamy days, but nevertheless she felt good. Snuggling up close she drifted off to sleep smiling happily.

Jilly Holden was tired and bad-tempered. After dancing nearly all night for not as much return as she would have liked, all she had wanted to do was fall into bed and sleep for a week but it was not to be.

She had arrived home at the same time as her friend Tara.

'Hi, Tara, I thought you had a night off. And if I remember rightly it was going to be an early night!'

'Yeah, I know, I know, but Col rang so I couldn't turn him down, could I? We went to Shakers, it was a really good night. Fuck, you should have been there. Everyone had turned out – it was fucking fantastic – and then I went back with Col. You should see his apartment. It is just so out of this world. Not only that, he's loaded, he's got the lot, and you'll never guess—'

Jilly interrupted her sharply. 'Just slow down. You're in overdrive and I can't keep up. I've been working all night.'

Jilly looked closely at Tara. The eighteen-year-old, who could easily have passed for Jilly's sister, was talking too quickly and waving her hands about as she stepped from foot to foot. She was as high as a kite.

'What have you been taking, you daft bitch? You're out of it!'

'No, I'm not,' Tara giggled happily. 'I'm with it enough

to know that your precious fella Petey was in Shakers with that Kit Carter and he was all over her like a rash. Almost shagging on the dance floor, they were so close. Mind you, so were me and Col. It was great! Fuck, I'm not in the least tired—'

'Well, I am. I'm knackered and I'm going to bed. So should you!'

Although desperate to know the details Jilly wasn't going to give Tara the satisfaction of responding. The girl was too wide-eyed and coked up to get into conversation with. She aimed Tara in the direction of her bed and then silently got into hers as tears of anger rolled on to her pillow.

It just wasn't fair and she knew she would have to do something positive if she wasn't going to lose Peter O'Brien to Kit Carter, the woman who, in her eyes, had everything she could possibly want without ever having to slut it out.

Chapter Thirteen

After Peter had crept out the next morning and hot-footed it through the gap in the hedge, Cathy's phone rang. Padding quickly across the room to get it before it woke Sammy-Jo she snatched it up.

'Hello?'

'I want to speak to Peter.'

'Peter?'

'Yes, Peter. I know he's there with you. I want to speak to him.'

'Who is this? I think you must have the wrong number—'

'Fuck off, Kit Carter. I've got the right number and I want to speak to Peter. I know he's there.'

Cathy looked at the receiver in amazement. She didn't know whether to slam it down or not. Still sleepy, she couldn't figure out who it was at the other end.

'Who is this?' she repeated.

'It's Jilly Holden, Peter's girlfriend, and I want to speak to him. I know he's with you – I've been told – I know

249

he's been there all night so put him on the fucking phone . . .'

Cathy remembered Jilly Holden was the lap-dancing blonde that Peter was with at the charity night.

Cathy was cross – with Jilly for phoning, with Peter for having put her in that situation and, even worse, cross with herself for making an error of judgement.

'Well, that's just tough. If you want to speak to Peter then I suggest you phone him in his own home at a reasonable hour of the day. If you're his girlfriend, which I doubt, then you'll have his home number, I'm sure.' Cathy slammed the phone down and looked at the clock. 6.30 a.m.

Still seething she prepared the coffee machine. Quietly she opened the shutters and looked out across the garden. Suddenly it hit her and she started to laugh at her own hypocrisy. She had already decided that Peter was handsome and fun and good in bed, but she certainly had no urge for an on-going relationship with him. So what if he was going out with Jilly the lap-dancing queen? It was actually amusing to think of the gorgeous long-limbed Jilly being jealous of her. If only the silly girl knew the truth behind the façade of Kit Carter!

Cathy, the Vietnamese double orphan and single mother, whose only family was crazy twin witches and a paedophile, money-grabbing, wife-beating husband! Cathy, who in her short life, had more than earned the money that lay in her bank account.

Smiling, she lay back on the lounger and fell into a deep sleep.

'Mummy! Wake up, Mummy. I want to go for a swim. Can I go to Mandi's now?'

Cathy forced herself awake and peered at her watch. Sammy-Jo was standing in front of her in her swimsuit with a towel over her shoulder.

Cathy cursed silently as she realised it was Sunday and it was 11 a.m.

Sunday mornings in the O'Brien pool, followed by drinks and a buffet lunch, were a ritual next door, and Cathy and Sammy-Jo were always included, along with half the neighbourhood.

'Just give me five minutes to have a shower and get dressed. Wait there, I'll be as quick as I can.'

For Mandi and Benny it was always any excuse for a celebration, and the usual Sunday do suddenly became a champagne farewell party for Peter with about twenty guests, even though he still had a week to go.

Jilly Holden was not one of them, but she was on the other side of the wall, listening to the celebrating. She had ridden up there with the intention of knocking and asking to see Peter but the thought of Mandi and Benny had suddenly put her off. She instinctively knew she was better off not upsetting them. Parking her moped a little way up the hill she had waited for Peter to come out but then the stream of guests had started to arrive and Jilly realised she was wasting her time.

It was a very sore point with her that she had never been invited inside the sumptuous property and when she realised Kit Carter and her daughter were in there she could have cried with frustration.

Racing home, risking life and limb on the bumpy winding roads, Jilly tried to figure out a way to get Kit Carter away from Peter O'Brien, preferably before he went back to London. It was a rock on her finger that she was after and it never occurred to her that even if she was the last person on earth, Mandi and Benny O'Brien would never consider her good enough for their beloved son.

'Smile at the camera, sweetheart. Give Uncle Paul a nice big smile . . . That's right. Now turn the other way, that's good. You're such a pretty little girl. Now hold this teddy, hold him close and look at him . . . That's lovely. Now shall we go and find your mummy?'

Nico watched through the one-way window and grinned. Paul was a natural, just as expected. He loved children and was excellent at gaining their confidence, but more importantly he was good at putting the more gullible parents at ease and separating them from their little kiddies for the photographs.

'They'll relax more if you're not there,' he would reassure them with a ready smile and perfect manners. 'We want them to smile for the camera, not be looking at you all the time. Your child has such potential . . . We'll do our best for you . . .' Paul had the patter down to a fine art. It didn't always work but on the occasions it did he always got the best shots for Nico.

The parents then only got to see copies of the straight-forward photos. They were totally unaware of the teddy bear-clutching and thumb-sucking that were essential for the under-the-counter sales. Very occasionally Paul took a gamble and persuaded the child to change outfits and that was when the hidden camera and camcorder in the changing cubicle came into play.

Paul led the child back out into the tastefully decorated waiting area where the little girl's mother was sitting with a glass of wine solicitously provided by a suited-up Nico, thrilled to bits that her child was 'a natural model'.

'Well, Paul, that went well, didn't it? How were the nudies from the changing room?'

'I'm not sure yet. I'll let you know, but I'm optimistic. Not a bad way to spend a Sunday, eh?'

Paul was a lot younger than Nico and had discovered his perversion at an early age courtesy of his little sisters. A spell in jail, with its accompanying abuse, hadn't cured him, just made him determined not to get caught again. The dark green eyes and long dark curly hair, combined with a slightly singsong Welsh lilt, were more feminine than masculine, giving him the ability to reassure and persuade. Visually Paul was a dream for paedophile activities: no one would ever suspect him. To Nico he was a gift, and between them they aroused no suspicion whatsoever.

'Any suitable candidates for the next step? We have to go the whole hog if we're to make the big bucks.'

'Well,' smiled Paul happily, 'it just so happens . . .' He paused for effect.

'Go on then, tell me,' Nico snapped impatiently.

'You remember that one yesterday, the flaxen-haired little brat Rachel, who looked like an angel but had the mouth of a guttersnipe? Well, her mother was giving me the eye a treat. I said I'd give her a call. It'll take time – you know how it works – but it's a definite possibility. I've got several of those on the go. Strange, isn't it? Some of those mothers would sell their fucking souls to get their kids thirty seconds of fame on the old telly.'

Nico rubbed his hands. 'Great, keep up the good work and keep me informed.'

Nico always made certain that he kept his hands clean. Paul did the dirty work, the front-line dangerous stuff, and Nico stayed firmly in the background ensuring that if the shit did hit the fan then it was Paul who would take the brunt. Nico would make sure of that. It was always in the back of his mind that his revenge on Cathy was outstanding and there was no way she was going to be able to prove he wasn't whiter than white. One day he would nail her to the wall and get his daughter back. One day!

'You're not still moping about after that geek Peter O'Brien, are you? You're wasting your time, you know. Mummy O'Brien would never in a million years let her baby go out with you, let alone anything else, and, as I told you, he was shagging Kit Carter last night.'

Jilly looked down her nose at Tara, who was stretched out full length face down on the beach beside her, talking into her beach towel.

'How the fuck do you know what tarty, mutton-dressed-as-lamb Mandi thinks? I've been out with him several times.'

'No you haven't,' Tara laughed. 'He's taken you for a few drinks and a quick shag, that's all. Face it, Jilly, he's too young for you. Eddie Harris is much more your type: stacks of cash that he can't bank, he's desperate to get in your knickers, and he lives here in one of the best apartments on the front so he can keep an eye on his own private QE II. And Petey? Off back to his student hovel in the UK this week.'

'Jesus, Tara, you can be so bloody coarse. Anyway, Eddie is a two-bit villain who looks like he's just gone ten rounds with Mike Tyson. I want better than that. Peter has class and money. He doesn't live in a hovel, he's got a bachelor pad in the Barbican, and when he finishes university he'll be earning a pile in the City, legit.'

Tara sat up and tried to brush the sand off her oily golden body. 'Who bought him a flat in the fucking up-your-arse Barbican, then? Daddy O'Brien. So you must think Benny O'Brien's money is better than Eddie's. I don't think so. Benny is even more of a two-bit villain, as you put it, than Eddie. Eddie's up there with the big guys, but Benny? Small fry who hit lucky once.' She flicked at the sand in the same way she would swat an annoying fly as she spoke. 'Peter has nothing himself – he's a fucking student, for God's sake. You've got carried away with his smart accent and education.'

'No I haven't. Peter's a cool guy.' Jilly was getting angrier by the second, mainly because she knew Tara was right: Tara was always right about men.

'When push comes to shove Peter is only Benny bank

robber O'Brien's son, and that's nothing to be proud of. It'll be a long old time before he gets his hands on any of shrewd Daddy's serious dosh. Your little friend Petey lives off an allowance and no matter how big it might be that's all it is – Daddy's handouts and he who pays the whatever calls the tune.'

Tara's laugh tinkled prettily, catching the attention of a couple of young lads walking along the beach. They walked over to where the friends were sitting topless and tanned on the sand.

'Mind if we join you?' they swaggered, completely confident in their alcohol-fuelled state that the answer would be yes.

'Do you understand English?' Tara asked them nicely, at the same time smiling her brightest smile.

'Yeah, of course. We are English.'

'Good. Then understand this: FUCK OFF, YOU CRETINS!'

As the pair of them slunk away humiliated, Tara screamed with laughter, and Jilly couldn't help but laugh with her.

'You are such a cow, Tara! Seriously, though, I really do like him a lot and it's not just the money. If it was money I was after I could pull any one of those sad arseholes who come in the club, but he seems taken with Kit Carter. Peter says she's just a friend but then he says that of me half the time and he did stay there last night, I'm sure.'

'Jilly, you daft cow, look at me and read my lips. He's too young for you. He's a boy! Anyway, I quite like Kit.

She's a character. You should try and be friends with her. That would faze your little friend Petey. If you can't beat 'em, join 'em.'

Jilly laughed out loud. 'You've got to be kidding. Stuck-up bitch. She looks down her nose at us.'

'Not at me, she doesn't. I met her at the pool the other day and she was fine. Quite a doll, in fact. All the men love her! Give it a whirl. She's good company to be seen with, she gets invited everywhere.' Tara smirked as she looked out of the corner of her eye at Jilly. She just knew Jilly would think about it.

Jilly snorted and flicked sand at Tara while, at the same time, considering the idea. Anything that brought her closer to Peter would be a bonus, and if she could start mixing in those circles maybe when he came back she would be nearer to him.

The pair of them trudged across the sand, back to where their mopeds were parked, fully aware of the admiring glances. Tara jumped straight on hers, wearing just a flimsy top over her designer tanga and flip-flops on her feet.

'I'll see you back there. I'm off to get sorted for tonight; it'll be a blast.'

'You wanna watch it, girl, you're turning into a real cokehead. You're going to regret it!' Jilly hesitated. 'Tara, if – and I say *if* – I take your advice, will you come to El Paraíso with me? Maybe this evening, just for an hour or so before we go on to the party? That's where they'll all be.'

'Sure, if you're buying I'm coming!'

They set off in different directions, waving happily to each other.

When Cathy had got the situation into perspective as far as her night with Peter was concerned, she enjoyed the day despite being worn out. Sammy-Jo had run mad for so long she was exhausted, and had fallen asleep in one of the vast overfilled armchairs in the O'Brien living room. Leaving her there with Anita, who was looking disapprovingly at the mess she had to clear up, they all trooped out noisily to invade the bar that was a popular ex-pat haunt.

Cathy's mood soon changed when she spotted Jilly and Tara holding court at the corner of the bar, dressed up to the nines, while she was still in her shorts and T-shirt, wearing no make-up, and her hair scraped up in an untidy and none-too-trendy ponytail.

Cathy headed straight for the ladies to try to tidy herself up but as she looked in the mirror she saw the door open behind her and Jilly Holden walked in.

'Hi. Look, I followed you in here on purpose. I'm really, really sorry about this morning. It was so stupid of me but I was still a bit drunk and got carried away. Sometimes I just don't think.'

Cathy turned to face her. 'You're right, it was stupid, but not because of Peter or even me, but because I've got a young daughter who might just have answered the phone and if you were pissed,' she paused to make the point, 'if you were pissed you could have said anything.'

Jilly smiled apologetically. 'I know and I do feel so sorry now. Can we start again? I know that you've already met Tara. We share a villa, along with four others, of course. It gets a bit cramped, but you're welcome to drop by for a drink, or a chat, if you're passing. It can get a bit boring, surrounded by all the oldies, I'm sure. We're not a bad crowd and we do enjoy ourselves. I'd like us to be friends.'

Cathy relaxed and smiled back. 'OK, forgotten. We all do stupid things we regret and I appreciate the apology. Anyway, I must get back to the others. I'll see you around, maybe go for a coffee sometime?'

She left the washroom, leaving Jilly unsure of where she stood. No mention had been made of her relationship with Peter.

Feeling a bit bemused by the conversation Cathy went over to Mandi.

'Guess what? Jilly Holden has just tried to be friendly to me – offered the hand of friendship so to speak, even invited me round . . .'

Mandi threw up her hands. 'You stay away from those little slappers or you'll get tarred with the same brush. The men flock round them and they take them out and about for decoration and anything else they fancy, but they don't respect them. They only get the kind of men they deserve and they're usually the dregs that hang around that bloody club.'

Cathy laughed loudly. 'I know, I know. They're all lap dancers. They slide up and down poles and they go out with all the rich old buggers that tuck peseta notes in their G-strings and then grope their boobs. I know! But at least they're earning a living for themselves.'

'Bullshit! They're upmarket whores, no other description for it. They're only working until they can get some poor idiot to marry them. You just keep away or you'll lose your reputation, you mark my words.'

'Yes Mand, of course Mand, whatever you say Mand!' Cathy smiled affectionately at the older woman and squeezed her hand. Although she was very fond of Mandi it fascinated her that the older woman was totally oblivious to her own tarty appearance. If the girls were classic Marbella beach babes then Mandi was classic old estuary poor, new dodgy money, but with strange double standards.

Still, Cathy always tried not to judge too harshly. She had seen what being different had done to the twins, and, of course, to herself to a lesser degree, although Cathy was now more realistic about her past. She had given it all a lot of thought and she knew that if she had listened to everyone then Nico could never have done what he did. But although she was prepared to take responsibility for Nico that was all. It had taken a lot of soul-searching but she had finally realised that the bombing of Vietnam and the fire at her family home were nothing whatsoever to do with her.

Sitting in the corner observing, Cathy wondered what Nico was up to. The crowd laughing and drinking in the bar would have horrified him because, perversions aside, Nico was quite old-fashioned and very class-conscious. The majority of the people in the bar, people who had been good to Cathy and made her welcome, would have been far too common for Nico. She hoped he had disappeared for good but in the back of her mind there was always her knowledge of his desire for revenge when crossed, and, boy, had she crossed him! A shiver went down her spine at the thought of what he could be capable of if they ever came face to face.

'You OK, Kit? You're miles away.' Peter appeared beside her.

'I'm fine, just a bit tired after last night, as you should be too.' She smiled into his eyes. 'I'm going to make a move now, collect Jo and have an early night.'

'I'll come with you.' The tone of his voice spoke volumes.

'No, Peter, you stay here. I have to spend time with Jo. I have things to talk about with her and she's got a school trip tomorrow up into the mountains so I need to sort out her stuff. I'll see you tomorrow.'

She got up from her seat and kissed him gently on the lips before turning on her heel and leaving.

Although she knew he would head straight over to Jilly Holden it didn't bother her too much. She didn't want him as anything permanent so she knew she had no say over what he did or didn't do with Jilly.

'Did Kit tell you I spoke to her? Offered the pipe of peace, so to speak. Oh, and I apologised. I suppose I ought to apologise to you as well—'

Peter interrupted her. 'Apologised for what? What do you have to apologise for?'

Jilly was nothing if not as sharp as a switchblade, and she realised instantly Kit hadn't told him about the early morning call.

'Oh, just for not being as friendly as I might have been. Anyway, Petey, what have you been up to lately? I haven't seen much of you.'

'This and that, doing the rounds of farewells before I head off. Will you be around when I get back? Be in about six weeks or so for a flying visit.'

Jilly took Tara's advice and played it cool. 'Oh, I should think so unless something too good to turn down offers itself to me.'

She had already planned her next move. She intended to become close friends with Kit Carter and to inveigle herself into the circle that she and the O'Briens were such a big part of. Then Mother O'Brien would find it harder to look down on her, and by the time Peter came back . . .

Paul was turning into a bit of a technophile. He had discovered a flair for video wizardry, and just for practice he had been busy enhancing some of the old footage that Nico had taken over the years. It was actually quite good – good enough for recycling if it was combined with some new stuff. He was incredibly proud of himself.

'Nico? Come and look at this. You'll be so impressed, man,' Paul shouted through to the luxurious outer office that Nico had created at the front of the industrial unit on the outskirts of town.

They had divided the unit into four sections: the reception area, the professional photographic studio, and the spacious changing rooms littered with outfits of all styles, sizes and colours and an assortment of toys. The rooms all led through from one to the other, finishing at a blank wall that was papered in heavy striped wallpaper. The stripes successfully concealed the last door that led into the fourth room, Paul's den, nicknamed the playroom. It contained a sectioned-off dark room for developing the photographs and a bank of video recorders, television monitors and editing equipment. It was from here that Paul was calling Nico.

'What have you got?'

'Look, Nico, look what I've done with your home movies . . .' He clicked one of the video recorders on.

The images of Cathy came to life with an essential clarity that had always been missing. In the old film Nico knew it was Cathy, but now he could see it was her as well. Nico could feel the old excitement mounting at the sight of her. The film was as good as most of the under-the-counter films that were on the market doing the rounds, and Cathy looked wonderful. A stark, childish terror was written all over her face as a naked but smiling Nico, his face deliberately turned away from the camera, headed towards her. This was far, far better than the ones of the young but experienced Tracy where she was well aware of what she was doing and was acting up for the camera. This was for real: Nico's honeymoon souvenir.

'Jesus, Paul, you're a genius. How did you do that?'

Paul, his bright, beautiful eyes gleaming, smiled the open and friendly smile that concealed such a nasty, vicious nature. 'Oh, a bit of cut and shut here and there. But never mind that, Nico, think what we can do with these . . . She looks about ten and truly fucking innocent. Where did you find her?'

Nico laughed fit to burst. 'I married her!'

'Wow! Well done, man, one up to you. Where is she now?'

'I have no idea; the bitch ran off and took my daughter with her, but I'm sure as hell going to find her and rub her nose in this. Now the goalposts have moved I can screw the bitch and her whole fucking loopy-loo family.' Standing stock-still, both men stared at the monitor. 'She is just so recognisable without all that fuzziness. Anyone who sees this will recognise her instantly. Christ, I can't wait to find her and show her this . . . show the movie queen exactly what is going out for distribution.'

Paul grinned. 'Should go down a bomb with the punters, this. She's too old for me, mind, even in this, but a treat for all those wankers sat at home with their imaginations running riot!'

Laughing excitedly, Nico and Paul went through to the front reception area. Anyone passing would never have given a thought to the two businessmen lounging back in their chairs, laughing and looking relaxed. Nico, middle-aged but still fashionably and expensively dressed; Paul, younger but with the air of a trendy college student, both tidy and well-mannered – just two ordinary blokes talking shop. The word 'paedophile' would never have occurred to anyone in connection with the pair of them.

'Are you still seeing Tracy?' Paul asked. 'She's OK, that one – for the films, I mean. What you see is what you get and she's always up for it, whatever it is. Worth hanging on to as a spare, if you ask me.'

'Yes I know, and yes I am still seeing her. There's mileage in her for a bit longer, but more than that . . .?' He shook his head. 'No, too common for me, unfortunately. Couldn't take her anywhere, and wouldn't want to wake up to her, that's for sure. Cathy was the best. She had class and, God, was she beautiful. She could charm any of the greasy dickheads that I had to deal with. Yep, with hindsight I should have kept a tighter grip on that one . . .'

His voice drifted off as he thought back over his time with Cathy. He really missed Sammy-Jo and it upset him to know that Cathy thought he would ever do anything to her. His first wife had thought the same but, for Christ's sake, he only took a few photos of his other two kids, nothing to warrant the way Joanna had treated him. Bloody protective mothers, they were all the same.

Nico was off in a trance, playing his usual self-justifying mind games. He put himself in a completely different category from Paul Evans. None of the women in his life had been children . . . young, maybe, but not children, he told himself. Joanna? She couldn't wait to marry him; Simonie was just the same, and then Cathy – he hadn't had to do much to get her married. He couldn't figure any of them out. They all wanted to be married to him but none of them could accept how he was.

Tracy? She was more than willing and would be down the register office before he could say wedding ring if she was old enough.

How could anyone call him a paedophile? They were all willing partners, as were all the other young teenagers that he used. But kids? No way. Nico knew that he would never actually touch a small child. The photographs and the films were just business, supply and demand. He might enjoy watching the finished product but he didn't actively participate and he found it offensive that Cathy had thought he would.

Now Paul – he was the real McCoy. He did it all for the love of it and money was a bonus. Nico could see clearly that Paul was dangerous and that no child, boy or girl, whatever age, was safe around him. He certainly would never trust Paul within a wide radius of Sammy-Jo . . .

Paul's voice broke through his thoughts. 'Knock knock! Anybody in there? I said how are the bookings for next week? Any response from the mailshots?'

'Yeah, they're coming fast and furious. If we continue at this rate we'll be able to take on a photographer for the legit shoots and we can concentrate on weeding out the others. Millionaires within the year at this rate. Just make sure you keep out of fucking trouble, though. No little sidelines that could send the vice squad sniffing. This outfit must be squeaky clean. Nothing, and I mean nothing, must lead back here.'

Paul laughed bitterly. 'Not a chance, man. Never in a million years am I going back inside. You can trust me on that – never, ever!'

Nico studied the face opposite him and remembered their trip to Thailand. As soon as the wheelings and dealings of business were over and the merchandise was being packed up for transport, Nico and Paul had headed for the coast and even Nico had felt uncomfortable.

Paul was an insatiable paedophile, and he had rarely come out of his beach bungalow in four days. Nico had seen the steady stream of children, boys and girls, some not much older than Sammy-Jo, who had filed in and out day and night. Some had come willingly, desperate for the minimal money he paid; others had been dragged in sobbing, by their minders. The screams echoed through the flimsy walls and eventually Nico had been forced to make Paul call a halt, terrified they were both going to be arrested. It had not been a happy experience for Nico and it had made him aware just how dangerous Paul Evans was.

'Well, Paul, I don't want you inside and I certainly don't want to be there myself so let's play this one really carefully, eh? We've got a cool little business coming on here. Don't blow it.'

Paul grinned boyishly. 'Right on, Mr Marcos!'

Chapter Fourteen

The only person concerned about Alison and Jane Carter was Sheila Miller. The rest of the village and half the county thought they were quite bizarre. Some laughed, some were frightened, but none was overly concerned about them as people.

In some ways they were almost a tourist attraction. Always described as 'The Twin Witches of the Forest', their reputation spread, and although it was good for their shop and their readings, they were both deeply disturbed. Unfortunately it was this behaviour that made them so popular as psychics. It was because they were so strange that everyone thought they had to be genuine.

The more Sheila heard, the more she worried, but the day that word got back to her that the shop was closed indefinitely she knew she had to find out what was going on.

Pulling into the drive of the house she looked around and found it hard to take in what she saw. The manicured lawns and pristine flowerbeds were now more like meadowland, with thistles as high as the window sills and sticky weeds strangling the once-regimented rose bushes. Although she still had a key she knocked at the front door. It was Sunday morning so she was sure the twins would both be there.

A dishevelled Jane opened the door and peered out through eyes that were looking but not really seeing.

'Hello, Jane, it's only me, Sheila.'

'What do you want?'

'Don't be so rude. I came to see how you both are. I'm worried about you, believe it or not.' Sheila was not in the mood for an argument on the doorstep in the pouring rain so she walked straight in, shedding her coat and boots as she did so, out of habit.

Alison appeared in the hall and stood beside her sister. Neither was dressed and not only were they scruffy they were also filthy. Their hair was hanging in matted strands and dirt was ingrained under their long, uncared-for fingernails.

As she stepped from the porch into the hallway the smell of stale body odour burned into Sheila's nostrils along with the distinctive smell of cat's urine.

'Have you got a cat? I'm sure I can smell cats . . .'

'So what if we have?' Alison and Jane shuffled barefoot off towards the kitchen, their raggedy dressing gowns trailing on the now grubby carpet that stuck to their feet.

Sheila followed them through determinedly after sneaking back to put her boots on again. She tried to keep a smile on her face but the state of the house made her feel physically sick.

There wasn't an inch of workspace in the expensive designer kitchen that wasn't covered in congealed crockery and filthy pots and pans. Ashtrays overflowed and the rubbish bin could barely be seen beneath the debris that had just been piled up on top.

Sheila turned in the direction of a persistent mewing and saw two pure black kittens scavenging among the mouldy leftovers caked around the sink.

'Oh dear, whatever is wrong, girls? Have you been ill or something?' Sheila looked around in horror. 'How could this happen in such a short space of time?'

Neither of them answered.

'Why didn't you ring me if you couldn't cope? Your parents would have had a fit if they'd seen their lovely home like this. Come on. If we all work together we can at least get the kitchen done this morning. I don't mind helping you.'

When there was no reply she looked at them both closely. Zombie-like they stared back, their eyes vacant. Their faces and teeth were tinged yellow, and bloodshot eyes peered out from under bird's-nest hair. With great difficulty Sheila refrained from commenting.

'All right then, I tell you what: you two go and have a good shower and wash your hair, then get dressed. I'll make a start.' Sheila tried to keep the concern out of her voice. 'Go on, off you both go, and then we'll all muck in together and get this sorted.'

The twins didn't move. 'Go on, off you go . . . GO ON!'

Robotically, they stood up and headed towards the staircase.

Sheila looked around the house with mounting horror. Every room was as bad except for Cathy's bedroom, which was untouched since the day she moved out apart from a heavy layer of dust on all the surfaces. The woman heaved a sigh of relief that at least that would be easy to clean.

Rolling up her sleeves, Sheila gathered up the flea-ridden kittens, put them outside with a bowl of tuna she had found at the back of the cupboard and determinedly got to work expunging the smell that permeated through the whole house.

Half an hour later there was still no sign of the twins.

'Are you all right up there? Jane? Alison? Can you hear me?'

When they didn't respond, Sheila made her way puffing and panting up to the top of the house.

'Jane? Alison?' She knocked on the door of one of the bedrooms but when there was no answer she cautiously opened it. Both women were sitting on the edge of the bed, side by side, neither of them washed or dressed.

'OK, girls, this is enough. Are you going to tell me what's wrong or do I have to call the doctor? This isn't right and I can't leave you like this. Now tell me, please, or I'm going to call the doctor now.'

Alison and Jane looked at each other and then at Sheila.

'We killed them.' Jane spoke first, followed quickly by Alison.

'That's right, we killed them.'

'Killed who?' Sheila was mystified.

'We killed Mum and Dad.'

'No, you didn't, it was an accident.'

'Nico said we killed them and he was going to the police and we'd be separated and locked up for ever. We killed them. We won't be locked up, will we?'

Sheila felt her knees start to wobble so she sat down quickly on a chair, pushing a pile of grubby clothes off it first.

'Hang on. I don't know what you're talking about. What's Nico got to do with this?'

'We had to pay him. We had to let him marry Cathy – what else could we do? He was going to tell the police that we killed Mum and Dad.'

Suddenly the twins were crying in unison. They tugged manically at their hair and clothes, before clasping each other tightly. It was a frightening sight and suddenly Sheila feared for their sanity. Aware that their grip on reality had always been tenuous, she was at a loss to know what to do except take control, like she had always had to do with the family.

'Stop this right now! Stop it! Get yourselves washed and dressed and come downstairs and then we'll discuss all this nonsense properly. I mean it.' She pulled herself to her feet and lumbered over to the door. 'I want you both downstairs in ten minutes and then I'll sort it all out for you, I promise. OK?'

Clearing up, Sheila counted the minutes, unsure what line to take next if they didn't do as she had said, but eventually she heard footsteps and the twins appeared in the kitchen. She guessed they hadn't really washed properly and they certainly hadn't cleaned their teeth for weeks but they had at least made a vague effort to wash their hair.

'That's better. Now I'll make us all a nice cup of tea and then you're going to tell me everything.'

Sheila listened and tried hard not to lose her temper with them. She wanted to shake them hard and bring them to their senses but she knew she had to stay calm to get the whole story out of them. But once she had heard it all she didn't know what to do. It was too late, Cathy had gone and no one knew where she was.

'OK. Now listen to me. The fire was an accident. Everyone said so and you know that too, so put those silly ideas out of your head. Nico Marcos is a liar and a thief so forget about him. The first thing we're going to do is get this place cleared up and you're going to help. Firstly it'll give me time to think, but also it'll be good for you to get back into a routine. I'm here now and I'll look after you, just like I always have, all right?'

Sheila was aware that she was talking to two grown women as if they were children but it was the only way she could get through to them. Jane and Alison nodded in unison and stood up, ready to get to work. Sheila knew the co-operation was only temporary but she wanted to keep them busy while she thought over everything they had told her.

'Tim? Hi there, it's Cathy, checking in!'

'And about time too. I was just going to try and get in touch with you, it's so long since I heard from you.'

The panic started to rise as Cathy took in Tim's obvious reprimand. 'What's wrong? What's happened? Is Nico—'

'Don't panic, there's still no sign of Nico. It's your sisters, they're not very well. Sheila has been running in circles like a headless chicken wondering how to find you. I've felt so guilty not telling her, but I did try to reassure her—'

'Are they ill?' Cathy interrupted sharply, firing questions without pause for breath. 'What's happened? Has there been an accident?'

'Not exactly.' His voice was cautious. 'They both went really . . . sort of . . .' he hesitated, trying to find the right words, 'well, mad I suppose is the only word. Sheila is looking after them. She's moved in there for a while. They're seeing a psychiatrist, apparently, the shop is closed and the house is in a state.' Tim was rattling on at an alarming speed, almost as if he was frightened they would get cut off at any moment. 'Sheila says they've got this weird idea that they killed your parents deliberately, that they murdered them! Nico had something to do with it, apparently. Sheila reckons he pushed them over the edge, has been taking money off them.'

There was such a long silence Tim thought he had been cut off. Deep down Cathy had always known the weak link was going to be Jane and Alison but still she was shocked, and suddenly frightened at the implications. If word got out then someone would tell the police. Cathy could hear the village gossip already.

'Cathy? Are you still there? Cathy?'

'Yes, I'm here. I'm going to have to come home and try and sort it out. I've got to do something, haven't I?'

'Well,' Tim hesitated, 'it might help, and I have heard that Nico has disappeared, left the Forest. Oh, I don't know. You have to decide for yourself what's best for everyone, where your priorities lie.'

'Shall I phone Sheila? What do you think?'

'I can't answer that, Cathy, but I do know Sheila is worrying herself silly and her health wasn't all that good to start with. She's so overweight now she has trouble with the stairs and her breathing is bad. She shouldn't be managing that bloody great big house on her own, not when it's in that state.'

'I'll have to think about it. Sammy-Jo still has to be my prime concern. Shall I give you my number? Do you feel safe having it?'

Tim's voice was grim. 'I'm not that much of a wimp, you know, Cathy. Just give it to me.'

She pictured Tim in the cluttered hallway of his home, carefully making note of the number as several dogs bounded round his feet, knocking over Wellington boots and shaking mud up the walls. She hoped it was still the same; she had always loved the atmosphere of organised chaos.

'Tell Simonie and Justin what's going on, will you? I'll phone them when I've decided what to do.'

'Cathy?'

'Yes?'

'Take care, won't you?'

Thoughtfully replacing the receiver, Cathy was in

turmoil, trying to figure out exactly what to do. Then she drove to her favourite place. It didn't have a name so she always called it Cathy's Cove, mainly because it sounded good. Not long after she arrived in Spain she had bought a car and one of her favourite pastimes was to drive around trying to get her bearings and, she always laughed when she told the tale, to get lost.

Driving up the coast one particular day she had turned off down a track in the direction of a small cove she had spotted by chance and ended up with her new sporty MG stuck in the muddy sand halfway down. It had cost her a fortune, and her pride, to be towed out by two laughing Spanish mechanics who had told her she should only venture there in a four-wheel-drive vehicle, preferably driven by a man.

With no intention of buying a new car or getting a man, she had eventually found a narrow trail to walk down, and the cove had become her escape. Very few people ventured there and she could sit peacefully on the natural breakwater, just watching the sea as it broke gently over the rocks.

Cathy was perched on the largest rock, absent-mindedly watching the yachts and windsurfers as she tried to think it all through. Sheila needed her, the twins needed her but probably didn't want her, but could she risk Nico finding out? Could she risk Nico snatching Sammy-Jo? She knew he had it in him to do that, same as she knew he had it in him to wreak terrible revenge on her.

She watched the crabs heading for her bare toes and

decided they were like Nico: fascinating, almost appealing, but given the opportunity to use their pincers to attach themselves to their unsuspecting prey they would, and they would pinch as hard as they could, causing maximum pain before scuttling off. Yes, she thought, Nico the crab, Nico the predator, Nico the paedophile.

The thought brought it all back and she knew she couldn't risk returning for good. Providing they agreed she decided she would make a flying visit to England and leave Sammy-Jo with Mandi and Benny for a few days.

'Hello, Sheila? It's me – Cathy.'

Cathy really thought Sheila was going to have a heart attack. She could hear her laboured breathing down the phone line as Sheila tried to ask and say everything at once.

'Calm down. I'm fine and so is Sammy-Jo. I'm so sorry, but I had to do it, I had to protect you all from Nico and that was the only way. I'm sorry, I'm sorry . . .' She tried not to but Cathy ended up sobbing down the phone as she took in the full extent of Sheila's distress.

'You didn't have to do it, you didn't. There's nothing we couldn't have dealt with. I've been so worried. Where are you?' The question was a plea.

'I can't tell you, but believe me, Sheila, you couldn't have dealt with something as big as this. Now tell me about the twins. Tim said they've tipped over the edge, that's why I knew I had to ring . . .' As soon as the words were out Cathy could have bitten off her tongue.

'Tim said? What do you mean, Tim said? Does he

know where you are? Why didn't he tell me? The little toerag, I'll kill him. He knew how worried I was but all he said was *someone* had heard from you.'

Sheila's Hampshire burr was getting stronger and stronger the more distressed she became and Cathy knew she had to cut the conversation short. The best way to deal with Sheila would be face to face.

'It's not Tim's fault. Look, I can't talk about it now. If I can arrange it I'm coming home for a few days or so but I have to leave Sammy-Jo behind. I don't want Nico ever finding her. I'll call tomorrow when I've made some arrangements. Sheila, all I can say is I'm really sorry!'

When Cathy approached Mandi and Benny she was confident they would agree to take Sammy-Jo; they had frequently offered in the past.

'Oh, Kit, we can't. I'm off to England myself for a couple of weeks, to see my sister and to check up on my Petey – make sure he's behaving back in the old country, and Benny has to keep nipping back and forth to bloody Gibraltar. You know what it's like. I'm sorry, darlin'. Why can't you take her with you?'

Cathy hid her disappointment. 'I can't really, but don't worry, Mandi. I'll think of something. I just didn't want to drag her out of her routine. Not to worry.' She smiled cheerily, not wanting Mandi to know how important it was. 'Is anything up with Peter? He hasn't been back in London any time at all.'

'Not that I know of,' Mandi cackled loudly; 'but I'll soon find out when I turn up on his doorstep with me cases!'

Cathy felt a fleeting sympathy for Peter. Mandi was having big problems cutting the cord and letting him go.

'Aren't you going to stay with your sister?'

'What? In Peckham? You're bloody joking, aren't you? Not a chance. No, I want nice London, then I can blitz the Knightsbridge shops – Harrods, Harvey Nicks – you name it, I'm going to hit it. It's easy to go stir crazy here and I'm ready for a bit of retail therapy in the real world. Mind you, I'm always pleased to get back.'

As Mandi chattered on, Cathy was thinking hard. She knew she could rely on Anita for minding Sammy-Jo mornings and evenings, it was just the nights that were difficult. Anita couldn't stop overnight. Her husband, Mandi and Benny's gardener and pool cleaner, was a macho man who gave Anita no credit for the hours she worked at the O'Briens' and for Cathy. He still expected her to wait on him hand, foot and finger, no matter how late she worked.

Suddenly a name flashed into Cathy's mind: Jilly. Jilly and Tara seemed to know everyone, and Cathy wondered if they might come up with someone who could live in for a few days – maybe an agency nanny. The only other options were to take Sammy-Jo with her to England or not to go at all, and she didn't want to have to choose either of those.

Cathy drove over to Jilly's villa straight away without telling Mandi. She knew she would talk her out of it. The more Mandi went on about Jilly and her friends the more it irritated Cathy. In fact Mandi and Benny irritated her a lot now that she really knew them. The more she thought about them, the crosser she became. Benny was a bit of a villain, Mandi was decidedly tarty, and yet they always had an opinion, and usually a criticism, on everyone and everything. Not only that, because Cathy rented their guest villa Mandi thought she had the right to interfere in every aspect of her and Sammy-Jo's lives. By the time Cathy pulled up outside she was feeling put upon and self-righteous.

The villa where the girls lived had probably once been someone's pride and joy but now it was run-down and neglected, an oasis of chaos amid the scented bougainvillaea and huge palms that lined the road. Fading pink and white emulsion was peeling off the building and the garden was overgrown and crawling with stray cats and kittens that lived and bred in the undergrowth.

Cathy nearly turned away again, the place looked so unwelcoming, but she heard singing and music from inside so she parked the car and went to the open door.

'Hello? Is anybody there?' Guessing no one would hear her above the music, she tentatively stepped inside and shouted again.

'Hellooooo . . .'

An unfamiliar figure appeared in front of her, dripping wet, with just a tiny hand towel almost, but not quite, wrapped around her long slender body.

'Sorry, I was in the shower, can I help you?'

'I'm looking for Jilly or Tara . . .'

'Tara's not in; Jilly's out the back, topping up her tan. Just go through.'

Tentatively Cathy picked her way through the debris

caused by six untidy females sharing two bedrooms. Towels and underwear were strewn everywhere and the kitchen was overflowing with empty wine bottles and dirty glasses. The smell of strong Spanish cigarettes got more powerful as she headed towards the terrace at the back of the villa.

'Kit, hi. What on earth are you doing here? I'm sorry about the state of the place, I'd have tidied up a bit if I'd known.'

Cathy didn't know where to look. Jilly had jumped up from her dilapidated sun-bed to greet her and Cathy was embarrassed to see she didn't have a stitch on apart from a sun-visor on her head. She tried not to focus on anything.

'Oh, that's OK. You said pop in, so I have. Your friend told me to just come through.'

'What would you like, vino? Ciggie?'

'No to both, I'm afraid. I don't smoke and I'm driving, sorry. I actually wanted a bit of advice.'

At that moment the other girl came through and Cathy saw them exchange glances. She realised she had sounded prissy.

'Can I change my mind? I will have a glass of wine – white, please, if you've got it.'

The girl with the small towel tiptoed barefoot around the corner and disappeared.

'Hannah's just gone to get another bottle from the garage. We've got a fucking great fridge out there full of booze and mixers. No food, mind, but enough alcohol to float a yacht. Now, what can I do you for?'

'I've got to go to England for a few days and I wondered if you knew of any nannies or agencies. I need someone to sleep in and look after my daughter, Jo. She's four.'

Jilly's face was a picture. 'You going to England? Are you going to see Peter O'Brien?'

Cathy laughed. 'No, I'm not! Peter and I are friends, I like him a lot, but that's it. No, I've got some family problems – illness and all that – and I have to go to Hampshire but I don't want to disrupt Jo and school. Any suggestions? I thought as you know everyone . . .'

Hannah came back round, waving two bottles; the towel had disappeared en route and she was now naked.

'Hannah, sweetie, I really think we ought to find our sarongs. We're embarrassing the poor girl. Can you drag a couple off the washing line?' Jilly turned back to Cathy. 'If, of course, she can find the washing line. Now where were we? Oh yes, you need a nanny . . . Oohh, that's a hard one, but I'll put the old brain cells to work and ask around.'

Hannah tiptoed back through the bushes with two sarongs in her hand and half a dozen hungry cats in tow. In the beginning it had bewildered Cathy how the girls could all look the same – lithe, blonde and tanned – but she knew now that those were the criteria at the lap-dancing club where they all worked.

Throwing one sarong on to Jilly's lap, she carelessly slung the other over her shoulder as she shooed the cats away.

'Fucking Tara and her fucking cats. I'm going to call in

the cat lady, get them all taken away and put down. It's fucking ridiculous.'

'I can probably help you if that's what you really want.' Cathy looked at Jilly. 'Remember that auction? For the animal rescue? Well, I know the woman who runs it. They neuter and rehome strays . . .'

'Sounds good to me! Mind you, I know more than a few old tom cats round here that could do with neutering and rehoming but they've only got two legs!'

All three of them laughed, and Cathy found to her surprise that she was enjoying herself, that it was nice to be chatting to people her own age.

Cathy had stayed longer than she intended to, and she also realised that after a couple of glasses of cheap but strong vino she would be pushing it if she drove home.

'Is it OK if I leave my car and collect it tomorrow? I don't often drink wine and I feel all light-headed.'

'No problem. Come in the afternoon, that's when we're usually here and awake!'

The deafening sound of several police cars, sirens blaring as they roared up the road, made them all jump.

'Christ Almighty, that's loud. I wonder what's going on?'

Jilly had barely finished her sentence before a large number of armed *guardia* came running round the villa from both sides. Another two appeared through the kitchen, shouting and pointing their guns at the three of them.

'What the fuck is going on here . . .?' Jilly was quickly silenced by a barked order from the man in charge.

The Spanish was rapid and hard to understand but the guns spoke volumes and the girls were quickly hand-cuffed and made to sit down in silence.

With no attempt at explanation, the police started ruthlessly to rip the place apart. Swarming in and out of the property and shouting to each other fiercely they systematically searched everywhere.

Cathy was terrified. She had absolutely no idea what was going on but she did realise that whatever it was, it was serious, very serious.

For a good hour they sat silently with their hands cuffed behind their backs, listening to the sound of falling furniture, slamming doors and loud voices. Then suddenly the noise stopped. One of the policemen came out from the garage with a basket full of dirty washing and, with a triumphant smile and a flourish made the girls look inside. The large brown paper bag looked innocent enough until he carefully opened it and, in best Paul Daniels tradition, pulled out a house-brick-sized block of cannabis followed by a see-through polythene bag containing a large quantity of white powder.

Jilly suddenly started screaming at the top of her voice, 'That fucking Tara, she promised! I'm going to fucking murder her. She's been fucking dealing again!'

Their protestations of innocence and their tears of panic were completely ignored, and all three were unceremoniously bundled into the back of the large *guardia* van and driven away at high speed, sirens full on.

Chapter Fifteen

Cathy felt she was in a nightmare. She kept closing her eyes and praying that when she opened them she would be back in the villa with Sammy-Jo, sitting on the sofa drinking their favourite non-alcoholic Sangria and watching Spanish cartoons she didn't understand.

But she wasn't. She was under arrest in a Spanish police station.

With no explanation from the police, Cathy was led away on her own and pushed through a door that was shut tight behind her, leaving her alone in a dingy room with only her overwhelming fear and a desperate desire to go to the toilet. Too frightened to call out, she just crossed her legs.

The heat in the tiny room was stifling despite the small ceiling fan that creaked and hummed ineffectually. The only furniture was a large rickety table and several ladder-back chairs with dirty rattan seats. The litter bin in the corner was overflowing with paper cups and empty cigarette packets and stubs.

Cathy looked around and tried hard to keep a rein on her emotions. She kept telling herself it was all a mistake, that they would soon realise it and then they would let her go back to Sammy-Jo. She didn't have a watch on but it seemed like hours that she sat there in silence, listening to the raised voices outside and trying to understand what was going on, before the door flew open and the room was suddenly full of people.

Jilly and Hannah were brought in and ordered to sit alongside Cathy. They were still dressed only in the sarongs they had luckily been holding as the raid started. They had begged to be allowed to dress but the police had allowed them to grab only sandals for their bare feet, before bundling them into the van.

On one side of the table Jilly, Hannah and Cathy sat in a line, and directly opposite, one of the plain-clothes policemen from the raid. Darkly handsome and casually dressed, he didn't look like a policeman until he smiled grimly and put his elbows on the table, clasping his hands in front of his mouth. He was noticeably in charge. In heavily accented English he introduced himself.

'I am an officer, and I am in charge of this investigation, and this is . . .'

He pointed to an indifferent-looking woman, who had come in at the same time. She told them in a bored monotone that she was the interpreter, there to ensure there was no problem with communication on either side. Mousy and miserable-faced, the Englishwoman made no secret of the fact that she disapproved of the girls.

'My name is Marian Rodriguez. I am English but

married to a Spaniard and I live here. I am bilingual and I will translate the questioning, which will be in Spanish, but only translate. I am *not* here on your behalf or to plead your case for you. I am here only to interpret literally everything that is said to ensure no misunderstandings.'

To compound her terror, behind them, standing on guard at the door, was the ugliest and most frightening woman Cathy had ever seen. Grim-faced and with her black hair pulled back tightly into a bun, she bulged out of her uniform at every seam. The buttons on her shirt were pulled back tight over gargantuan breasts that were trying to fight their way out in every direction and her trouser pockets were nearly inside out with the strain. Glaring into the middle distance she stood still with her feet apart and her hands behind her back.

The silence that followed was broken only by the creaking of the fan; no one said a word, but the Polaroid photos of the 'find' laid out on the table facing the girls silently mocked them.

Jilly and Hannah sat mutely – they had already said they would answer nothing without a lawyer – but Cathy frantically tried to explain that she was only visiting, that it was the first time she had been there, that she knew nothing of the drugs found at the villa. All she wanted to do was get out and back to Sammy-Jo.

The single phone call she had been allowed she had used to phone Mandi, to tell her what had happened and to ask her to take care of Sammy-Jo. Mandi had predictably launched into a diatribe about Jilly Holden and her friends but she promised to contact the consul and a lawyer that Benny knew, before screeching almost hysterically down the phone, 'Don't say anything until the lawyer gets there!'

Very soon, though, Cathy, who naively thought that if she told the truth she would shortly be home, was being questioned so rapidly and aggressively even the interpreter was having trouble keeping up.

'Your name is Kit Carter?'

'Yes, that's right.'

'Your passport says something different.'

'My real name is Cathy but I am called Kit.'

'The surname on your passport, your driving licence, it is not Carter . . .'

'No, that's right, it's Marcos. My married name is Marcos but I am separated from my husband and I use my maiden name.'

'You are not British, why do you have a British passport? Is it stolen? Is it counterfeit? You are in Spain using a false name, tell me why?'

The man opposite stared accusingly at Cathy, absentmindedly pushing his thick black hair from his forehead. Cathy noticed the beads of sweat running down the side of his face and ending up in the thick bushy moustache that completely covered his upper lip.

It was almost a relief to see him sweating as well. She was drenched from head to foot, perspiration even running down her legs and forming uncomfortable puddles in her deck shoes.

One after another the questions were fired at her, and

before too long Cathy realised where the questioning was going. She was frightened, and too late, she remembered Mandi telling her not to say anything. The whole thing looked decidedly suspicious and when Mandi and Benny's names were mentioned the questioning became even more quick-fire, more aggressive.

'You are related to Mr and Mrs O'Brien?'

Out of the corner of her eye she could see Jilly's head moving fractionally from side to side. She remembered what she had been told: 'If anyone asks, we're related,' but she couldn't bring herself to lie outright.

'Not exactly, but I call them my aunt and uncle . . . They're good friends to me and my daughter.'

Jilly's sharp intake of breath told her that was the wrong thing to say but Cathy couldn't understand it.

'Tell me about the drugs . . .'

'Tell me where they came from . . .'

'Tell me how they got to the villa . . .'

Cathy realised that she was getting nowhere fast. Jilly and Hannah were leaning silently back on their chairs and Cathy was copping the full force of the police officer's questioning.

'I'm not answering any more questions until my lawyer gets here,' she finally declared.

After about five minutes' non-response, the man stood up, forcefully kicking his chair so hard it toppled to the floor with a crash. Cathy visibly jumped. Silently the three officials all left the room, leaving the girls together.

'Jilly, what is going on? What are we going to do?' Cathy was still crying, her terror written all over her face.

Jilly didn't answer; she glared a warning and put her finger to her lips in a silencing motion. As soon as she patted her ear Cathy got the message. The police were listening in on the other side of the door.

A strange conversation then took place that consisted only of hand signs and mouthed words. Cathy realised that the culprit had to be Tara, that she was a known dealer but only a small cog in the big wheel of drug smuggling and distribution that centred on the waters off the coast that divided North Africa and Spain and were easily crossed with a good cruiser. Tara had promised them all that she only took the stuff, that she no longer had anything to do with dealing.

Suddenly the door flew open and the scary policewoman pulled Jilly and Hannah by their arms out of the room, then someone else came in.

'Miss Carter?' The man who held out his hand was dressed from top to toe in black, and reminded Cathy visually of Nico. The outstretched hand, the charming smile and the friendly approach meant to put her at ease made her even more jumpy, and the overpowering scent of strong aftershave made her feel nauseous.

'I am Javier Alfonso, a lawyer. Mrs O'Brien called me to act for you. I have to tell you, you are in a lot of trouble. Now you have to be honest with me and tell me everything if I am to help you. But first, do you want the interpreter back in or are you happy to speak with me?'

The man's command of English was excellent but he retained the strong Spanish accent that Cathy had previously always found so attractive. She declined the interpreter with a slight smile; the woman was so sullen it was a relief not to have her in the room.

'There's nothing to tell because I don't know anything. I was only visiting. I don't even know them really. I've met Jilly and Tara just once or twice and I'd never even seen Hannah before.'

The man looked directly into her eyes and smiled slightly. 'Then what were you doing there drinking alcohol? Smoking cannabis? Sunbathing nude?'

'I wasn't nude, I was wearing what I have on now.' Cathy pointed to her shorts and T-shirt indignantly. 'Jilly and Hannah were but I wasn't, and I wasn't smoking anything. I don't smoke. Jilly was, but I just thought it was an ordinary cigarette. *I was just visiting.*'

'Why were you visiting if you didn't know them? It is strange to socialise with people in their own home, people who are naked, whom you don't know, is it not?'

The same smile. If the lawyer didn't believe her then no one would.

Cathy went over it again – why she was there, what went on while she was there, why her passport gave a different name. Over and over she repeated it all, hoping that he would believe her.

Eventually Javier got up, excused himself and went over to the door. He spoke quickly to the guard outside and again Cathy cursed her lack of Spanish. Sammy-Jo would have understood more than she did.

Javier disappeared, leaving Cathy alone in the room with the policewoman who menacingly removed her baton from her huge belt and nonchalantly waved it back and forth. Cathy's fear was so strong that she was physically shaking as she irrationally wondered if she was going to get beaten into submission, made to admit the charges, locked away for ever from Sammy-Jo. However, the woman just kept on juggling, sadistically being provocative and enjoying every second of Cathy's obvious terror.

Javier came back into the room and barked a short sharp sentence at the woman, who slowly, with a sarcastic smile, put the baton back into its strap and left the room.

'I'm sorry, Miss Carter – Cathy – they are going to keep you in custody tonight and you will appear in court in the morning. I shall ask for bail but, even if they agree, they will retain your passport and documents and you will possibly be under house arrest.' His face was apologetic. 'It's the best I can do at this moment. I'm sure you are innocent, your statement is too simple to be false, but a night here and then bail is better than months awaiting trial in one of our jails, I can assure you.'

'Trial? What do you mean, trial? I haven't done anything, nothing at all . . .'

'You were there, Miss Carter, socialising in a house with known drug dealers where a considerable amount of illegal drugs were found. Of course, they will think you were there for that purpose, either to buy or sell.'

Cathy gave up arguing. 'OK, I see your point, but will you call Mandi for me? Explain? My daughter is with the O'Briens. She's only four.'

'Of course. I will see you at court tomorrow morning, Miss Carter. Don't worry too much, I will do everything

I can. Mr and Mrs O'Brien are good clients and, of course, good friends of mine.'

With a vicious smile the policewoman led the three young women downstairs into the depths of the building and then pushed them happily into a small dank concrete room with an old-fashioned iron-barred door. By now Cathy was really desperate for the toilet but all the woman did was hand a metal bucket in to them.

They spent the night huddled up to each other in what appeared to be a single cell, one of a line of four that were all occupied but they couldn't see, didn't want to see, by whom. It was hot and airless and the noise was incessant.

Despite her anger Cathy realised it was pointless blaming Jilly and Hannah. They were in the same boat because of Tara. A lawyer had been to see Jilly and Hannah too, but the bad news for them all was that Tara had done a runner and no one knew where she was. The other girls from the villa had been questioned and released without charge. The focus was now solely on the three in custody – the three caught on the property with a substantial haul of drugs hidden in the garage under the villa.

'What's going to happen now, do you think?' Cathy asked timidly. 'I don't understand any of this. Why did you try and warn me off saying anything about Benny and Mandi? I don't understand . . .'

Pulling the thin cotton blanket around her shoulders, more for comfort than anything else, Cathy pulled her knees up tight to her chest as she looked curiously at the two girls who were now pulling faces at each other.

'Oh, come on, Kit, Cathy, whatever your name is,'
Jilly's tone was sarcastic in the extreme, 'you must know
Benny's into wheeling and dodgy dealing. How else
would they be able to live as they do? You're guilty by
association, regardless of what you say. Related to them?
Living rent free? Using a different name? Come on, do
you think we came over on the last fucking boat?'

'But I'm not related to them and I paid rent up front
and my name really is Cathy Carter. It's my maiden name
and I can use it if I bloody well want to. There's no law
against it!'

For the first time Hannah joined in. 'I know that and
you know that but the *guardia* see it differently. You, you
stupid cow, are in big trouble and you've made it worse
for us now with all your fucking lies.'

Cathy's intake of breath was inaudible. She couldn't
believe what she was hearing – that they were actually
blaming her.

'You're joking! You're the ones who lived with a junkie
dealer and let her use the place as a clearing house, and
how do I know you weren't part and parcel of it? I don't
know anything about you apart from the fact you're
bloody sleazy lap dancers in a sleazy dive that calls itself a
club. Don't try and tell me that little titbit helped your
case!'

As Cathy's eyes filled up again Jilly tried to mediate.
'Look, it's no one's fault and we're not doing ourselves
any favours by fighting with each other. Hopefully, it'll
get sorted tomorrow. There's three lawyers involved now
and if they can't sort it out between them then they all

want firing. Let's try and get some sleep. We're going to need all our wits about us in the morning.'

Despite their efforts none of them slept; they were all dreading the next morning.

After a cup of muddy coffee and a stale croissant each they were given clothes, handcuffed again and led out of the police station to a waiting police van. It took off at breakneck speed, throwing them and the female guard all around the windowless vehicle until it braked sharply and the doors were opened.

Cathy looked around in horror as they were led into a court room surrounded by armed guards. Javier the lawyer and the same interpreter were already there, along with the two men representing Jilly and Hannah. The arguments bounced back and forth in Spanish and it wasn't until the end of the hearing that the interpreter spoke to them.

'It's not good. The police are opposing bail but your lawyers have persuaded the magistrate. You can be released on bail on condition you hand over your passports and bail of two and a half million pesetas – about ten thousand English pounds each – to the Court. You will also stay within the perimeters of your properties.'

'But I have to go to England. My sisters are ill—' Cathy turned to speak to the magistrate but her lawyer silenced her and pulled her away.

'Do not argue unless you wish to go to jail. Just agree to everything and pay the money, it's the only way.'

Her shoulders sagged noticeably and she looked over to Jilly and her friend. They were both crying helplessly and pleading with their lawyers.

'They cannot raise the bail.' Javier's voice was very matter of fact.

'I'll pay it for them. They can't go to jail. It wasn't them, it was Tara.'

He held up his hand in front of her, much in the same way the *guardia* stop traffic. 'Do not do that, Mrs Marcos. If you do, it will reflect badly on your story about not knowing them. They have to deal with it themselves. It is not your problem. I'm sorry.'

'But I can't let them go to jail. I can afford it.'

'It doesn't matter if you can afford it. Do not do it!'

Cathy's guilt as she left the court was overwhelming, knowing that the others were going to be heading off to the notorious women's prison, but as soon as she got outside she found Mandi waiting for her in a real strop.

'You silly, silly girl. I told you they were trouble. Not only have you dropped yourself in it but me and Benny as well. The police are always on the lookout for any ex-crims, ever since it was nicknamed the Costa del Crime round here. My Benny was too small and too ancient a fish to be of any interest to them, but now . . . I don't know, they've already been to our home and they've turned your villa over as well. Jeez, Benny is going to go ape about this when he gets back.'

Cathy was mortified. 'I'm sorry, Mand. Do you want me to find somewhere else to live?'

'No way, girl, no way. That would only make it look worse. No, let Javier deal with it, but I warn you, he's bleedin' expensive.'

★ ★ ★

Fortunately Mandi had kept control of her tongue for once and all Sammy-Jo knew was that Cathy had gone to see some friends and stayed the night – almost true and nothing too complex for Cathy to follow through. The big problem was that she couldn't go home to see the twins and Sheila.

However, a shock was in store for her when she phoned three days later.

'Sheila, I've got some bad news . . .'

'Don't I just know it, young lady, don't I just know it. You've been in the *Gazette*, you know. Now tell me what you've been up to and where you are because I'm ready and packed.'

Cathy was stunned. 'I haven't done anything, Sheila. It was all a mistake. How did the papers pick up on that?' As soon as she said it she realised the answer. A reporter from the local English paper had been in the court building; she had recognised him but stupidly thought nothing of it. He had obviously picked up on where the girls came from and had passed it on.

'That's not what I read. According to the *Gazette* you've been arrested and charged with drug smuggling and now you're out on bail and the other two friends of yours have been carted off to jail.' Cathy could picture Sheila's indignant face and despite the circumstances she managed a smile.

'Trust me, Sheila, it'll be OK. It really is a mistake and I don't want you travelling. Please stay with Jane and Alison. They need you and they haven't got anyone else.

I've got friends here and a good lawyer. I'll keep you up to date, I promise.'

Eventually Sheila agreed, although reluctantly. There was no point in trying to hide her location now it had been spread all over the papers so she gave Sheila her phone number and address.

She phoned Simonie herself, who informed her Justin was just thinking about catching a flight out there.

'He can't do that, the baby's due soon. Tell him he has to stay with you! Listen, I've just told Sheila and now I'm telling you, I'm fine, it's all a big misunderstanding and when it goes back to court in a few weeks it'll all get thrown out, my lawyer is confident.' Cathy crossed her fingers as she said it, hoping that she wasn't pushing her luck.

'Cathy, supposing Nico reads it? He'll know where you are, and now you're on bail you can't leave. That's what Justin is worried about.'

Cathy sank back into the chair. The feeling that gripped her was one of overpowering fear and anger that she hadn't thought of that herself. Simonie was right. Once again she would be a sitting target.

'Oh, don't worry about that. I've got enough friends here to protect me and Sammy-Jo. It's no problem, really. Anyway, Nico never reads newspapers. He's not into that sort of thing, is he? Do you think you could mail me a copy, just so that I know what's been said and can put it right eventually?'

For Simonie's sake she tried to be light-hearted about it, and even managed a gentle laugh but all she wanted to do was get off the phone and think.

'Well, if you're certain . . .' Cathy could hear the relief in Simonie's voice and knew she had said the right thing.

Nico. What could she do about him? She guessed if Nico did read about her he would be on the first plane out to Spain, and until she was proved innocent he would make wonderful mileage out of Cathy's arrest. The only glimmer of hope on her horizon was that he was apparently no longer in the area, so possibly unable to read a newspaper local to the New Forest.

Gingerly Cathy walked through the gap in the hedge to see Mandi. She knew Benny was home because she could see his car and she knew she had to face him.

To her amazement Benny treated her like a long-lost friend. There was no hint of recriminations. At first she had wondered if Mandi hadn't told him but when she broached the subject herself Benny was fine about it.

'Don't worry, these things happen. Javier will get it all done and dusted for you, no problem. One of the disadvantages of Marbella is that every so often they have a bit of a purge and turn your drum over, make sure you know who's boss, but then it all blows over again. They know I'm not into drugs.'

'But I thought you'd be furious, that you'd chuck me out . . . Mandi said—'

'Don't you worry about Mand. She gets upset when they come calling. I'm just furious that those little tarts sucked you into their mucky little scams – but apart from that, forget it, pet; it comes with the territory.'

Cathy wanted to throw her arms around his neck and

kiss him but she had seen the way Mandi could turn into a wildcat if a female of any age so much as looked at her Benny.

'That's a weight off my mind. I'm really grateful.'

'Good, because I think it's time we had a little chat, Mrs Cathy Marcos, as opposed to Ms Kit Carter!' Benny's face creased into a grin, a big wide grin that split his face in half and framed his well-constructed tombstone-like dentures. Benny didn't so much have wrinkles as crevices that slewed across his features like a complex road map. Thirty-odd years in the sun had taken their toll on his body and instead of golden and smooth the tan was now chestnut and gnarled.

Cathy still sat silently, unsure of where she would stand if she told them everything.

Mandi came into the room and sat down, looking accusingly from one to the other.

'Well?'

'Well what?'

'Have you given the silly mare a bollocking? I told her you'd be furious.'

Benny's laugh was raucous. 'Get off your high horse, darlin', and get us a drink. We've got a lot of talking to do.'

Cathy knew she had no option if she wanted to stay where she was and keep Sammy-Jo safe. She had to tell them and trust that her story would stay secret. She was sure it would, especially as Mandi and Benny had their own secrets!

'Dear, oh Lord, babe. I've never heard nothing like it

in my life.' Mandy had stayed silent as Cathy gave them a précis of her problems but suddenly she was vocal again. 'Our lively little corner of Spain must have seemed a haven of boredom after that lot. No wonder your mate twisted our arms to let you stay here. Shame you got caught up with Jilly Holden and co, though. Still, I did warn you. It's a good job they're still locked up—'

Sharply, Benny interrupted. 'No more, Mand. It doesn't help nothing to go on and on!'

Cathy's face crumpled visibly as the tears crept slowly down her cheeks. Embarrassed, she flicked them away with the back of her hand.

'Oh, don't. I feel so sorry for them. It was bad enough in the cells in town, but from what I've heard about the prison . . . I should have bailed them, I know I should. I can afford it and it wasn't them, it was Tara.'

'It was all of them. I'm telling you again, they're all money-grabbing little whores and they deserve to be where they are. Now what would you like to drink?'

Cathy knew the subject was closed.

Chapter Sixteen

As the days turned into weeks and Cathy heard nothing from or about Nico she began to relax. The thought of going back to court had almost been back-boilered by the fear of Nico turning up.

Sammy-Jo's school was on alert in case he appeared there and charmed his way in. Cathy had employed a security firm that placed a guard outside day and night, and Benny was on the ball with it all. Villain he may once have been, involved in dubious activities he no doubt still was, but anything connected with children and predators would see him up on his soapbox in an instant.

'If you get so much as a sniff of that little pervert being even in the country, then we'll deal with him. There's not many here got any time for scum like that. Should be strung up by their nuts, the lot of them. I'd do it meself if I came across him, and enjoy it.'

The expression on his face was frightening and the movement Benny made with his hands left Cathy in no doubt as to what he meant. It passed through her mind that she wouldn't like to be on the wrong side of him.

Then just as suddenly he had smiled and continued, 'Still, the main thing to concentrate on now is sorting out this other business. Javier seems to think you'll get off. He believes you, and the statements he's collected support everything you've said, so let's hope!'

Cathy wasn't so confident but she wanted it all over and done with. It was a nightmare having to stay within the property boundaries, and she found she was spending more time with Mandi than she would have chosen to do under other circumstances. She was going stir crazy, and it was in the worst moments that she thought of Jilly and Hannah, locked away in the prison up in the hills. It upset her to think of them there but she could also see that Javier was right; if she didn't know them, if she had been innocently caught up in the drugs crime, then why would she pay their bail money, especially as it was so high? Mandi argued, in her own inimitable way, that they had slept their way round most of the loaded men in Marbella and beyond, so let one of them cough up. But they didn't – none of them. As always when a scandal broke, everyone ran for cover, desperate to distance themselves, as Jilly and Hannah were now finding out to their cost.

In a desperate bid to alleviate her boredom, Cathy had taken to writing everything down – not quite a diary nor a memoir, but all her recollections from childhood through to the present, including her time with Nico and her thoughts about the mess she was caught up in. It gave her a purpose when Sammy-Jo was at school. Benny had given her his old word processor and she spent hours typing laboriously in no particular order with the shutters closed and the fan on to stay cool.

One afternoon a few weeks after she was bailed, she was concentrating so hard on her typing that she didn't hear a car pull up on to the drive outside, nor did she hear someone getting out and walking up the steps to the front terrace. The first thing she heard was her name being called, followed by a loud knocking on the door.

'Cathy?'

Peering through the half-open shutters at the shadowy figure outside, Cathy panicked. She jumped back out of sight and tried to get her brain in gear.

Nico must have found her.

In the course of about twenty seconds, with her back flattened against the wall, Cathy thought about phoning the police, phoning Mandi, whether she could get out the back way, even using her kitchen knives. Her heart palpitated so hard she was sure he could hear it and beads of sweat broke out on her forehead.

Another knock, louder this time, was followed by footsteps up and down the terrace. Someone was looking through the shutters. The door latch lifted and Cathy started to move slowly and silently towards the back door, her escape route.

'Cathy?' The voice was louder. 'Cathy, it's Tim. Are you in there?'

Moving back to the windows she opened one shutter carefully and studied the man outside, still unsure until he moved into the light and she caught his smile.

'Tim, what are you doing here? God, you just scared the shit out of me. I thought it was Nico.'

'I'm not surprised, and I don't think much of your security guard. I could have been Nico, or even the mad axeman. He just asked my name and told me to park on the drive!'

She threw the door open and flung her arms around his neck in relief. Too late, she realised what she had done and blushed red, the first time she had blushed in ages.

'It's good to see you, even if you did frighten me half to death!'

'Well, as you can't get to come home I thought I'd come to you – update you, support you and all that. God, it's hot out here, how do you stand it?'

It was blisteringly hot and the sun was beating relentlessly on Tim's pale face and neck, which were already turning salmon pink.

'That's why I was shuttered away inside in the cool. Come in, I'll turn the fan up as it's you. I'll even get you some iced tea to cool you down!'

Laughing excitedly, she led him in and motioned to a chair carefully placed to get the full benefit of the cooling breeze from the fan blades.

'Who knows you're here? Does Sheila? Simonie? Oh, Tim, I can't believe it. I've been going crazy shut up here with only the couple next door for company. They're lovely but they think they have to parent me and I don't need that. I need conversation – real conversation. Oh, it's so good to see you.'

'OK, OK,' Tim held up his hands, 'I get the message and I'm pleased to see you. You look great, actually, really fit and well – much better than I expected. It must suit you here.'

'Yes and no. I look fit and well because I'm confined to barracks so to speak so I'm eating too much and sunbathing too much. Any longer and I shall be a fat dried-out old prune.'

'Never!'

Cathy felt suddenly shy at the way Tim was looking at her appreciatively. Most men did, but Tim? Well, he was just Tim. Good old Tim. Looking at him, the man instead of the boy, she felt a tingling, a pull towards him, towards Tim the man.

No, she told herself, not now. There's too much going on and he's only here to be a friend. But as she was telling herself that, she could hear Simonie's voice: *He's always been in love with you* . . . No, no, no, she remonstrated silently.

Tim broke the silence. 'Have you heard anything about a court date yet?'

'No, nothing. The system here is quite strange compared to England, but I'm actually waiting to hear today. The police are still gathering evidence, according to my lawyer. He's cautiously optimistic that I'll be released. There's really nothing to link me to the charges other than that I was there. I mean, I could have been anyone who just happened to be there, even a passing policeman! Oh well, not much longer to wait. We'll see what happens. I don't want to count chickens and all that.'

Tim looked across at her sympathetically. 'I do hope everything turns out OK. I'm sure it will.' She could see he was choosing his words carefully. 'Do you want to hear about the twins or is that too much on top of everything else?'

'Go on, hit me with it – it can't be any worse than this – but let me show you round at the same time. We can talk as we walk and you may even get to meet Mandi and Benny, your friend of a friend who actually owns this place and the one next door. By the way, where are you staying?'

'A big sprawling hotel down by the beach, full to overflowing with Brits with sunburn and kids, but it'll do. I'm hoping I won't be there too much.'

The phone call, although expected, was still a shock.

'It is Javier here. I have been informed today that you have been summoned back to court next Tuesday. We have been lucky, I think. The police have found Miss Tara in Benidorm and she was in possession. At the moment she is still denying anything to do with the drugs at the property but I am hopeful.'

Cathy replaced the phone and looked silently at Tim.

'Is this it?' Tim asked quietly.

Nodding her head, she tried to smile but it was more a quiver around the edge of her lips that she couldn't control before bursting into tears.

Even Nico was getting concerned about Paul. The more he got to know him the more worried he was that Paul would go too far one day, and he knew he had to confront him. Paul's hunger for ever more violent child pornography, more violent than even Nico considered acceptable, scared him. He was only too aware that the further Paul pushed back the boundaries personally, the more likely they were to get caught.

Nico wanted out but didn't know how to go about it. Paul knew far too much about him, both personally and businesswise. He still lived at the Devon farm and still co-ordinated the distribution of the imported films, and although Paul was under orders not to take anyone back there Nico was certain he did. Paul wouldn't be able to resist it.

Deciding to play it by ear, he went to the studio. Paul was in his 'playroom', editing some footage of the angel-faced but obviously petrified Rachel. Nico picked up another tape thrown on the floor.

'What's this one, Paul?'

'Waste of good camera time – me and the mother. She was up for it and it gave me a good excuse to set the equipment up. Mummy went out and left me to babysit . . . bingo!'

Nico tried to choose his words carefully; he didn't want to upset Paul. 'I think we need to pull back a bit, slow down. We're going to get caught if we're not careful. I want you to toddle off to Thailand for a couple of weeks and chill out, leave me to hold the fort and cool it all down. Maybe actually find a child model!'

Paul looked over his shoulder at Nico and the boyishly good-looking face broke into his easy charming smile, the smile that had women falling at his feet.

'You worry too much. Those stupid, conceited old slags will never in a million years make a complaint. Just imagine how it would look: they invited me round, they let me set up the camera and then they went out, leaving me alone with their spoiled little brats! No, man, we're safe as houses, but I wouldn't say no to Thailand just the same!'

Nico breathed out hard with relief. He vaguely wondered if he could get away with closing down the operation while Paul was running amok in Thailand. Smiling at Paul he reached over and rewound the tape.

'Good. You arrange it and bill it to the company. I'll spend the time you're away being legit. That'll be fun, won't it, ha, ha, ha.'

Both men laughed but Nico's thoughts were somewhere else, his brain in overdrive, plotting the best way to deal with the increasingly maverick Paul.

He wondered about going respectable again and starting up another business. He loved the idea of going back to Hampshire and setting up in competition with Simonie and Justin. Thanks to the 'model agency' he had more than enough funds offshore to give them a good run for their money.

Smiling to himself he decided that as soon as Paul was away he would start the process. Providing enough compensation was paid into Paul's account he couldn't complain.

The nearer the crucial day got, the worse the headaches became, and Cathy was functioning on autopilot.

Because of Sammy-Jo she knew she had to prepare for the worst, to think the unthinkable, because if she was jailed then there had to be some contingency plans for her daughter. She also had to prepare her, but at four years old, Sammy-Jo would find it difficult to understand. Tim agreed that if Cathy was imprisoned he would take Sammy-Jo back to England, to Sheila, who would look after her. Cathy knew Sheila would do it but she also knew she couldn't ask first because that would send everyone into a panic, maybe unnecessarily. The day before the hearing she kept her daughter at home and they spent the time at the pool next door with Tim.

'What exactly have you told her? I need to know just in case. If I suddenly drag her off to London I think we can safely say she'll ask a few questions!'

Cathy fiddled nervously with the strands of hair that were stuck to the side of her face in the heat.

'All I've said is that I may have to go away for a while, and if I do then Uncle Tim will take her to England to see her family. That's it. If the worst comes to the worst then Mandi and Benny, who she adores, will enlarge on it and deal with it as best they can. There's nothing else I can do without scaring her, possibly without reason.'

Tim reached over and gently took her hand. 'It'll be OK, it has to be. I can't imagine it any other way . . .'

Cathy leaned forward and rested her elbows on her knees, her face so close to his they were almost touching.

'Mummy, Mummy.' The interruption made them both jump and separate like scalded cats. 'Look at me! I can dive backwards. Mummy look at me!'

Cathy's eyes moved reluctantly from Tim to Sammy-Jo. 'That's lovely, darling. Keep practising. We'll join you in a minute.'

She looked back at Tim, their eyes suddenly locked, and Cathy could feel the surge of emotion again, the feeling that hadn't been there since Nico had first looked at her all those years ago.

'I have to go and play with Sammy-Jo. I'm not being fair to her; it may be her last day with me for a long time.' Gently she reached her hand up and touched his face. 'Stay with me tonight, Tim. I don't want to be on my own. Don't go back to the hotel . . .'

Jumping up, she ran over to the pool and leaped in, a huge bomb of a jump with her knees pulled up. Sammy-Jo screamed with laughter as the water flowed over the edge of the pool, flooding the mosaic border. As she surfaced, Cathy saw a figure looking over the side.

'For someone so small that was one big splash!'

'Peter! What are you doing here?' Cathy pulled herself out and sat on the side.

'I came to offer some support but I can see you've already got some. This is . . .?' Peter looked in the direction of a bemused Tim and back again, raising an eyebrow at Cathy.

'Oh, that's Tim, an old friend from England. If it all goes wrong then he's going to take Sammy-Jo back to my sisters.' Cathy smiled openly. 'Come and meet him. I've known him for so long . . .'

'Hi, Tim, I'm Peter. My parents own this villa.'

'How absolutely lovely for you.' Tim's voice oozed sarcasm.

Naively Cathy couldn't understand the slight atmosphere but still chattered on speedily in an attempt to relieve it. Peter and Tim stood squarely opposite each other as Cathy looked from one to the other.

'I take it Mandi updated you when she visited? I haven't heard from Jilly, needless to say, but I have heard that, understandably, she and Hannah are both really scared and depressed. Are you going to see her?'

Peter looked at the ground. 'Not a chance. Mum and Dad would go ape.'

'But you were so close and she's crazy about you. It would give her such a boost.'

'No way. Not a good idea. I don't want to be high profile in all this.'

Puzzled, Cathy glared at him. 'Then why are you here? With me? I'm in court with them.'

'Yes, I know, but Mum and Dad like you, whereas Jilly . . .' he paused and grimaced dramatically, 'well, you know what Jilly's like.'

'Crap, Peter, absolute crap. You should have the courage of your convictions. Go and see her . . . You saw enough of her before, it shouldn't be any different now. Friends are friends.'

She looked over at Sammy-Jo, who was out of the water and drying her hair on one of Mandi's big fluffy towels. 'Come on, Jo, we're going back now.'

Peter looked genuinely bemused at Cathy's abruptness. 'Can you imagine how it would appear if I was seen with her? Look what's happened to you – at least I had the sense never to go to their villa . . .'

'Yes, Peter, and who was it who introduced me to her? Who told me she was all right really? *A good laugh*, if I remember your description correctly.'

Peter adopted his little-boy stance, head hung with hair flopping over his face and eyes peering up apologetically.

'I know, I'm sorry! Forgive me?'

Cathy couldn't help but laugh, completely oblivious to Tim's expression behind her, his irritation barely concealed.

'Only if you promise to at least acknowledge Jilly tomorrow. She'll have had a really shitty few weeks and she needs all the real friends she can get. All those pervs who were more than happy to shag the beautiful sexy dancer have fallen over each other to distance themselves from her and her trouble. Now you're not like that, are you, Petey?'

Sammy-Jo ran on home ahead, leaving Tim and Cathy to follow slowly, close together but not touching, both unaware of Peter watching them, his face set in a frown as he tried to figure out the dynamics of the couple strolling away, deep in conversation.

'Well, that's someone you've got wrapped around your little finger, another one all the way from England to support you,' said Tim. 'Any more to arrive tonight?'

Cathy laughed. 'Peter is lovely. He helped me back on to my feet when I arrived here, and cheered me up. At the same time he was quite openly seeing half the females in town. He's a Casanova and I love him . . . as a friend, but he's also a mummy's boy, an only child, spoiled rotten and used to being pampered.'

As they clambered through the gap in the hedge, Tim took Cathy's hand.

'Whoever takes him on permanently will have their work cut out,' she continued. 'Jilly Holden is completely besotted with him but Mandi and Benny disapprove and, ultimately, Peter does as he's told.'

'Sounds a bit of a wimp to me.'

'Not really, just brainwashed by years of mothering. Anyway, enough about Peter. I've spoken to Guy – he owns my local restaurant and he's going to deliver a full five-course meal at ten o'clock for us. Last meal for the condemned and all that.'

'Sounds a bit late to me, ten . . . past my bedtime.'

'Not in Spain it isn't, and, anyway, Jo will be in bed by then. She's tired already. I really need some normal adult company, especially tonight, which I think is going to be long and drawn out.'

Tim looked at her. She noticed that the red glow of sunburn was fading and a slight tan was taking over, along with an attractive sprinkling of freckles across his nose and forehead. Unlike the confident and openly sexy Peter, Tim had an air of vulnerability about him. Cathy alone knew this was a throwback to the childhood bullying that he had endured as a skinny, spotty youth, but as an adult it was very attractive. She could imagine that there was no shortage of local girls back home who would love to mother him!

His voice interrupted her thoughts. 'What are you

thinking? You're miles away . . .'

'If I told you, you wouldn't believe me. I'm going to have a shower and freshen up. Help yourself to a drink, or whatever. Maybe you could have a chat with Jo? She needs to know you a little better, just in case . . .'

On the dot of ten a van pulled up and two waiters delivered the meal, laying it out on the ready-laid table and presenting Cathy with two bottles of wine and a bottle of champagne with a message tied around its neck. 'This is for tomorrow when it's all over. Dinner's on me. Love Guy.'

Tim read the card. 'You seem to have a regular menagerie of pet admirers. Can I compete at this level, I ask myself. You're certainly not little Cathy any more, are you?'

'If I'm not it's only because I had to grow up quickly. One day I'll tell you all about it, but tonight we're just going to eat, drink and chat, and act like nothing's wrong. So take a seat and we can pretend we're out to eat in a super exclusive restaurant instead of housebound in a rented villa!'

As he sat down she ruffled his hair and lightly kissed the top of his head.

Mandi and Benny were eating at the same time, seated either end of their enormous ornate dining table laid with gold-rimmed crockery and heavy gold-plated cutlery. Peter sat alone between the couple, slouched on the upholstered dining chair with his elbows on the table.

'Petey, I wish you'd listen to me. I don't like you sitting

down to dinner in shorts and T-shirt. It looks so uncouth in front of Anita. Nice slacks and a polo shirt – that's all I ask – a bit of class and some manners.'

Peter was hard pushed not to laugh as he took in the tableau in front of him: his mother in her skintight leopard-print Lycra trousers and more hair and make-up than Joan Collins on TV, and his father in tight chinos stretched across his flabby thighs and a short-sleeved shirt that emphasised his gross beer belly. But common sense told him not to comment, just to change the subject.

'Come on then, Dad, tell me what you really think will happen tomorrow. What does Javier think or know even? I can't believe that crook isn't well aware of what's going to happen.'

'I really dunno, son. You know lawyers – they make their living out of dragging things out. That daft kid Tara will be hung out to dry regardless and she could get the others off the hook if she admits to it, but she hasn't and she's not in court tomorrow—'

'Sod off, Ben,' Mandi interrupted. 'They've been looking for a good excuse to close the lap-dancing club down and all this hands it to 'em on a bloody plate. Three of the so-called dancers convicted of drug dealing? They'll screw 'em all, and Kit for good measure, and then close the club, or up the protection charges.'

Peter looked from one to the other, unsure which one to go with. He loved both his parents but it annoyed him that they could be so pretentious – snobs, in fact, in a strange way.

Peter's good education had given him a different perspective on life. His flat in the Barbican was tastefully and sparsely furnished, very light, strikingly minimalist and the complete opposite of the ostentatious villa in Spain that he truly hated. The drawerful of heavy gold chains, bracelets and rings that he had been given over the years never saw the light of day and he took a perverse pleasure in dressing down.

'Couldn't you have done something behind the scenes, Dad? You've got more than a few cops in your back pocket. Why does Kit have to go through this just because you fancy getting Jilly Holden out of Marbella? I wasn't intending to marry her, you know.'

Benny's face was a picture of fury. His already battered features turned bright red as he tried hard to control his temper. For a moment Peter thought he was going to get a smack around the head, the way Benny used to clip him when he was younger.

'Don't you fucking talk to me like that, boy. You know nothing, nothing . . .'

'That's where you're wrong. I know a lot more than you think, especially when it comes to the lap-dancing club . . . I know everything there is to know about it—'

Before he could continue, Benny was on his feet. 'Shut your mouth now or I'll shut it for you. You need to learn a little respect, especially for your mother. Now get out of my sight.'

Peter looked at them and laughed. 'Same old parents, same old argument, same old response. OK, I'm going . . .'

'Petey, don't go, your dad doesn't mean it.' Mandi was in tears, her thick black mascara running down her overtanned face. 'Come on, you're only here for a couple of days – why spoil it rowing over that little tart Jilly Holden? We'll all be well shot if you ask me.'

Peter smiled. 'Did I tell you I'm going to see her tomorrow? I might even speak up for her in court—'

'Fucking get out now and don't come back until you're ready to apologise for upsetting your mother. Speaking up for Jilly Holden? Not if you want to keep your flat, your car, your fucking enormous allowance you won't.'

Peter had quietly closed the door before his father even finished the sentence. He didn't have to wait for the end because he'd heard it all before.

Pausing only to grab his wallet and cigarettes, he made his way over the floodlit grounds to the guest villa.

'Hi, guys, mind if I join you? I'm *persona non grata* at the moment and it's all your fault. I told them I was going to see Jilly tomorrow in court.'

Peter looked from one to the other, quickly taking in the situation between Cathy and Tim. Quickly he carried on, innocently pretending not to notice. He had no intention of making a tactful departure.

'Any chance of a glass of vino and a morsel from your overflowing table for a poor homeless person who's going to have to sleep on your couch tonight?'

Cathy and Tim looked at each other in horror as Peter helped himself and then pulled a chair up to the table.

'There's more than enough for three by the look of it.'

'Benny, darling, what did Petey mean about the lap-dancing club? That's not anything to do with you, is it? There isn't going to be any trouble, is there?'

"Course not, babe! You know I potter about with all sorts, but I'm not actively involved. That's for the management company to deal with. I might have invested a few quid in the beginning, but that's all; no different to the time-shares and the bars. It's all just business. I don't get involved in any of it directly. Nothing for you to worry about, that's for sure.'

Mandi knew exactly what that meant but she had no intention of questioning him further. She loved her lifestyle with everything that it entailed, and she had no intention of jeopardising it. Never in a million years was she ever going back to Peckham and poverty, and if that meant burying her head in the sand then so be it.

It was a long and frustrating evening for Cathy that ended with Tim unhappily alone in Cathy's bed, Cathy wide-eyed and sick with fear in the spare bed in Sammy-Jo's room, and Peter smug on the sofa bed in the lounge.

Cathy made a lot of decisions as daylight dawned but then put them on hold. There was still the hearing to go through.

Saying goodbye to Sammy-Jo was the hardest thing, unsure of whether she would see her again that evening or not for maybe several years.

'If I do have to go away today, sweetheart, then Uncle Tim is going to take you on holiday to England.' She knew she couldn't be seen to cry or even be upset so she talked to the child in the bedroom with the shutters closed. 'You'll stay with Aunty Sheila and see the twins. You'll have a great time.'

'What about Daddy? Why can't I see Daddy? I miss him.'

'I know you miss him, I know you do, but we don't know where he is.'

'But if you go away as well then you might not come back. I won't have anybody.'

Cathy took the child by her shoulders and looked into her eyes, the familiar deep dark eyes that charmed everyone but were offset by the slightly mean-looking twist of her mouth. Again it hit her how much like Nico she was, both in looks and temperament.

'Jo, you will always have me, I promise you. Now I have to get ready to go out and you have to go to school so shoo, off to the bathroom!'

The laughing that followed completely disguised the tension that was rising in Cathy's chest and threatening to suffocate her.

Javier turned up right on time to collect Cathy, and Tim was going to follow in his hire car. Peter had long since made his way sheepishly back through the hedge and Cathy knew as he left that he would bow to his parents: he wouldn't turn up at the courthouse for Jilly.

Cathy had been dreading coming face to face with the other girls but she was totally unprepared for the vehemence of Jilly's attack as she and Hannah were brought into the room.

'You fucking little bitch,' she screamed for everyone to

hear. 'You could have helped me, you could fucking afford it. Do you know what it was like in that stinking hole? Do you? While you were swanning around we were rotting in a sweltering hovel.'

'I was under house arrest. I couldn't go out anywhere.'

With a screech Jilly made as if about to jump Cathy, but Hannah pulled her back, aware of the approaching policewoman with her baton drawn. Jilly was in a fighting mood, her face so close Cathy could feel her hot breath. 'House arrest? Oh, you poor baby . . . I shall make you pay for this. You wanted me locked up because of Peter O'fucking Brien but you'll be sorry. You watch your back because one day, Kit Carter, or whatever your name is, I'll pay you back.'

As Jilly suddenly lunged towards the bewildered Cathy all hell broke out. Javier pulled Cathy into a side room as Jilly and Hannah were dragged roughly back down to the cell. Tim just watched it all but he had heard, and taken in, every word.

Because of the fracas the hearing was held without any of them present, only magistrates and the legal eagles, and Cathy was taken down to the cells as well, although she was separated from the others.

Two long hours later they were taken up into the courtroom, the same formidable room as before but with a different, much older interpreter, than they had seen originally at the police station, who smiled encouragingly and promised to make sure they understood everything.

The words flowed fast and furious and before the interpreter could even start, the magistrates got up and left the room. Javier went straight over to Cathy.

'Case dismissed against you and also the others. Tara sent her lawyer to the court with a signed document taking full responsibility and confirming that no one else was involved.' He shook her hand. 'You are free to go, but first you must collect your passport.'

Cathy couldn't believe what she was hearing. It was all over. Or that was what she thought until Jilly came over, eyes ablaze with anger and frustration.

'Remember, you spoiled bitch, you're going to regret doing this to me, just remember that!'

Turning sharply on her heel she stormed out purposely, ignoring Cathy's voice behind her: 'But it wasn't my fault. I didn't do anything . . .'

Javier moved over and stood protectively between her and Jilly. 'She is angry. The prison is not a nice place and she has been there for many, many weeks but she will forget soon.'

Tim wasn't so convinced. 'Personally I think not. Cathy, don't you think you'd be safer back home? This is all a bit much here. I can't get my head around it. I feel as if I've been watching a film in glorious Technicolor – larger than life and very, very strange.'

Cathy smiled and flung her arms around his neck. 'Come on, let's get out of here. If I never see this place again it'll be too soon!'

Chapter Seventeen

'Good news, girls! Cathy has been rightly cleared and she should be on her way home soon to visit us all. She's even changed her mind about bringing Sammy-Jo. I can't wait to see them both.'

Sheila was at the house cooking dinner for Alison and Jane. She couldn't make up her mind whether they were actually improving or just learning how to disguise their illness a bit better.

'Haven't you got anything to say, either of you? You should be pleased it's all turned out right. Your sister could easily have been in big trouble.'

'Makes a change from getting us into it. Serves her right . . .'

'What did you say, Alison?'

'Nothing, nothing at all.'

Now Sheila was getting a little deaf the twins spitefully enjoyed speaking quietly to each other and often giggled behind the woman's back like two naughty children. Sheila knew they were doing it on purpose but at least they seemed to be improving, communicating a bit more, so she usually let it go.

'As I was saying, Cathy and Sammy-Jo will be visiting soon. They're coming home with Tim and they'll be staying here. I'll have to get Cathy's room ready.'

'They won't be staying here. This is our house and Cathy hasn't got a room any more. She's got her own money, she can go to a hotel. She's not staying here.'

This time Jane made sure she spoke loudly enough for Sheila to hear, looking at her sister for backup as she spoke.

Alison quickly joined in: 'She's given us enough trouble. Our doctor says it's all Cathy's fault that we've been ill – Cathy and that bastard she married.'

'That's right, he made us ill and it was Cathy's fault – all her fault.'

Sheila ignored the twins. She had spent too many hours trying to reason with Jane and Alison about the situation but they wouldn't listen. She was also sure the psychiatrist had said nothing of the sort but the twins only ever heard what they wanted to hear.

'As I said, Cathy will be home soon and Tim is with her. Oh, wouldn't it be nice if they could get together? Properly, I mean . . .'

'When will dinner be ready? We're starving.'

Sheila checked herself again. It took all her willpower lately not to fly off the handle with them. It was wearing her out doing everything in the house for them, her health was deteriorating, and they didn't care in the least. They sat around all day every day, sniping and sniggering as Sheila washed, cleaned and shopped and they didn't offer her a penny. If Cathy hadn't stepped in without even being asked then Sheila would have been on the breadline.

'When are you going to open the shop up again? It might do you good to have something to do, keep you busy . . . There's lots of people asking about you, wondering how you are.'

Alison and Jane carried on as if Sheila hadn't spoken; they muttered and mumbled to each other, low enough for Sheila not to hear a word.

Sheila raised her voice over theirs. 'So you're telling me that you don't want your sister and your little niece staying here? You don't want them even though they're desperate to see the both of you? Well, that's OK then, they can stay with me.' Sheila turned away from them. 'I'm ashamed of you both.'

The twins spluttered and laughed.

Sheila put their dinner in front of them and left the room to sort out her belongings. Sadly she accepted that it was time for her to move back home.

The phone was ringing in the distance and she waited for one of them to answer it but eventually she gave in and dragged her swollen ankles down the hall.

'Sheila? Hi, it's me! I'm just ringing to let you know we're booked on a flight out on Friday morning so we'll be there late afternoon . . . Sheila? . . . Is everything OK?'

'Cathy, I'm sorry but you know how difficult the twins can be. They don't want you to stay at the house, I'm afraid . . .'

Cathy erupted. 'Put one of them on the phone, self-centred cows. It's my home as well and I can stay there anytime I like.'

Sheila was desperate to smooth things over; she couldn't face the thought of any more bickering. 'They're not in at the moment. Look, Cathy, I'm moving back to my house tomorrow, why don't you stay there with me? Leave the twins be. They'll come round in time, once they see you and Sammy-Jo. They're better than they were.'

'Do you really think they are ever going to be well? They've been like it all their lives – why should it change now?'

Sheila knew she had to be truthful; Cathy would soon be back and would see for herself. 'No, I don't think they'll get much better than they are and you're right, they're the same as they always have been. Maybe you'll be able to talk to their doctor. He won't, can't, talk to me.' She stopped talking for a few seconds trying hard to gain control over the quiver in her voice. 'But enough for now . . . I can't wait to see you both. It'll be just like the old days when you used to come and stay with me.' Sheila hesitated; she wanted to ask the question but didn't really want the answer. 'Are you coming back for good?'

'I don't know. I'll decide when I get there. I still have to think of Sammy-Jo. I don't want her to have anything to do with Nico – ever.'

Nico wanted to close down the agency but keep the farm. He had it all planned out. The only uncertainty was how to deal with Paul. As soon as he got back from Thailand, Nico approached him carefully, ready to work his way up to the news.

'How did it go? Any new contacts?'

Paul's face shone, his eyes were bright and he was very fidgety from too many dubious substances and not enough sleep. 'Brilliant mate, fucking brilliant. I'm thinking of moving out there. I could still work for you but from there. How about it? An on-the-spot agent personally checking the merchandise . . . We could even diversify, give the Internet a go.'

Trying hard not to smile Nico pretended to hesitate. 'I don't know about that, Paul. How would it work? What's in it for me? I really need you here at the farm.'

'No problem, I've got it all sussed for you. My old cellmate is out soon and he needs to lay low. He can run the farm. He's OK is Damien. Believe it or not he was brought up on a huge farm so he can be legit on that side as well. *And,*' Paul paused for effect, 'he's got more contacts than you can shake a stick at, *and* he's a computer nerd – just think what we could do with that! Onwards and upwards, I reckon. The market is out there for anything we can get.'

Nico looked quizzically at the young man moving excitedly from foot to foot in front of him. '*Damien?* Is that for real? I didn't think anyone was really called Damien.'

'Yep, straight up – public school, university, the lot. Never pick him out in a million years. So with Damien on the farm with a few computers and me in Thailand with the real thing you could be a gentleman of leisure, just sit back and watch the profits roll in.'

Again Nico feigned indifference. 'I'll give it some thought but in the meantime we need to wind down the agency and transfer the equipment back to the farm. I'm off back to Hampshire soon. I'm going to be based there again, I think. I just need to find somewhere decent to live without any of the notoriously nosy neighbours. Sniff on one side of the Forest and they talk about it on the other.'

'Why go back then?'

Nico raised his thick eyebrows and drew his lips back over his teeth in a spiteful fake smile. 'I've got scores to settle. So many scores, so little time!'

Watching the sun set over the Mediterranean Sea in the distance, and savouring the scents of various plants that blended together to form an overpowering perfume in the air, Cathy decided she didn't want to go home for good.

Cathy loved the laid-back atmosphere and it was a good lifestyle for Sammy-Jo. The child was brown as a berry, spoke fluent Spanish and spent most of her days after school either in the pool or the sea. But more than anything, the child was healthy and content, and Cathy intended she should stay that way.

Tim hadn't been impressed when Cathy had insisted that they spend the last evening eating out with Mandi and Benny. He didn't like them but Cathy was certain that was more because they were Peter's parents than anything personal.

'Well? Have you decided yet what you're doing? If

you're coming back then you're welcome to carry on renting for another six months, but we're not selling, I'm afraid. We've discussed it and we're going to keep the villa for our Petey.' Mandi was pressing the point, wanting an answer.

Cathy decided, for Tim's sake, to be evasive. 'I'm not sure but I'll pay your rent up front anyway. I haven't got time right now to sort out all the stuff I've accumulated since I've been here.'

Feeling his eyes on her she deliberately didn't look at Tim.

'You are going to look Petey up when you get back, aren't you? He'd love to see you . . .'

Benny was all too aware of the expression on Tim's face so he intervened sharply. 'Give over, Mand. The girl's going to have enough to do when she gets back, sorting out her sisters and keeping out of that pervert's way—'

'What pervert?' Tim interrupted.

'That dirty paedophile she was married to, of course,' Mandi answered innocently, unaware that Tim didn't know the full story. 'Disgusting little child molester, should be castrated and locked up.'

Tim said nothing and Cathy still couldn't bring herself to look at him.

'I don't want to talk about that tonight,' she smiled brightly. 'Let's just have a nice evening together. I have so much to thank you both for – and Tim as well. I couldn't have chosen a nicer place to live, despite everything that happened!'

Smiling at each of them Cathy noticed the set of Tim's face and knew that she was going to have to tell him the whole story before they left for England.

'And we've loved having you here. You've been like a daughter to us – and little Jo as well, of course. She's turned into a great little kid. You're almost family now!'

After dinner and a long-drawn-out farewell, Cathy and Tim drove down to the beach, leaving Sammy-Jo with a tearful Anita.

'Family? Are you sure you want to be part of that family? They're a bit odd, the lot of them. Even the housekeeper looks like she's out of the Addams Family.'

'Maybe,' Cathy snapped as they walked along the beach for the last time, 'but isn't that what everyone used to say about the Carters? About all of us?'

'Mmm, I suppose so.' Tim pulled her hand and swung her round to face him. 'Truth be told, I suppose I'm just jealous – jealous of that smarmy Peter and jealous that you're so happy here. I really want you to hate it here and come home with me, to stay.'

Taking his face in both her hands Cathy kissed him hard, full on the lips. 'Peter is a friend, that's all, I promise. We had a bit of a fling once but that was all it was for both of us. Mandi and Benny? For all their faults they did their best for me, and I owe them big time for Javier. I was at an all-time low when I arrived here and they took me under their wing and turned everything around. For that I will always be indebted to them, and to you, of course!'

Tim shuffled his feet in the sand and looked down, concentrating on his toes.

'I don't want you to be indebted to me, Cathy, I want you to be in love with me, like I am with you – like I always have been.'

'But you don't really know me, not really . . .'

'I do know you. I might not know exactly what's happened to you but it makes no difference to how I feel. I want you and Sammy-Jo in England with me, but I'm not sure that's going to happen.' He still didn't look up at her, didn't see her smile.

'Let's take it one step at a time. Don't forget I'm still married to Nico. I have to deal with all that at some point.' She took his hand.

'Come on, let's go home. There's no silly Peter to interrupt us tonight!' Together they walked back to the car and drove home.

Nico was on yet another visit to his old territory in Hampshire, this time to put in an offer. He had found the ideal property to buy after a few trips back and forth from Devon – a large secluded house with no noticeable neighbours and two miles from the nearest village. It had taken all his willpower not to march into Simonie and Justin's office and slap the cash for a house on the desk but he knew that would raise their awareness of him. It had been quite a surprise when he was doing the rounds of the estate agents and had seen their name above the office, but despite his anger at their apparent success he had decided to bide his time for them.

With everything nearly signed and sealed he parked his car and wandered through the town, looking for a newsagent's to get some cigarettes. Standing impatiently in the queue of schoolchildren buying mountains of sweets and crisps he glanced at the papers on the rack beside him. He looked and then did a double take before grabbing the local paper off the shelf. The headlines jumped out at him: 'Local woman on drugs charge in Spain released.' The woman in the photograph taken outside the court was, without doubt, Cathy, and standing next to her, an arm protectively round her waist was Tim O'Connor.

Nico could feel his heart pounding as the excitement coursed through his veins. He had found her, and hopefully also his daughter. Then and there he knew what he was going to do. He took off almost at a run down the road until he came to the local travel agent. Throwing the door open he pushed to the front of the queue.

'I want to go to Marbella as soon as possible, preferably tonight. I'll pay whatever it takes.'

As the plane touched down at Heathrow Cathy felt a tremor of panic. Supposing Nico was still around? But everyone had assured her that he had disappeared, that he had moved away.

'I don't think I'm going to be able to stay in England, Tim. I'm frightened already and we haven't even got off the plane.'

Tim gripped her hand. 'There's nothing to worry

about any more. First thing tomorrow we'll go and see a solicitor and get some proper advice. You can't keep running away, you shouldn't have to.'

The previous night, Cathy had told Tim the whole story, everything bar a few gory details that she couldn't bring herself to put into words. He had listened open-mouthed. Despite being the same age as Cathy, Tim was still naïve in the ways of the world and he couldn't understand how anyone could be as depraved as Nico.

'Tim, there's lots like him. If you could have seen the steady stream of apparently respectable men that beat a path to Nico's door, prepared to pay a small fortune for the stuff he had to sell. Some looked the part, but others? You probably know some of them but you'd never guess. Child porn is big business across the spectrum and Nico is just a cog in the wheel that keeps it going.'

She had seen Tim was finding it hard to take on board and she'd hated having to tell him about it all.

'Why didn't you tell anyone? Why didn't you just go to the police?'

She'd hesitated, still protective of the twins, but she'd known that if she wanted to have a relationship with Tim then she had to be honest.

'Because of the twins. Because he convinced them that they would be sent to jail for the fire that killed Mum and Dad. They were terrified of being separated, terrified of being sent to jail. They believed him – still believe him, according to Sheila. That's why they cracked up. The pressure became too much for them. He blackmailed

337

them, Tim. They handed over a fortune. And now they hate me for it!'

That last night in Spain they'd slept fitfully, wrapped tightly around each other, despite the heat, each fearful, for different reasons, that it might be their last night together; neither with any idea what the future could hold for them.

Nico parked his car in the lane and walked up the gravel drive, tiptoeing so as not to make any noise. He rang the bell gently and waited out of sight of the spyhole. The second the door started to open he had his foot in it and pushed his way in.

'Hello, girls. Long time no see. It's your favourite brother-in-law, come to pay you a little visit.' He looked from one to the other, taking in the twins' terrified faces, and laughed. 'What's the matter? Not pleased to see me at the coven?'

With a flight to Spain booked for the next night Nico just couldn't resist paying a visit to the twins. He thought of them as a bit like puppets: he could pull their strings and make them dance to whatever tune he fancied.

Once again he held all the aces and he intended to use them, just as soon as he found Cathy and Sammy-Jo. There was no doubt in his mind that he was going to get Sammy-Jo and pay Cathy back tenfold.

Swaggering down the hallway he looked from side to side into every room.

'Not up to the normal standards of Aunty Sheila, I have to say. It all looks just a bit tacky. No self-respecting witch would call this a coven.'

Still they said nothing. They just watched as he sauntered around, following at a safe distance in silence. He made his way into the kitchen and nonchalantly looked out of the window at the vast expanse of garden.

On the wide window ledge, among the potted plants, his eagle eyes spotted a dog-eared little address book. He waited for a few seconds before running his hands over, pretending to check for dust while at the same time palming the book.

'Guess what, girls? I'm off to see your little sister tomorrow. I'm going to Spain. Do you think she'll be pleased to see me?' Putting his hand in his pocket and sliding the book inside, he suddenly found the silence disconcerting. Something was different but he couldn't figure out what. He turned sharply.

'Talk to me then, talk to Nico . . .'

His eyes didn't have time to register the carving knife before it was at his throat. Alison was in front of him as he turned, with Jane so close he could have counted her teeth.

'Hey, come on now, girls, there's no need for that. I'm only being friendly. I don't want anything. Come on, put that down, you'll get in trouble . . .'

Still they didn't speak but their faces were no longer frightened; they were frightening. Nico stood stock-still. He could see that they were both quite deranged.

The tableau was frozen in time – Alison with the knife, Jane close behind and Nico leaning back as they leered at him. No one said a word but the tension was palpable.

After several seconds that felt like hours Nico suddenly felt the knife move away from his throat, and his eyes followed it as Alison used it to point silently in the direction of the front door.

Nico put both his hands in the air. 'OK, OK, I'm going. Just put that thing away. It's dangerous.' Walking backwards down the hall, he tried to focus on the knife and both of them just in case Jane had one as well. Roughly Jane pushed past him and opened the door. Suddenly her fist reached out and hit him full on the jaw. He fell out of the door and it slammed shut behind him.

Stumbling back up the driveway all he could hear was the pair of them cackling with laughter. Nico had the feeling that he had come face to face with madness and it scared the life out of him. He had never tasted fear like it in his life, and when he got to his car he leaned on the bonnet, trying to stifle the nausea that was rising from his stomach. As he breathed deeply in and out and the fear faded, the anger took over. Anger that they had made him look foolish and anger at himself for not fighting back.

It wasn't until the next morning, as he was getting ready to leave for the airport, that he found the address book in his pocket, but it wasn't the twins', it was Sheila's.

The first number in Spain that he found rang and rang. He cursed the phone and was about to throw it across the room in his usual manner when he found a second Spanish number.

'Mandi O'Brien speaking.'

'Hi, I wanted to speak to Cathy. This is her solicitor in England.'

'Oh, you've got the wrong number, love. She doesn't live here, and anyway she's on holiday for a few weeks.'

'Of course. I completely forgot. I really need to speak to her urgently. You haven't got a contact number for her, have you?'

'I have somewhere, but if you're in England she'll probably be visiting you. That's where she is, seeing her family.'

'Right, I should have remembered that. I'll try her sisters' number. Thanks for your help. I'm sorry I disturbed you.

'Yeessss!' Nico punched the air. 'Gotcha, you bitches, every single one of you!'

Laughing and dancing round his hotel room, he tipped everything out of his case. He didn't have to go to Spain after all.

Chapter Eighteen

After three weeks of wet and windy weather, Cathy was itching to get back to Spain. The life she had previously enjoyed was suddenly claustrophobic. The closed-in houses and pubs governed by ridiculous licensing hours made her quite homesick for the free-and-easy way of life in Marbella. There she was Kit Carter, an independent young woman; in England she was still 'little Cathy'. She had grown up rapidly in her time away but no one seemed to recognise it.

'I can't get used to calling you Kit – it doesn't suit you – and as for "Jo", sounds like a boy's name to me.'

Sheila was stretched out in her decrepit favourite armchair with her swollen feet on a strangely pretty pink footstool. Her weight had ballooned so much that she had to lower herself down slowly and wedge herself in the chair, and once settled it was hard for her to move again without help.

Cathy reckoned she was probably creeping towards twenty-odd stone, and at little more than five foot tall, she was dangerously obese. The heating was turned up too high in the small room and as Sheila sweated profusely and her face reddened, Cathy feared for her health.

'I don't really care what I'm called but everyone in Spain calls me Kit and I quite like it. It's not so babyish as Cathy or rather, "little Cathy".' She smiled as she spoke but her eyes were focused on Sheila's heaving chest that moved up and down dramatically as she breathed.

'Sheila, I really think you should go to the doctor and I also think it's time you stopped running round after the twins. They don't appreciate it. Maybe without you constantly available they'd get their act together and you'd get some rest. It's just not fair on you and you'd still get paid. You've always done over and above.'

'I doubt it. You should have seen the state of the place last time. It was a hovel and no one else would have cleared it up unless the health people had come in! I don't want to do it but they won't have anyone else in. Anyway, I owe it to your mum and dad.'

'You don't owe them your health, that's for sure. Just go to the doctor; if not for yourself then go for me. In fact, I'm going to make an appointment and take you myself. Tomorrow. No argument!'

Cathy called out of the window, 'Jo? Where are you? It's time for dinner. Do you want to come to the fish and chip shop with me?' Opening the back door she looked all around and called again.

'I can't see her. I bet she's over with Tim and his horses again. She spends more time with him than she does with me lately. I'll give him a ring when I get back. It's nice that she gets on with him.' She looked over at Sheila for confirmation. 'They do seem to get on all right, don't they?'

Sheila smiled smugly. 'Of course they do. She's your daughter and I always knew you and Tim were right for each other!'

Grabbing her car keys Cathy planted a huge kiss on the top of the older woman's head. 'I love you, Sheila. I hereby nominate you my new mum!'

'Get away with you, you daft little thing. Go and get the dinner.' Sheila's eyes glazed over with sheer happiness.

Queuing up in the shop Cathy looked out of the window at the ponies wandering aimlessly about in the road, blissfully unaware of the traffic jam they were causing. Smiling she wondered vaguely if she ought to let Sammy-Jo have some proper riding lessons before they went back to Spain. She loved the ponies and even relished the really smelly mucking out that Cathy had never been able to stomach.

Almost subconsciously she saw an expensive car carefully negotiating the bend in the road. The driver hooted at the ponies, trying to make them move before impatiently driving round them, a bit too close for comfort. The car was big and silver and there was a child in the front. Cathy only caught a glimpse but the bewildered face looking, but not seeing, out of the passenger window in her direction seemed familiar. She watched the car as it drove away from her.

Sammy-Jo! By the time the thought registered, the car

had negotiated the animals and disappeared off down the main road.

Rushing out of the shop door, she peered into the distance but there was nothing left to see. The road was clear.

For a split second she wondered if she had imagined it, whether she was getting paranoid, but deep down she knew she wasn't. She knew the child was Sammy-Jo.

'Help me! I think someone has taken my daughter.' She shouted the words but no one knew what to do and before they could react she was tipping her handbag all over the floor of the shop. She couldn't believe she had left her mobile phone at home, the one Tim had got her specifically for such an emergency. Leaving everything spread where she dropped it, she grabbed her purse and ran to the phone box opposite.

'Sheila? Is Sammy-Jo with you? Has she come home yet? . . . Well, bloody well look! Phone Tim, I'll be back in five minutes . . . I think she's been taken . . .'

By the time she got back to Sheila's cottage the woman was in tears at the door and Tim was racing up and down the road like a madman.

'She wasn't with me, I haven't seen her. Tell me what's going on.'

Cathy was so hysterical she could barely get the words out. 'I saw a car, I think she was in it. It must be Nico, he's snatched her, just like I thought he would . . .'

Before she had finished the sentence Sheila groaned and clutched her chest, falling forwards on to the ground like a carelessly thrown sack of coal. She looked up at

Cathy for a split second before closing her eyes and slipping into unconsciousness, her lips turning blue as Cathy and Tim watched.

'Call an ambulance, she's having a fucking heart attack. Quick, do something, Tim, help her . . . Tim, what about Jo?' Cathy was beside herself, unable to decide what to do first.

Tim grabbed her arm so hard she could feel his fingers through her coat. 'First, keep calm. You stay with Sheila, try and keep her warm. I'll call 999 and then go and look for Sammy-Jo. She's probably just wandered off. I'll be back as soon as I find her. Look after Sheila. She looks really poorly.'

For as long as she could remember Cathy had had nothing to do with religion, but as she crouched shivering on the damp grass at the kerbside holding Sheila's hand, she found herself praying silently. 'Please, God, don't let him have her. Please, please, don't let Nico have her . . . Please let Sheila be all right. Please, don't let her die . . .'

As the ambulance pulled up, Tim reappeared, his face a picture of misery.

'Have you found her? What's happened?' As soon as Cathy saw the expression on his face she feared the worst. 'TELL ME!' she screamed at the top of her voice. 'Tell me what's happened, Tim. Tell me before I smash your fucking face in.'

'Nico has her. He's left a note and a package for you.'

Tim held out his hand and offered her the large padded envelope that she turned over and over in her hands, feeling what was inside the same way a child would, trying to guess a birthday present.

All the time the paramedics were conscientiously attaching breathing equipment and monitors to Sheila before transferring her on to a stretcher and then into the ambulance.

'We have to get a move on. Do either of you want to come in the ambulance with her?' The man looked at the pallid, almost vacant faces. 'We're going now . . . We have to get her to hospital as soon as possible.'

'You go, we'll follow as soon as we can.' Tim took Cathy by the arm and led her back down the path as the ambulance pulled away and raced off, lights and sirens full on.

The outside of the envelope was covered in Nico's instantly recognisable scrawl: 'I have my daughter. If you go to the police I shall show them, and everyone else, the video. Fit mother? Not! *Touché*. Nico.'

Without thinking, Cathy frantically tore open the envelope, pushed the videotape into the machine and pressed the play button. The screen flickered slightly and then suddenly, in full explicit colour Cathy could see herself, the star of a movie that left nothing to the imagination. Frozen to the spot she watched in horror for a few seconds before panicking and pushing all the buttons in an attempt to stop it. She looked at Tim but his face was still focused on the screen, expressionless and empty. He looked as if he had been zapped with a stun gun.

'He made me do it, I had to do it, it's not what you think, I had no choice . . .'

Tim's gaze moved in slow motion from the screen to

Cathy's face. 'I can't deal with this now,' he said. 'I'll go to the hospital. You call the police so they can start searching for Sammy-Jo. The sooner the better . . .'

'I can't call the police. Can you imagine what they would think if they saw that? He's her father, he's allowed to have her. There's nothing I can do, nothing I can do . . . nothing I can do . . .' Screaming and crying she started banging her head on the door frame, head-butting the woodwork harder and harder until she actually dented her forehead and ripped the skin.

As soon as he saw the blood trickling down into Cathy's eyes Tim visibly pulled himself together. Grabbing her, he wrapped his arms tightly around her from behind and pulled her away from the door. He held her so tightly she couldn't move, whispering in her ear quietly over and over again, 'It'll be OK, I promise, it'll be OK. We'll find her, I promise we'll find her, but you have to tell the police. You have to!'

Slowly the sobbing subsided and Cathy calmed enough for him to ease his hold. Her tiny body heaved as she gulped in air and tried to speak coherently. Carefully he led her over to the sofa and sat her down beside him.

'One of us has to go to the hospital, Sheila hasn't got anyone else. You go, Tim. I'll decide what to do. I have to speak to my sisters . . . Go on, I'll be OK. You go and see to Sheila.'

'I'm staying with you. I'll phone Mum – she's Sheila's best friend. She'll go to the hospital and she can let us know what's happening. Sheila would want us to look for

Sammy-Jo. Sheila's in the best place but Sammy-Jo could be in danger.'

Cathy's eyes were wide and wild as she tugged frantically at her hair the way she used to as a child. 'What are you saying? He's her father – he wouldn't hurt her. Tell me he wouldn't hurt her, not his own daughter . . .'

Tim's face would have told her he wasn't convinced but she was fortunately too distraught to notice so he tried gently to reassure her; there was no point in anything else.

'I'm sure he won't, but she's probably frightened. She hasn't seen him for . . .' he hesitated, 'how long? Well over a year? That's a long time for a child. He'll be a stranger to her. Now, please, call the police. It's the only way.'

'I can't. I just can't face having to show them . . .' she found it hard even to say the words, 'having to show them that, that *thing* . . . You do believe me, don't you? He made me do it. I was only sixteen, for Christ's sake. I didn't have a clue.'

'Who was that with you?'

'You stupid dumb bastard, it was Nico – clever, clever Nico with his face away from the camera. See what I mean? If you don't recognise him do you think the police will believe me? And if they catch up with him he'll deny it.'

'What about the stuff that Simonie and Justin have? You told me it was your insurance. Insurance isn't any damn good if you don't use it when you need it. Let's go and get it and then we'll decide what to do.'

Cathy looked closely at the young man sitting beside her, a young man who had probably never come across anything like it before in his life. She felt light years away from him.

'Tim, if you want to just walk away I'll understand. It's not fair on you – all this. You don't want me after what you've seen on that screen. It made me feel sick so God knows what it did to you. I saw the look on your face: you're disgusted with me.'

Tim put his arm around her. 'I was shocked, and yes, I was disgusted, but not at you. I've always wanted you, ever since I was six and you took on the role of my protector. I still want you and now it's my turn to protect you. And your daughter as well.' Kissing her lightly on the end of her nose, he stood up and pulled her with him. 'Now, no more nonsense. Let's go and see Simonie and Justin, and collect the insurance. I'll let them know we're coming.'

On their way in the car the mobile rang. Cathy answered it.

'That was your mum. Sheila *has* had a heart attack but she's holding on. She's critical but they're hopeful. Oh, Tim, this is all my fault. I've ruined so many lives with my stupidity. You all told me about Nico but I didn't listen.'

'It's not your fault, how many more times do I have to say it? Now we have to be positive to be any help to Sammy-Jo. Look, we're here . . .'

Swinging the car sharply off the road he hooted and Justin came running out of the house.

'I thought you were never going to get here. What's happening? What did the police say?'

Tim climbed quickly out of his Jeep. He fired a warning glance at Justin. 'We'll talk about it inside.'

Justin looked bewildered but took the hint. 'By the way, I'm sorry but can I ask you to be ever so quiet? Tamara's only just settled, just as it seemed like she was never going to stop crying ever again. We love her to bits but she's wearing us out.'

Cathy smiled weakly. 'I remember. When Sammy-Jo was tiny it was constant. Sometimes I almost hated her, but look at me now.' She tried and tried not to crumble but the pressure was too much, the tears built up until they overflowed but she stayed silent, terrified that if she let go again she wouldn't be able to stop.

Nico wasn't as happy as he had anticipated. The child hadn't been over the moon to see him – in fact she hadn't even recognised him at first, refusing even to acknowledge him, and then he had had almost to force her into the car, bribing her as he did so.

'Come on now, Sammy-Jo. Daddy's come all this way to see you. Now, let's just walk to my car and we'll go for a ride. I've got Smarties and Coke in the glove box.'

At nearly five Sammy-Jo was well versed in the 'stranger danger' routine, and although she vaguely recognised the man she was also aware that her mother didn't know where she was.

'I'm not allowed. Mummy's indoors. I'll go and get her—'

'Come on! We'll go for a burger – Mummy won't mind. She'll be pleased we're getting to know each other again. I tell you what, you get in the car and look for the sweets and then I'll go and see her for you. You can look after the car for me.'

As he took her hand he could feel the reluctance and that irritated him so he pulled her along faster than he had intended. As soon as she got into the car he did her seat belt up.

'Stay there, Sammy-Jo, I'm just going to give Mummy this present I brought for her. I can tell her where you are as well, then she won't worry.'

As he got out of the car he clicked the remote-control central locking.

He guessed that Sheila would be in the kitchen, as always; he had never even seen in the other rooms. The bloody woman seemed to live quite happily in the kitchen.

Creeping up towards the front door in the dusky early evening light, he pulled the hood of his waxed jacket up and kept his head down. Very softly he opened the unlocked porch door and left the parcel propped up against a small vase on the table in the corner. Running back to the car, he jumped in and raced off, not even noticing the terrified little face beside him that was suddenly aware of something being wrong but not sure what.

Mummy had told her that Daddy was not always very nice . . . that Daddy had disappeared . . . that Daddy was . . . She tried to rack her young brain to decide if she had done something naughty.

For Nico, getting Sammy-Jo had been so easy it had almost taken the fun out of it. The very first drive past Sheila's cottage had given him a glimpse of Cathy as she was getting out of her car with bags of shopping and Sammy-Jo. His daughter. The daughter that he had been deprived of, the daughter he was going to get back and have all to himself for the time being. Cathy was going to have to dig deep into her pockets if it was the last thing he ever did. He would have all the cards once again.

Humming happily, Nico had rushed back to his hotel and phoned Paul.

'You know that video you tarted up? The one of my beloved wife doing her stuff? Well, I need a copy and I need it urgently. Get it in the post to me Special Delivery tonight.'

Next day he had parked in a small clearing from where he had just about been able to see the cottage through the bushes and had stayed there most of the day, observing. He had been busy deciding the best way to get into the cottage and get Sammy-Jo when lo and behold he had spotted her on her own, playing on the grass verge. He had nearly had a seizure when, just as Sammy-Jo had got into his car, he'd caught sight of Cathy driving away, but she hadn't noticed them and the little girl hadn't seen her mother. Almost too easy for Nico Marcos, who loved a challenge.

Very soon he was getting irritated. He had driven as fast as he dared out of the Forest and up to the motorway. He wanted to get back to Devon as quickly as possible, but to try to cheer the child up he'd stopped at the services. Again he pretended to phone Cathy.

'It is all right for Sammy-Jo to come away with me, isn't it? Good. OK, I'll tell her . . .'

'I want to speak to Mummy. Let me speak to Mummy . . .'

'Sorry, sweetheart, it's a bad line. Mummy sends her love and says you're to be good and enjoy yourself. Now let's get something nice to eat, we've got a long drive ahead of us.'

'I want to go to the toilet . . .' The child was looking at him tearfully and he was shocked to see fear in her eyes.

Shit, he hadn't thought of that one. 'It's just over there. You go in and I'll wait outside. Don't talk to anyone or Mummy will be very, very cross. Hurry up now.'

He waited by the door as the tearful little girl made her way in. A couple of minutes passed, then another couple of minutes. Nico was starting to panic but eventually she walked out very slowly, looking at him suspiciously. She was a lot thinner than he remembered, and taller, and her long thick hair was not quite as dark. Her skinny arms were wrapped around her concave chest as she walked beside him, refusing his offer of a hand to hold.

'I'm cold. Why haven't I got any clothes with me?'

'Because we're going to buy you lots of new ones and take you to the hairdresser. You're going to have a lovely time. Daddy's got a farm . . .'

'Uncle Tim's got a farm as well, I help him look after his horse and feed his chickens. When we were in Spain

355

he stayed with us and I taught him Spanish so now he's going to teach me to ride.'

Nico could feel his blood pressure soaring; he had a terrible urge to slap Sammy-Jo around her smug little face. How could she mention that little shit in his presence? He was her father, for God's sake, not that jumped-up little boy Tim O'Connor.

'Well, I'm here so you're not going to need Uncle bloody Tim any more. Now we're going to the car and you're going to get in the back with the blanket and go to sleep. When you wake up we'll be at the farm.'

'I don't want to go to sleep, I don't want to go to your farm, I want Mummy. I want to go home.' The wail echoed across the car park and Nico had to catch her sharply as she backed away from him. He could see she was about to turn and flee.

'And which home's that, you spoiled little brat? The one in Spain that you ran away to? Or that poky little dolls' house that fat Sheila lives in? Or maybe the witches coven where your crazy aunts hang out?' He pulled her by the arm and dragged her to the car, aware that passers-by were watching. He smiled after a fashion, raising his eyebrows as if to say 'kids', and whispered at her through gritted teeth, 'Now just get in the back of the bloody car and go to sleep. If I hear another sound from you I'm going to smack you so hard . . .'

She didn't say another word but he could hear her sobbing under the blanket, sobbing and sobbing until she fell asleep.

It was a long tiring drive, despite the comfort of the

top-of-the-range saloon, and Nico knew Sammy-Jo was awake for a lot of the time but she never said a word and neither did he. The silence suited him. He really didn't want to listen to her grizzling and whining, and the child was too frightened to open her mouth.

He thought about that all the way back to Devon. It wasn't turning out like he had expected it to. Nico had anticipated her hurling herself at him in pleasure, thrilled to be going off with him, not constantly crying for her bitch of a mother. He was her father – she should be pleased to be with him. His romantic image of his long-lost daughter being delighted to run off on an adventure with him was rapidly fading.

'We're here, Sammy-Jo, we're at the farm. Come on, out you get.' Silently she sat up and looked around at the uncared for and isolated farmhouse in the middle of nowhere.

Almost immediately the front door flew open and Paul rushed out to greet them. As Sammy-Jo reluctantly got out of the car Paul went over to her and, smiling widely, ruffled her hair gently.

'Hello, beautiful. I bet you're tired and hungry after that stupid long drive. You come with Uncle Paul and I'll make you a real grown-up breakfast – eggs and bacon, sausage and tomato – then you can tell me all about yourself.' He held his hand out to her and she took it with a watery smile.

At that moment Nico suddenly realised exactly what he had done. He watched as they walked hand in hand towards the farmhouse and he could see, as clearly as if it was happening again, Paul walking into his beach house in Thailand with little girls and boys with the same easy smile and charming manner and a bag of sweets. Those children had smiled back as well at the beginning as Paul played at being Mr Friendly, but it hadn't been too long before they were screaming in agony as Paul satisfied his own particular sadistic urges.

As Nico raced in after them, Paul turned and grinned. 'What a gorgeous little daughter you have, Nico my man. Now this one really could be a model.' He turned back to Sammy-Jo. 'You and I are going to get on just fine, aren't we, little one? Your Uncle Paul will look after you while you're here.' Gently he stroked her hair and pushed it back off her face. 'Has anyone ever told you how beautiful you are?'

Sammy-Jo looked up at him, her eyes full of trust.

The thought of putting Sammy-Jo in such danger sickened Nico. He couldn't understand why he hadn't thought it all out a bit better, instead of jumping in on impulse . . . again. Naively he had thought that Paul wouldn't dare touch his daughter but he could see that he had underestimated the man. Paul was talking to Sammy-Jo in exactly the same way he talked to the children who had innocently walked through the agency doors. Many had walked out again untouched, but for the chosen few it had slowly but surely turned into a nightmare as Paul lured them and their mothers into his web.

Furiously Nico pulled Paul to one side.

'You lay one finger on my daughter and I'll kill you,

that's a promise. I'll kill you stone dead without a second thought. She is mine.'

Paul laughed; his eyes wrinkled humorously, making him look friendly and approachable to the unknowing. 'Oh, and there was me thinking you'd brought me a present!'

Nico felt the cold grip of fear and suddenly he regretted snatching the child but it was too late. Now he had Sammy-Jo he couldn't just admit defeat and take her back to her whore of a mother and her boyfriend; he had to follow it through. If she went back, then it was going to be in exchange for a large dollop of cash from that trust fund that Cathy had filched from under his nose.

But he also knew he would have to watch her every minute of the day when Paul was around.

Cathy was getting angry as her friends bombarded her with advice. She had a slight niggle in the back of her head that Justin and Simonie had their own axe to grind with Nico, as had the twins and even Tim. She knew that she needed neutral advice from someone who didn't know her or Nico.

'I'm going to see a solicitor in the morning, I've decided, not the police.'

'Cathy, you can't. You have to tell the police. There's no alternative. They've seen this sort of thing loads of times. They're not going to judge you. He needs locking up, punishing.'

'Oh right. OK. Let's take it from the top. I starred in a porno film at sixteen, I left my husband on the day my inheritance was due and ran off to Spain with his daughter and the money. I was arrested on drugs charges, my sisters are the local mad witches who, deliberately or not, with or without my help, torched the family home and killed two people. Oh yes, and I'm a Vietnamese orphan. I'm sure they're going to try really hard to find Nico and Sammy-Jo . . . and if they do, then *what* will they find? They'll find Nico Marcos, the smooth, charming businessman, who could talk his way out of everything.' Cathy looked round at the faces of the three silently listening. 'They'll probably even decide she's better off with him. Even the twins have said they won't co-operate, they don't give a shit about all this. All Jane said was, "Serves you right." Selfish cows – and would the police listen to them if they do decide to help me? Not a chance.'

'But, Cathy love—'

'Don't Cathy love me. Why do you all want to treat me like I'm still a child? Little Cathy died the day she got married. I know you mean well but you're not going to railroad me, any of you. On this I'm going to make my own decisions.'

Suddenly Justin and Simonie's baby started crying. The kittenlike mewing that started gently and then gradually got louder echoed eerily through the baby monitor on the wall. Cathy looked at her friend, her eyes ringed black from lack of sleep and her hair lank and tied back. The guilt washed over her like a bowl of ice-cold water. Cathy jumped up out of her chair like a scalded cat.

'Simonie, you go and see to Tamara. We shouldn't have come and laid this on you. If I can just have the bag of documents then we'll be off. You've got more than enough on your hands.'

'Don't be silly.' Justin was up from his chair. 'We want to help.'

'I know you do but all we're doing at the moment is going round in circles. I have to deal with this myself. Just do one thing for me, please. As far as anyone else is concerned, Sammy-Jo has gone to stay with friends for a few days, OK? Just leave it at that for the time being.'

Sheepishly Tim stood up as well, looking apologetically at the couple. 'I'll phone you tomorrow, let you know what's happening.'

As soon as the car pulled away Cathy dissolved, clutching the bag of documents tightly to her. 'I'm sorry, but I couldn't listen to the baby crying, I just couldn't. All I want to do is to go home and sort through all this. There might just be some clue in there as to where he might be.'

Tim concentrated on the road in front of him. 'I think you should go and see the twins face to face. They'll come round, I'm sure they will.'

'They won't – anything that remotely suggests the police sends them off. Nico planted the seed in their minds and now it's a full-grown tree eating through their disturbed brains. He's clever, I have to give him that. He managed to find their weak spot.'

Tim gripped the wheel. 'No, Cathy, he's not clever, he's evil, pure evil. There's no other explanation for how he is and I hate him.'

361

★ ★ ★

Dominic Bingham was working his way towards retirement. After forty years the legal profession bored him, the everyday crud of divorces, wedded disputes and wills reminded him constantly of his self-perceived failure. Despite his age and experience he was still only a junior partner with his name last on the sign over the door. His late wife had always told him it was because he was too nice, too kind and that to be a high-flying legal eagle an inbuilt ruthlessness was essential, and he just didn't have it. She had also said that she loved him for it.

After she died he had been very lonely and had occasionally taken solace in comparatively mild pornography – nothing too heavy, just the male/female explicit kind that was readily available. But on one occasion he had bought a film from under the counter of a sex shop in Soho and had nearly gone into shock when he'd viewed it.

It had started out as the usual stuff he was used to, but halfway through it looked as if it had been accidentally, or maybe carelessly, over-recorded, and the faces of the young children in the short section haunted him. Paedophilia at its worst had jumped off the screen into his living room and hit him full speed in the solar plexus. He desperately wanted to do something but he was trapped. He couldn't take it back, he couldn't take it to the police, all he could do was have bad dreams about it.

The day Cathy went into his office at random to seek advice about her husband was the day he decided fate had taken a hand. He took up his crusade. He decided his legal swan song would be to help nail at least one of the bastard perpetrators of the filth that was circulating, and from what he had heard about him, Nico would fit the bill nicely. He knew just the man to help him. As soon as Cathy had left his office, Dominic picked up the phone and dialled the number.

'Hello, Jack? I need your help. I've got a job that's right up your street. Does the name Nico Marcos mean anything to you?'

Chapter Nineteen

'Get us a drink, darlin', and if you're really good and show us your tits you can have one yerself.' The young man in the beer-sodden football shirt was leaning on the bar, leering down her cleavage.

Jilly Holden gritted her teeth. She had been on her feet behind the bar for seven solid hours and was still trying to serve several customers at once. The group of mouthy young lads were barely more than teenagers and they were all semi-paralytic.

'Come on, sweetheart, smile, it might never 'appen. Come back to my hotel room and I'll cheer you up. My nickname's shaggy, you know.'

'That's right. If it moves, shag it – that's his motto.'

'Line 'em up, gorgeous, before he drags you off round the back for a quickie.'

Putting her elbows slowly on the bar Jilly leaned forward seductively. All of them gazed at her 'in and up' breasts.

'Read my lips, boys. Fuck off, all of you. I don't play

with little boys, especially little boys who can't hold their booze.' She snarled the words, knowing that if Del heard her he'd go ape.

'Wwooohh,' the three main offenders jeered and laughed as she flounced off to the other end of the bar.

Jilly hated it in Del's Bar. It represented everything she hated about the other side of life in Marbella, but it was better than nothing, better than having to go back home to England with her tail between her legs instead of a millionaire on her arm.

The small airless bar with its Union Jacks, karaoke machine and satellite television was filled to overflowing with drunken British yobs who were preprogrammed by the licensing hours back home. After several more drinking hours than usual spent pigging out on local beer washed down with cheap brandy chasers, they were ready to fight or throw up and fall over – quite often both. But Del had offered her a job when no one else had wanted to know.

Jilly Holden bore a grudge against Cathy that was so big it gnawed at her. With convenient blindness she blamed Cathy for all her ills.

When the court case had finished and she was released, Jilly had expected to carry on with her life as before, but she had soon found out that mud sticks, and in a place like Marbella, with its own secrets, the last thing the community wanted was a police interest. Suddenly, not only was she *persona non grata* among the very people she wanted to be in with, but she had no job and nowhere to live.

Even worse, Peter O'Brien had cut her dead when he was visiting his parents – on Daddy's orders, no doubt, but that didn't matter to Jilly. All that mattered was that he didn't want to know.

Benny O'Brien's business dealings were quite diverse. Among many other things he had an interest in the lap-dancing club, his property management included the villa the girls had rented, and he was Peter's father. Jilly was out in the cold on all fronts and for that she blamed Cathy. If Cathy had paid her bail then she would have been OK. People would have accepted her innocence the same as they had accepted Cathy's, but a spell in jail had cast a cloud and put her at the top of the unwelcome list, while the inscrutable Cathy had managed to come out of it shining white. Smarmy, sweet and dainty, independently wealthy and orientally attractive, everyone loved her, including, no doubt, Peter O'Brien.

'All right, girl? I know you're pissed off with your fall from grace but smile, please. Your face is putting the punters off.'

Del put his arm round Jilly's shoulder and much as she wanted to shrug it off she couldn't, not without offending him. The job and the accompanying poky flat was all that was on offer so she had to make the best of it for the time being. She had other plans but they would take a while.

'Sorry, Del, but those little pissheads give the Brits a bad name. I don't know why they don't just go to their local holiday camp for a fortnight. They could drink themselves into a stupor there and save the air fare.'

'And if they did, I'd soon be out of business. Now

367

don't be so snooty. It's horses for courses in this business and they're the clientele that pay for us to live and laugh in the sun, so smile please and get serving if you want to get any kip tonight.'

Jilly smiled at Del, the same fixed smile that she learned to turn on like a light bulb when she had been writhing ecstatically around an inanimate and very boring pole.

'Sorry, Del, I am grateful to you, really. You've done me a big favour and I don't know what I'd have done without you – probably ended up on the beach. I'll get back to work and smile at the bastards. I'll even shine like the star of Bethlehem if that's what you want.'

'That's what I like to hear.' He patted her Lycra-clad bottom and smiled appreciatively as she wiggled back to the front line, to a chorus of drunken cheers.

Del Warren was a bit of a wide boy who had jumped at the chance of voluntary redundancy from the monotony of the ailing steel works back home, conveniently forgotten to tell his wife of twenty-five years about it, and taken off to the Costa del Sol. He had always fancied the idea of a bar in Spain so took a chance and bought a run-down place off the main street in Marbella and turned it into a little bit of Britain. The lager louts loved it and he loved them. They drank themselves into oblivion and were blissfully unaware of the jacked-up prices that took effect around midnight when they were too out of it to notice.

Often Del had a bit of an after-hours gents' party that catered for a select few of his friends and went a little bit further, pulling in a bit more cash to be stashed away from the ice-cold but beautiful Birgitte. Altogether it had bought him a fairly nice villa outside of town and a Danish girlfriend who looked good but disinterestedly spent all her days on the beach topping up her tan or shopping with his credit cards. He knew he had to dump her but not until there was someone else to replace her. On the surface Jilly Holden looked as if she might fit the bill.

'Jilly!' Del's voice roared over the loud music. 'Got a sec?'

She finished serving and went over to him. 'What now?' Her voice was tired and resigned. 'Don't give me another bollocking, Del. I'm pretty well done in. Your star of Bethlehem is about to fall out of the sky.'

'I know, but I just wondered if you'd help out at my gentlemen's night tonight? I'll make it worth your while. Natasha's just phoned. She's leaving me in the lurch: she's off to sea tonight on a yacht or, more likely, a beautiful pea-green boat. I know you don't like the blueys but all you've got to do is look the other way and keep the drinks flowing. I'm closing up now and then the lads will come in round the back.'

Jilly's face dropped like a stone. 'Oh, Del, can't you do it tomorrow instead?'

He shook his head. 'Sorry. Now or never. It's worth double pay and an extra night off . . . please? I'm in a bit of a spot.'

Pouting and holding his hands together as if in prayer, he looked at her wide-eyed. With his slicked-back Elvis hair and shiny clothes and a medallion round his neck the size of a tin lid he always looked as if he was about to burst into song. He was nicknamed the karaoke king of Marbella and was always first up to sing on the pretext of encouraging the punters.

She smiled, knowing she wouldn't turn him down. 'Throw in a bottle of Jack Daniel's and you're on.'

Jilly was on autopilot. The drinks were flowing and the till was ringing as the dozen or so men tipped spirits down their necks and shouted insults at the large television screen. She could hear the grunts and groans of the soundtracks but she couldn't even be bothered to look up. They bored her and, anyway, it was 4 a.m. Del's 'gentlemen's nights' often went on until the early hours.

Dragging a stool round to the back of the bar where she couldn't see the screen, Jilly slid on to it gratefully and pulled an old magazine out from under the counter. It had been a long night and she was struggling to stay awake.

Suddenly the whooping and jeering stopped.

'Fuck me, Del, we don't want to watch that. It's kids . . .'

'Bloody hell, they've done their party piece, taped over and left the last bit. Christ, that's a bit off, isn't it?'

'Hang on,' a voice echoed into Jilly's aching head, 'that's that Kit Carter, isn't it? You know, the Chinese bird that hangs around with Benny and Mand O'Brien . . .'

As she jumped down and shot to the other side of the room, she caught a glimpse of Cathy just before Del clicked the machine off.

'No, that wasn't her. Sorry to disappoint you, lads!' Jilly was instantly wide awake and plotting. All she had to do was get her hands on Del's video tape and watch it properly.

'It was Kit Carter. I'd swear to it.'

'Don't be so stupid, Bas. If anyone knows her it's me, remember? And it isn't – just looks like her. Now come on, who wants a top-up?'

Her spirits soared. She feigned disinterest as Del switched everything off but her eyes were following him. She had to get the video. The O'Briens could put that in their sniffy pipe and smoke it. Their precious little prospective daughter-in-law was a porn queen. No wonder she had so much money.

Jilly Holden was as happy as the proverbial dog with two tails, three even. The image of pound signs and the concept of revenge were alternating in her head.

Cathy was racing down the hall, nearly tripping over the carpet runner.

Every knock on the door, every ring on the phone sent her into a frenzy of expectation. She couldn't believe that Nico wouldn't be in contact, although deep down she expected it to be a while; she knew he would have to punish her first.

Opening the door, she was stunned to be confronted by a smiling Peter O'Brien.

'Hello there. I thought I'd take a drive in the country, and look where I've ended up!'

'Peter! How did you know I was here?' She looked at him as if he was an apparition that she couldn't quite make out.

'Well,' he stated dramatically, 'I went to your home address. I was planning to surprise you and, lo and behold, I met your sisters! They sent me in this direction in no uncertain terms, the second word they used being "off"! Right pair of charmers, those two – unlike their little sister.'

Cathy tried to smile but found it impossible.

Peter raised one eyebrow. 'Well? I've driven all the way from London, don't I even get invited in?'

Cathy moved back and gestured him into the hall. 'Sorry, I'm a bit distracted at the moment. Sheila – this is her cottage – is in hospital. She had a heart attack.'

'Where's Jo?' He looked all around as he walked through in the direction Cathy was indicating.

'She's not here, why? What's it to you?'

Peter smiled widely, his straight white teeth, which had cost his parents a small fortune in orthodontists' bills, gleaming alarmingly. 'Oh dear, touchy, touchy. It was only a polite question.' He looked at her clearly for the first time. The sallow skin and dark-edged eyes were not what he was used to seeing on the effervescent Kit Carter. 'Hey, whatever's wrong? You look awful. What's been happening to you?'

Suddenly Peter found himself on the horns of a dilemma. He had been dispatched in person by his parents to warn Cathy about the video circulating selectively around Marbella.

Jilly Holden, once she had got her hands on it, had made sure that it was common knowledge and those that hadn't seen it had definitely heard about it. He also had to warn her that Jilly had been asking about to find out Cathy's address in England.

Mandi and Benny knew all about Nico and his dubious habits, but had found it difficult to stick up for Cathy without breaking her confidence. Peter, in person, to break it to her gently, had seemed the kindest way to alert her, but he could see there was something desperately wrong. He wondered if she knew about the video already.

'Tell me, Kit. I know you, I know there's something wrong – tell me!'

She looked at him and he could see she was thinking about it. Her eyes were moving all over the place and her hands were clenching and unclenching almost in rhythm.

'I can't . . .'

'Yes you can.' He reached out to her but she shrank back, almost in fear. 'We're friends, aren't we? Come on, come and sit down and tell me what's wrong.'

Cathy looked away as she spoke. 'Nico's got Sammy-Jo. He took her three weeks ago and I haven't heard anything.' Her voice was a monotone, belying the enormity of her statement.

'Oh Christ, Kit, I'm so sorry, I had no idea . . .'

'No one knows except immediate family, and, of course, Tim. That's when Sheila had the heart attack. It was the shock.'

'What about the police? What have they said? Have they got any leads on where he might be?'

'I can't go to the police. Nico has a video of me that he threatens to make public if I do . . .'

Peter was torn. He didn't want to lay any more bad news on her but in a way it could also be good news. If Nico was already circulating the film then Cathy would have nothing to lose. As he was chewing it over the back door opened and Tim came in with a flourish and looked directly at Peter, his eyes saying far more than words ever could.

'I saw a strange car outside but I certainly never expected it to be you. What brings you down from the bright lights of London to our gentle neck of the woods?' The antagonism in his voice was certainly not disguised as he stared aggressively at his perceived adversary.

Peter was determined not to bite; he could see how upset Cathy was.

'Just called by to say hi. That's not a problem, is it? I didn't intend to intrude.'

Tim continued to glare. 'Well, you are intruding, actually. It's really not a good time so it might be better if you leave. Cathy's not up to it.'

Cathy shook her head slightly as if to clear it, almost as if she had heard the conversation on time-delay.

'Excuse me, Tim, but I'm not mentally incapable. I can make my own decisions. Peter is a friend of mine and is welcome here any time. Now I'm going to put the kettle on and make a drink for *all* of us.' She looked from one to the other. 'Peter, tell me about your visit to the twins. I do know they're both quite mad but they used to have some manners . . . not many, but some.'

Her watery smile affected him deeply but he had no intention of showing it in front of Tim.

Peter took a deep breath. Relaxed, he smiled again. 'God, but they're scary, those two. I felt as if I'd taken a wrong turn and ended up in the depths of spooky Transylvania. Honestly, I was genuinely frightened, and when the two black cats started rubbing round my ankles, well, Devil's kitchen nothing, I was out of there like the proverbial bat out of hell . . .'

For the first time in weeks Cathy laughed. Peter always could tell a good story.

Tim looked at Cathy, the scowl still painted on his face. 'I've got to get back to work now – are you going to be all right on your own?'

Peter controlled his expression. 'It's OK, Tim, I'm not here to rape and pillage, just to say hello. Kit's perfectly safe with me.'

'Her name's not Kit, it's Cathy!'

The slamming of the door reverberated around the small room.

'Well, I never! What exactly is your friend's problem?'

Cathy was embarrassed. 'There's been a lot going on. He's stressed out at the moment; it's all getting to him.'

Peter wagged his finger in front of her. 'Now, now, no porkie pies to Petey. Tim's behaving like an adolescent with a crush who doesn't get out much. I was like that at about twelve years old! If anyone is stressed out it's you, but you're managing to be civil.'

'Yes, well, we're all different. Now tell me what you're doing here? The New Forest is hardly on your doorstep.'

Another deep breath! 'Well, can you take another shock? And it is a shock, a not very nice shock but . . .' he paused and looked her straight in the eye, 'after what you've told me it may just be of help to you.'

Peter told her all about the video Jilly was circulating.

Cathy's screech could probably have been heard half-way down the road. 'She did what? How could she? How could she do that to anyone? Fucking bitch!'

'I know, I know, she's really blown it for herself now, but Mum and Dad weren't sure what to do and they didn't want to tell you over the phone, so here I am. They're sticking up for you as best they can but without telling the whole story . . . Well, you can imagine some of the old buggers out there.'

'Bloody hell, Peter, just what else can go wrong? It's one thing after another. Why is Jilly doing it?'

He gave her an old-fashioned look. 'Because she blames you for everything that happened to her and, as she's after finding you, I think she probably sees the video tape as a cash cow. But that's all by the by. Now you've got nothing to lose by going to the police about Nico and your daughter. The video's in the public arena already!'

Like a punch in the stomach all the implications hit her. 'Have you seen it? Did she show it to you?'

'She tried but I gave her her marching orders. I also tried to get my hands on it but she's too clever for that. There's a copy locked away, or so she says.'

'Peter, what shall I do? Tell me what to do.'

'For starters I suggest you don't tell Tim. I'm not being funny but he's too protective to be constructive. Talk to your solicitor and see what he suggests. Also, I know you're up to your eyes in it but give Mum and Dad a ring. They think the world of you and if they can help they will. Dad has contacts, maybe he can help with the search for Jo, unofficially, of course.'

Cathy didn't answer. She could feel the tears starting up again despite feeling all cried out.

'Hey!' Peter smiled at her. 'Don't you give up. Listen, I've booked into The Stag for three nights. I don't have to go back to London until Monday so I'm here to help, yeah? Let me know if I can do anything. I intended to turn this trip into a bit of a holiday but with the news about Jo . . .' He pulled her close and hugged her, a great big bear hug that completely enveloped her. 'Anything you want, anything at all . . .'

'Good afternoon, Mrs Marcos. Take a seat. And this is . . .?' Dominic Bingham smiled questioningly.

'This is Peter O'Brien, a good friend of mine from Spain, but he lives in London some of the time. He's visiting with both good and bad news. But tell me, have you had a chance to go through all the documents I left with you? Were there any clues there? Have you any idea where Sammy-Jo might be?'

The man laughed and held up his hands. 'Whoa, hold up there. One thing at a time. Yes, I have been through the papers and yes, there may be some clues there but I have to sift a lot more thoroughly. No, I don't have any information about your daughter, I'm sorry to say. Now tell me your news, calmly and slowly so that I can make notes and you can catch your breath.'

Taking Peter's advice, Cathy had rung Dominic, and got an appointment for that afternoon. And, despite feeling guilty about doing it, she took Peter with her. She hated the idea of not being completely honest with Tim but the more she thought about it the more she realised Peter was right – Tim was getting over-possessive, and Cathy knew she didn't need that sort of pressure. She needed support and that was what Peter was offering. She couldn't believe that in the midst of all the trauma Peter had actually been able to make her laugh!

As she updated Dominic about Jilly and the video she could feel herself relaxing fractionally. Now it was all in the open, there was nothing left to hide and she could concentrate on finding Sammy-Jo by whatever means.

'Mrs Marcos, the decision whether or not to go to the police is entirely in your hands. The evidence I have here, that I've admittedly only looked at superficially, isn't actually an awful lot. Mr Marcos could get round most of it, I suspect, as he is her father, as there are no orders for custody in place, and as, on the surface, he can claim you are an unfit mother. As for blackmail, Mr Marcos can easily claim that the money from your sisters was a family gift. I don't think they will be able to do very much.'

Cathy was visibly collapsing in front of him and he felt deeply sorry for her. Sometimes he had to act for clients he disliked and despised, clients he knew were lying, but Cathy Marcos was different. He believed every word she said and he was even beginning to fear for the child himself. He smiled as he continued, trying his best to reassure her just a little.

'However, I do know an excellent private detective who used to be in the police force on the vice squad, and who is prepared to help. His name is Jack Bayliss and he's brilliant, I promise you! Lots of good contacts. If you agree I'll hand the papers et cetera over to him and he'll go through them with a fine-tooth comb. Think about what you want to do and let me know.'

'I don't have to think, I'll do anything it takes. I'd like to meet him.'

When they left Dominic Bingham's office Peter was ready to drive Cathy back to the cottage but on a whim she directed him to the big house, the Carter family home. Marching up to the front door with a reluctant Peter in tow, she rang the bell and knocked on the door at the same time. There was no reply.

'Come on, I know you're in there. Now open the bloody door or I'll break it in.' Cathy was screaming through the letter box, and when the twins didn't reply she grabbed her mobile phone out of her coat pocket and dialled the number, whispering to Peter, 'They're too unworldly to think it's me . . .' one of them answered and Cathy bellowed down the phone at her, 'You've got five seconds to open the door or I'll get the police to do it.'

The door opened and two sullen faces looked out. 'There's no need to threaten us, you know.' Looking over Cathy's shoulder, they spotted Peter.

'Who's that?' Their terror was apparent as they shrank

back, trying unsuccessfully to hide behind the door together. 'He was here earlier – what does he want?'

'It's OK, he's a friend. Now we're both coming in to talk to you so let's have no more nonsense and certainly no bad language. I'm getting sick of you two showing me up.'

Cathy could see Peter's chin starting to dimple as he tried to smile.

'Now this is Peter – he's a friend of mine from Spain and he's helping me – I want you to do something for me, but it's something you'll enjoy, I'm sure!'

They were both silent and both suspicious but Cathy marched inside with Peter in tow.

'Someone else might come here looking for me. Now I know you sent Peter away with a flea in his ear but that's not what I want you to do. If a very attractive young woman called Jilly Holden turns up here asking about me then I want you to invite her in and then scare the shit out of her, and then keep her here. Then call me. OK?'

'Why should we?'

'Because I'm fed up with always giving. Give, give, give, and I never get anything back. It's time you gave me a bit of support in all this. You've been no fucking help to me so far—'

'We have been. We scared the shit out of bastard Nico. He thought we were going to slit his throat with the carving knife.' Jane and Alison giggled in unison.

Cathy could feel herself starting to palpitate. 'Well, I don't want you to go that far with Jilly but she needs a good fright and I know you're the best ones to do it. Now

I'm going into the kitchen, I'm going to make a drink and then we're all going to sit down together and be civilised for a little while before you come with me to visit Sheila in hospital, got it? Good. Now be nice to Peter while I'm out of the room.'

Peter sat on the opposite side of the vast lounge, looking far more relaxed than he felt as two pairs of eyes drilled into him. The silence in the room was deafening.

'Well, Jane and Alison, isn't it? It's nice to meet you properly. I've heard all about you. Kit, I mean Cathy, is very fond of you.'

Their humourless laugh grated on his nerves but he smiled regardless, despite their lack of communication.

'That Nico's a bit of a shit by the sound of it – made everyone's life a misery from what I can gather.' There was still no response but he was determined to get through. 'Cathy is distraught about him taking Sammy-Jo and we're trying to track them down. You haven't any ideas, have you? Imagine you'd both like to see him dealt with, mmm?'

'Bastard, I wish we had slit his throat. Is Cathy really fond of us? We thought she hated us.'

Peter turned on his conciliatory voice. 'God no, she gets a bit frustrated with you both but she loves you to bits.'

'Devon!' Jane spat the word out.

'What about Devon?'

'Just Devon. Try Devon.'

'What makes you say Devon?'

'We're psychics, you arsehole!'

Cathy came back into the room with a tray just as Alison snarled the word.

'Are you insulting Peter? I said no bad language.'

Peter smiled at each of the three of them in turn. 'Your sisters reckon Nico has some connection with Devon – know anything about it?'

'No, what makes you say that?' Puzzled, she looked at her sisters.

Peter answered quickly, 'Because they're psychics; they know these things.'

Cathy was beside herself with frustration. 'Don't talk that crap. It's not fair in this situation. I'm desperate—'

Alison interrupted her sharply. 'See? That's why we never tell you anything. They're in Devon, in the country. Nico and Sammy-Jo together. And there's someone else with them.' Their staccato speech faltered for a few seconds as they both looked puzzled. 'This Peter fellow is right for you. You have to marry him!'

Peter and Cathy had both reddened, neither looking at the other.

The twins had eventually conceded ungracefully and they had all tripped into the hospital to see a delighted Sheila.

After she and Peter had dropped the twins off home, Cathy confided, 'See? I told you they were both barking.'

'You should have an open mind on these things. You know, even the police use psychics when they've run out of other options. Think about Devon. Even if it's something they heard and didn't realise, they seemed positive.'

'Maybe. I'll mention it to Dominic but I'm sure he'll think I've lost the plot.'

Neither of them mentioned the other insight the sisters had revealed.

Cathy didn't tell Tim any of it and afterwards she wondered if that was a bad omen for their relationship. She thought about what the twins had said about Peter. Absolute bullshit, she told herself. Peter was just a friend.

Chapter Twenty

Nico was in a quandary. Virtually housebound on the farm because he knew he had to watch his daughter constantly, he was going crazy. He didn't dare take her far in case they were spotted. Despite checking the newspapers and watching the news he wasn't totally sure Cathy hadn't gone to the police. His gut instinct was to protect his daughter and deep down he knew that the best way to do that would be to take her home to Cathy. Paul on his own was bad enough but Paul together with his friend Damien was Nico's worst nightmare. It was made worse because Sammy-Jo adored the two young men who played with her, made her laugh and treated her like a princess, but was one hundred per cent wary of her father. Even the presence of Tracy as unofficial child-minder didn't ease Nico's concerns: she was young and vulnerable herself.

Nico was backed into a corner and he knew it. He knew he shouldn't have Sammy-Jo in the same vicinity as Paul and Damien but his ego wouldn't let him take her back. Not without some face-saving exercise.

After considerable thought he picked up the phone and made his first call.

'It's Nico. If you want Sammy-Jo back then the package includes me as well and a substantial cash reward. Think about it.'

He spoke quickly and quietly, then put the phone back on to its base before Cathy even had time to speak.

'Sammy-Jo? Where are you? Come on, we're going into town for some shopping . . .'

Nico wanted to get away from the farm and the local shops were safe enough.

Sullen-faced, the child appeared in the doorway, keeping herself distant from her father.

'I want to stay with Paul and Tracy, I don't want to come with you. Paul is going to take me to get a pony – a Dartmoor pony, he said – and then I can ride again, like I did with Uncle Tim.'

Nico felt everything closing in on him. Paul and Damien were, on the surface, behaving themselves but he knew from experience that wouldn't last long. Their insatiable appetites for child sex could only be contained for short periods of time.

Nico couldn't be bothered to argue with the child – she never took any notice of him anyway – but he knew he had to get away from the atmosphere for a short time at least. The farmhouse was a rambling decrepit old building that hadn't had any maintenance done on it for donkey's years but it had a certain charm despite the dubious plumbing and wiring and the lack of modern appliances. It was also surrounded by acres of land; nothing was produced but Damien and Paul occasionally tidied up the fields to avoid raising the interest of the local farmers. Nico had often thought about doing it up and living there permanently but without Paul! He had let the new property in Hampshire go, and now the farmhouse was his only base.

Nico wanted out of the business completely. It had all got out of control and it had taken Sammy-Jo to make him realise it.

He knocked on the door of Paul's permanently locked den. 'It's only me. Let me in.' The key clicked and Nico went into the room that to all intents and purposes was a fairly comprehensive home office. Paul and Damien were side by side, each working at separate computer terminals with different pornographic images on the monitors.

'Here, Nico, look at this.' Paul pointed to one of the monitors. 'Isn't that great? I can't believe all the time we spent pissing about with cameras and camcorders and all that crap. This is just mind-blowing. The wonders of modern technology! We're going to set up our own site. Damien's well into it all, learned it at university – before he was nicked, of course – and then picked up a few valuable tips inside!'

Lately Nico had felt disgusted by the antics of the two young men. The original idea of Paul being based in Thailand and Damien down on the farm looking after the video distribution had disappeared down a black hole once they had discovered the joys of the Internet. Nico's initial enthusiasm had waned as the material that they downloaded was becoming more and more gruesome and the two young men got more and more excited about it all. They spent most of the day and night closeted away, trawling all the paedophile sites and networks for material and clients. They were happy as could be, copying and logging the disks for hours on end. Nothing was beyond the pale for them.

Nico looked away from the screens. 'I'm going out. Tracy is with Sammy-Jo. Remember what I said: one wrong move and you'll be crippled first and dead second.'

They both spun on their wheelie office chairs and smiled innocently.

'We've promised already. We wouldn't do that, would we, Paulie?' Damien smiled and, again, Nico thought that he deserved the name. There was something demonic about him.

'Of course not, man. We do have some morals, you know!'

They both laughed and turned back to the screens.

But Nico didn't trust them an inch. Pulling away he leaned out of the car window and called Tracy over. 'Don't take your eyes off her for a second, Tracy. I mean it.'

Cathy was frantic. The call had come when she least expected it and Nico hadn't given her time to ask even one question before the line had gone dead. An instant 1471 told her only that the number had been withheld.

She quickly phoned Dominic and told him the news.

'That's good,' he reassured her. 'He's obviously thinking about it and if the number came up as withheld then he's still in the country. Now Jack is going through all the paperwork you provided. The police complain about their paperwork but it gives them good practice for when they become private eyes. Jack is an expert after all his years on the force.'

Tim was not impressed with the details of the phone call. 'So he thinks you're going to go back to him, does he? He's got some front, that man. You wouldn't . . . would you?'

Lately he was getting on her nerves. He was only interested in anything that might affect their relationship and his reaction to the latest news was typical of his attitude.

'I don't know. I might if it meant getting Sammy-Jo back . . .' She didn't mean it and didn't really know why she said it but his response was enlightening to her.

'Oh yes, right, just shut me out of it and go back to the bastard.' He was on his feet, leaning over her. 'Where do I fit in here? I don't know why you have to spend all your time looking for the child. She went off with him happily enough and he *is* her father. You're only doing this to spite him.'

She could see he instantly regretted his outburst but it was too late. He'd said it and that to Cathy meant he'd thought it.

Calmly she looked at him. 'Are you saying you think you should be more important to me than my daughter? That I should ignore the fact that she is with a child abuser? Tim, we have our whole lives ahead of us to think of ourselves. Right now it's only Sammy-Jo that I'm concerned with.'

'Not so concerned that you can't find time for that smoothie O'Brien who's trying to smarm his way back into your life – not to mention Nico Marcos. How are you ever going to be able to choose between the three of us? Are you going to lure Nico back here, then announce your decision to us all?'

The sarcasm in his voice hit her like a speeding bullet. Frowning she tried to take in what he meant.

'Are you saying this is somehow all my fault?' Still her voice was calm and reasonable, belying the turmoil she was feeling.

'I don't know. I just think you're stringing us all along while you decide which one is most beneficial to you.'

Cathy was about to launch into a verbal attack when she heard Sheila calling her from the garden. She decided Tim would keep for another time; Sheila didn't need the stress of hearing them rowing on top of everything else.

Recently out of hospital and en route to her sister who lived in Yorkshire for some convalescence, Sheila was having to be almost physically restrained by Cathy from doing too much.

Cathy turned away from Tim without a word and went out to see Sheila.

'Cathy dear, I know I keep asking you but you won't tell me so I'm going to keep asking until you do. What is going on? I need to know. Even if it's bad news it would be better than guessing. Why are the twins coming here? They never go anywhere.'

'Well, I've decided it's time for everyone to know everything. I'm not going to have compartments any more, so I've invited the twins, Simonie and Justin, Tim, Peter and of course you – everyone that matters to me. I'm going to put you all completely in the picture. Once I've done that then I can concentrate on the best way to find Sammy-Jo.'

'But is it bad news you're going to tell us? Is that why you're doing it?'

Cathy crouched down beside the seated woman who now looked old and drawn from the strain of her illness and the weight loss. 'No, Sheila, it's not. In fact it's good news because this is clear-the-air time. This is the time when I put the record straight. I admit I may have made mistakes but I've done nothing wrong.'

Sheila reached out and ruffled Cathy's hair affectionately. 'I know you haven't. Cathy dear, I don't know how I'd have got through the last few weeks without you. Even with everything you've got on your plate you still found time for your old Aunty Sheila. Even those silly sisters of yours haven't been too bad. I'm so lucky!'

'Nonsense, we could never ever pay you back for everything you've done over the years – nearly all my life, in fact.'

Two clear bulbous tears rolled down Sheila's cheeks as she looked at the young woman beside her – grown up now, but still little Cathy to her.

Cathy stood up. 'Come on, enough of that now. Let's

go in and make you beautiful before our guests arrive.'

Peter collected the twins en route and Simonie and Justin arrived together a bit later, minus baby Tamara. Sheila was already regally ensconced in the armchair in her 'best' room with her hair done and a touch of make-up that Cathy had applied. The only person missing was Tim, who had gone off home in a huff earlier.

Cathy decided to start without him.

'You all OK for a drink?'

'Get on with it. We've got to get back.' Alison and Jane were sitting side by side, huffing and puffing in exasperation at being dragged from their house by Peter.

'No you haven't. This is a one-off and I want you to listen. It matters to me what you think, and up until now I haven't told everyone everything although I did it to protect each of you.'

Looking around at them all she took a deep breath and was just about to start when Tim threw the door open. No one had heard him come in the back way.

'You could have waited for me. Some of us have to work, you know . . .'

Justin stood up and laughed gently. 'Just sit down and shut up. You sound like an old tart having a hissy fit.'

Tim's face reddened and he looked at the floor, the way he always used to as a young boy. Cathy realised in that instant that Tim the boy was what he still was, deep down.

'I'll start at the beginning. When Mum and Dad died—'

'Don't you dare go into all that,' Alison interrupted.

'And you can shut up as well.' Cathy glared at her sisters. 'Now, where was I?'

Dominic Bingham and Jack Bayliss were sharing a bottle of Scotch in Jack's office. It was getting late and both had decided their working day was over.

The two men had known each other for forty-odd years and although they were hardly best friends, they were good buddies, they respected each other and had a lot of working history between them. Both were widowers and lived alone, but whereas Dominic was lonely Jack quite enjoyed being alone.

'Just one more thing, Jack, before we forget about work. The Marcos case – have you managed to find anything out about our Nico Marcos?'

'Not a lot, but I'm getting there. I've got a couple of people still to get back to me. He's a problem because he's never had so much as a speeding fine, let alone anything serious. The name often rings a bell but nothing concrete . . . yet.'

Jack Bayliss was a working private detective from the old school of policing. His patience was legendary and he had always got his results the same way fanatics of complicated jigsaw puzzles got theirs. Every single piece was meticulously examined, and if there was nowhere obvious for it to go at the time, then it was put to one side but never discarded, never forgotten. It had to fit in the end. Finally all the pieces are joined up and there in front of you was the whole picture, complete and telling its own story.

'The name is known, but, asking around, there's a lot of nothing known about him. You know the scenario: "Nico Marcos? I know the name but I can't place him . . . don't remember him . . . might have met him . . . not very nice but I don't know why" – all that sort of thing. But I'll find something eventually.'

'What do you think about the little snippet from the bizarre sisters that their psychic talents say Devon?' Dominic wasn't smiling as he asked the question. Stranger things had happened than a psychic pulling the answer out of her mind.

'I don't know. I have to keep going through the papers and bank account details. It would help if they could dig a bit deeper into their subconscious and find an address, though.'

They grinned at each other at the thought of it.

Jack Bayliss stretched his long legs and put his feet up on his desk, slowly sipping his Scotch and licking his lips as he blissfully savoured it.

From the other side of the desk the lanky Jack looked all arms and legs to the short, rotund Dominic. They were complete opposites in appearance but something had clicked between them all those years ago. Jack was as straight as a die and, like his friend, had never been a high-flyer. Both had worked hard and plodded through their working lives, doing the best they could without consciously trampling over heads en route.

'Did you watch the video?' Dominic asked curiously.

'I certainly did. That is one sick bastard. I've been seeing stuff like that for years and to the trained eye it's easy to see that kid was terrified. She wasn't acting up, no way. And if he can do that to the girl he's just married then he can do anything. Boundaries don't exist for sickos like that, so my instinct tells me that the daughter isn't safe.'

'Exactly what I thought. That's why I wanted to take the case on. You haven't met Cathy yet, have you? She's tiny and vulnerable and doesn't deserve this. I can't believe that a man old enough to be her father could do that sort of thing to her and then to take the daughter maybe for the same thing?'

Jack grimaced. 'This is a man with a big problem. He's a control freak with a perversion – dangerous, truly dangerous. I've seen it all before. I've found his ex-wife and I'm going to see her. She wasn't happy but I know how to lean gently! Oh, and I'm also paying a visit to Antonio, my pet ex-grass in Soho. There's not a lot he doesn't know or he can't find out for a fee.'

'Good. I really want to find that child and get her back where she belongs. I feel so strongly about it I'm surprising myself.'

Dominic leaned back in his chair and crossed his hands on his large belly. With his round, dark-rimmed glasses and slightly untidy hair he always reminded Jack of a jovial Billy Bunter. 'Now, enough business talk. Do you want to shut up shop and adjourn to the pub? We can make a night of it if you've nothing else on.'

Tracy watched Nico's car as it pulled away.

'Come on, Sammy-Jo. Let's go and watch telly for a

while and then you can help me cook some dinner. I'm
not very good at it.'

'I want to go and see Paul. Can we go into his den?'

'No, you know you're not allowed in there. Anyway, I
want to watch telly.' Tracy studied the child's face closely.
'Have you ever been in Paul's den, Sammy-Jo? Has he
ever asked you to go in there?'

'Nooo.' The child hesitated and Tracy knew instinctively that she was lying.

'Go on, you can tell me. I won't tell your dad.'

'No, I haven't been in there, I haven't, I haven't . . .' As
Sammy-Jo's long dark lashes fluttered down over her eyes
and a secretive expression appeared on the child's face,
Tracy was frightened.

She took Sammy-Jo's hand. She knew there was no
point in pushing it but Tracy intended to keep a closer
eye on the child; even she knew that Sammy-Jo shouldn't
be anywhere near the men behind the door.

Tracy Jones was young but she was worldly wise. There
wasn't much she hadn't seen and done in her short life.
Life on the run-down estate where she was brought up
was hard, and only the strongest survived intact. The
youngest of five siblings, two of whom had died from
heroin overdoses, she had, from as far back as she could
remember, been determined to drag herself out from
under it all.

Nico Marcos, or Nicholas as she knew him then, had
seemed like a gift from the gods to her, an escape route
from the family that she despised and that didn't really
give a toss about her. She hadn't chosen to be on the

streets so young but it had happened, and with cunning and a sharp brain she had made the best of it. She had known from the start that Nico was a pervert but he had always rewarded her well by her standards so she could easily switch off and act out his silly perverted games on autopilot.

But Paul Evans? He was in a completely different league. The man frightened the hell out of her, as did his friend Damien. She knew full well what they were up to in the den with their computers, and they certainly weren't playing solitaire.

Tracy reasoned that what she did, she did willingly for either money or payment in kind, but a young child like Sammy-Jo would be permanently damaged, maybe even killed if Paul and Damien got their hands on her. Tracy was certain that was what they were planning. She had seen the way they each looked at Sammy-Jo when they thought no one was watching. Tracy knew she would somehow have to get Sammy-Jo away from the farm, even if it meant blowing her chances with Nico.

'Where does your mummy live, Sammy-Jo?'

'We live in Spain.'

'Yes, I know that, but where is she now? Where were you staying before you came here?'

'At Aunty Sheila's . . .'

Tracy felt she was pulling teeth, the answers were so hard to get, but eventually she extracted the name of the village. She just hoped it was a small place.

'You sit and watch *Neighbours*, Sammy-Jo. I've got a letter to write.'

★ ★ ★

Cathy finished her description of events. 'And all I can say is I'm sorry for involving you all but I can't apologise for what has happened in the past. It was not my fault.' She looked at Peter, who was watching her closely. 'As Peter said, I can beat myself up for ever or get on with the really important business of finding Sammy-Jo and then getting on with my life.'

Tim looked as if he was scowling for England at the mention of Peter, but Cathy didn't care. If their relationship was to have a chance then she knew he would have to grow up.

Cathy had held it all together and was feeling quite proud of herself. She had left nothing out and had still managed to hold her head up instead of crawling away in shame, but then the twins had come over and put their arms round her.

'We're sorry, we shouldn't have . . .' Then Cathy couldn't hold back any longer. Crying, she hugged them both and to her surprise they almost responded normally. The natural reticence was there but it was tempered with an effort.

In the midst of all the emotion, the phone rang. Instantly calm, Cathy rushed to get it, clambering over all the legs in the small room to reach it.

'It's Nico. Have you decided yet? If you come back to me we can be a family again – just you, me and Sammy-Jo – forget the past and start again . . .'

Playing for time, Cathy tried to sound neutral. 'Nico, I'm not sure . . .'

Before she could say any more Tim snatched the receiver from her hand.

'Just piss off, you fucking little pervert. She doesn't want you and the police are looking for you . . .' He held the receiver away from himself and looked round at the silent, horrified faces in the room. 'He hung up on me, the bastard!'

Instantly the room erupted as Cathy threw herself at Tim and grabbed the phone. As soon as she confirmed it was dead she went berserk, trying to beat him around the head with it. Peter pulled her off him and took her forcibly into the kitchen, slamming the door behind them and then leaning on it to prevent her getting out.

Back in the lounge, Sheila and Simonie were both panic-stricken. Justin pulled back his arm and punched a surprised Tim in the solar plexus, while the twins just sat still, quietly observing the chaos with slight smiles on their faces.

Peter waited until Cathy was breathing normally before trying to talk to her.

'Come on, it's OK. We'll sort it out. Nico will ring again!'

'No, he won't. You don't know him. He'll be so angry he's likely to take it out on Sammy-Jo. Christ knows where he'll take her now, but if he thinks the police are looking for him he'll run for cover. That's it with Tim now. I don't want him involved in any of it. I can't understand him: I can't understand why he's changed.'

The distressed expression on her face made Peter want to go back in and beat the other man to a pulp. It was such a stupid and self-centred thing to have done. Instead of considering Sammy-Jo he had used the situation to try to score points off Nico. Nico, the man everyone knew was dangerous and unpredictable.

'Love does strange things to people, Kit, and he's not in control of his emotions at all. He's so obsessed with you it's affecting his sensibilities. He sees everyone and everything as a threat to your relationship.'

'We don't have a relationship, not any more. It's over. God, how am I going to tell Sheila? It was the highlight of her life, the thought of me and Tim being together, just as she had predicted.'

Peter pulled her to him. 'Now isn't the time to think about sparing other people's feelings. You need to get in touch with Dominic first thing on Monday. I'm going to phone the Uni and tell them I'm not going back again for personal reasons. It's time I stopped playing at being the eternal student. Post-graduate? More like never-ending student! It's off to work now. Playtime is over, I've decided.'

'You can't do that. Mandi and Benny will string me up for it, they're so proud of you.'

'I can and I will. This is more important. Now, are you up to going back into the other room?'

His hands gently brushed her hair back off her face before using his hankie to wipe her tear-stained cheeks. Smiling he tapped her under the chin with his forefinger.

'Chin up, chicken! Let's go and confront the warring factions!'

The scene that confronted them would have been

laughable had it not been so serious. The twins were sitting po-faced on the sofa with an angry red-faced Tim between them. Sheila was being comforted by Simonie, and Justin was looking completely bewildered. He'd never been violent in his life before.

Cathy was the first to speak. 'You've really blown it for me now, Tim. You know what Nico is like; his pride won't let him phone me again. I could have persuaded him . . .'

'Oh yeah, that's right, persuaded him right back to you. You were going to dump me for him . . . again.' Eyes bulging with anger, and nostrils flaring, Tim glared round the room, looking for support. 'Don't any of you agree with me? After all he's supposed to have done she's still being nice to him, still even considering going back to him. Why? Why shouldn't I have told him his fortune?'

Peter's voice was low and calm as he replied, 'Because he has her daughter and if that was the only way to get her back then that was the only thing to do – play along with him. Now I think it's time you left before you say something else you might regret.'

'Don't you tell me what to do, you jumped-up fucking *student*.' The word was said with such poison even Peter looked surprised. 'I don't take orders from a mummy's boy who's never done a day's work in his life. I'm not going anywhere. If Cathy wants me to go then she has to say so herself.'

Looking at him sadly, Cathy said the only thing possible. 'I want you to go.'

401

Nico couldn't believe what he had heard. He guessed it was Tim O'Connor who had shouted at him down the phone and nearly burst his eardrum, but he couldn't be completely sure.

Driving round aimlessly after leaving the farm Nico had found himself on the outskirts of Torquay. On the spur of the moment he had driven into the town, parked overlooking the sea and tried hard to think of a way out of the mess he had created. Suddenly the fun had gone out of his business and he didn't want to be involved with the likes of Paul and Damien any more. Looking in the vanity mirror at himself, he saw a middle-aged man rushing towards fifty, a man with no purpose in his life, a wife who hated him, one child who was frightened of him and two others who had probably forgotten he ever existed. Added to that was the knowledge that he had taken his own daughter to a house that was now full of evil in the forms of Paul and Damien. For the first time in his life Nico hated himself. They were right, he was a pervert.

Pulling out his mobile phone he flipped it open and dialled the number again, determined to right things with Cathy, but he hadn't had a chance. Someone else had got to the phone before he could explain.

Driving quickly back to the farm, Nico made a decision. He would go back to Hampshire, without Sammy-Jo, his bargaining tool, and see Cathy, speak to her face to face, make her see reason. But first he had to ensure Sammy-Jo's safety. He decided he would have to pay Paul and Damien to leave, send them off to Thailand or Cuba for a holiday –

anything to get them away from his daughter.

Pulling up at the farm, he was surprised when Tracy came out to meet him with Sammy-Jo hot on her heels.

'Nico, we've run out of milk and bread. I'm just going to walk down to the post office. I need some exercise, I won't be long. Can Sammy-Jo come as well?'

Nico was just about to agree. Normally he was suspicious by nature but he was distracted, and anyway, the less time he had to spend with Sammy-Jo's accusing eyes fixed on him the better. One look from that child was enough to make Satan himself feel guilty. But then he thought of the possibility of Cathy snatching her the same way he had.

'No, leave her here with me.'

'But I want to go with Tracy. You can't make me stay here, you can't. I'm going with her.'

Nico was at a loss. Everything was spiralling out of his control.

'You are not going, Sammy-Jo, and that is that. Now get back inside before I lose my temper. If I hear one more sound from your miserable little mouth . . .'

Tracy scuttled away up the farm track with the letter safely tucked down her T-shirt. She had seriously thought about not going back but now she knew she had to, for the child's sake.

Paul and Damien were standing side by side, looking out of the window at the scene below.

'What do you reckon, Pauly? Can we really pull it off?'

'No doubt about it. We just have to plan it properly.

Jesus, it'll be such a coup. I reckon we might even crash the system with this one!'

'Any timescale in mind?'

'Not yet, but we have to start arranging it. It'll need to be planned down to the last second, a bit like a space launch.'

'If we do it then there'll be more than a few rockets going off all over the world!'

Paul and Damien smiled at each other in anticipation. 'Right then, let's get arranging. The site is set up. All we have to do is announce the date and time.'

Chapter Twenty-One

Fortunately Marshwood was only a small village with one main road and one papershop and post office combined, so the letter addressed to 'CATHY MARCOS c/o SHEILA MILLER' arrived in the second post the next day.

The childish handwriting wasn't familiar so Cathy opened it curiously.

Please come and get Sammy-Jo, she is with Nico on a
big farm near Torquay. You have to come and get her,
I don't like Paul and Damien.

Cathy squealed out loud, but her relief at having some news was drastically tempered by the wording of the letter. She rushed to phone Dominic.

'Cathy, I have to ask you, do you want to go to the police or do you want to talk to Jack? The choice is yours. I can't tell you what to do, I can only advise you, and my advice now is to go to the police. This appears to be more than just a parental abduction.'

'I'm not going to do that right now. I have to protect the twins. They're still under the psychiatrist and I don't want any setbacks. If Jack doesn't get anywhere in the next few days then I know I have to, but let's give him a chance. Nico won't harm Sammy-Jo. He's just using her to get back at me. That's why he phoned.'

Dominic wasn't sure who she was trying to convince, him or herself.

'I'll speak to Jack straight away and get him to phone you. Can you bring the letter over as soon as you've spoken to him?'

'I'll wait for him to phone and I'll phone Peter as well. I need him here.'

Although she was expecting him, Cathy still jumped when Peter rang the doorbell. Impatiently standing by the door with her car keys in her hand she flung it open.

'I'm waiting for Jack Bayliss to ring me, then I'm going to see Dominic. Will you come with me to see him?' Cathy was hovering over the telephone willing it to ring. Her heart was thumping away in anticipation.

'Look at this note. Who the fuck do you think Paul and Damien could be? Maybe they just own the farm where Nico is staying? If it's in Devon it could be a B and B. I've never even heard their names before. There just isn't enough information. Who could have sent it?'

The letter was already dog-eared from being read and reread as Cathy frantically tried to figure it out and look for further clues that deep down she knew weren't there.

'We have to go to Torquay . . . we have to go straight away.'

'Torquay is a big town and it's spread over such a wide area, we wouldn't stand a chance. Let's wait and see what Jack says. He'll know what to do.' Peter paused, then:

'Cathy, don't you think it's time for the police? You can't sacrifice your daughter for your adult sisters. The fire was accidental – they haven't got anything to be frightened of.'

'But that's the trouble, I'm not sure! You can see what they're like – supposing they did do it? Supposing they really did torch the house like he said, where does that leave me? I actually don't want to know. I couldn't deal with it if it's true.'

'Well, well,' Jack smiled down the phone, 'so the witches were right, Devon does come into it. What was the postmark on the envelope?' As soon as Dominic had phoned and given him the news Jack was more optimistic: in the light of other information he had gleaned, the letter was important. It gave other names, and several together were always easier to trace than just one.

'The postmark is well and truly smudged, apparently. It looks like it's something "ford" with two or three letters before it. It was posted yesterday. What do you think the relevance is of three men, a child and possibly another young female all holed up on a farm?'

'I think you and I can both guess the relevance of that and before very long I'm going to have to talk young Cathy into going to the police. I'll give it a good shot first, though. If we can get the child out and away we can decide what to do about the paedo Nico and his mates after that.'

Jack rang Cathy and arranged to meet her at Dominic's office.

'I'm leaving for Torquay in the morning. I'll keep you updated regularly, of course—'

Cathy was sharp. 'You won't need to do that, I'm coming with you.' She looked across at Peter. 'Do you mind staying here? Just in case he phones again or even turns up? He doesn't know you, so you can pretend to be a relative of Sheila's.'

'Whatever you think is best, but you will let me know how it's going, won't you? And you will be careful?'

Cathy looked at him affectionately, well aware that Tim would have sulked and stamped and inferred that she was trying to shut him out. There was no doubt about it, Peter O'Brien was growing on her!

As a private investigator Jack Bayliss was the best. He could be kind and gently persuasive or he could be assertive and aggressive if the situation called for it. His visit to Nico's ex-wife had called for a bit of everything.

Pulling up outside the fairly ordinary semi in a quiet suburb of Manchester, he'd predicted that his reception would be hostile. Joanna Marks, as she now called herself, had been cautious when he had first contacted her and furious that her sister had been tricked into revealing her whereabouts, but Jack had been politely persistent and not averse to a bit of emotional blackmail.

He rang the bell and waited, aware that there was someone watching him from behind the net curtains at the front window. Eventually the door, with its shining brass furniture, opened and a very well-maintained middle-aged woman invited him in grudgingly.

'I'm Jack Bayliss. I am very sorry to intrude on you but this is really important.'

The woman smiled politely as she looked him up and down.

'That's for me to judge. Important, to me, is not being found by my ex-husband; important, to me, is making sure he never finds where my, our, children are. Now, you tell me exactly what you deem important compared to that?'

He could see the woman was trying to size him up and he guessed she had been expecting a scruffy down-at-heel bloke with the statutory grubby mac. He had long ago discovered that far too many people thought that all private eyes looked like the television stereotype and always ensured he was smart and clean, despite being deliberately nondescript.

'Oh, I'm sure once I tell you why I'm here you'll agree that it is important. But first let me reassure you, I have no intention of letting Mr Marcos know where you are. I am acting for the second Mrs Marcos, whom I'm sure you can relate to. Do you mind if I sit down?'

Jack wanted the woman sitting; a standing conversation was always far too stilted for his liking.

'Of course, we'll go into the lounge. Would you like a drink? Tea? Coffee?'

'Tea, please,' he smiled as he went ahead of her in the direction of her pointing arm, 'white, no sugar.'

As soon as he was in the room the door closed firmly behind him, setting the boundaries of where he could go.

Sitting quickly on the nearest armchair he surreptitiously looked around. The room was immaculately clean and tidy, not a spec of dust nor anything out of place, but cluttered with ornaments and bric-a-brac, and chronological photographs of a boy and girl.

Regimentally pleated net curtains hung at the sparkling clean windows and the rugs on the floor were lined up exactly parallel to each other. Even the pot plants with bright green polished leaves were strategically placed to form a pattern.

Jack's immediate assessment was that Joanna Marks was one really uptight woman. The door opened again and she came back into the room with a tray.

'Come along now, Mr Bayliss, this isn't a social occasion. Tell me what you want from me exactly.'

'I want to know a little about your separation from your husband – sorry, ex-husband. I want you to give me any information you can because as we speak Nico Marcos is hidden away somewhere with his young daughter, whom he has abducted from her mother, and we need to find them quickly. I'm looking for anything that might help.'

'Are the police going to be calling here? I don't want the children upset. You see, they think he is dead.'

'The police aren't involved at the moment but they will be very soon unless we find him and the child. Now you

410

tell me, Mrs Marks, are we right to be concerned? What can you tell me?'

Jack looked away as he picked up the bone-china cup and saucer in one hand and a biscuit from the plate in the other. He knew that if women especially had something distasteful to say they were more likely to come out with it if there was no eye contact. He sipped his tea and nibbled on the biscuit, to all intents and purposes engrossed in what he was doing.

'I don't know if Nico is a danger to that child or not but I left him after I found out that he liked reading dirty magazines about you know what with young girls – filthy, filthy magazines, full of old men with the young tarts. Then I found some photographs he had taken of his own children in the bath, with no clothes on, posing, touching each other. I found them in his briefcase, a whole set of them.'

The woman's voice was breaking so Jack still concentrated on his cup.

'He went mad, called me frigid and sexless, so I sent him packing. I told him I would call the police and tell them. The children were punished for letting him do it, then he left and I moved away. That's it. Now you tell me about the latest Mrs Marcos.'

Jack told her the outline of what had happened.

'Sixteen years old?' Joanna Marks nearly choked on her drink. 'The little whore, what was she doing with a man his age? She must have been after his money or something.'

'On the contrary,' Jack was trying hard to keep his cool,

411

'he was after her money. Cathy is a lovely young woman who was conned by a man old enough to be her father. But that's by the by. Do you know if Nico has any connections in Devon?'

Visibly annoyed, the woman snapped back, 'No, I haven't got a clue. We did go to Devon once, somewhere near Torquay, on our honeymoon, but that was all.'

'Where did you stay?'

'I don't remember, somewhere out in the sticks. Nico rented a little cottage. He loved it but I hated every minute of it. I loathe the country, it's dirty and smelly. I couldn't wait to get home.'

Jack looked back at his cup and tried to keep his voice even. 'Can you remember the name of the place? It would be helpful. It could be where he's gone back to.'

'Good Lord, how do you expect me to remember something from nearly thirty years ago? It probably isn't even there any more. It was about to disintegrate then.'

'How old are your children now, Mrs Marks? They must be adults . . .?'

'I'm not prepared to discuss them with you. It's none of your business.'

Jack made some more small talk and then left, leaving the woman with a business card that she looked at as if it was somehow contagious.

Nico was becoming paranoid. Backed into a corner, he was unsure where to turn first to get out of the mess with his ego intact. He was yearning for normality and he knew all he had to do was drive off with Sammy-Jo and everything would be all right, but he also knew that would be admitting failure. He couldn't give Cathy the satisfaction of that, not after what she'd done to him. Cathy had to pay a price. There was no alternative.

Nico looked around and wondered if there was any way to retrieve the situation, maybe get Cathy to live at the farm with them – after, of course, she had handed over whatever was left of her trust fund and Paul and Damien had gone.

The lounge in the farmhouse was spacious and cold even in summer. When he had first bought it he had made an attempt at décor just in case anyone came calling. A lot of the furniture and fittings had come with the building that was an executors' sale and he hadn't bothered to replace them. All he had done was hire a cleaning company to come in and blitz away the smell of the previous owner, and then he had bought a few personal items from a junk shop to make the place look homely.

The chintzy curtains at the windows were thin and faded, and an assortment of chairs that didn't match littered the room; the only thing in the whole building that he really liked was the big old pine table that was battered and worn.

He gently ran his fingers over the grooves that crisscrossed the top. It reminded him of his early childhood when the whole family would sit around the table and eat long-drawn-out meals in the balmy Mediterranean afternoons; but that was before he had started to grow up and his father had taken to whipping him into line.

He sat in the old rocking chair in the corner and rocked back and forth, chain-smoking.

He reasoned with himself that Paul and Damien wouldn't do anything that might send them back into the prison system; no one with any sense craps on their own doorstep. No, he decided, he would go and see Cathy. Tracy was bright enough to look after Sammy-Jo for a day or so while he sorted it all out, and after that he and Cathy could maybe start again.

He tried to figure out a way to deal with Tim O'Connor other than killing him with his own bare hands. Just the thought of that little shit sleeping with Cathy was disgusting, but then maybe she hadn't? He tried to convince himself that Cathy would never do that. She was still married to him; she was still his wife, after all!

He went out into the old-fashioned kitchen and dug about in the back of the filthy cupboard in the outhouse until he found the carefully hidden bottle of Scotch and a large wrap of white powder. His nerves were as taut as guitar strings and he needed to chill out a little.

It hit Tracy like a thunderbolt as she lay awake in the bedroom that she shared with Sammy-Jo. Why hadn't she thought of it before? While she had been busy wondering if they were going to do something to Sammy-Jo, she hadn't actually thought about where she herself might figure in it all. Supposing they were after her as well? Suppose Nico had brought her to the farm for that reason? Paul had filmed her in the past acting up for the camera, all plaited hair and white ankle socks and looking innocent. Suppose he had moved on? The more she thought about it, the more scared she became. Tracy had been in the den and she had seen the stuff that they were downloading and it was scary. The young girl knew then she had to get away from the farm and take Sammy-Jo with her. It was just a matter of planning it carefully so they didn't get caught.

Tracy desperately wanted to go to the toilet but to do so she had to get out of bed and make her way across the landing where the floorboards creaked and groaned. In the bedroom, at least she could lock the door and know they were both safe but once on the landing anything could happen to her or to Sammy-Jo. By opting to stay in the room she spent all night awake, scared out of her wits, waiting impatiently for dawn and the noise of the squawking cockerels.

Pulling the covers up tight to her chin and facing the sleeping Sammy-Jo she decided that the next day she would at least have to try to make a run for it with the child.

Daylight dawned and Tracy felt safe enough at last to go out to the toilet. The house was quiet so she took a chance on going downstairs to get a drink of water as well. As she tiptoed down she could see into the lounge where Nico was crashed out on the floor, fully clothed and unconscious, with vomit all over his shirt. To Tracy the empty bottle on the floor beside him was a good indicator that he would sleep for a while.

On the spur of the moment Tracy picked up his mobile

phone that was on the table and took a twenty-pound note out of his wallet.

She rushed back upstairs and shook the sleeping Sammy-Jo awake.

'Come on, get up. It's a lovely morning for a walk. Get dressed and we'll walk to the shop and buy some sweets . . .'

'Daddy will be angry. I'm not allowed . . .' The child was upright in the bed, looking surprised. Normally she was awake long before her adolescent room-mate.

'No he won't, he's still asleep. We'll let him have a lie-in. He'll like that, but be quiet so we don't wake him and put your coat on in case it rains.'

Slowly they crept down the creaky stairs together and opened the back door. Tracy hesitated for a moment to check that there was no movement from Paul and Damien's room, before bundling the surprised child outside.

'Come on, I'll race you up the road . . .'

Paul looked out of the bedroom window just in time to see the pair of them hot-footing it up the farm track.

'Damien, quick, it looks like they're doing a runner . . . Tracy and the kid are haring up the fucking track like rats.'

'Don't be stupid. They're probably playing. Nico would throw one if they ran off. Tracy isn't that stupid, she knows he'd kill her.'

'We'd better tell him, though. It'll screw all our plans up if the kid has gone.'

Without bothering to get dressed they both went downstairs.

'Nico? Nico, wake up, mate.' Paul pushed him with his bare foot. 'Nico, your kid's gone walkabout, did you know?' He glanced at Damien. 'Looks like he overdid it a bit last night.'

Nico didn't stir and as Damien leaned over him he swore fiercely. 'The bastard's dead, he's fucking dead. He must have OD'd. What the fuck are we going to do?'

'First thing is to get the kids back. We have to go through with the live filming, it's all set. Just leave him there for now, worry about it when we get back.'

Even Damien looked surprised at Paul's response.

'Well, come on, get dressed and we'll go and catch them. If Tracy saw him she may well be off to the Old Bill. We can't have them swarming all over the place, can we? Now move!'

Tracy heard the chugging of Paul's rust-bucket car before she saw it. Grabbing Sammy-Jo by the scruff of the neck, she pulled her through the hedge into the ditch and put her hand over her mouth.

'Don't make a sound. Paul and Damien want to hurt us. We mustn't let them catch us, so not a sound.'

She could see Sammy-Jo was petrified but that was tough; she knew petrified was better than what Paul could do to her.

Suddenly she remembered Nico's mobile phone. Keeping one hand on Sammy-Jo's coat she pulled it out of her own pocket with the other and scrolled down the numbers.

Cathy . . . there were two numbers. She didn't know which one to dial so she chose the first.

'Sammy-Jo, listen to me. I'm going to let go of you but you must stay still, please? For me?'

Someone answered the phone. 'Is that Cathy? I must speak to Cathy. I've got Sammy-Jo and we're hiding, and Paul and Damien are looking for us . . .'

'Hang on a minute, who is this? I don't know what you're talking about . . .'

'Is Cathy there?' Tracy was whispering loudly.

'Cathy doesn't live here. She—'

Tracy pressed the button and scrolled to the next one. She could hear the chugging heading back towards them, only this time it was slower.

'Cathy . . . I want to speak to Cathy . . .' she gulped, crying at the same time.

Peter was taken aback. He could hear the voice at the other end of the phone was hysterical but he didn't know who it was.

'Calm down. Who is this?'

'I'm Tracy and I'm with Sammy-Jo. We've run away and we're in a ditch and Paul and Damien are looking for us. I must speak to Cathy.'

The sheer panic that overtook Peter was so intense he thought for a second his heart had stopped beating. 'Tell me where you are.'

'I don't know where we are. We're in a ditch and I can hear the car. It's coming back really slowly . . .' The urgency in the girl's voice was permeating down the line and Peter could hear that she was absolutely terrified.

'Now listen carefully, Tracy. Stay right where you are and don't hang up. I'll call the police from my mobile. Maybe they can put a trace on the line and find you. *Don't hang up* unless I tell you.'

Peter could hear whimpering in the background. 'Give the phone to Sammy-Jo . . . Hello, Jo? This is Uncle Peter, remember me? From Spain? Now I want you to do everything that Tracy tells you, do you understand? Everything! Now give the phone back to Tracy and don't cry. You'll be back with Mummy really soon.'

With the landline phone to one ear and the mobile to the other Peter called the police and tried to explain, but midway through he heard Tracy crying, 'They've stopped and they're walking. They're looking in the hedge . . .'

The next thing he heard was a distant male voice. 'So there you are, you girls. Where do you think you're going?'

'We're not going anywhere, Paul. We were playing hide-and-seek. We're going to the sweet shop . . .'

Peter said a silent prayer for the young girl's presence of mind. She had obviously put the phone down still switched on. He put receiver to receiver so the police could listen in. He just prayed they could hear it all.

'Now why would you do that, Tracy darling? Why would you suddenly go looking for sweets at this hour of the morning?'

Peter heard a different male voice: 'You were doing a runner, weren't you? You found his fucking body and you were doing a runner.' Peter winced as he heard the thud of a hand on flesh and Tracy squeal. Sammy-Jo was sobbing in the background. He felt completely impotent but at the same time he was grateful it was he that had answered the phone; that Cathy wasn't there to hear it.

'Now get your arses in the car. We've got plans and you two are not going to fuck them up . . .'

Tracy knew that they had to try to stay away from the farm one way or another so she pretended to trip and grabbed her ankle, pleading all the while.

'Please, Paul, we weren't going anywhere. Please, my ankle hurts. I can't move. Please, Paul, I promise we weren't . . . We'll walk back to the farm and see you there . . .'

Paul kicked her viciously in the middle of her stomach.

Peter heard the girl scream in pain. He could only guess at the scene.

'Shut up, slut, and get in the car. Come on, both of you.'

As Tracy started to get up she could see a vehicle in the distance. She looked sideways, trying not to let the men see what she was looking at. Her eyes focused and she saw that it was the milk float trundling slowly towards them. She knew she had to play for time.

'I can't move, I really can't. Sammy-Jo, help me get up . . .' As the child automatically reached out her hand, Tracy pulled her fiercely backwards on top of her.

The milk float was nearly close enough.

'Get up and get in the fucking car . . .' The man's voice echoed across to the mobile phone.

Tracy took her chance. 'Help, help, we're being

kidnapped.' Screaming at the top of her voice she scrambled to her feet and dragged Sammy-Jo into the middle of the road. 'Help us, please. Call the police, we're being abducted . . .'

The screams were piercing, and Peter felt physically sick as he heard them.

The milk float was nearly there and Tracy could see the milkman's shocked face as he recognised the two girls from Willowbrook Farm.

Paul and Damien looked round and saw him.

'Quick, Paul, let's get out of here.'

'Not without the fucking kid.'

'No, it's too late, I'm going. Come on . . .'

Paul hesitated and as Tracy bent down to comfort the child, he aimed a well-placed high kick on to the side of Tracy's head. She dropped to the road like a stone but luckily landed on top of Sammy-Jo, making it impossible for the men to make a last pull at the child. They jumped in the car and disappeared off down the road as the milkman concentrated his efforts on the two children in front of his wheels.

Sammy-Jo crawled out from under Tracy, rushed back into the hedge and retrieved the mobile phone, handing it over cautiously to the milkman.

'Hello?'

'Who's that?'

'It's the milkman. Do you know what's going on?'

'No, just tell me if the girls are OK and where exactly you are!'

421

While Jack and Cathy were on their way to Devon the mobile phone rang twice.

The first call was from Joanna. 'I've remembered the name of the village, it's Hedford.'

Just as they were jubilantly looking at the map the phone rang again. It was Peter.

'It's over. You need to go to the hospital in Torquay. Sammy-Jo is there with another girl, Tracy. They're OK. The police will tell you the rest but I'm afraid Nico is dead and the other two, Paul and Damien, have disappeared.'

Cathy thought it would take for ever. The traffic was a nightmare and the reception on her mobile was poor so she didn't catch everything. In the end she gave up and stared grimly ahead, hurling the occasional abuse out of the window at the leisurely holiday drivers.

Jack drove the car straight up to the hospital and abandoned it there. Sometimes there were more important things than wheel clamps or fifty-pound fines, he decided.

'I'm Mrs Marcos. You have my daughter, Sammy-Jo, here?'

The woman at the reception gave Cathy an old-fashioned look of total boredom and clicked on to her computer, slowly scrolling down with a detachment that inferred her mind was elsewhere – planning the evening meal? Thinking about her boyfriend? Cathy could feel herself losing patience.

'Excuse me but this is urgent . . .'

'Take a seat and I'll get someone—'

Cathy didn't even wait for the woman to finish the sentence. She was off and running through the doors into the A & E department, looking in cubicles and down corridors. Despite his long legs Jack was having trouble keeping up with the much younger woman on a mission. Suddenly she caught sight of her daughter in a small side office with a nurse and another woman. Throwing the door open, she rushed in and burst into tears as she snatched Sammy-Jo up. The emotion was too much for both of them; neither could speak.

'Mrs Marcos? I'm Sally McDonald, the hospital social worker. I know you're pleased to see your daughter but I really need to talk to you . . . alone. Do you mind if the nurse takes her off for a drink?'

As soon as the nurse had left the room, holding hands with a tearful Sammy-Jo, two men came in. Despite the casual clothes Jack knew instantly that they were police. He had guessed they would be there waiting, and he had warned Cathy that there would have to be some stiff questions and answers.

He was right.

By the time the police had arrived at the scene and gone to the farm, Nico's body was still on the floor in the lounge, and Paul and Damien had disappeared. The computer expert was still at the scene, trying to unravel the complex network of hidden websites that the pair had set up. He knew there was something really sinister here – the disks alone showed that – but the rest would take time.

Meanwhile, the police were searching for Paul and

Damien, two known and convicted paedophiles, both dangerous and both still on the loose.

The main question that was so very difficult to answer was *why didn't you tell the police?* Without wanting to lie, Cathy was economical with the truth. Now Nico was dead all the threats had been lifted.

Jack intervened and halted the questions, telling them politely but bluntly that it was not the right time for recriminations.

They told her about Tracy, and Cathy insisted on seeing her. Cathy wasn't sure what she was expecting but it certainly wasn't the scared young girl she came face to face with. The two black eyes were almost framed by the livid red and blue bruise on the side of her head and a drip was attached to her hand.

'Hello, Tracy, I'm Sammy-Jo's mum, Cathy. I understand I have a lot to thank you for. I don't know how I can ever repay you. You saved her life.'

Tracy smiled half-heartedly. She was still in a lot of pain from the kicking.

'Makes a change for me to do something good. I'm sorry about it all. I did want to take her home but I didn't dare. Nico would have—'

'It's OK, Tracy.' Cathy gently touched the girl's hand. 'There's nothing you can tell me about Nico that I don't already know, and now he's dead.' The sadness she felt surprised her; she had expected only relief.

'He wasn't too bad really.' Cathy looked back at the girl in surprise as she continued, 'That's why I was there. He brought me to the farm to protect Sammy-Jo from Paul and Damien. Nico loved her but once he'd got her he didn't know what to do.'

Cathy had to leave the small side room, before her emotions got the better of her.

'I'll see you later, I have to talk to the police,' she told Tracy.

Jack was waiting outside the door with a plastic cup of murky coffee.

'Shall we go and find a hotel? So long as they know where we are then anything else they want to know, they'll get in touch. You realise this won't be the end of it, don't you? There'll be questions galore and you need to be ready for them.'

'What about Tracy? We can't just leave her there on her own. Are her family coming?'

Jack laughed drily. 'Oh, I think not. To quote their response to the police phone call: "Torquay? I'm not going all the way to Torquay for that little slut", and they haven't!' He saw the shock on her face. 'I'll fill you in later but Tracy has to stay in for observation, at least until tomorrow. Then it will be foster care for her, I suppose – she's still so young.'

When the doorbell rang the next day Peter couldn't believe his eyes to find Jilly Holden standing on the step. But if he was shocked then it was nothing compared to how she felt to see him.

'Well, hello, Jilly. What brings you here?'

The bright blonde hair and deep suntan that had always looked so attractive to him in Spain looked brassy and common in the weak English sunshine. He smiled charmingly nevertheless.

She was wrong-footed in more ways than one. Her strappy shoes didn't provide much protection as she tried to avoid the carpet of leaves on the path, and her prepared speech went out of her mind completely.

'I was in England and I thought I'd come and see Kit. I didn't expect to see you here though.'

'Well, you know how it is. Kit's out at the moment. Do you want to come in – catch up on old times?'

Her spirits rose slightly and she tripped over the step into the cottage, blissfully unaware of what had been going on.

Peter shut the front door and leaned on it. 'Can I have the film, please?'

'What film?'

'The film in your handbag, the film you were intending to blackmail Kit with. Now hand it over and, believe me, if I hear you've said one more word about it to anyone then I'll have no option but to let Dad deal with it. Do you get my meaning?'

'I don't know what you're talking about. The film is in Spain . . .'

Peter smiled and suddenly Jilly was frightened. 'The film, please, just give it to me and then you can fuck off. You have caused far more grief than you can ever imagine. One day maybe I'll tell you all about it but in the meantime, give me the fucking film.'

Jilly never took her eyes off his face as she rifled in her suitcase-sized handbag.

Peter took the cassette off her. 'Any more mention of this to anyone and you, my friend, will be dead. *Comprendes?* Benny's tentacles are long and vicious, remember that! Now get out!'

Jilly tottered off down the path, trying hard to retain a little poise.

'Just one thing,' Peter called after her, 'how did you get this address?'

'Two fucking crazy old witches who live at the other house said I'd find Cathy here.'

Stupid old crones. Peter smiled to himself. *They missed their chance. Unless, of course, they had sent Jilly round on purpose!*

No one would ever know.

'Right, Sammy-Jo, we can leave now.' Cathy's bright smile barely disguised the engulfing misery that she felt. Both Sammy-Jo and Tracy had been kept in the hospital overnight for observation and Cathy had stayed there, sleeping fitfully in an armchair beside her daughter's bed. It had been a long night for everyone.

'Where are we going?'

'Well sweetie, we have to talk to that nice policewoman again and then we can go home at last.'

As she pulled the child close and tried to hug her, instead of the usual response Sammy-Jo remained rigid and unbending, her face expressionless.

'What about Daddy? And Tracy?'

Cathy inhaled deeply before replying. Sammy-Jo had

been told about Nico's accidental death in the kindest possible terms but she was not accepting it.

'I've told you, darling, Daddy died. He had an accident and died. That's why he couldn't help you when those men were chasing you. He would have helped you if he could . . .'

'I want him to come home with us.' Sammy-Jo was sitting on the edge of the high bed, shoulders hunched, swinging her legs rhythmically back and forth. Her huge eyes looked everywhere except at Cathy.

'Daddy said he wanted us all to be together but you wouldn't let him come back. It's your fault he's dead.'

All Cathy wanted to do was to run out of the room, to run and run away from her daughter's accusing expression. But she knew she couldn't; she had to deal with it and try to help Sammy-Jo. Just the thought of it all frightened her.

She turned to Jack, who was standing in the doorway watching. Silently she pleaded for help. His head moved a fraction in the direction of the open door before turning to leave.

'I'll be back in just a minute. Mummy's got to go and see the nurse before we leave.'

Cathy caught up with Jack halfway down the corridor. 'What can I do? She won't listen to me.' Her voice was flat and despairing.

'Of course she won't, not yet. The poor child is in denial. This is going to be a long hard slog for you, but she'll be OK eventually. You, more than anyone, should know what it's like for her. Her daddy is dead and she doesn't want him to be. She doesn't know the details and she doesn't need to know.'

Putting a paternal arm around her shoulder he gave her a gentle hug. 'One step at a time, eh? Let her find her own pace. Now what do you want to do about Tracy? Do you want her to visit or would that be too painful for you? She really wants to keep in touch with Sammy-Jo.'

Smiling weakly, Cathy looked up at the kindly man towering over her. 'I don't matter in this – it's Sammy-Jo that matters, and of course Tracy. She's just as much a victim of it, yet another victim of Nico. Of course she can come and visit. Let's see what the police and her social worker have to say about it all.'

'Good. Let's go and see them and then I'll take you both home. Familiar surroundings will make all the difference to you both.'

As the car pulled up, Peter was already on the pavement waiting. Moving forward, arms wide open to welcome them, he suddenly spotted the warning in Jack's expression as the detective gently shook his head.

Putting his hands into his pockets instead, Peter smiled warmly. 'Hello everyone, shall I go and put the kettle on? Sheila's inside waiting for you both, and of course Sally.'

Seeing Cathy and Sammy-Jo both engulfed in misery Peter felt an unusual rage building up inside him. He knew quite clearly that if Nico had not already died then he himself would have made sure he was dead. Punching the wall in frustration, he was angry at his own anger.

'What are you doing?' Cathy's voice behind him made him jump visibly. 'Please don't, Peter. I don't want any more . . .'

Suddenly she was in his arms shaking from head to toe.

'I'm sorry Cathy, but seeing Jo like that . . . I don't know, she's not the same, is she? The bubbly little wild child, she's suddenly a miniature adult. I hate and despise Nico and I feel ashamed that someone of my own sex could do that, especially to his own daughter.' He buried his face in Cathy's hair and held her as tightly as he could.

'I know, but now we have to all get over it. I just want to get away from here, to give Sammy-Jo something to look forward to.'

Peter released her and stood back. 'Let's go back to Spain together. We could have a good life there. Marry me, Cathy.'

Closing her eyes Cathy sighed. 'I'd love to say yes, but it's too soon. In the future? Maybe . . . Probably.' She reached her hand up and stroked his cheek thoughtfully. 'Spain again sounds good, but what about that fucking video? Everyone's seen it. How can I go back there now? And what about the twins? And Sheila?'

'The video is sorted, Jilly Holden is sorted, and as for the twins and Sheila, I'll let them tell you all about it. Give it some thought, discuss it with Jo and let me know, eh? It's all going to be OK. Trust me, I'm a doctor.'

Cathy laughed out loud. 'No, you're not!'

'All right I'm not, but you can still trust me. I'll look after you both and we'll have a wonderful time in the end.'

Chapter Twenty-Two

The faces were long and the mood was sombre as they all gathered at the big house after the funeral of Nico Marcos. Cathy had felt strangely sad at the small turnout; all the scumbags who had previously hung on his every word and been lavishly entertained in his home were noticeable by their absence, as was any representation from Joanna and his children. Cathy had tried approaching her through Jack, but despite the children being Nico's son and daughter, Sammy-Jo's half siblings, the door was firmly shut.

The bare bones of the story, carefully reported to protect Sammy-Jo and Tracy, had been big news for a couple of days and nearly everyone had been either frantically distancing themselves from all knowledge of Nico or scurrying for cover away from police interest for fear of being linked to him and his lifestyle.

Looking around now, Cathy could see her life confined in just one room.

The twins, as usual, appeared quite bored as Simonie

and Justin regaled them with tales of baby Tamara, and Sheila was busy berating Tim for looking so sullen, even at a funeral, and despite the obvious adoration from the young Tracy! Jack and Dominic were busy discussing another case but their minds were still firmly on Paul and Damien. Jack was determined that, one way or another, those two would be caged for ever, and he was going to do his bit regardless of the police investigation. Peter stayed firmly glued to Cathy and Sammy-Jo, doing his best to support them both through the dreadful day.

But that was it – the sum total of the turnout for Nico – and Cathy knew that not a single one of them had come for him. Every person at the sparse gathering was there under pressure from Cathy to make a showing for Sammy-Jo's sake.

Peter appeared at her side. 'Oh well, at least the twins look the part for a change, very funereal!'

'Come for a walk with me.' She took his hand and led him down through the grounds to the summerhouse of her childhood. It was no longer her father's old den, more like a glorified shed full of all the gardening overflow, but, unless she was imagining it, the smell was still there.

Slowly she looked around and inhaled. Suddenly she was aware of a feeling of presence, a ghostly but comfortable feeling that washed over her soothingly. She imagined that her parents were there, watching her, sympathising with her but encouraging her at the same time. *If you can get over your past then so can Sammy-Jo.*

'I used to spend hours here as a child. Mum and Dad would be pottering about and I would paddle in the water or swing on my swing. I was so happy then. The nightmare of Vietnam had faded and everything was right for me. Even the day before the fire we were down here having lunch.' Looking at him intensely, she continued, 'Do you think the twins did start the fire deliberately? Would they have done that? Could they have done that?'

Peter looked back at her. He knew that the ghost of the past had to be laid to rest if she was to move on. There was nothing to be gained by dragging any of it out.

'Of course they didn't. You have to believe that and you have to let it be now. Nico has gone so it's not an issue any more. Forget all that and let's move on. Everything will be easier to put into perspective with a bit of sun on your back!' Hand in hand they clambered out of the overfilled summerhouse, laughing gently together as they stumbled and tripped over the sit-on lawnmower.

'I've always fancied a go on one of these.'

'Come on then.'

'We can't, not today.'

Cathy laughed excitedly. 'Oh yes we can!'

Together they dragged the machine on to the lawn and fired it up. With Peter in his best suit and black tie in the driving seat and Cathy, still resplendent in her funeral outfit complete with hat, perched precariously behind him, they bumped up and down the grounds as the mower roared its disapproval.

'Not exactly quad-biking, is it?' he shouted over his shoulder at her.

'Look over there.' Cathy pointed in the direction of the house.

Agog on the patio were all the funeral guests, along with Sammy-Jo, who was clapping her hands and actually smiling for the first time.

Alison and Jane stood together looking on in resigned indifference.

'And she says *we're* crazy . . .'

'Maybe everyone is. Come on, we've got to get back to the shop. We've got customers waiting.'

As they turned to go back into the house Cathy noticed them and shouted loudly, waving her hat frantically to get their attention.

'Wait a minute, Janey, Ali, wait for me.' Rushing up the lawn, she hurled herself at them. 'Nothing like this is ever going to happen again, is it? We're sisters, don't forget, we have to stick together whatever!'

The twins linked arms either side of her and they walked slowly into the house together.

'Mummy, Mummy, wait for me. I'm coming as well.' Sammy-Jo ran after them, her new shoes clomping across the patio.

Peter grinned as he dumped the lawnmower where it had stopped and wandered over to Jack and Dominic.

'This is still a fine old mess, isn't it? I can't believe that two dangerous bastards like Paul and Damien can just disappear off the face of the earth. How can it happen? Why didn't someone keep tabs on them when they were released?'

The two older men exchanged grimaces as Peter ranted.

'We agree with you, Peter,' Jack touched his arm, 'but

it happens all the time. There's changes afoot but they won't help Cathy. They could even be abroad by now – our borders leak like a sieve at the best of times. I'd put money on Thailand myself.'

Dominic interrupted quickly. 'We have to let the police get on with all that. The main thing to focus on now is helping Cathy and Sammy-Jo through it all. The only thing that will help them is time.'

'Dominic is right, Peter. Cathy's biggest problem right now is guilt. As she sees it, if she hadn't insisted on marrying Nico, none of this would have happened. You have to help her see that the main villain was – is – Nico.'

Peter chewed at his lip. 'The twins' psychiatrist has recommended a counsellor for both Cathy and Sammy-Jo but at the moment she's determined to deal with—' Out of the corner of his eye Peter could see Tim making his way towards them so he broke off midsentence and smiled. Tim didn't return it.

'Shouldn't you have gone back to sunny Spain by now?' Tim squared up in front of Peter, not trying to hide his dislike. 'I hear you're actually going to join the real world of work at last.'

Peter grinned at him, determined not to take the bait. 'Well, sort of. I'm actually going to start my own business out there, just tying together the loose ends here first. Kit's got a lot to deal with.'

'What loose ends might they be? *Cathy* has all the support she needs here – you're superfluous to requirements now.' Tim smiled superciliously. 'You can go right this minute if you want, we won't miss you!'

'Not until Kit's ready. She has things to arrange before we can go . . .' Peter hesitated and feigned surprise. 'Oh, I'm sorry Tim, didn't you know? Kit's coming with me, and little Jo. We're going to have a villa built on the coast. But in the meantime we're going back to Mum and Dad's for a good long holiday. Young Tracy is going to come as well for a while, if the authorities, and her no-good parents, allow it.'

As Tim's face darkened Peter continued to smile.

'Come on Tim, no hard feelings, eh? So much has happened and you and Kit have been friends for so long—'

'Fuck off, Mr High and Mighty. First you live off your parents and now you're going to live off Cathy. You're nothing but a leech. You and I could never be friends, and if *Cathy* is going with you then she's as mad as her fucking sisters. They're all barking mad, the lot of them. It must be infectious!'

As he turned angrily on his heel to storm off he suddenly noticed Cathy standing nearby, listening to it all. She said nothing, but exactly what she thought was written all over her face.

She watched Tim marching angrily around the side of the house. He quickly disappeared from sight, and Cathy felt another door in her life close.

'Peter, can we go somewhere quiet?' She turned towards Jack and Dominic. 'Excuse us for a minute.'

She started back towards the house leaving Peter to follow.

'I'm sorry about that, Kit.'

She waved her hand in the air dismissively. 'I don't even want to talk about it. Tim will never change. I thought he would grow up and lose the chip on his shoulder but all that's happened is it's turned into a great big plank. But enough about him, Tim O'Connor can look after himself. Now the twins are going to sell the big house and all its memories, it will help them. They want something smaller and easier to manage that's nearer to the shop, and of course to Sheila.'

'Poor old Sheila.' Peter smiled sadly.

'Not really – in her own way she needs them as much as they need her, so hopefully,' Cathy paused and turned towards him, taking both his hands in hers, 'hopefully now things can only get better and I can leave them all with a clear conscience this time!'

She poured two glasses of wine. 'To us.'

'To us and our future!'

'To us and changing the future . . .'

'Mummy, Mummy, where are you? I want a drink.' Sammy-Jo's piercing voice penetrated from the hallway at the second they clinked their glasses.

Cathy and Peter locked eyes and then arms.

'See? She's getting better already!'

Broken

Martina Cole

DI Kate Burrows thought she'd never face a killer like the Grantley Ripper again. But she was wrong.

One by one, children are being abandoned. Thankfully, they're rescued from harm. Then one victim is not so lucky, and Kate knows she's in a race against time to save lives.

As a parent herself, Kate's finding the case tough and she needs the support of her lover, Patrick Kelly, more than ever. But Patrick's got problems of his own . . .

The unforgettable heroine from THE LADYKILLER is back with her toughest case yet.

Praise for Martina Cole's sensational bestseller:

'You won't be able to put this one down' *Company*

'A powerful novel' *Express*

'Set to be another winner' *Woman's Weekly*

'A major new talent' *Best*

'Martina Cole again explores the shady criminal under-world, a setting she is fast making her own' *Sunday Express*

'A cracking yarn . . . Cole writes with huge authority' *Ms London*

0 7472 5541 5

headline

Now you can buy any of these other bestselling
Headline books from your bookshop or
direct from the publisher.

FREE P&P AND UK DELIVERY
(Overseas and Ireland £3.50 per book)

Backpack	Emily Barr	£5.99
Icebox	Mark Bastable	£5.99
Killing Helen	Sarah Challis	£6.99
Broken	Martina Cole	£6.99
Redemption Blues	Tim Griggs	£5.99
Relative Strangers	Val Hopkirk	£5.99
Homegrown	Gareth Joseph	£5.99
Everything is not Enough	Bernardine Kennedy	£5.99
High on a Cliff	Colin Shindler	£5.99
Winning Through	Marcia Willett	£5.99

TO ORDER SIMPLY CALL THIS NUMBER

01235 400 414

or e-mail <u>orders@bookpoint.co.uk</u>

Prices and availability subject to change without notice.